It was Evan.

What in the world was he *doing* here? Was this a mirage?

The last time I'd seen Evan, we'd stood outside on the docks, shrouded in fog, hugging, and I was crying because summer was over and he was leaving the island.

"Hey, you." He slid off the freezer and wrapped his arms around my waist.

And there it was. What it had taken me so many months to forget. That feeling.

"So. Are you working here?" I asked. "Nobody said you were working here." I can be a bit blunt when I'm feeling cornered.

"What, am I required to file papers with the government?" Evan joked. "The island's cracking down on outsiders?"

No, I thought, *but maybe they should be.*

maine
squeeze

Banana
Splitsville

Catherine Clark

An Imprint of HarperCollinsPublishers

HarperTeen is an imprint of HarperCollins Publishers.

Maine Squeeze
Copyright © 2004 by Catherine Clark
Banana Splitsville
(Previously published as Truth or Dairy)
Copyright © 2000 by Catherine Clark

Library of Congress catalog card number: 2010938191
ISBN 978-0-06-206489-9

Typography by Sasha Illingworth
11 12 13 14 15   LP/BV   10 9 8 7 6 5 4 3 2 1
❖
First Edition

CONTENTS

maine squeeze

Chapter 1

"You're not just going to leave me behind, are you?

You're not going to strand me on this island. Are you?"

"Don't make fun of me. Just don't." I looked at my boyfriend, Ben, and raised one eyebrow. "But are you seriously that upset about my being gone for a day?"

"Well, no. But it is kind of lousy," Ben said.

Ben and I had just gone for an early-morning walk so we could have a little time together before I drove my parents to the airport. When they first told me they were leaving the island for the summer, I'd had that exact same reaction, which was why Ben was teasing me about it.

I'd kind of panicked at first. I don't know why. It wasn't like it was a deserted island or that I would be stranded—I lived there year-round. By the way, it's just referred to as "the island," like a lot of islands off the coast of Maine, and I'll keep it that way because (a) I'm too lazy to change everyone's names, and (b) I don't want to incriminate anyone. If you've been there, you might recognize it, but I'm going to keep some things mysterious in that Jessica Fletcher/Cabot Cove/*Murder She Wrote*–reruns kind of way.

Not that there will be any murder in this story. Unless crimes of passion, crimes of the heart, count.

Anyway, my parents would be landing in Frankfurt, Germany, tomorrow, while I'd be showing up for my first

3

day of work at Bobb's Lobster. Something about it didn't seem quite fair.

"When do you think you'll be back tonight?" Ben lingered in the doorway of my house, his hands on my waist.

"Maybe seven? Not too late," I said. I'd drop my parents at the airport in Portland—from there they'd fly to Boston, then overseas—then I'd pick up my friend Erica and drive back.

"I wish I could go with you."

"Would you really want to listen to my parents chanting along to German-language tapes in the car because they haven't quite mastered the language yet?" I asked. Not that they'd gotten the hang of French, Spanish, or Italian, for that matter, but that wouldn't keep them from spending ten weeks in Europe. Nothing would. Not even the prospect of leaving me and Ben alone all summer. (Well, only if *his* parents would leave, too. . . .) I wasn't actually going to be "alone" alone, anyway, because three of my best friends were moving in.

I thought back to the night two months before when my parents told me they were going to Europe for ten weeks. At first I thought we were all going together. I was really excited, but then I realized I was not included, that they'd be sipping wine in the Alps while I schlepped melted butter at sea level.

But I couldn't begrudge them this second honeymoon concept—they deserved it. And did I really want to trek all over the world with my parents? I pictured my dad wearing a pair of lederhosen and doing a jig around a beer hall in Austria, while I cowered in the corner, hoping no one would guess we were related.

Then I pictured me, here, alone in this house. Me and Ben. Alone. It sounded too good to be true. I was afraid that they'd make me stay with Uncle Frank and Aunt Sue.

It's not that I don't like my aunt and uncle. I just didn't want to live with them. My aunt has this blueberry addiction—she spends the whole summer trying to invent new recipes using blueberries. She eats so many that I could swear her skin sometimes has a blue tint. And if my uncle told me one more time that I should *paint* instead of doing collage art . . . I would go nuts.

Fortunately, my parents suggested my friends move in here, rather than me move in with my aunt and uncle. I'd be eternally grateful for that.

Ben smiled. "You're right. I can probably skip the German lesson in the car."

"Yeah," I said.

"But it's our first day off from school—and our last day off before we start working full-time. It'd be great if we could just go hang out on the beach or something."

"Tell me about it," I said. "We'll just have to make up for it—we'll find an extra day somewhere," I said. "We'll both call in sick or something. Middle of July."

"Okay, it's a plan." Ben nodded. "Maybe we'll be sick for two or three days. No, wait. I don't want to lose my job."

Ben was so psyched about his first summer on the island. He'd gotten a job working on the ferry, which we called "Moby" for obvious reasons—it was large, white, swam, and carried lots of people inside it. He'd be one of the guys taking tickets, tying up at the dock, loading bags of mail and unloading carts of groceries and other supplies, handing out life jackets in the event of an emergency—whatever was needed, except for the actual navigation and driving of the ferry. That was left to a few guys on the mainland and a couple on the island: John Hyland, a grumpy, retired fisherman who hated "summer people" and never smiled (his wife, Molly, ran the island post office and wasn't much friendlier), and "Cap" Green, who talked your ear off and told you more about the tide, the neighbors, and his health than you ever wanted to know.

Ben and I actually met on the ferry to school one morning. Everyone from seventh grade and up goes to the mainland for school, which means I'd been catching the ferry at seven o'clock every morning for the past six years for the forty-five-minute trip. But enough about my tragic life.

Meeting someone on the ferry probably sounds really romantic, but you haven't known nausea until you've ridden a ferry that smelled like diesel and you've had to sit inside because it was cold and raining very hard. Even someone like me, who'd been taking the boat for years, had trouble on days like that.

Ben was new to the island, and he was looking *completely* green. My friend Haley and I felt so sorry for him that we went over to him and asked how he was doing. Haley told him to look at the horizon, which is a trick for not getting seasick. Then I gave him some of my still-half-frozen cinnamon-raisin bagel and told him to come stand in the doorway with me, because it's better when you have something in your stomach and when you get a little fresh air, even if it's cold and wet outside.

"What's your name?" I asked him.

"B—Ben," he stammered, looking around nervously.

"Colleen Templeton," I said, shaking his hand, trying to distract him by making small talk and introducing myself.

"Colleen?" He nodded, biting his lip. "I really don't want to puke on my first day."

"You won't," I assured him. "Just have another bite of the bagel and you won't. But at least if you do? We're all wearing raincoats."

He laughed and then clutched his stomach.

I don't know how I could have found someone so green, so cute. But he was.

And I don't know if he asked me out a couple of months later out of gratitude for that day, or what. By that time I was starting to realize Evan—who I thought was the love of my life *last* summer—had moved on, so I decided I might as well, too. It was good timing, which was a first for me. My family's notorious for bad timing.

So now it was kind of funny that Ben would be spending eight to ten hours a day on the ferry. There's an expression, "getting your sea legs." Ben had those now, and very nice sea legs at that.

I was really looking forward to spending the summer with him. This year would be so different from last year. I wouldn't have any big ups and downs, like with Evan, who my friend Samantha had dubbed "the drama king." I wouldn't have to worry about how Evan felt about me, or whether Evan and I were going to get together, or whether, after we *did* get together, anyone would catch us making out in the walk-in fridge at work, which in retrospect seems a little tacky. Fun at the time, though, I have to admit. But my life was a lot less racy, now. I was a lot calmer—and happier.

As Ben and I were standing on the porch, saying good-bye, an old, faded blue-and-white pickup truck came rattling up the road. "Here comes trouble," Ben said as Haley Boudreau pulled into the driveway.

Haley slammed the driver's door shut. "What are you doing here?" she asked Ben.

"He came over for breakfast—to say good-bye to my parents," I told her, looking at all the boxes and bags in the back of the truck. Haley was moving into my brother Richard's old room, and Samantha would be coming up from Boston tomorrow and taking the guest room. I was going to pick up Erica when I drove my parents to the Portland airport that afternoon.

"You knew I was here, right? That's why you came over, so I could help you carry all that stuff in," Ben said as Haley unlatched the truck's tailgate.

"Yeah. Do you think you can lift this?" Haley picked up a small duffel bag and tossed it to Ben. "We'll do the heavy stuff. What do you think, we're not strong enough?"

Haley could be so stubbornly independent. You'd never know from the way she was talking to Ben that they were such good friends. The three of us did practically everything together.

She pulled a large cardboard box out of the back of her family's beat-up pickup truck. "How much did you *bring*?" I asked as I went over to help.

"I'm glad this is the last box," I said as we climbed the stairs. "Remind me again why we told Ben to leave and let us do this on our own?"

"Come on, it's good for you," Haley said. "You'll be ready to carry those big heavy trays."

"Strength training? Okay. Consider me strong." I dropped the box of CDs onto the floor in Richard's old room. It was funny to think of Haley moving in here when she only lived about five minutes away. It was like when we were ten and had sleepovers at each other's houses every Saturday night. We used to annoy Richard to no end; I wondered how he'd feel about "Horrible Haley" living in his room.

Haley and I have been friends ever since my family moved to the island, when I was eight. My mom grew up here, but went away to college and lived in Chicago for a while, which is where she met my dad and where Richard and I were born. Then her parents needed help, and Mom and Dad were sick of big-city life, so they turned their summer vacations on the island into year-round living. First one job at the elementary school on the island opened, and my dad took it, and then another, and my mom took that. (They're like the tag team of silliness when it comes to working with little kids. Maybe it's because they spend so much time with little kids that they're slightly, well, goofy. I mean, they've definitely spent too much time inhaling glue, paste, and Magic Markers.)

Haley is the shortest person I know—not that it matters, but it's a fact. Her father and her uncle are lobstermen, just like her grandfather, and his father before him, etc. etc. They've been on the island for decades—probably a century or two, for all I know. They call everyone who arrived since 1900 "from away." But they're not standoffish about it, the way some people can be.

I once asked her why she'd decided to work at the Landing, instead of with her family, this summer. "My family's crazy," she'd said. "You know that. They wouldn't even *pay* me. Or they'd say they were going to, but then they'd tell me they needed the money for something else, and would I mind waiting a few weeks . . . you know how it was last summer. I made about ten dollars."

Haley had a strong Maine accent, so when she said words like *summer* and *dollar*, they sounded like "summah" and "dollah."

"So you'd rather sell postcards and ice cream cones?" I'd asked. "Really?"

"Yes, really," she'd said. "You have no idea how stubborn my mother can be."

Actually, I did, because I knew how stubborn *Haley* could be. Like this latest standoff with her mother—it could last for months. Haley and I had had a few standoffs ourselves over the years. We always got over them and apologized to each other, but sometimes it had taken weeks.

"Good. Fine," Mrs. Boudreau had said when Haley told her about our summer plan to share the house. She was already mad about Haley's going to work for someone else, and it showed. "Have a wonderful time," she said coldly. "See you in September." Which, of course, sounded like "Septembah."

I'll quit talking about their accent now—I just really like the way it sounds. I always wanted to have an accent, but I could never pull it off since I wasn't born here.

Unlike me, Haley didn't have a serious boyfriend. She was determined not to get too serious or tied down with anybody while she was still young. Her older sister had gotten married by the time she was twenty, and then had two kids right away. Haley wanted to get off the island and go to college and see the world before she did that. She'd earned a scholarship to Dartmouth—she was brilliant in science and calculus—and was looking forward to getting off the island and meeting people who'd never even heard of it. Or so she said. I wondered how she was going to handle being so far away from the ocean when she'd never lived anywhere else. (I'd be attending Bates College, which isn't on the coast, either, but it's not far from it.)

"So, how do you think Richard's going to take the news?" Haley asked as she sat on the bed. "Do you think he'll even come out here this summer?"

I fixed the bulletin board, which was hanging crooked. The board was covered with photos of Richard and his freshman-year girlfriend, Richard and his sophomore-year girlfriend. . . . He always went out with beautiful girls, but he had a time limit on his relationships, it seemed. Two or three months and he was moving on. *Tick, tick, tick.*

It was hard to think that my big brother, who I'd worshiped for years (because he was five years older, he was just old enough to be really nice toward me most of the time, at least once he got past the new-baby-hatred phase—and I really looked up to him), was maybe not all that different from other guys, or that he did typical guy things that made him sort of a jerk.

"He's supposed to be coming for July Fourth. He doesn't get much vacation time because he's so new at his job," I told Haley. "So he's only coming for the long weekends—Labor Day, too."

"But we'll be gone then," Haley said. "Isn't that weird to think about?" She opened the box on the bed beside her and pulled out a few books. "Did I say weird? I meant incredibly great."

"And we'll be unpacking then, too," I said. "Is that why you brought so much stuff? Are you practicing?"

"I brought my favorite things," Haley said. "Because who knows when my mother's going to get mad at me again and decide to throw out all of my stuff."

"She wouldn't do that," I said.

"She would. When my sister announced she was getting married, my mother put all of her belongings at the end of the driveway. Remember that?"

"She doesn't like being left . . . I guess," I said.

"What does she think? That we're going to stay home and live with her forever?" Haley started putting books into Richard's empty bookcase. "I wish *she* would go to Europe for the summer, instead of your parents."

In a way, I almost wished that, too. Now that my parents were actually leaving that afternoon, I was thinking about how much I would miss them.

There was a knock on the door. "Colleen? Could you come downstairs?" my mother asked.

"Is it time to go?"

"Not yet. But there's something important we have to discuss before we leave."

"What to do when Starsky and Hutch get upset when they realize that you're gone?" I asked, referring to our cats. My dad named them after his favorite old television show.

"No. The house rules," my mother said.

Haley and I exchanged a look. *What* house rules?

Chapter 2

Haley drove off in the truck, the shocks bouncing along as she backed down the bumpy gravel driveway.

I saw that my parents had loaded their luggage into the back of the old Volvo wagon. (You almost don't need a car on the island, really—you could practically walk everywhere you need to. Mostly you just need cars and trucks to haul things. But if you want one when you get to the mainland, you have to keep it somewhere.)

Dad was sitting on the top porch step, petting Starsky and saying good-bye. Starsky always seemed to know when someone was going away, and then he tried not to let you out of his sight.

"Hutch is obviously crushed you're leaving." I pointed at Hutch, who was sprawled on top of one of the Adirondack chair cushions, his legs hanging off, about to fall but completely oblivious to the world.

My family had this ongoing debate about how cats ever got onto the island in the first place. My mother theorized that the original feline residents of the island must have sneaked off a pirate ship in search of a better life. My father always said, "Actually, there was that one cat that took the ferry. No, wait. There had to be two." He was working on a children's picture book about a ferry cat and an ex-pirate cat that fell madly in love. As I said, he can be pretty goofy. Naturally, the two cats in his book looked exactly like Starsky and Hutch. Starsky is a gray tortoiseshell tabby with a white tail, and Hutch is a blond marmalade-colored tabby cat. They're brothers.

I wondered which one was more like a pirate. Starsky did have a habit of knocking my earrings from the top of my dresser to the floor, so maybe he had more of a yearning for stealing—and wearing—gold. Hutch had a habit of sleeping through everything, major and minor.

"You know what? Hutch is great. Hutch is cool. I yearn to be as relaxed as he is sometime in my life," Dad said, and I laughed.

Mom came outside, carrying a large sheet of hot pink poster board.

"What's that?" I asked.

"This is your contract," she said, looking it over. "Just want to make sure I didn't leave anything out. Honey, do you have a pen?"

My dad pulled a felt-tip marker out of his pants pocket. I don't think he's written with an actual pen in years. He even writes and signs checks with Magic Markers.

"You know how we talked about setting some ground rules, so we wrote them down to make them official and binding. This is a very big deal, you know. Us leaving you here by yourself. In fact, I'm almost having second thoughts about it." Mom tapped the marker against the porch railing.

Second thoughts? She couldn't. She wouldn't. Haley had already moved in. And I had the perfect picture of my perfect summer in my head. It definitely did not include Mom and Dad hanging around, crowding in at the corners of the photograph, waving hello.

"Mom, we've been over this. I'll be responsible," I said.

"Yes, I think you will be," she said, "but I'm not so sure about the other girls. I just . . . I'd hate it if anything happened."

"To the house?" I asked.

"Not just the house. To *them*," she said. "And to *you*."

"Oh." She did have a point there. "But, Mom, we'll all look after each other—we always do."

"But I won't be here to make sure of it," she said, her voice quavering.

"Mom, don't worry." I put my arm around her shoulder and gave her a little squeeze. It was a warm and fuzzy moment.

Then she stepped out of the hug and slapped the poster board on the slatted table. "Read, initial, and sign."

RULES—SUMMER RESIDENCE

1. No drugs or alcohol allowed.
2. No sleepovers. Especially of the boyfriend variety.
3. The house will be kept clean. To that end, the house will be cleaned once weekly. Uncle Frank and Aunt Sue will be dropping by for random inspections. In fact, the house is subject to inspections by your aunt and uncle at any time.
4. No loud parties. Small gatherings are fine, but do not annoy the neighbors.
5. Each girl will be responsible for her own long-distance phone calls made on the house phone, as well as for excessive Internet connection charges.

6. Any damage done to the house—not that there will be any—will be repaired by the time we get home.
7. The Volvo is only to be driven by you and Colleen—nobody else.
8. No changes will be made around the house.
9. Anyone breaking any of the above rules will be asked to leave the house.
10. I don't have anything else; it just seemed like there should be 10. Have fun!

I smiled as I scrawled my signature in purple ink on the first line marked "Signed and Agreed By."

Mom carefully inspected my signature, as if I could have forged it. "It's up to you to post the rules in the kitchen—and get each girl to sign this." Then, out of nowhere, she started crying. "I don't want to go," she said, hugging me, her tears dropping onto my shoulders.

"Mom, please," I said. "You *do* want to go. You're not setting Dad loose on the Continent by himself, are you? I mean, he could really give Americans a bad name."

My father cleared his throat. "Ahem."

"Okay, a worse name," I amended.

"That's not what I was thinking about!" he said with a laugh. "Anyway, it's not as if I'm an embarrassment to anyone." He stood there, saying this, wearing a long-sleeved T-shirt Mom had given him last Christmas that said "I'm a Mainiac" over the outline of a moose.

"Are you wearing that on the *plane*?" I asked.

"Good point." He ran upstairs to get changed into his traveling clothes, and Mom and I just laughed as we taped the poster board onto the kitchen door.

I headed to Erica's house in Portland that afternoon around four o'clock, after a dreadfully sobby drop-off at the airport.

Dad kept cracking bad jokes about what souvenirs he would bring home for the cats, and Mom kept telling me how to look after the garden, even though she knew I was hopeless when it came to having a green thumb. And she kept crying, too. I guess we never had been separated for as long as we would be that summer. Maybe it was good practice for my leaving home in the fall, like she said, but neither one of us liked it. And okay, so I cried, too. Miserably. Embarrassingly.

Now, while I was at a stoplight, I glanced in the rearview mirror and saw that my eyes were only starting to unpuff. I reached over to the passenger seat for my sunglasses and slipped them back on, then stuffed a crumpled Kleenex into the pocket on the driver's-side door.

I wasn't going to cry—I didn't think I would. But after we unloaded their suitcases and bags, as Mom and Dad were hugging me good-bye, this police officer started yelling at us because we were staying in the pickup and drop-off area too long and we were getting in the way of other people. Also, I hadn't parked quite as close to the curb as a person should, and this hotel shuttle bus was sort of stuck until the driver went up onto the *other* curb. It was chaotic, to say the least. I was about to be blamed for something.

Naturally, I burst into tears.

I think in some weird way that made my parents happy, though, because then they shifted into their "take care of Colleen" mode and suddenly stopped being upset themselves. Mom gave me a tissue (with a teddy bear print, of course) from her purse, and Dad gave me a Lifesaver, and off they went through the doors for their first flight. They just whisked away and left me there with the scowling police officer and a wet face. They'd land in Frankfurt in the morning. I'd wake up at home, without them. It was a bit hard to fathom.

Good thing my three best friends in the world would be there with me.

I pulled up in front of Erica's house and parked. She lived on top of a hill, in a large brick colonial house with a great view of the water. The last time I'd seen Erica was in May, when she came out to the island for her grandfather's birthday. We usually saw each other every other month or so—either she came up or I went to Portland with my mom and dad to shop, or eat out, or visit their friends.

Erica was going to the University of New Hampshire in the fall, so she could be close to home. Erica's parents were a tad overprotective.

Erica was the sweetest, nicest person in the world. She worked as a hostess at Bobb's, which was a perfect fit for her. Even when people got angry about waiting too long for a table or were rude to her, she'd just "kill them with kindness," as the saying goes. She earned a lot of overtime money because she couldn't say no when others asked her to cover their shifts—great for the money part, but bad because she'd work too many hours and get completely exhausted. (Being too nice occasionally has its downsides. That's why I try not to go overboard. That, and the fact it doesn't come naturally to me.)

"Look who's here!" Erica's mother cried when she

opened the front door. "It's Colleen Templeton!" She always says this, as if she's announcing my arrival at a fancy dress ball. Instead, I was standing on their doorstep wearing cut-off khaki shorts, a bright pink tank top, and unlaced sneakers.

Erica came running to the door and we gave each other a quick hug. After talking to her for a few minutes, we quickly tossed two large duffel bags and a box of Erica's stuff into the back of the car, grabbed some juice and sodas from the fridge, and were about to be on our way when Mrs. Kuhar caught up to us.

Erica's parents were coming up to the island the next weekend, but her mom acted as though Erica was leaving the country when she said good-bye (and I knew what that looked like, having just been through it myself). She gave Erica several instructions on when to call home, how to dress for the changing weather, how to arrange her schedule at Bobb's so she didn't get overworked like last summer. . . . Then Erica and her mother hugged, then her mother hugged *me*, and eventually we were on the road.

"We're on the way!" Erica said, putting down her window and resting her arm on the door as we hit Interstate 295. "Wow, what a nice day, huh?"

"Can you believe we're really doing this? I mean, we've been talking about it since April, and now it's finally happening." I took a sip of orange soda. "Isn't this great? This summer is going to be *so* amazing." I reached down to turn up the radio.

Seconds later, Erica leaned over and turned down the radio. "The thing is, Colleen," she said, sounding a little nervous. "I can't actually live with you."

Chapter 3

"You can't?"

Already there were some glitches in the perfect plan, some "flies in the ointment," as my father would say, only he always made a point of mentioning they were black flies, because that's the fly variety here in Maine that will bite you until it hurts.

Anyway. The fact that Erica wasn't going to live in the house with us came as a complete and utter shock to me. She was more reliable, nice, and—maybe it's shallow to say, but she's really skilled at cooking, and I'd been relying on her to feed me all summer—than the rest of us put together. What would we do without her? What would I eat? Toast only got you so far. Now I was looking at toast and leftovers from Bobb's. Leftover reheated lobster stew on toast. Yuck.

I told myself to stop thinking about my stomach and get this figured out. "But wait. If your parents won't let you live with us, then how come they're letting you ride up with me today?" I asked. It didn't sound exactly logical.

"I needed to get there?" she said meekly. "And you were coming down anyway to drop off your parents?"

I laughed. "Well, true. But why are they against the idea of you living at my house? I mean, when have you ever given them a reason not to trust you?" I asked.

Erica fiddled with the knob on the glove compartment. "Well, uh . . ."

I couldn't believe it—Erica was almost acting guilty. "What? Did you do something?"

"No! I was going to say . . . well, it's not me they're worried about," Erica said slowly.

I nearly slammed on the brakes, which was not a good thing because we were on the highway. "What? It's *me*?" I felt terrible. Did Mr. and Mrs. Kuhar really think so poorly of me? They'd always acted so friendly toward me, so *nice*. Just like Erica—they were almost *too* nice sometimes. And since when could I not be trusted? I was extremely . . . trusty. Trustworthy. Whatever.

"No, no! I mean, it's not you," Erica assured me. "It's the entire situation. Four girls on their own. My parents think I'm still too young for something like that. You know how they treat me as if I'm ten sometimes. Plus, they said that they want me to look after my grandparents this summer."

"Your grandparents are sixty-five, going on thirty!" I said. "I held the door for your grandmother last week at the store? And she stared at me and said, 'Are you working here now? Well, what are you waiting for? Are you doing arm-strengthening exercises? No? Then go *in* already.'"

Erica laughed as she leaned down to adjust the back straps of her brown sandals. "Yeah, that sounds like her, all right. I know, they're completely self-reliant. And, Coll, I'm *really* sorry. I should have told you sooner. I just kept hoping I'd convince my parents to change their minds."

"Don't apologize!" I said. "I mean, I'm disappointed. I wish you *could* live with us. But it's perfectly fine. You'll be over all the time anyway. Right?"

"Of course! I just won't be able to sleep there, that's all. And hey, that means you'll have a guest room now."

I swear, she could put a positive spin on anything. She was amazing that way.

When we pulled up in front of the house it was getting close to seven thirty and dusk was falling, but I immediately spotted Samantha sitting on the porch with Haley.

"Sam!" I closed the car door and ran over to the porch steps. We could unpack the groceries later.

"Colleen!" Samantha jumped up and gave me a big hug. "How's it going?"

"Wow, you look fantastic," I said, stepping back to admire her. She wore faded stretch boot-cut jeans, boots, and a light-orange T-shirt with cap sleeves that looked great against her dark brown skin. She wore her hair pulled back in a gold barrette at the base of her neck. "Did you get taller over the winter or what?"

"No, you got shorter," she replied. "It's the heels, of course. Hey, Erica!" Sam quickly hugged Erica, and then Erica hugged Haley.

I ran inside and brought out four glasses and a pitcher of iced tea while Erica put all the cold groceries in the fridge and freezer. Then we all sat on the porch, talking and laughing. It felt exactly like the end of last summer, sort of like no time had elapsed at all. I love that about summer.

Sam and her family had rented a place on the island last summer, after coming the year before that for a shorter vacation and falling in love with the place. They lived in Richmond, Virginia, for the rest of the year, and her parents were both university professors, which gave them the summers off. I've never been to Virginia, but from what Sam has told me, it sounds pretty different from here. I know it's a lot *warmer*, which is why Sam had decided to stay down there for college and attend the University of Virginia. I was kind of envious of that, and planned on visiting her during key months of the year—like February. And March. And April. (It usually doesn't get really warm and springlike here until May.)

Sam and I e-mailed each other once a week, at least, so we knew everything that had been going on over the past year in each other's lives. I knew how she'd done on her college entrance exams, who she'd gone to her prom with, how her parents had taken her cell phone away during finals week, which senior awards she'd won, that she was still addicted to Heath candy bars, and that her parents were spending a week in late August on the island and the rest of the summer researching new books.

So catching up when she got to the island didn't take long. But of course we went over it all again anyway. Sometimes it was hard for us to shut up and let someone else do the talking.

One thing I really like about Sam is that she always speaks her mind. You don't have to worry about where you stand or what she thinks of a person or a situation. She'll tell you. But not in a mean way—she's just very honest and forthright. You can trust her not to lie to you. If you ask her, "Does this shirt look all right?" she might say, "It's perfect," or she might say, "Not with those pants, no." And she'd immediately go to your—or her—closet and find something that looked better.

She could even make her Bobb's outfit look okay. And she was such a good server, too. She could remember twenty orders and get all the details right. Her tips always outnumbered mine, but she didn't brag about it.

She was the kind of person who'd pitch in when someone else got slammed with too many tables wanting too many things. And she always tipped out the bussers and dishwashers really well. She was generous to a fault, sort of like Erica, but it was a great fault when you were her friend.

At the end of last summer, Samantha had treated me, Erica, Haley, and some other friends to an all-day sailboat cruise on the ocean. It was something tourists always did, but we never thought of doing it ourselves. For one thing, it was expensive. For another, it was . . . touristy. It was the equivalent of us tying on plastic lobster-eating bibs and saddling up at picnic tables outside Bobb's for the Friday night early-bird special lobster boil: "Reserve Now—the Early Bird Catches the Lobster!" As if birds caught lobsters. But whatever.

After we got over feeling slightly embarrassed, we had an amazing time, cruising from the island over to and around other islands, making our way along the rocky coast, sitting in the sun drinking spritzers and eating a gourmet lunch while getting what was essentially a tour of our own backyard.

"Genius. Pure genius. You're coming back next year—you *have* to," Haley had told her—Haley, who'd initially thought the sailboat cruise idea was ludicrous and a waste of time.

I suddenly remembered that Evan had been there on the sailboat, too. I remembered leaning back against him and the wind whipping my hair and him giving me his baseball cap and the sun sparkling on the water and the sound of the hull slicing through the water.

There were so many memories with Evan that I'd been trying to forget over the last year. Fortunately, he wouldn't be around this summer to remind me. Nobody had heard he was coming—not my boss, Trudy; and not his cousin Jake, who he lived with last summer. And especially not *me*. I hadn't heard he was coming—or what he was doing this summer.

Of course, he'd quit writing me back in November. Not that I was feeling angry and bitter about it—at least, not anymore. I was taking the whole fun-while-it-lasted approach. Apparently, Evan was the type of guy who was completely and utterly devoted to you—until suddenly one day he wasn't, and you never heard from him again.

You know that type. A terrible, horrible person.

"So. Now what?" I asked after we'd drained the pitcher of iced tea, the ice in our glasses had melted, and we'd gone through the short versions of all of our lives.

"Now we unpack the rest of the groceries," Erica said. She had helped me stock up on things at the supermarket before we caught the ferry to the island. We have only a small market here, and it's more expensive, so we'd tried to buy in bulk. "Then we decide what we're grilling for dinner. But first I'd better call my grandparents and tell them I'm here, so they don't worry—and so they don't call my parents and make *them* worry."

We all filed into the house, and while Erica was on the telephone with her grandparents, Haley, Sam, and I went upstairs. "So, which room did you choose?" I asked Sam as we stood at the top of the stairs.

"The guest room," she said. "Since I slept in it a few

times last summer, it sort of felt like home already."

"Okay. So that leaves my parents' room open, since Erica won't be here. Maybe one of you guys wants to move in there?"

Wait a second. It was the biggest room in the house, with the best view. Maybe *I* wanted to move in there.

But no, that would be weird. It would have my parents' vibes. Not that there was anything wrong with them, but it would just feel strange, and giving up my room would be strange, too.

"No. Let's just keep this room vacant," Sam suggested. "That way, when people come to visit they'll have a really nice place to stay."

"Who's coming to visit?" I asked.

"I don't know. Your brother. My parents. Orlando Bloom." Samantha smiled.

Haley and I laughed. We'd all thought we saw Orlando Bloom getting off the ferry last year, and had been convinced he was summering somewhere on the island. We rode our bikes all over the place, hung out at the general store, stalked a few B&Bs, did everything we could to find out where he might be staying. But we never spotted Orlando—or his very-good-looking look-alike—again, until someone reported they'd seen him getting back *on* the ferry and leaving the island.

I brushed my hair and headed downstairs to help get dinner ready. I was good at setting the table. I could do that, and dishes, quite well. The rest of the meal should be left to other people with actual skill.

Almost as soon as Erica hung up the phone, promising her grandparents she'd be over when we finished dinner, it rang again. I grabbed it.

"Hey, you're there!" Ben said. "I thought you were going to call when you got home from Portland."

"I was, I was! But I kind of got caught up in . . . catching up. You know." I laughed.

"So how was the drive? Did it go okay? How's Erica?" Ben asked.

"You know, it was fine, but my parents got pretty upset at the airport." Best to lay it all on my parents. After all, they were in Europe now and couldn't defend themselves. "And then it turns out Erica can't live with us, but that's okay—she's here now, making dinner. I'll take her over to her grandparents' later."

"So what are you doing tonight?" Ben asked.

"We're just going to eat and hang out," I said. "I think it's kind of a girls' night thing. But I'll see you tomorrow—after work?"

"Sounds good. Hey, tell Sam I'm looking forward to meeting her, okay?"

"I will. I missed you today. Bye, sweetie!" I clicked off the phone. "That was Ben. He said to tell you he's looking forward to meeting you tomorrow."

"So what's this Ben guy *really* like?" Sam asked as she chopped vegetables for a salad.

"He's great. We hang out all the time," Haley said as she got four glasses out of the cabinet. "And he treats Colleen really well. In comparison to certain other boyfriends she's had."

I groaned. "Did you have to mention him? I've been trying so hard not to think about him."

"So don't. He's not worth it," Haley declared. "Ben's

taller. And nicer. Sweeter. I like him a lot more than I ever liked Evan," she said. "And you can actually trust him, too."

"What? All that and a cute face, too? Sounds too good to be true," Sam commented. "How did you get so lucky, Coll?"

"I know!" Haley said. "Not that I think Evan was great, but this is a place with a limited population. We get one new, nice, cute guy, and she gets to go out with him. *Again.*"

"Come on!" I laughed. "There are a lot more guys around here. Or at least there will be this summer."

"And who cares, really? Because it's not all about the guys. In fact, it's not even *half* about them," Sam declared.

"Yeah. It's about earning tons of money for next year—"

"And hanging out together—"

"And the book club."

"Of course. We can't forget the book club."

"When's our first meeting?" Haley asked.

"Friday at three. Of course, just like always," Sam said with a smile.

Chapter 4

The next morning at ten o'clock, Sam, Erica, and I walked to work together. Erica had come over at nine to make sure Sam and I were awake and getting ready—she had a tendency to look after other people like that.

Sam and I had stayed up so late talking and watching TV the night before that the walk to Bobb's felt a lot longer than a mile to me. I had no energy, which wasn't exactly a good way to start off a forty-plus-hour workweek.

"We should have driven," I said as we trudged down the road for our first lunch shift of the summer. Bobb's was only open on weekends during the off-season, and wasn't busy enough to hire me for that. It would be hard, getting back into the swing of work again. I felt more like lying in bed until noon, then taking a long, hot shower, then sitting in the sun. Eventually getting around to making something to eat. Meeting Ben when he got through with work. You know.

"We're going to walk to Bobb's all summer. It's our exercise plan, remember?" Sam said. "One of them, anyway."

"Whose dumb idea was that," I grumbled.

"Mine," Sam said. "Thanks."

"Sorry." I reached up to push a lock of hair off my cheek. I have these short parts in my hair that are layered, and they insist on escaping barrettes. My hair was shaping up to be a real frizzone that day. Frizzone, by the way, isn't an Italian pastry; it's the name we came up with last summer for out-of-control hair after we kept calling the island the Frizz Zone. In fact, you can pretty much forecast the weather here by what your hair does. It would be humid today, with a chance of rain tonight. Those of us with long-ish, wavy-ish hair were natural-born forecasters.

I'd been working at Bobb's since I was fourteen years old. I started out behind the takeout window, taking and ringing up customer orders. "To go or to eat here?" was the line of that summer. (At the takeout window, "here" meant sitting at a couple of picnic tables right beside the parking lot, so not very glam.) When it was slow, we'd watch people walk up toward the restaurant and we'd bet on whether they were coming in to eat or would get their food to go and sit at the little picnic area.

Yes, we were bored.

Personally, my favorite Bobb's item was the fried haddock sandwich. Whenever a customer asked, "What's good here?" I'd tell them to get the sandwich. Then they'd say, "I'll have the fried clam basket." Somehow I wasn't convincing in my pitch, but oh well, that left more haddock for me.

At Bobb's we didn't use computers. Everything was shorthand, abbreviations, or had a nickname. We used white notepads to take orders. "You're actually writing this down? How quaint," tourists would say when they saw me jotting on the notepad.

Quaint was a top-ten tourist word. Some of the others were: *clam chowdah*, which they loved pronouncing in a bad fake accent; and *gift shop*. Trudy had even started selling Bobb's T-shirts and ball caps because customers kept asking for them. She sold two tees with goofy slogans, but luckily our uniform tees just had a logo on the front and a red lobster on the back.

We had an old cash register, too—not a computer, just a big, fat calculator with a cash drawer attached. "It works. Why replace it?" Trudy would say.

That was the philosophy of a lot of people on the island. For instance, my parents and this twenty-five-year-old Volvo with 200,000 miles on the odometer that I now drove. There was no point replacing something that still worked because you'd probably have to leave the island to find whatever it was you wanted. And then you'd have to haul whatever you didn't want *off* of the island, or else find someone else on the island who wanted your old stuff. Which was weird, when you saw someone walking down the road pushing the very stroller that you, Colleen Templeton, once graced, wearing your old baby clothes. I'm all in favor of recycling everything we can, but it's still strange to see your past walking around with a new identity.

Anyway, Trudy put a lot of money into having good food at the restaurant, the best and freshest seafood catches, along with some cool, old standard family recipes.

There were old wooden booths near the windows, and long tables in the middle of the restaurant for large groups. There was also a "banquet room," where people had private parties for weddings, birthdays, promotions . . . basically, any excuse would do. There were little lamps fashioned after lighthouses on each table. For

31

a while the salt and pepper shakers were shaped like lobster claws, but they were so cute that people kept stealing them, so Trudy went back to using plain glass ones. One of my jobs when I was fifteen used to be Salt and Pepper Girl, which was nothing at all like the groundbreaking rap hip-hop group Salt-N-Pepa. It involved refilling and pouring and wiping off greasy fingerprints.

There used to be a lobster tank near the salad bar, but it caused too much confusion because some people didn't understand why the lobsters were dark blue-green instead of red. They only turn red when they're cooked, which I think is a very good metaphor—I know *I* turn red when I'm cooked, figuratively.

So anyway, back to the Bobb's language. Here were some of the order nicknames: fried clams were rubber-neckers; a tuna sandwich was shark on toast; sea scallops were bottomfeeders; a fried seafood basket was a frantic Atlantic; lobster stew was floating fish; a lobster roll was a rock 'n' roll.

This didn't make sense to me at first because the nicknames were just as long as the actual order names, but Trudy explained that it was part of the restaurant culture, that having nicknames made us close as a team, because we had our own language. So, okay. But you definitely didn't want the out-of-town customers to hear you calling out some of your orders in the kitchen. For one thing, some of them didn't sound all that appetizing. For another, they'd probably say, "How quaint!"

"They should say 'How *Maint*,' not 'How quaint,'" Sam had said last summer.

"We're not quaint. We're Maine-ahs," one of the cooks said.

"Did you hear that accent? How *quaint*!" Sam had teased him.

Despite the goofy names, the food at Bobb's *was* incredibly good. We always had people waiting for tables, crowding the dock outside, mingling, and sipping drinks in plastic cups while they waited, and once or twice falling into the water.

You didn't want to fall in, not out there. The water near Bobb's and the marina was not only as cold as the rest of the ocean could be, and full of seaweed, but it was also tainted with boat engine fuel run-off, scraps of fish, etc. It was rather disgusting, if you really stopped to look at it.

Cats roamed around the docks; kittens lounged on the docks in the sun. They lived for, and on, the fish that escaped from nets being hauled in, bait that was dropped out of buckets, and of course, dropped fried shrimp and clams. They had to compete with some very fast seagulls, the pigeons of the ocean.

I stepped around a couple of cats now, as we walked into Bobb's.

"You know, some places you can be away from for months, and then as soon as you see them again, it's like you never left. Know what I mean?" Sam commented. "I swear, this same loop of rope was lying here when I left last August."

"That's because we don't actually do anything in the off-season," I said. "We wait for the tourists like you to come back before we actually—"

"Tourists like me? Excuse me, but I worked side by side with you last summer," Sam replied. "I'm no tourist."

"So define what you are exactly," I teased.

"She's a part-time resident," Erica said.

We were arguing about how to define a Maine native—which, technically, I wasn't, since I hadn't been born here, which meant I too was "from away"—when we walked into the kitchen and I lost my breath completely. It wasn't the smell of bleach, from everything being disinfected to the umpteenth level of cleanliness for opening day. It wasn't the onions on the chopping board, or the tomato bisque simmering on the stove.

It was Evan.

What in the world was he *doing* here? Was this a mirage? I exchanged panicked looks with Sam and Erica. No, it couldn't be Evan.

But it was.

He was sitting on top of the stainless steel ice cream freezer. He had a semi-scruffy look, like he hadn't shaved in a day or two. He could make stubble look good. I hated that about him.

He was wearing a faded yellow long-sleeved T-shirt with a hole in it, and long khaki shorts. His long legs nearly stretched down to the floor.

I found myself staring at his legs, at his feet. So he had nice ankles. So what? How could I be so shallow as to fall for someone because of his *ankles*? Ankles didn't mean anything. They just held you up. Shinbone connected to the anklebone connected to the footbone, etc.

He was wearing the same Birkenstock sandals he wore last summer.

Last summer. The last time I'd seen Evan, we'd stood outside on the docks at five A.M., shrouded in fog, hugging each other, and I was crying because summer was over and he was catching the ferry and leaving the island to go back to Philadelphia.

It was like something out of my grandmother Templeton's favorite movie, *Casablanca*, which I must have watched with her at least ten times. Instead of the ferry, there should have been an airplane whirring its propeller blades behind us. We should have been in black-and-white, not color. And Evan should have been wearing a fedora hat and a trench coat, instead of a T-shirt and shorts and Birkenstocks, and talking about our problems not amounting to a hill of beans.

What is a hill of beans, anyway?

A hill of blueberries I could understand.

Anyway, whenever I thought about that awful morning, I remembered Evan's faded blue T-shirt, and pressing my face against his chest, how soft the cotton shirt was and how it smelled.

I used to think Evan wore this really cool cologne, because he always smelled so good, no matter what. But it turned out to be his Ultimate Endurance antiperspirant.

I could have used some Ultimate Endurance right about then.

"What—what are you . . . doing here?" I stammered.

"Hey, you." He slid off the freezer and wrapped his arms around my waist.

And there it was. What it had taken me so many months to forget. That feeling. That scent. Us. Lying on the beach together. Swimming together. Walking together. Being together.

"Are you . . . working here?" I finally managed to get out. "Or something?" My voice came out as a pathetic whisper, as if the words *or something* could ever be sultry.

Without answering me, he stepped back and spotted

Samantha standing behind me. "Hey you, too." He gave her a quick hug, and she playfully kicked up her leg behind her as if this was her prom, or an end-of-World-War-II V-Day photo. Evan dipped her, lowering her toward the freezer, and they both laughed.

Why was their hug more romantic than ours? No fair.

Erica acknowledged him with a shy nod. "Hi."

"Hey, Erica. How's it going? What's up?" Evan replied.

He had the nerve to ask what was *up*. How about my *pulse*, buddy?

"So. Are you working here?" I asked. "Nobody said you were working here." I can be a bit blunt when I'm feeling cornered.

"What, am I required to file papers with the government?" Evan joked. "The island's cracking down on outsiders?"

No, I thought, *but maybe they should be.*

"Funny, we were just talking about that," Sam started to tell him.

"But . . . *are* you working here?" I asked again.

Evan raised his eyebrows.

"Because, I mean, Trudy said you weren't working here." In fact, I think I asked her to swear to it in blood, like something out of *The Adventures of Huckleberry Finn*. We had a pact, or at least I did. Since when did Trudy lie to me? I'd been working here for four years, and I couldn't ever remember her lying to me. Well, except for that one time when she told me Saturday nights would not be "all that busy."

Evan shrugged. "I changed my mind. My other plans fell through—"

"What other plans?" I asked.

I couldn't help feeling angry to see him again. He'd blown me off. He'd dropped me. Completely. Sure, we were hundreds of miles apart, and maybe it *was* pointless to have a long-distance relationship. But he could have kept in touch. He could have warned me he'd be here again. Not to mention the fact that Trudy and Robert could have warned me when I asked them, repeatedly, whether they'd heard from him and whether he'd be back. I was furious with Trudy and Robert, I decided. I'd quit if I didn't like working here so much.

Not, I guess, that I would have planned my summer any differently if I'd known Evan was returning. I wanted to be here with my friends—and with Ben. This could be the last time it'd be so easy for us all to be here together. If I'd known Evan was coming, I wouldn't have run off to, say, Europe or something. At least not without seriously thinking it over first and deciding it was the best possible move.

"So. When did you get here?" I asked Evan.

"Well, I got in last night—but it was dicey," he said.

About as dicey as this is, right now? I just stared at the freezer, wishing it wasn't as newly cleaned as it was, that it was the end of the season, not the beginning, and that I couldn't see my distorted reflection on its side. Was my hair seriously going to look that bad on the day I saw him, after nine months of perfect hair and not seeing him? (Maybe the two things were related. He really was evil.)

"Dicey?" I finally said. "How?"

"I was supposed to catch a ride with a friend heading up north to work at a summer camp," he said. "But his car broke down outside Boston." Evan laughed. "It was

37

such a rust heap that we took out our bags, and he just sold it to a junkyard for twenty-five bucks. They towed it away and we just stood there on the side of the highway. Then it started raining. Not just raining, actually— pouring. With lightning flashing and these huge cracks of thunder. So it was impossible to hitch a ride when we were crouched down, holding our backpacks over our heads."

What an amusing little story, I thought. But I was dying inside, dying. I'd never had heartburn in my life, so I wasn't sure if that nauseous churning in the pit of my stomach was heartburn or just disgust.

Soon Evan had Sam, Erica, and the rest of the summer crew laughing at his tale of hitching a ride from a police officer to the train station, getting as far as they could with what little money they had, then camping at a New Hampshire rest area, and finally finding a ride the next day with two nuns and mistakenly swearing as they got into the car because Evan's friend hit his head on the door.

"So, anyway, I made it, safe and sound. Someone was looking out for me, I guess," Evan said.

Darn that someone.

"Technically, I was supposed to be here three days ago," he said.

And what a loss for all of us that you weren't, I thought. I was so (a) angry at the nuns, which is horrible, I know; (b) angry at his attitude; (c) angry at the way he was telling this long, drawn-out story that really only illustrated his stupidity and poor planning. When a random nun has to save your butt—I'm sorry, but you're really counting on luck or divine intervention.

Nuns. Come on! Like they'd let Evan ride with them for more than ten minutes. Didn't they automatically recognize Satan? Weren't they specifically trained for that sort of thing?

Then again, maybe the nun bit wasn't even true—Evan had a habit of embellishing things, of saying things that were obviously exaggerated. Such as: "I love you, Colleen."

"Why didn't you just call someone to come pick you up?" I asked.

"What would the fun in that be?" He stepped closer to me. "Unless, of course, you were the one who came. Still got that Volvo?"

No. I drove it into the ocean when you broke my heart. Sadly, however, I survived.

"Of course," I said.

And there we were, the last place I expected to be, just standing in Bobb's kitchen, looking into each other's eyes.

And I was thinking:

I will kill Trudy with my own bare hands for hiring him back.

"Well, I'm not starting until tomorrow, so I guess I'll see you then," Evan said. "Bye for now."

"Okay. Whatever," I mumbled under my breath.

As he walked away, I looked over at Sam, who was studying the schedule, which was on a clipboard hanging from the back of the storeroom door. Trudy did the schedule in pencil. Sometimes it was tempting to erase an entire week . . . like now, for instance.

When Sam met my gaze, I mouthed the words, "What the . . ."

And she whispered back, "I know!"

It was a good thing the lunch shift at the restaurant was beginning. I kept my mind off Evan by visiting with the kitchen staff, the cooks and busboys and dishwashers—most of them had worked at Bobb's the summers before, like I had, so it was more of a reunion.

Even though it was a Tuesday, the restaurant was very busy. Lots of islanders came in to celebrate the beginning of summer, to mark the fact that Bobb's was even open for lunch. And there was a ferry full of retirees from Florida who were traveling together across New England on a bus tour. They kept making jokes about the ferry being worse even than the bus, which was saying a lot, apparently.

One table took so long to order that my mind completely started to wander. I couldn't get over the fact that Evan was here, that I'd just talked to him. I had a hundred questions I wanted to ask him. I was so angry and so excited at the same time. It was a really bad combination; I wanted to talk to him, but if I did, I'd only yell and scream at him.

There it was, that intense pull I felt toward Evan. I could say I'd keep my distance from him. But this was Bobb's, where we both worked. And we were on the island. There weren't that many places to hide.

For some reason I suddenly remembered how we'd sneaked into the old, abandoned lighthouse last summer, after an open-house party at our neighbors' place. We'd sprinted up to the top, climbing up the circular stairs, laughing and pushing each other, until we were standing on the little ledge, looking out at the water. Then we started kissing and soon we were moving on to other things. "Nobody can see in, don't worry," Evan had whispered in my ear.

We'd gotten into enough trouble when my parents were around to keep an eye on me. What would it be like *now*?

But wait! Colleen! I scolded myself. Evan and I weren't together, and I didn't want to be. He'd been fun last summer—but that was all it ever was with him. Fun. Ben and I had something deeper, more serious. Everyone thought we'd get married one day, and we probably would.

I smiled and looked at the first retiree to finally decide on her order. "Would you like soup or coleslaw with that?"

Behind her, I saw Evan outside through the plate glass window. He was standing on the dock, talking and laughing with Stan Mathews, one of the lobstermen who supplied the restaurant. As they talked, Evan was skipping rocks on the water.

The older woman cleared her throat. "Excuse me, doll. But what's the soup again?"

"Oh! Ah." I had to glance at my order pad to remember, which was rather pathetic. We had the same soups every Tuesday last summer. "Clam chowder or tomato bisque," I said.

"Did you say *chowdah*?" a man at the table asked. "Come on, say it. Chowdah!"

I smiled politely, said "Chowdah" as best as I could, and finished taking everyone's orders. Then I went into the kitchen, clipped the slip to the carousel, and came back to the table with rolls in a plastic basket shaped like a lobster trap.

"Look at that! Oh, Bill, look at that. How quaint!" one of the women said.

Before I could go over to the bar for their drinks, I caught Evan looking at me through the window. When he saw me looking at him, he smiled and waved.

How quaint, indeed. How ridiculously, nauseatingly, shockingly quaint.

Chapter 5

"So. *That* was awkward," Sam said as we walked to the house that night after the dinner shift, at about ten o'clock. She smoothed back her dark brown hair and refastened one of her small gold barrettes.

My feet were so tired from being on them all day that I was starting to rethink this walk-to-work-and-back exercise plan. I was going to need new sneakers. I was going to need a new bike, and not the one-speed hand-me-down from my grandmother that I usually rode all over the island. (Though I couldn't imagine getting rid of the cute wicker basket on the handlebars. My grandmother made it herself. She was so multitalented—she could sew, knit, and draw like nobody's business.)

"What was awkward?" I asked. "Running out of the special at five thirty and then having to tell everyone we were out of clams at six? I mean, what seafood restaurant runs out of clams? Trudy must have lost her predicting skills over the winter."

"No, it wasn't about the *menu* selections." Sam laughed. "You know what I'm talking about, Coll!"

"Oh, right. When that guy at table nine asked you if you would be working tomorrow, too? What was he . . . like, forty, forty-five?" I'd seen a guy wearing a goofy khaki hat with earflaps smiling and flirting with Sam.

"If I were working tomorrow, which of course I *am*, do you think I'd tell him?" Sam shuddered.

"Too bad there aren't more restaurants on the island," I said—and as soon as I did, I realized how very, very, very true that was. More places to eat would mean more places to *work*. And that would mean I wouldn't have to work with Evan again.

"Yeah, we know that," Sam said, sounding exasperated. "So anyway. What about *Evan*?"

Sam and I had had a brief chance to talk in the kitchen about how freaked out I was, but it wasn't easy to really dish while Cole, the dishwasher, was trying to eavesdrop (and not dishdrop). We were short two people that night, and things had gotten so busy that I hadn't spent that much time thinking about Evan. Which was a blessing not even in disguise, but a flat-out obvious blessing for which I would be eternally grateful.

"I mean, how shocked were you when you saw him?" Sam asked.

"Let's just say that my blood pressure hasn't quite gone back to normal yet." In fact, it felt as though maybe there was a *new* normal that was going to be a lot higher than it used to be. Evan and Ben and me. In the same town. Surrounded by water. Oh, joy.

"He looks, I hate to say it, good," Sam commented. "Really good. He's definitely still working out a lot, or doing triathlons or whatever—you can tell."

"Maybe you should go out with him this summer, then," I suggested.

"Are you serious? No way!"

"Come on, I saw the way you guys were hugging each other."

"Yeah. Very moving, wasn't it?" Sam scoffed. "He was just being a drama king, as always. You said he wanted to major in drama, right?"

"Last I knew, yeah." I let out a sigh. "He looks . . . older or something." I thought about Evan's face. I thought about the way Evan had put his hands on my waist when he saw me. I thought about our tragic good-bye scene in the fog, on the docks, last summer, when I felt like I would fall apart when I saw him get onto the ferry. And how did I not go *with* him, so I could draw the pain out another forty-five minutes?

Then again, it was okay to make a fool of myself on the island—people knew me here. It wouldn't be okay to be crying the entire way there and back on the ferry.

"You're right, he did look older. Except I think he was wearing the same exact things he wore last year. But then, maybe I am, too," Sam said.

"Just the Bobb's uniform. That doesn't count."

"At least they got us a few new T-shirts. My old ones were so worn out, it was ridiculous. But okay, why did he just show up like that? Why do you think he didn't tell anyone, like *you*?"

"He probably feels too guilty for blowing me off last fall. You know?" I asked.

"Evan? Guilty?" Sam shook her head. "He doesn't strike me as the kind of person to feel guilt. Or remorse. Or have regrets."

"Or feelings," I added.

Sam laughed. "Come on, don't get upset. All I meant was that he's more of a live-for-the-moment type."

"Yeah, live for *his* moments, anyway," I said. "He could care less about my . . . moments. Whatever that means. God, listen to me, I'm ranting about *moments* now."

"So the summer's not starting off exactly as we expected," Sam said. "But you know, Evan can go his way this year, and you can go yours. You don't have to worry about him—you're with Ben now."

I smiled, thinking what perfect revenge it was that I had an even better boyfriend now. Ben never ignored me; he was never rude to me; he respected me; he loved me; he'd never cheated on me; we'd never even fought about anything more serious than what pizza toppings to get. Ben wasn't like Evan, and I loved that about him. He was dependable, reliable, and even unflappable when I got into my anxious college-application-due mode and yelled at him for photocopying my collage art in the wrong reduction size.

(Temperamental artist. Yuck, I know. I try not to live up—or is it down—to that stereotype, but sometimes I can't help myself. Honestly.)

Anyway, it all boiled down to one thing: Evan was more flash, less substance.

Flash was overrated.

Flash was like a tall hot fudge brownie sundae with extra whipped cream that tasted great at the time but gave you a stomachache later.

Flash left you sobbing as you stared at your empty e-mail inbox.

I was through with flash.

When we walked up the driveway, Haley and Ben were sitting on the front porch of the house, talking and laughing.

"Hey!" I said, walking up to them. "No fair having fun without us, while we're still wiping down tables."

"And no fair sleeping in, while *we're* already at work for two and a half hours," Haley replied. "Right?" she asked, turning to Ben.

"Yeah, we have a much worse deal. Do you know how cold it is at six A.M.?" He smiled at Samantha and got to his feet. He was wearing a hooded sweatshirt, shorts, and untied basketball sneakers. "You must be Sam. Hi."

"Hey, Ben, nice to meet you." Sam shook his hand.

"I've heard a lot about you," Ben said, smiling. "I'm sure about half of it is true, right?"

"Well, all of the *good* stories are true, anyway," Sam said. "Disregard any of the others."

"Come on, there aren't any bad stories about you," I said. "Unless you count the time you made the tartest lemonade in history for a rude customer."

Sam grinned. "Well, that wasn't necessarily bad. She left, didn't she?"

"Hey, what's that?" I asked, pointing to a familiar-looking orange backpack that was sitting beside the porch swing.

"I heard you have an extra spot in the house, so . . ." Ben shrugged.

"Uh-huh. *Right*," I replied.

"No, actually, I brought back some books I borrowed from your dad," Ben said.

"*The Very Hungry Caterpillar*?" Haley joked. "Or *The Cat in the Hat Comes Back*?"

"Ha ha," Ben said.

"It's nice to meet you, Ben, but I'm beat," Sam said. "I've got to go take a shower and hit the sack—I'll see you guys tomorrow, okay?" She walked over to the door.

Haley covered her mouth as she yawned. "Yeah, I was

thinking of turning in, myself. Good night, Ben. Night, Coll."

"Good night," we both said. I felt bad that Haley and Sam felt they had to bolt as soon as Ben and I were together. I mean, I wanted time alone with him, but hanging out as a group was okay with me, too. This was their house for the summer, and they should be able to hang out wherever and whenever they wanted.

"So, how was work?" Ben asked once we were by ourselves.

"Work was—" Suddenly I remembered. *Evan.* Sitting on the freezer, giving me a hug, waving at me through the window. Reminding me of his stupid nice ankles. "Um. It wasn't exactly what I expected."

"Why not?" Ben asked. "Come on, how much could that place change?"

"You'd be surprised," I said with a faint smile. I really needed to tell Ben about Evan. I'd have to tell Ben who he was, that we'd dated, that he was back in town. Sooner or later, I'd have to tell Ben the whole story, or at least part of it.

But as he wrapped his arms around my waist, I decided the story could wait. I snuggled close to him, enjoying the feeling of being in his arms. I felt safe and warm.

"You know what? You smell like . . . lobster and melted butter," he said.

I stepped out of his embrace and slapped him on the shoulder. "You'll never be asked to live here if you go around saying things like that."

"Sorry," he said, laughing. "I was only joking."

"No, you're not. You know what? Let me go change

and I'll be right down," I said.

"Okay, but hurry—I can only stay for another half hour at the most," Ben said. He gave me a quick kiss, then went back over to the porch swing and sat down.

Upstairs, I ran into Sam in the hallway outside the bathroom. "Coll, I know we have the extra room, but . . . he's not really moving in," she said. "Is he?"

"No!" I laughed. "It's just this running joke we have."

"Okay. But is he staying over? I mean . . . is that cool with your parents?"

"No, definitely not. It's on the list, remember? 'No sleepovers, especially of the boyfriend variety,'" I quoted.

"Then again, they *are* a few thousand miles away," Sam said. "How would they—"

"Don't even think it," I said. "Well, okay, think it, but don't do anything else. Anyway, Ben and I aren't exactly . . . we don't. You know. Sleep together."

"No?" Sam asked.

"Not yet, anyway," I said. For some reason Ben and I were both still waiting to take that last step. Maybe I was waiting because I felt like I'd jumped into that too quickly with Evan and it had made the breakup that much worse. I was a little tentative now, I guess.

I quickly changed into a pair of striped pink Adidas workout pants and a long-sleeved navy fleece, and went back downstairs. On the way, I grabbed an apple from the bowl on the kitchen table.

"So did you really bring a change of clothes?" I asked, pointing to the backpack, now propped against the porch chair. I sat next to him on the porch swing and took a bite of the apple.

"Sure. I mean, why not? I can always sleep out here

on the porch." Ben laughed. "No, *your* parents might be gone, but mine are still very much here. And they're expecting me home in a half hour."

"Right. Parents." I snuggled a little closer to him. "I remember those."

Ben put his arm around my shoulders and squeezed me tightly. Then he turned and started to nuzzle my neck, giving me little kisses. I turned to him and kissed his chin, his cheeks, his mouth. I just needed to be reminded of how wonderful Ben was, how he was nothing like Evan, how he worshiped me completely . . . ?

Suddenly the telephone rang, jarring me out of the fantasy that I was worshiped by—well, anybody. Who was calling so late at night? Maybe Haley's mom, I thought. To tell her to go to bed or she'd be tired tomorrow.

"Ignore it," Ben whispered in my ear as the phone rang again.

"Done," I said, trying to lose myself in his kisses.

The phone stopped ringing. Seconds later, there was a loud knock on the screen door. "Um, sorry," Haley said. I pulled away from Ben and looked up to see Haley standing there holding the telephone out to me. "Coll? It's your parents."

"What? My parents?" Somehow they knew that if they called right now, they'd ruin the one half hour I had to spend with Ben. It was amazing.

"Hello?" I said into the receiver.

"Colleen!" my father's voice cried. "How are you?"

"I'm fine—but are you? I mean, is there an emergency or something?" I asked.

"Goodness, no."

"Then why are you calling *now*? It's like four in the

morning there—isn't it?"

"It costs less to call now," my father said. "Plus, we have jet lag, and knew you'd just be getting home from work. How was it?"

"Fine, the same as always," I said, my brain flashing back to the freezer moment, when I first saw Evan. In some ways, yes, work was the same as always, but in some ways it was completely different. I decided to spare my father that particular detail—and it wasn't just that Ben was still sitting beside me. It was that my dad wouldn't enjoy hearing about Evan any more than Ben would.

"And how are all the girls? Did everyone arrive okay?" he asked.

I got up off the swing and went into the house to grab a glass of water. "Yes. One thing, though—Erica is going to live at her grandparents' house instead of here. So we have a free bedroom—yours, in case you decide to come home early."

Why did I say that? I missed them, but I didn't want them to come home early.

"Oh, no chance of that. I mean, we aren't planning to cut the trip short—but if there's an emergency, or if you need us—"

"No, don't worry, everything's fine. It's going to *stay* fine, too," I told him.

My mother got onto the phone next, and I talked to her for a couple of minutes. Before I hung up, I had to promise her that I'd stick to every single one of the posted rules and that everyone in the house would stick to them, too—and everyone on the island would, too. I'm actually not sure what I promised. I was really tired, and I wanted to get back to Ben, who was patiently waiting outside for me, even though it was getting chilly. "Yes, Mom. Love you, too. Good-bye!"

She rattled off a few German phrases and then she was gone. Despite the fact they had kind of annoyed me, I was really glad they'd called. It was great to hear their voices. It was just . . . couldn't I have heard their voices the next morning?

"Your parents have incredibly bad timing," Ben said when I rejoined him on the porch. I sat on the swing and cuddled up next to him. "Do you think they have a web cam set up or something? You know, 'Let's see what Colleen's up to'?"

"No, you know what it is. My family, my entire extended gene pool, has really poor timing," I said. I patted my mouth to cover a wide yawn. "You know that."

"And yet, I still hang out with you." Ben lightly rubbed my shoulders. "Why do you think that is?"

"I have no idea," I said. "Maybe because you know you owe me."

Ben laughed. "I *owe* you?"

"Yes. You'd never have your summer job now if you'd puked on the ferry that first day of school," I reminded him.

"You're so romantic." Ben tilted my face toward his and we kissed.

Telling Ben about Evan now would be a case of bad Templeton timing. Wouldn't it? I mean, here we were, enjoying ourselves, feeling really close. If I told him now, it would be a horrible end to a pleasant evening. We only had about ten minutes left before Ben had to go home.

So, it was settled. I'd tell Ben about Evan tomorrow.

Chapter 6

When Erica, Samantha, and I walked into Bobb's for our staff meeting the next day, I expected to see everyone sitting in the dining room, where we usually got together for these occasional meetings.

Instead, the meeting was in the kitchen. Evan was sitting on top of the stainless freezer once again. Standing beside him was a girl I'd never seen before. I felt my heart start pounding nervously, and my palms got sweaty. *Don't tell me that's his new girlfriend,* I thought. *Please don't tell me it's bring-your-latest-conquest-to-work day.*

She had long, straight blond hair, and wore khaki capris, white sneakers, and a Bobb's T-shirt with the sleeves rolled up, showing off tan, sculpted arms. She looked like a tennis player. Maybe it was the K-Swiss court shoes that made me think that.

Trudy started off by saying something about how being in the kitchen brought us closer to the heart of the restaurant, and how that would bring us all closer together. She talked a lot about needing to be *close*. She was somewhat of a hippie, but she'd also apparently read a lot of business books over the winter and she was just dying to try out their theories.

"So, crew, there are a few new people I want you all to meet. Well, one is new, and one is a returning favorite." Trudy winked at Evan.

I nearly tossed my cookies into the sink I was standing

beside. "Returning favorite"? As if this were a game show and Evan was a former champion or something. Or a feature on the menu. Tonight's returning favorite: Evan the cold-hearted. Served with a side of slaw, also cold.

Maybe I felt so grumpy because I was sleepy from staying up so late with Ben the night before. I couldn't imagine how *he* felt—he'd already been at work for four hours. Poor Ben. He had to be at work at six. Our summer schedules weren't going to work very well together. He kept trying to get the later shift, but since he was the new guy he got last choice.

The new person at Bobb's was the blond-haired girl standing beside Evan. Her name was Blair, and she was taking the place of Kelley, who'd decided at the last minute to work at the Spindrift B&B instead of at Bobb's. (Why anyone would want to make beds and muffins is beyond me, but to each her own, I guess.)

"Blair came to visit for a weekend but decided to stay on," Trudy said.

That still didn't answer my question: Did she *know* Evan before now? What did she know and when did she know it? Etc.

"Where are you from?" I asked her, smiling and trying to be polite about the fact I was prying.

"The most boring town in the United States," she said with a sigh. "I am *so* glad to be here."

Everyone laughed, and I thought, Could she be a little *less* forthcoming? That description didn't sound like Philadelphia, Evan's hometown. But you never knew. Anyhow, my invitation to visit that particular city had been rescinded, so what did *I* know?

"Is this the first time you've ever been here?" I asked.

She nodded. "Yeah."

"What made you want to stay for the whole summer?" I went on.

"Isn't it obvious?" she asked.

I just smiled at her. *Um, no? That's why I'm asking? Because if it has anything to do with Freezer Boy there, I need to know. Now.*

"This place is heaven!" she said. "I love the ocean, and I love the feel of it here."

"Yeah, well—see how you feel in July, when you're waiting on a table of spoiled ten-year-olds who just flew in from New York and they expect you to shell their lobsters *for* them," Evan told her.

"Now, Evan, that's enough of that," Trudy scolded. "We don't need any negatives here in this kitchen, just positives." She smiled at everyone, and Evan looked at me and the corner of his mouth curled up in a half smile.

I just looked at him, remembering the day last summer when that happened, and how hard we'd laughed when Evan had intentionally cracked a claw so that it shot pulpy liquid into one of the kids' faces.

Then Trudy was off on one of her let's-all-pretend-we're-crustaceans-and-bond lectures.

"Remember, we all have to work together as a team if we're going to make it through another crazy summer. A lobster has eight legs and two claws, and needs every one of them to walk." Trudy was constantly trying to integrate things about lobsters into her management technique. It was funny—when it wasn't extremely annoying. Because right now there were some legs on this team that I wouldn't mind losing. Legs with Birks attached to them. Why did he have to be in such good shape? I hated that about him. Running around the island, Little Mr. Triathlon.

It was appropriate that he was sitting on the freezer all the time. He could be so cold. All those times I called him, E-mailed him, told him that I wanted to visit. And he totally encouraged me, until push came to shove and it was time to set a date, and then he dropped me.

"Colleen?" Trudy asked.

"Oh. Yes?"

"Are you still with us?" Trudy waved her hand in front of my face.

For the moment, I thought. If I could find another job on the island, then . . . no.

"Are you getting enough sleep?"

"Not last night," Samantha commented.

"Oh, really." Trudy frowned at me.

Evan was staring at me, and I felt this heat rising from my toes all the way up to my face, and I knew I was turning bright red. Almost cooked-lobster-like.

"Well, I was wondering: If you could be a sea creature, Colleen, what would you be?"

"Anything with a hard shell," Evan said before I could think of anything, and everyone laughed. Me, with a hard shell? He was the one who'd retreated, not me. I was the one who'd gotten hurt.

"Soft-shell crab," I said, staring right back at Evan, who had this idiotic grin on his face. "With a baked potato on the side."

"Yeah, well, I think I'm more of a squid," Evan said. "Squids are the smart ones, right?"

No, squids are the slippery, elusive ones. So yes, that fits you perfectly, I thought.

"Now, one last announcement before we throw open the doors and meet our public," Trudy said when she wrapped up the meeting about five minutes later. "Blair is still looking for a place to live this summer. For now she's camped out on our living room floor, but I'm sure she'd like something a little more permanent and private. If anyone knows of anything . . . please don't hesitate to speak up. All right, you guys. Let's have a great summer!"

Erica, Samantha, and I immediately headed off to a corner of the kitchen where we could talk privately.

"So what do you think?" Sam asked me. "Should we tell her we have space in the house? Would you be okay with that?"

"We don't really know her. I mean, we don't know her, period," I pointed out. "We have no idea what she's like."

"No, but she seems nice," Erica said. "Doesn't she? And you have that empty bedroom that used to be for me, right?"

"Unless Ben sneaked in there when we weren't looking," Sam joked.

"I don't know, Erica. My parents . . . they wanted to approve of everyone living there," I said.

"So what's not to approve?" Sam asked. "She's employed. She must be okay or Trudy wouldn't have hired her. How about we invite her over and show her the rules? Ask if she wants to agree to the terms? If she does, great. If not, then no big deal—she can keep looking. But . . . you know how hard it is to find a place to stay here, Coll."

"And she seems really nice," Erica said again. "She even volunteered for the Monday and Tuesday lunches because no one else did, because everyone knows you don't make good money."

"I wonder if her parents would let her live with three total strangers," I said.

"We're not strangers, we're co-workers," Sam said. "All you can do is ask." As I said earlier, she has a way of cutting to the chase and making things seem simple—things that I could obsess and worry about.

I nodded. "Okay." The three of us approached Blair, who was studying the back-of-the-house menu of abbreviations, no doubt trying to memorize some of Trudy's bizarre nicknames.

"Blair? How about living with us?" I asked. "We're all splitting a house, and we have an extra bedroom."

"You're kidding. Really?" Blair asked.

"I was going to live there, but then my parents changed their minds and said I had to stay with my grandparents instead," Erica said. "So yes, really. It's available."

"There's no rent," I said, "but you'd have to kick in some money for basic house expenses, split the groceries, all that. It's about a mile from here—" I felt a tap on my shoulder, and turned to see Evan standing at my elbow.

"What are you talking about—you're all living at your house?" Evan asked. "Where are your parents, Coll?"

"In Europe," I said, trying to ignore the fact that (a) he had just called me "Coll," (b) he still had his hand on my shoulder, and (c) it was making me feel very uncomfortable.

"You're kidding!" Evan said. "They left for the whole summer?"

"Practically, yeah," I said. "They'll be back at the end of August."

"Oh. That's too bad. I was looking forward to seeing them again," Evan said.

Don't take that tone with me, I thought. That I-know-your-family tone. So aggravating. "Yeah, well. Too bad."

Actually, if my parents had known Evan was coming back, they probably wouldn't have left me here by myself. They thought he was "semi-dangerous." At least that was how my dad put it when he was trying to console me during the days when I was trying to get over Evan and spent every spare moment moping around the house.

Maybe I should spare them the bad news and not tell them Evan was back for the summer, so they didn't spend time worrying on the Continent and ruin their trip. He wasn't that important.

Evan shrugged. "I guess there's a lot that's been going on that we don't know about each other."

Um . . . yeah. For instance, I didn't know if he had a heart or whether he was running on battery power. How many Duracells would it take to make someone appear human?

Suddenly I realized that Sam, Blair, and Erica had drifted away, leaving me and Evan alone. "Um, yeah," I said. "There probably is a lot we don't know. For instance, where are you going to college?"

"Actually, I'm going to B—"

"Not Bates," I interrupted him. "You're not going to Bates. You can't."

"I can't?" he asked.

"No—"

"Can I finish what I was going to say?" he asked.

"But Bates—that's not fair, because *I'm* going to Bates—"

"Oh, and you have to approve who can be there at the same time with you? You're on the admissions board?" Evan asked.

"No. I just thought . . . maybe we shouldn't be at the same college because maybe that would be weird. Right?"

"Maybe it would be. Yeah, it probably would be," Evan said. "But you don't have to worry about that, because what I was trying to say was that I'm going to Boston University," he said. "That's where I'm going. BU."

"Oh." I felt like a complete idiot. Why couldn't I just shut up now and then and wait for people to speak? Did I have to rush in and embarrass myself like that? "So, BU." I smiled weakly. "That sounds great."

"Yeah. What is that—a three-hour road trip from Bates?" he mused.

As if it mattered, I thought. As if I were going there, or he would come see me. "More like two and a half," I said, and then I could have kicked myself. Why did I want it to sound shorter?

We exchanged awkward glances. The last time we discussed a road trip, it was me to Philadelphia. And as we both knew, that never happened, which was part of the reason I was standing there feeling like I wanted to shove him into the walk-in freezer and lock the door behind him.

Not that I would. But picturing icicles on his stupid stubbled face *really* made me smile.

Evan, not knowing what I was thinking, smiled back at me.

"It really is good to see you."

Don't! Don't be nice like that, I thought. "Yeah. You too," I said.

And then the lunch shift began. It was completely busy, and I didn't get a chance to take a break until two thirty. Sam was finishing up with a large party, so I signaled to her that I was heading outside, and grabbed a bottle of chocolate milk from the fridge. Then I went outside to get some fresh air. The air doesn't circulate all that well at Bobb's—or at least not in the kitchen, with the giant steaming pots of hot water and soup simmering all day long.

I got a shock when I opened the back door. The wind had shifted direction so that it was now blowing off the water towards, well, *me*—and it was getting really cold. It felt good, though, and I knew I would cool down in about two minutes. Then I could go back inside, wipe down my section's tables, and wrap some silverware in napkins (Trudy called it "bundling") before the end of my first shift of the day.

I cracked open the twist top on the chocolate milk and leaned back in the doorway, taking a few gulps. I was in mid swallow when Evan came up to me, carrying a bag of garbage for the Dumpster.

I was going to offer to move when he squeezed past me in the narrow doorway. And then he stopped and stood there for a second.

"So. Still got milk, huh?" he asked.

I just glared at him. He thought he was so funny. Him and his Ultimate Endurance, which somehow got activated to smell even better when he was standing that close to me. He wore it, he lived it . . . and I had to suffer because of it. I didn't have high endurance for this. I had low tolerance. And now he was cracking jokes about my beverage preference.

"What? Why are you looking at me like that?" Evan smiled.

"You know why," I said.

"Not really, no," he said.

And there was this electric feeling in the air all of a sudden, as if a storm were about to hit. Suddenly it didn't feel chilly.

"That trash bag is touching my leg," I said. "What else?" I wriggled out from the doorway and went back into the kitchen to safety. I wasn't ready to be alone with Evan like that. I didn't think I'd ever be ready for that again.

Chapter 7

"This is it? No way!" Blair said as we walked up to the house. The four of us were sneaking in a visit between shifts at the restaurant so we could show Blair the place. "How long have you lived here? You're so lucky!"

"Well, we moved here about ten years ago," I said. "When my grandparents died, we moved into their old house. Well, first we moved back to help take care of my grandfather, and then we stayed here."

"Your grandparents died?" Blair gave me a sympathetic look. "I'm sorry. They must have been pretty young."

"Yeah, they were. In their sixties." I still missed them, and I wished we could have all lived here together—if not in this house, then at least on the island. I had lots of great memories of the weeks we'd spent here together when I was little.

I'd inherited not only my grandmother's bike, but also a little of her artistic skill. She had done illustrations for a book about the island, and it had become so popular that she'd been asked to work on a few other books—one was all botanical illustrations, and another was about the ocean. She'd had a fatal stroke about ten years ago, and I'd always regretted that I hadn't gotten to know her better. After she passed away, my grandfather didn't do very well. He ended up with heart trouble, and he died about two years later.

"Wow. That's terrible," Blair said when I told her the story. "Sorry if I brought up a painful subject."

"It's okay," I said. "I don't mind talking about it."

"Still, you live here all year? That is so cool. I'd love to do that. This makes my town look pathetic—well, more pathetic than it *usually* does." She laughed.

It was fun to watch someone new to the island see the place for the first time. You know how you get so used to something that you don't realize how great it is until someone else points it out?

"Wait until you see your room," I told Blair as we walked through the kitchen. On the way in, I grabbed the sheet of poster board off the bulletin board. Blair was so busy looking around the house that she didn't notice.

After a quick tour of the first floor, she and I headed up the stairs together. "It's usually my parents' bedroom, so you'll have to be really careful and make sure you don't, um, wreck anything."

"No problem," Blair replied.

During a break at work, I'd called my parents and asked them whether it was okay for me to offer the extra room to Blair, since Erica couldn't take it. They'd said it was fine, that they trusted my judgment.

Sometimes I wished they didn't trust me or my judgment so much. It felt as if I could only go *down* in their estimation of me—and that it might happen fairly soon. But Blair seemed cool, and I just couldn't see that we'd have any problems. She was really making an effort to get to know all of us, and so far she was a great co-worker. Okay, so we'd only worked together one shift so far, but you could learn a lot about a person in that short time.

"It's huge!" Blair cried when she walked into the bed-room. She wandered around the room and looked out the windows. "Ocean view. King-size bed. The color's a little drab, but I can deal with that. So why has no one else taken this gorgeous room?"

"Well, it was set aside for Erica, remember?" I explained again how her family had decided she should stay with her grandparents this summer instead of here. "And then we decided to leave this room vacant for guests."

"Wow. And you'd really let me just live here? Free of charge?" Blair looked at me.

"Well, yeah—I mean, you'd need to pitch in on house stuff with the rest of us, like groceries and the phone bill," I said.

"You're the best!" Blair said, throwing her arms around me.

"Okay, but before we go any further, there's some-thing you have to see."

"The bathroom? Oooh, is it connected—a master bath?"

"No, not quite." I laughed. "Feel free to go check it out, though, third door on your right. But I was talking about this." I handed her the poster board. "It's a list of house rules, which my parents wrote up and made me agree to. It's important to them, so if you could look at it and make sure you're okay with the ground rules, that'd be great."

"Ground rules?" she said, beginning to scan the list.

"Yeah. If you don't mind. Just review them. I know it sounds dumb, but—"

"No, it's fine. I know how parents can be."

"I'm going downstairs. Come on down when you're ready," I said.

As I started down the stairs, I heard Haley's voice. She didn't sound happy.

"You guys asked her to *live* here? Without asking me about it first? Without even letting me meet her?"

I gulped. Oh, no. Why hadn't I thought of that? Of course Haley would have to approve of the plan, too. And there was nothing Haley hated more than being out of the loop.

"But she's really nice," Erica said.

"So what? You know, you don't even live here!" Haley cried. "How can you make decisions that affect the rest of us?"

"I'm so sorry," I said as I walked into the kitchen. "We shouldn't have asked her without asking you."

Haley just glared at me.

"Come on, Haley—I'm sorry. We got carried away—we just felt so bad because she didn't have a place to live. She's been sleeping on Trudy and Robert's living room floor," I explained.

"But we all agreed that we'd decide who was in the group together. We're fine with just the three of us, aren't we? It's not like we *need* a fourth person so we can pay less rent. We *have* no rent! And then *you* always have a place to sleep when you stay over," she said to Erica.

Erica shrugged. "I can sleep on the sofa."

Haley rolled her eyes. "Come on."

"Nothing's final yet," I told Haley. "Meet Blair first, okay? If for some reason you don't like her," I said in a soft voice, "we'll just tell her that we changed our minds."

"We can't do that," Sam said. "That'll come off really rude. We already *offered* it to her. And she really needs a place."

"What's she doing up there, anyway? Moving in already?" Haley asked.

"I'll go get her," I said. I headed for the stairs, but before I could go up them, I saw Blair heading down. "Hey, Haley's home—you've got to meet her."

"Oh, sure. Great. Love to," she said with a smile.

"So what did you think of the rules?" I asked as she reached the bottom of the stairs. "Are you going to be okay with them?"

Blair handed the poster board back to me. "They're exactly the kind of rules my father would write up for me. In fact, I think he has, already. So it's no problem. I'm ready to sign on, if you guys are."

"Um . . . well, let's see. Blair, this is Haley. Haley, Blair."

"Cool name." Blair smiled at Haley.

"Thanks." Haley wouldn't quite look at her, at first.

I went to the fridge and got out a pitcher of lemonade. I sliced a few fresh wedges of lemon and tossed them into the pitcher. "So, let's go outside and talk. We still have some time before we have to get back to work."

"Where are you working?" Blair asked Haley as we filed out onto the porch.

On the way, Samantha grabbed four wineglasses from the cupboard. "Just to make it fun," she said to me.

"Or, are you working, I guess I should ask," Blair said to Haley as she settled into a chair. "Not everyone has to."

"Oh, I have to, all right," Haley said. "I work at the Landing—you know, the shack down by the water with coffee and ice cream—"

"Where are you from?" Blair interrupted.

"Here," Haley said.

"You have that accent. I love that accent," Blair said.

Haley shrugged. "I can't help it. I'm going to try to get rid of it in college."

"Oh, yeah? Where are you going—Paris or something?"

"Not quite. Dartmouth."

"Oh, God. Dartmouth. I got rejected by them before I even submitted my application. When I requested a catalog they sent it to me with this big DON'T EVEN BOTHER sticker on the front cover."

Haley laughed. "They didn't."

"Pretty much," Blair said. "Ivy League . . . I mean, I'd kill to be Ivy League. I'm actually taking a year off so I can reapply and try to get in somewhere good next time."

"I don't care that much about whether it's Ivy League," Haley said. "I just want to be somewhere where the other people are smart. It's a lot of pressure, you know?"

"Yeah, but it's your ticket to everything when you graduate," Blair said.

"My ticket's going to be to Europe. One way," Sam said. "Right, Colleen? We're going to Europe for three months after we finish college."

"Right," I said. "Just as soon as my parents do all the groundwork this summer and figure out where we should go."

"Yeah, but you wouldn't want to go or stay where your *parents* like. Would you?" Blair asked.

"She has a point," Sam agreed.

"Colleen's parents think classical music is fun," Haley

said. "They read about ten books a week, and their last big road trip was to . . . Where was it? Historic Colonial Inns of Massachusetts?"

Everyone laughed.

"Hey, at least they have a great house, and we're all really lucky to be here." Sam raised her glass. "To the Templetons."

"To Starsky and Hutch!" Haley grinned at me.

"Starsky and Hutch?" Blair said.

"Our cats. Are you okay with cats?" I asked.

"Um. Sure," Blair said. "Are they nice?"

"Supersweet." Erica raised her glass in the air. "To a great summer!" She turned to Blair. "Your turn."

"To . . . oh, my gosh, I can't think of anything original," Blair said. "To . . . the ocean! And my new view of it. Thanks, guys."

To ex-boyfriends, I thought. *To new boyfriends.* "To friends!" I said.

We all reached forward to clink our glasses together.

I guess I must have clinked too hard, because my wineglass splintered into a hundred pieces and we all jumped back to avoid the shattered glass.

Maybe I should have taken that as an omen, but I didn't. It just seemed like something clumsy at the time.

Chapter 8

"Colleen?" Trudy stopped me on my way back into the kitchen on Friday. I was done, for the moment, with my lunch tables. "Could you help me out with something? There was just a woman here who insisted on looking at every single T-shirt we had for sale, and she and her kids must have tried on about twenty shirts. Could you do me a favor and go refold them all?"

"Sure," I said.

"And there's some additional stock in the drawer underneath the cabinet. If you wouldn't mind restocking, too, while you're at it?"

"No problem." I quickly washed my hands in the sink and then went out front. No one was working at the register, and Erica was nowhere in sight, which was odd. But, knowing Erica, she was probably carrying leftover boxes of food out to someone's car, or driving them home, or something. The phrase "above and beyond" was created for her.

I picked up the pile of T-shirts from the counter and moved them over, away from the register, so they wouldn't be in the way. I shook the first one out and laid it on the counter, then neatly folded it into a small square, with the Bobb's logo showing above the pocket.

When I finished folding the first stack, I crouched down to put them into the glass display case. I was doing some rearranging when someone else walked behind the counter and legs slammed into my shoulder. "Ow!" I cried.

"Sorry!" a voice above me said. Evan reached down and put his hand on my shoulder. "Colleen, you okay?"

I pushed his hand away and resisted the urge to spit on his sandals before standing up. "I'm fine."

"How was everything today?" Evan asked as he ran through a credit card for a customer.

Everything was fine, I thought, pulling myself to my feet, *until you showed up.*

"Great. Delicious," the man said. "We'll definitely be back." After he'd signed the receipt, and after he and his family left the restaurant, Evan leaned against the counter, watching me fold shirts for a second.

"I can ring up the next person," I said. "I mean, I'm here. I could have rung up the *last* person."

"I didn't see you," Evan said. "I didn't think anyone was over here."

"Yeah, right," I murmured.

"What—you think I'd intentionally crash into you? Why would I do that?"

I shrugged and didn't say anything. I tried to slide open the cabinet door closest to him so I could put the size small T-shirts away. But it wouldn't open from the side I was on, so I looked up at him. "Do you mind? Moving?"

He took a few steps to get around me, but he didn't walk all the way out from behind the counter. In fact, he was standing about a foot away from me, giving me no room at all to work. "I don't want to leave because someone might come up, and, you know, you are busy with those shirts. Busy busy busy." He smiled at me.

I let out a deep, annoyed sigh and just kept restocking the case, trying to get it done as quickly as I could, and also trying to ignore what it felt like to be in such close proximity to him again. He smelled the same as always. And I caught myself looking at his ankles again as I crouched down to pull out overstock from the bottom drawer. And then I started thinking about the time he came to my house for dinner last year and I played footsie with those ankles under the table. Or would that be "anklesie." Whatever. Wrong, wrong, wrong to be thinking about it now.

I couldn't get those shirts folded quickly enough. As soon as I was done, I marched straight past him to Trudy's back office and knocked on the door. "Trudy? Could I maybe change my schedule around?" I asked.

"Sorry. No changes for the first month," she said.

"The first *month*? Why?"

"People need routine. A restaurant needs routine," she said.

Yes, but I need a routine that doesn't involve seeing Evan every day, I thought. Couldn't she be more sensitive?

"Why? Is there a problem?" Trudy asked.

"Yes. No—it's fine," I said. I closed her office door and went back down the hallway into the kitchen. Evan smiled at me as he walked past, carrying a tray of desserts out to the dining room.

Drop them, I thought, staring at the tray. *Drop them.*

After the lunch shift, Sam, Erica, and I headed down to the Landing. I was glad to be getting out of Bobb's for a while, and away from Evan.

The three of us were going to our weekly book club

meeting with Haley—at least that's what we said we were doing when anyone asked, and occasionally we did talk about what books we were reading. But in reality we were going down there to watch the ferry come in. Later on Friday afternoons was when it got crowded with tourists coming for the weekend. Haley and I had started out as kids, watching people get off the ferry in order to write stories about them. We played a game of making up details about their lives; she wrote stories about them and I did sketches.

Then when we got older it became part celebrity watch and part looking for hotties who might be coming to the island for the weekend. We could also see people cruising into the harbor on their sailboats.

Not that I was looking for a guy now—in fact, I hadn't been for the past year, or for last summer, either. But that didn't mean I couldn't look. I mean, help my *friends* look.

We called it our book club so that we had an excuse for being there every Friday. *Book* was an acronym for "boys on our kiss-list." Okay, so we came up with that in the fifth grade and it sounds dumb now, but at the time? It was brilliant.

"Where are you guys going?" Blair asked when we didn't turn off on the road to our house. "Or am I totally lost?"

"We're going to the Landing," Erica said. "Want to come along? It's time for book club." I cast a sideways glance at Erica. I wasn't sure if I wanted to invite Blair, but it was too late now to take back the invitation.

Blair looked confused. "But I probably haven't read the book. What is it?"

Erica quickly explained what our book club was all about.

"I like the sound of this. But how about if we stop by the house and change our clothes first?" Blair suggested.

"I don't know," Sam said. "See, I kind of like letting people know where we work. Just in case, you know, it's Orlando Bloom for real this time, and he starts wondering where he should go for dinner, and he looks at our T-shirts and voilà. He's at Bobb's."

"You have it all planned, huh?" Blair teased.

"Anyway, we'll get all bogged down in changing, and then we'll miss the three o'clock, and we'll have to come back and change before we go back to work at four thirty . . ."

"Hey, say no more." Blair held up her hands. "Let's go! My parents are going to be so impressed when I tell them I'm in a book club." She grinned.

I'm sure Ben wondered why Haley and I were always there hanging out on Fridays, but we never told him the real reason, because that would ruin everything. We said it was our Friday-afternoon book club. "Then why don't you have books with you?" Ben had asked more than once.

"We remember it all—we just read the book this week. What do we need the book for?" Haley said.

Not very convincing, but he didn't push the issue. He was nice, and trusting, like that.

Last summer Evan had been a little more suspicious. He'd always asked, "What book is it this week?" and I'd have to come up with something, and then if it was something he'd already read and I hadn't, I'd have to read it just to keep from blowing our cover. Yes, our cover *was* that important. It was a fun game for us that we didn't want to see end.

Evan had even pulled up a chair once last summer and tried to butt in on our "meeting." Samantha politely told him it was a *female* book club.

When we got down to the Landing, Blair and Erica went over to Haley's window, while Sam and I sat down on one of the wooden benches facing the dock.

"So that was pretty uncomfortable at work today," Sam commented, loosening the laces on her sneakers.

"Your feet?" I asked.

"Um, no," she said. "You and Evan. There's so much *tension* between you guys—it's like painful to watch sometimes. Are you going to try to switch shifts, so you don't work with him so often?"

"I tried, but Trudy said she doesn't want anything to change for a month. She's anti-change. Which is odd, because lobsters get to molt, so shouldn't we be able to?"

"Molting isn't your problem, Coll. I mean, did you even *tell* Ben yet?" Sam asked.

"Tell him?" I asked.

"About Evan being here this summer." She slid her sunglasses down her nose and looked at me over the top of the frames. "Oh, no. You guys haven't talked about it, have you?"

I shifted uneasily in my chair. "Well . . . no, not exactly."

I was overdue on a couple of talks.

Evan and I hadn't had The Talk, or any talk, yet. Maybe there wasn't all that much to say, I thought. We were together . . . and now we're not. We were totally crazy about each other . . . and now we're not. We were in love . . . or so I thought.

It was all sounding like bad poetry. That was what bad poems were about: lost love, love in general. Of course, there were good poems about that subject, too. I'd had plenty of time to find them in my *Norton Anthology of Poetry* when Evan was not calling me.

And yes, I was procrastinating about telling Ben about Evan, and about the fact he was back and working at Bobb's with me. It wasn't as if I'd never said *anything*. I mean, before we went out the first time, I'd told him I'd had a couple of boyfriends before him. Of course, I'd focused more on Walter, my second grade sweetheart, and Clifford, who took me to our freshman winter formal.

"Walter and Clifford?" Ben had laughed. "You're making this up, right? Freshman winter formal? So what does that mean—down jackets and black ski pants?"

"It was a *very* sexy evening. Actually. Very sexy," I insisted.

"Not exactly?" Sam was saying now. "Meaning what?"

"Well, I did tell Ben that there were lots of, um, familiar returning employees at Bobb's."

Samantha raised her eyebrow. "*Familiar?* Is that seriously what you said? *Familiar?* How about extremely—"

"I know, I know," I interrupted her. "Slightly more than familiar." I tried to kick a rock with my sandal, but I ended up hitting it with my toe instead. "There just hasn't been a good time to talk to him about it yet."

"Ahem. You've spent at least a couple of nights hanging out with Ben this week," Sam pointed out. "Like last night. You've had time."

"Oh, sure, *time*. But not . . . the right time."

Sam laughed. "Listen to you—'the right time.' There's never going to be a *good* time! Just get it over with, because if you don't, he's going to hear about it from someone else, and that'll be really bad."

"I know. I know I have to tell him. It's just . . . I don't want it to be awkward. I don't want him to feel threatened. That's why I have to pick the perfect time. I know—why don't you come with me when I talk to him?" I said.

"Yeah. Right," Sam said. "*That's* what I want to do."

"Why not?"

"I don't even know Ben yet. Do you know how awkward that would be? And why would I be there for such a personal conversation?"

"Because you're nosy?" I suggested.

"What are you being nosy about now?" Haley dropped into a chair beside me and handed us both fudge bars. "Make it quick, I only have a ten-minute break. As soon as everyone gets off Moby, I've got to run back."

"Oh, nothing," Sam said. "Just talking about some people at work." I knew she was covering for me so I wouldn't have to tell Blair and Haley what a coward I was being, which was awfully nice of her. Haley would be mad if she thought I was hiding *anything* from Ben.

"So I was wondering something. How come you don't work at Bobb's?" Blair asked Haley.

"It's kind of dumb. But my mother has this feud going with Trudy and Robert. I can't even remember how it started, but she'd disinherit me if I ever worked there. Not that there's anything to inherit," Haley said.

"So about this club. Have any of you ever actually

met a celebrity getting off the ferry?" Blair asked as we watched the boat approaching.

"I met a senator once," Haley said. "That was pretty cool."

"Oh, yeah," Blair teased. "Bet he was a real hottie."

"She," Haley said. "And no."

We all laughed.

"Speaking of hotties, you know who's really cute?" Blair took a sip of water. "That Evan guy."

That Evan . . . guy. It was weird to hear someone else talk about him that way. Was Blair interested in him? Should I tell her that we'd gone out? Or should I just warn her about what a jerk he could be?

Blair and Evan . . . if they got involved, I wouldn't be able to handle it, I realized. Why hadn't I thought of that before I asked her to live with us? I mean, I knew none of my close friends would date him . . . but what if Blair did?

"Colleen went out with him last summer," Erica said before I could say anything myself. Because I was just sitting there having an anxiety attack and letting my Fudgsicle melt.

"Yeah, they had a *thing*. A pretty serious thing, actually," Sam added while I rubbed at the melted chocolate with a napkin.

"Oh, *really*." Blair gave me what seemed like a look of newfound respect. I smiled awkwardly. "A thing? Cool. So, what's he like? How long did you guys have this . . . thing?" She laughed.

"Um, well." I wondered how much I should tell her. We'd only met a couple of days ago, so I didn't feel comfortable going into complete detail. "He's . . . well, he *can* be . . . fun," I said. That was pretty vague. "We went out for a month or so."

"No, it was longer than that, wasn't it?" Erica said. "Two months."

"Yeah, I guess. But then summer ended and he went home, and so . . . you know." I shrugged.

"No point keeping up a long-distance relationship," Blair said. "That's exactly how I feel about things."

I smiled. It wasn't exactly how *I'd* felt, but whatever. I really didn't feel comfortable talking about Evan with her. And even worse, now Blair knew about me and Evan, while Ben still didn't. That wasn't cool. What if it got back to Ben from her? Or what if Haley mentioned it? They were friends; they'd talk like that. But she knew I wanted to be the one to break the news, or at least I hoped she did.

The ferry pulled up and we all watched as first several cars drove off it, and then a varied collection of middle-aged-looking men and women strolled off the ramp and onto the dock. Small children screamed and raced each other to the end of the dock and were chased by their parents. A few teenaged boys were there, but they were boys we knew from the island—boys I knew nobody either would be, or should be, interested in.

In other words, no prospects.

"See you guys later!" Haley jumped up as she saw someone approach the takeout window.

I smiled as I saw Ben helping an older woman walk carefully from one surface to another. He was carrying her luggage for her, too.

"You know what? Out of everyone?" Blair pointed toward Ben with her red straw. "*That's* the best-looking guy here."

I cleared my throat. Did we have the same taste in guys or what? "Blair? That's my boyfriend. Ben. You met him at the house the other night. Remember?"

"Oh, my gosh—I'm sorry. You're right—I didn't recognize him in his uniform. Sorry," Blair said. But she kept looking at him—staring, in fact.

He walked right up to where we were sitting. "Hey, guys. How's it going?"

"Good," I said, looking up at him and smiling. He leaned over and kissed me on the cheek. "How was work?"

"Crazy, as usual on Fridays," Ben said. "How's the book club?"

"We were just finishing up our discussion," Sam said. "Metaphors, similes. You know."

Ben stretched his arms over his head. "I'm so beat. I'm going home to take a shower and change—I'll see you when you get off work tonight, okay?" He gave me another quick kiss and went over to the bike rack to unlock his bike.

"Your schedules really suck this summer, huh?" Sam commented. "Not like when you were dating Evan and you could see each other at work all the time."

"Sh!" I said.

"Sh, what?" Blair asked.

"He doesn't know about Evan yet. I still have to tell him."

"Why would you do that?" Blair said.

"Uh, because I have to?" I said. "Because it's the only right and honest and decent thing to do?"

"Maybe, but it's stupid, too. I never tell guys about ex-boyfriends," Blair said. "It just makes them mad, or it makes them think they're better than him, or even worse, it makes them think they have to go out and *prove* that they're better than him."

Why did it sound as if she'd had a hundred boyfriends already? "So you just don't say anything?" I asked.

"I keep it vague. Extremely vague. I think secrecy is underrated these days," Blair said.

I nodded, smiling. Maybe she was onto something.

"I mean, has *he* told you about all of his ex-girlfriends?" Blair asked.

"I think so. I mean . . . well, how would I know? He only moved here last year."

"Exactly. And how would Ben know about Evan if you don't tell him?"

Sam cleared her throat. "He'd know."

"Why?" Blair asked.

"Because she and Evan act like freaks whenever they're around each other."

"Freaks?" I laughed. "We do not!"

"Okay, then. Whatever you say. But why don't you go walk Ben home?" Sam suggested.

I glanced over my shoulder and saw Ben talking to one of his neighbors. "Good idea. See you guys in an hour!"

I jogged over to catch Ben before he rode off on his bike. We walked down the road together, catching up on things.

Tell him! Tell him! my brain screamed as I babbled on about an E-mail from my parents and a description of Trudy's latest dessert concoction (a peanut butter fudge brownie sundae with fresh strawberries and whipped cream—what I'd had for lunch).

"I'm going to have to come by for that," Ben said, sounding very interested. "I should do that, huh? Come see you at work sometime this weekend?"

"Um . . . maybe not this weekend, because it's going to be swamped," I said. "How about sometime during the week? Like, ah . . ." I hadn't seen the schedule yet for next week, but there must be a day that I worked and Evan didn't. And if there wasn't? I'd create one.

Tell him, tell him right now!

But we only had an hour to spend together. Why should I ruin it? I'd wait for my day off. Monday. I'd tell him then, for sure.

Chapter 9

Any day that starts off with you getting canned cat food on your sunglasses is not a good day.

Maybe I don't even have to point that out, because it's pretty obvious, but take my word for it: When your small, perfectly oval, slightly green and slightly pink framed sunglasses, that you found only after trying on fifty other pairs and annoying your mother to no end at a department store, because all the other shapes made your face look big, or small, or wrong, only she couldn't see that, only *you* could see that . . . well, when something happens to *those* glasses, you should take it as a sign.

I was feeding the cats before I went to work, and I had leaned over to set down the bowls, but my sunglasses were perched on my head and they tumbled right into the ocean fish catch (or, rather, can) of the day. The lenses went smush into the gloppy, fishy part. If that image isn't disgusting, I don't know what is. In fact, I could not stop thinking about it even after I washed them in hot soapy water for five minutes, so I wasn't wearing sunglasses, which could have been part of my problem. Any bright sunny day near the ocean without sunglasses? Not a good idea.

Also, someone had used up the coffee the day before without replacing it. I added Rule 11 to the pink poster board:

No using up coffee without buying more.

Then I made myself a cup of herbal spearmint tea—which is what I usually drink before going to sleep at night—and made a bowl of instant oatmeal, because we were also out of milk for cereal. Halfway through eating, I noticed the oatmeal had a strange-looking black seed floating in it. The rest of it went down the garbage disposal. Then I added Rule 12 to the list:

No using up the last of the milk without buying more to replace it.

It was my day off, but not Ben's, so I'd decided to do a round-trip on the ferry. That way, we could spend some time together. The way the day started off, maybe I should have given up on my plan to talk to Ben about Evan that afternoon, but I didn't. I even begged Sam for assistance, but she turned me down, saying she wanted to spend the day reading and hanging out on the beach. She promised to stop at the store for milk and coffee, so I was officially out of excuses.

I was riding my bike down to the Landing when I turned a corner in the road and saw Evan riding toward me. Could this island *get* any smaller? Could there not be more than three main roads?

Of course, as I got closer I noticed that Evan had a nice road bike, while I was cruising along on my trusty fifty-year-old one-speed.

"Hey!" He turned around and started riding beside me. "What's up?"

"Oh . . . not much." *Just going to tell my boyfriend about you.*

"You're not—" I stopped myself before I blurted it

84

out, for once. If I told him where I was going, he'd probably follow me there, or ask me why I was going to the mainland.

"I'm not what?" he asked.

Not that nice. Not very considerate. Not as good-looking when your ankles are covered up with white socks. "You're not, ah, training for a triathlon, are you?"

Evan squinted at me, which was funny considering I couldn't stop squinting. Having light blue eyes makes you very sensitive to bright sunlight. "No, not right now. Why?"

"Just, you know . . ." I shrugged. "Wondering."

"And you? Where are you headed?"

"I'm, ah, going to visit Haley. At work."

"Oh, yeah? Well, tell her I said hi."

"Sure thing," I said. "I'll do that."

Haley was no fan of Evan's, though, so maybe I wouldn't do that. I heaved a sigh of relief as he turned back around and rode away.

"Could you get me two large root beers?" I asked Haley. "No, wait. Maybe I should make those banana splits."

"Having a bad day?" she teased.

"Not yet," I said. "Well, kind of." I explained about the cat food and the sunglasses while she filled the cups with root beer.

"Thanks for making me lose my appetite," she said as she handed me the large plastic cups.

"Thanks. I'm bringing one of these to Ben—I thought I'd catch Moby and ride a round-trip with him."

"That sounds like fun." Haley rested her elbows on the takeout window and we both gazed out at the people getting off the ferry.

I saw Ben talking with a tall girl with long red hair who was carrying a classic off-white L. L. Bean "Boat and Tote" canvas bag. (I used to think they were stupid, until I realized how much stuff you could carry in them.) "Who is that girl?" I asked as I watched her give Ben a big smile and wave good-bye as she disembarked.

"I have no idea," Haley said.

"Isn't she on the ferry like every day?" I asked. I'd seen her every day that I came down here, anyway. Why was she boating and what was she toting? And did it have to be with Ben?

"Almost. Usually at three, though. She's early today."

As she walked past, I couldn't help noticing that she was flat-out gorgeous. She was tall, and she wore a black skirt, a pink-pattern wispy blouse, and black sandals. Her legs were model material. "Do we hate her, maybe?"

"Maybe a little bit." Haley nodded. "Yeah."

I stepped aside as a customer approached the window. "Wish me luck."

"Luck," she said. "For what? Drinking a root beer?"

"Yeah, something like that." I laughed. The way my day had begun, I wouldn't be surprised if I (a) dropped it off the boat, (b) got the hiccups after drinking it, or (c) laughed too hard while drinking it and had root beer come out my nose.

"Actually . . . I'm going to tell Ben about Evan," I confessed.

"Oh. Oh? Well, then. *Luck*," Haley said. "Lots of it."

When I stepped up to the ferry to get on, Ben just stared at me.

"Colleen? What are you doing here? What's this?"

I handed Ben a ticket. "For me." Then I handed him the root beer. "For you."

"Wow. Thanks."

"I'll go sit down. Come and find me when you get some free time, okay?" I said.

"More than okay." He smiled and kissed my cheek as I walked past him.

I sat up front, on the upper deck, enjoying the sun on my face with my eyes closed against the brightness of it. I was exhausted from last night's shift. We'd been fairly busy when a table of twelve came in without a reservation. It was a birthday party for a four-year-old, and by the time we could get them a table all of the kids were in pretty rotten moods. While I went to get their sodas, Evan had brought them a couple of trays of French fries to keep them happy, and then entertained them all by doing some simple magic tricks, like pulling out quarters from behind their ears. Then they'd laughed and yelled and made Evan be their waiter, instead of me. What can I say? They were easily entertained. I was a bit put out, until he shared his eighteen-percent tip with me.

"Hey."

I opened my eyes and saw Ben standing there. "Hi!"

He sat down beside me and we gave each other a hug. "This was so nice of you to come for a cruise. You didn't have to buy a ticket, though."

"Well, I didn't want to get you in trouble or anything," I said. I looked into his eyes, squinting against the bright sun. Why did I feel so guilty, like I had done something wrong? It was what I *hadn't* done that was the problem. I gave myself a mini pep talk while he finished off his root beer.

If I tell him about Evan, that will make it seem less weird. Once I tell him, it'll be out in the open and we can all go back to our normal, or semi-normal, lives.

"So, there's something I have to tell you," I began.

"This doesn't sound good. What's wrong?"

"Nothing! Nothing's *wrong*." I put my hand on his leg and gave his thigh a reassuring squeeze. "I just need to let you know about something that happened last summer, before you lived here." I paused for a second and then reminded him, "You didn't live here then. I didn't know you."

Ben just stared at me. "Yeah, I know I didn't live here last summer. I'm the one who moved."

"Right. Right!" I laughed nervously. "I really have to stop saying that so much. *Right.* I'm constantly saying that, aren't I? It must be annoying."

"Colleen? I only have a couple of minutes, so . . ."

"Okay. Last summer." A strong breeze blew the strap from my knapsack against the ferry railing. For a minute, I just sat there and listened to the sound of it snapping. "I probably mentioned I went out with this guy named Evan. Right?" Darn. I said it again.

"No, I don't remember anything about a guy named Evan," Ben said.

"Sure, I told you. Evan. From Philadelphia?" I finally got the nerve to look at his face, and tried to gauge his reaction to this news. "Anyway, it wasn't like it was anything serious. We dated for a couple of months—you know, typical summer . . . fling. Thing."

"A couple of months isn't exactly a fling."

Darn Ben and his definitions.

He looked at me, then down at the deck, then back

up at me. "One or two dates is a fling. Not two months."

"But see, sometimes the way you feel about a person is that they're like a fling, like that's how *un*important they are to you."

"And you spent two months with a guy you didn't care about. Wow. That really makes me feel good about us."

"No! I didn't mean . . . Sorry. Okay, so it wasn't just a fling. That was a poor choice of words. We . . . we went out last summer."

"So why are you telling me about this now?"

Because I have to? And because Sam won't be my friend if I don't? "Well, it's just . . . this guy, Evan? He came back this summer. I didn't *know* he was coming. I hadn't even heard from him in months. I mean, I'd barely heard from him since the day he left."

Annoyingly, the image of our painful good-bye scene actually had the nerve to flit through my brain the split second I said that. The early-morning fog, the long romantic hug, the never wanting to let go. . . .

"We didn't keep in touch," I said to Ben. Or at least I did, but he didn't. "So I had no idea he'd be here again. Which is maybe why I never mentioned him. Anyway, he's here."

"Really. Where did you see him?" Ben's voice was flat, almost like a monotone.

"Bobb's."

"He came in for dinner or something?" Ben asked.

"Well, uh, yeah. In a manner of speaking." This was going to be so, so awkward. "He works at Bobb's."

"When did he start? Last night?" Ben asked.

"Actually . . . maybe a few days ago."

"And you're just telling me this now," Ben said, not as a question.

Oh, no. I knew I shouldn't have waited so long. He was really angry. I'd never seen him like this. "We hardly have any of the same shifts, so I haven't seen him much, and I didn't think it was a big deal," I babbled. Now, on top of everything, I was lying.

"Just . . . don't. Look, I have stuff to do." Ben stood up and walked over to the steps that led down to the main deck.

That could have gone a lot better, I thought as I watched him glide down the steps. I mean, it could hardly have gone *worse*.

Right?

After a few minutes, I tried moving down to the lower deck to see if I could talk to him. First he walked past me without making eye contact. Then when he was standing beside Cap Green, I went to try to join the conversation. But Ben moved away, leaving me alone with Cap, the chatterbox of the ferry industry.

I was stuck on Moby with Ben, who hated me now. I looked longingly at the inflatable life rafts hanging on the wall and the preservers stacked beside the door. Making a run for it sounded tempting. Ben would probably help by giving me a push in the direction of the island.

I had a new rule. It didn't have anything to do with the house, but just for fun let's call it Rule 13, because it felt so unlucky.

Never have important discussions on a boat when you are halfway through a round-trip.

Chapter 10

"So, I'll see you later?" I asked.

Ben mumbled something as he leaned over to unlock his bicycle, but I didn't quite catch it. I decided not to push my luck right now. He was still angry with me. He probably didn't want to see me later, or even *think* about seeing me later. He hadn't spoken to me on the way back to the island. (Me, I had made small talk with tourists, and it was the longest forty-five minutes of my life.) I had to give him some time to let him deal with the news about Evan, and me and Evan.

"Okay, well, um, take care," I said awkwardly as he pulled his mountain bike out of the rack beside the Landing.

"Ben! Where are you going?" Haley shouted from the takeout window.

"Hi, Haley!" he called back.

Well, at least he was talking to *her*. He wasn't doing that hate-by-association thing.

"Where are you going?" Haley asked.

"I've got to get home," Ben said. He didn't explain what the big rush was. Obviously it involved getting away from me.

"Hey, you want a FrozFruit for the road?" Haley offered. "We got more coconut in today."

"No thanks. Tomorrow, though! See you later." Ben gave me a cursory glance, and immediately his grin

91

faded. Then he climbed onto his bike and started pedaling away.

"Bye!" I called after him, trying to sound as sweet as I possibly could, hoping I'd erase this new, bad impression I'd apparently made on him. Then I walked over to Haley. No, more like crawled.

"So, how did it go?" Haley asked.

"Couldn't you tell? Ben hates me now."

"Hates you? Come on, be serious. What flavor do you want?"

"I'm not hungry. Anyway, you saw how he was," I said. "Not even talking to me." I stared at the tubs of ice cream. "Cookies and cream," I sighed.

Haley scooped ice cream into a sugar cone and molded the scoop so that it would stay in the cone. "So he's a little put out," she said. "I wouldn't worry about it."

"I don't know. I think I *would*," I said.

She dipped the ice cream into the bowl of chocolate sprinkles—we call them "jimmies," but I know not everyone does, because I ordered them that way once when we went back to Chicago to visit and everyone treated me like I was a freak. "How did he really react?"

"He kind of didn't say anything. I mean, he was mad at first. And he's still mad. That pretty much wraps it up, I think."

Haley handed me the cone, then rang up the sale and slipped a dollar into the register. "Don't worry. He'll be angry for a while, but he'll get over it. He loves you. He'll understand."

"Thanks for saying that." I started to lick the ice cream. "I hope you're right."

"Of course I'm right," Haley said. "I'm a Boudreau,

and Boudreaus are always right. Or at least they always think they are."

I laughed. "Haley, what if he doesn't forgive me? What if he gets mad at—at Evan, and they fight or something?"

Haley looked at me and frowned. She seemed annoyed by the suggestion. "Ben's not like that. When he's mad at someone, he keeps his distance. Now be quiet and eat your ice cream and forget about those guys for a second. Put your feet up. Relax."

"Okay, Mom," I said.

"I'm not acting like—" Haley stopped as she noticed she was about to unfold a napkin for me. "Anyway, eat."

"So, speaking of. Have you seen your parents lately?" I asked.

"Oh, yeah. I went over there to see how they're doing. They're still mad I'm not working for them. They kept saying pitiful stuff like, 'Well, we're about to go under, not that you'd care about that.'"

I smiled. I could just picture Haley's mom saying that. "She thinks guilt is one of the food groups."

"Oh, yeah. She's horrible. And she's *good* at it, too, which is the worst part. So I'm going over there at two to help out." She rolled her eyes. "I cannot *wait* for September."

I was on my way back into the kitchen to put in two orders and grab some food when I saw Evan delivering a trayful of plates to one of my tables.

There. He was doing it again.

I hated how he kept bringing food to my tables, as if I needed help, as if I couldn't handle it on my own.

Ten minutes later, I walked into the kitchen to pick

up another order that was ready and caught him doing the same thing. "What are you doing?" I asked. "I can get those."

"I know, but I'm right here." Evan shrugged. "Besides, all my tables are parking right now. I don't have much to do."

"Yeah, but I can still handle it," I said. "I don't need your help."

Evan turned to look at me. "You know, last summer you loved it when I did this."

"Yeah, well, last summer I loved a lot of things you did," I said before I could stop myself. I bit my lip, wishing I could take it back. I couldn't believe I'd just said that. I had to follow up with a witty retort immediately. Danger, danger! Actual feelings emerging!

Evan was grinning at me in that annoyingly seductive way of his. It's amazing how far nice green-blue eyes can *get* a person in life. It's like a get-out-of-jail-free card.

"But, you know, as the saying goes . . . that was then. This is now." I gave him what I hoped was a withering, devastating look. Probably I just seemed really crabby. Not the soft-shell kind, either.

"Wow. Deep. *Insightful.*" Evan nodded. "I bet Bates can't wait to get a hold of your mind."

I took the plates of food off his tray, briefly considered tossing them into his face, thought he might get burned, and instead started loading them onto my own. If only I were closer to the refrigerated pie case, I thought. I'd love to see his annoying, charming smile covered in blueberry or coconut cream.

"We *could* just swap trays," Evan said. "You know, an empty one for a full one? Or do you have a close personal attachment to that one—you guys go way back or something?"

I heard a laugh behind me, and glanced back at the coffee machine. Blair was standing there, laughing at Evan's ridiculous tray joke. Great. Now we were amusing other people. Even more than we usually did.

I hoisted the heavy tray and headed out to the dining room. When I walked through the swinging door, somehow the tray slipped from my fingers—sweaty, no doubt, from my Evan encounter—and tipped a little, and I jostled a side dish of coleslaw off the tray. Of all the luck. It landed right on my foot, then I almost slipped on it and fell down.

I hate coleslaw. What or who is "cole" and what is "slaw" about cabbage and mayo, anyway? If I ever had a side dish named after me, I hoped it would not resemble a "slaw." Colleenslaw. That's about how good I felt about myself as I scraped it off the carpet five minutes later.

It was all Evan's fault. Everything was.

(a) The fact that I had coleslaw shoe.

(b) The fact that I'd just had to get up close and personal with the carpet.

(c) The fact that Ben wasn't speaking to me and probably wouldn't be for the rest of the day.

I pulled off my apron and tossed it into the laundry hamper beside the kitchen door. "What are you doing?" Evan asked. "You're not leaving, are you?"

"No. I'm taking a break." I walked through the kitchen to the back door and stepped outside. For some reason he was following me.

"You okay?" he asked.

"I'm fine." As I was walking onto the docks, it started

to rain. As if my day could get any worse. I should have known it was about to rain because the kittens that hung around the docks were nowhere in sight. They have cat-dar. They can tell when storms are coming, sort of like my hair.

"This is all your fault, you know," I said.

"Me? What did I do?" Evan asked.

"You know, you have a way of ruining things just by standing there."

Evan started to laugh. "I think you're giving me a little too much credit. I can't actually make the weather change."

And then we just stood there for a minute, not saying anything. I couldn't think of anything *to* say. I was speechless. I'd spent hours rehearsing all the things I'd say if I ever saw him again, if we were ever alone again. Now I couldn't open my mouth. Which was so ridiculous, considering.

"So, what was your winter like?" Evan finally asked.

I knew he was trying to be nice, to make conversation, but it made me so angry that he had absolutely no clue what my winter had been like. *And my fall, and my spring?* I wanted to ask him. *And basically everything since last August 29th, or whatever day it was in November when you just vanished?*

"Colleen?"

"Oh—fine," I said. "Just fine."

"Fine. Really? Did you want to give me any details?"

"I just . . . I don't know why you're asking. Now. I mean, it's a little late. You could have asked me back when it was actually semi-relevant."

"Yeah, but what would be the fun in that?"

I was so sick of hearing him say that. The *fun*. Was that how it felt, completely ignoring someone by not keeping in touch? *Fun?*

I started thinking that I must have really bad taste when it came to boyfriends. Maybe that was it; maybe that was why I'd had two of them while my friends didn't, because I'd picked guys who were no doubt available because they were horrible, evil losers.

But that didn't make sense, because Ben was a totally nice person with zero flaws except (a) nearly vomiting when he met me, which technically had nothing to do with me, and (b) being too nice sometimes, to a fault.

Ben wasn't the problem. Evan was.

"I can't believe you're still wearing your Birks to work. I thought Trudy banned sandals as footwear. Didn't we go over that, like, a hundred times?"

Evan just looked at me with a small smile turning up the corners of his mouth. "Funny."

"What?"

"You never struck me as the nagging girlfriend type."

"That's because (a), I'm not nagging, and (b), I'm not your girlfriend."

Before I knew what I was doing, I'd stepped closer to Evan, and I gave him a little shove, a bit more forceful a shove than I'd meant to. His sandals slipped on the slick docks, and he lost his balance. Then he plunged backward into the harbor, landing butt-first with a loud smack in the dirty, fishy, disgusting cold water.

"Oh, no—oh, Evan—I'm sorry!" I cried, running over to him when he surfaced.

I expected him to be coughing and sputtering and yelling at me, but he wasn't. He was actually smiling.

"Are you okay? Are you freezing?" I asked. "Come on, get out."

"You know what? It's refreshing, actually," he said.

"Refreshing? You're literally swimming with the fishes." I could see a fish skeleton bobbing in the water beside Evan.

Erica ran out of Bobb's toward us, holding a couple of towels. "Evan, are you all right? Do you want help getting out?"

"Thanks, Erica. That would be nice." He swam toward the dock and held on to it with his fingers, which already looked slightly blue. I watched as he reached up for Erica's hand, while she dumped the towels in my arms.

Suddenly, Evan grabbed my ankles instead of Erica's hands—and pulled me facefirst into the water. I threw the towels over my head as I dove in.

The water hit me like a wall of ice cubes. I think my heart actually stopped beating for a second as my head submerged, and I closed my eyes and mouth against the freezing, murky water.

When I surfaced, I saw Evan smiling at me. He hadn't even started to get out of the water yet. "You . . . This is so dangerous!" I said.

"So . . . it's okay for *me*, but it might hurt you?" Evan's hair was slicked back, and he looked so good to me that for a few seconds I just treaded water and stared at him. I started remembering a night last summer when we'd dared each other to go swimming. Not just swimming, actually. Skinny-dipping.

We were walking home from a party, and we took a detour down a dirt road, by this private cove, to check out the full moon.

And yeah, we both did the dare. And then—

Erica cleared her throat loudly. "So, don't you think you guys should get out now? We should all get back inside."

"Right!" I said quickly, swimming to the edge. I hauled myself up onto the dock, with Erica's help, and grabbed one of the towels from her, quickly covering the wet T-shirt and shorts that were now clinging to my body. I rubbed my hair with the towel, trying to dry it a little bit.

"I lost a sandal." Evan was crouching at the edge of the dock, peering into the water.

"So dive down and find it," I said.

"Like I could." He stood up and looked at me, giving a slight laugh as he reached down to slip off the one remaining Birkenstock. It was dripping wet. "It's your fault, and they're like ninety-dollar sandals."

"You only lost one. So that's forty-five."

"But I can't buy just one, I have to buy a new pair. So you owe me ninety bucks."

"Yeah, but they were at least two years old, so they weren't worth that much."

"So? Replacing them will still cost me ninety." Evan rubbed his head with a towel. "You can start paying me tomorrow, out of your tips. Unless you have ninety on you right now."

I quickly reached into my pocket, hoping I hadn't lost my wad of bills to the harbor along with Evan's stupid sandal. Nope, it was still there. But I wasn't handing it over.

"No. I don't. And I can't give you all the money I make tomorrow. I need it."

"Well, you should have thought of that before you pushed me in." He turned and walked up the dock and then up the ramp to the restaurant's back door.

If I could have found that missing sandal, I would have thrown it at the back of his head.

We had a shower in the basement that he was probably going to use. I'd stay out of his way until he was finished. Me, maybe I'd just go home and shower, so I could change my clothes. And if I didn't work any more tonight, I wouldn't make any more tips, so then I wouldn't have to pay him back.

Right?

I started shivering and realized I needed to get inside. I called home and asked Haley if she could bring me a change of clothes.

"Why do you need new clothes?" she asked.

"Don't ask."

"I just asked."

I let out a sigh. "Because I fell into the water and my clothes are sopping wet and I smell like bait."

"Gross. Why didn't you just say so?"

As soon as she dropped off the clothes, and when Evan was done, I went into the bathroom and took a long, hot shower, trying to wash away the entire day: the cat food on my sunglasses, the bad talk on the ferry with Ben, the nasty harbor smell in my hair.

The way Evan had looked, treading water beside me. How it reminded me of last summer.

And how I shouldn't be thinking those kinds of things anymore.

Ben wasn't waiting for me when I got home that

night, and I can't say I was surprised. In a way, I was a little relieved, because I was so exhausted that I didn't know if I could (a) deal with his being mad at me, (b) explain why my shoe smelled of coleslaw, and (c) explain why I'd acted so secretive about the whole thing with Evan.

I shouldn't have secrets from Ben. Should I?

But I did.

Chapter 11

It was still raining the next morning, so I decided to take advantage of the bad weather to work on a new collage piece.

I've been doing collage art since I was about nine. It started out as an art project for school—I'd always loved children's books by Eric Carle, Leo Lionni, and Lois Ehlert, to name a few. So I tried to imitate their techniques, but it didn't come out quite right. Dad helped me improve, though, and I started small, making Mother's Day and birthday cards, then worked up to bigger pieces. I made mini-yearbooks for my friends, and even taught art in my parents' classes a few times a year. We sometimes used discarded lobster, clam, and mussel shells and stones from the beach to make glued collages—a different type than I usually made, but it was still fun.

My dad, Magic Marker Man, couldn't have been more thrilled by my decision to pursue an art major. After Richard gave up liberal arts to become a stockbroker, Dad had been convinced he'd failed somewhere along the line. Now, sadly, I would apparently uphold the Templeton tradition of doing lots of work for no pay.

But maybe it wouldn't come to that. I was working on some new pieces, and getting slides made of others so that I could start putting my portfolio together and maybe someday have a gallery show. Portland has a lot of galleries and a really active arts scene.

"Why don't you paint? You should paint," my uncle Frank would say whenever he saw my work. "You know, Betty McGonagle sold over *fifty* paintings last summer."

Which might sound impressive, except that:

(a) Betty McGonagle paints only one thing.

(b) It's the ocean.

(c) She does the same thing over and over again and they're all 5"x7".

(d) They're sold at the Landing gift shop, and you could put old, expired, rancid *meat* at that gift shop and it would sell, as long as it had the word *Maine* imprinted on it. (People get desperate when they see the ferry about to leave, and they reach for something—anything—quaint.)

(e) Betty McGonagle is like seventy-five years old and has all day to paint.

Don't get me wrong. I love paintings of the ocean. Winslow Homer really knocks me out. But I just can't get excited about Betty McGonagle's paint-by-numbers . . . numbers.

Suddenly I realized there was a reason I was thinking so much about Betty McGonagle. And it wasn't jealousy over her sales figures or ability to capture moving water.

The smell of paint was wafting down the hallway and sneaking into my room. Was there another artist in residence that I didn't know about? I set down my glue and wandered out into the hall. Then I followed my nose to Blair's room. I knocked on the door. "What's that smell?"

"Paint!" she called out. "Come on in—check out how good it looks!"

I walked into my parents' bedroom and nearly tripped on a bucket of paint as Blair switched on the overhead light to give me a better view.

"Purple?" I cried. "You painted my parents' bedroom bright purple?"

"No. It's lupine, actually," she said. She leaned down to look at the can of paint sitting on newspapers on the floor. "Late-afternoon lupine." She was wearing overalls and a white T-shirt, with a baseball cap over her hair.

"It's still . . . purple, though," I said.

In a way, it looked sort of cool. And my parents could be fun, and it fit into the category of playful elementary school colors. But she had a lot of nerve, painting a room that was only going to be hers for a couple of months. And who was going to get into trouble? Not her. *Me.* "How could you do this?"

"What?" She seemed surprised by the question.

"You just . . . paint someone's room? Without asking? You're only living here for two months!"

"But I needed a change," Blair said. "That light blue— it was bringing me down. So washed out. When I wake up in the morning, I need a blast of energy, not to look at myself in the mirror and just seem . . . faded and tired."

"But it was new. And it matches—excuse me, *matched*—everything," I said. "And it's my parents', and my mother picked out the color and she spent like a year choosing it." One of the most aggravating years of my *life*, I could add—the great Templeton redecorating project of the new millennium. Poring over home improvement books and comparing color palettes until the break of dawn, night after night. It was my mother's reaction to Richard leaving home for college. (Of course, she didn't finish all the work until well after he graduated.) I wondered what she was going to do when I left home.

First, probably repaint my room and turn it into something else.

Or maybe Mom would deal with my leaving home by going to Europe without me for the summer. Hold on. How did that make sense?

Anyway. Blair wasn't all that apologetic about it, and I wasn't the kind of person to fight and fight over it. I strongly believed in that old adage "What's done is done," maybe because my father said it all the time, usually whenever he botched a home improvement project. I told Blair that we'd have to repaint before the summer was over, then I went downstairs, took down the house rules list, and wrote:

13. Do not paint or redecorate any rooms
    without asking first.

It was too late, and it kind of repeated some other rules on the list, but whatever. Doing it made me feel better, as if I'd proved some sort of point, which of course I hadn't.

I went back up to my room and tried to work some more, but I couldn't stop racking my brain for the name of that light blue paint shade that my mother loved so much. I could ask her in an E-mail, but that might make her suspicious.

I knew—I'd ask at the hardware store. Eddie would remember the name of it, and I could see if he had some in stock. I grabbed the car keys from the counter and went outside.

I was about half a mile from the store when I saw him running on the side of the road.

My first thought was to pull over and ask if he wanted a ride. It was raining, after all.

My second thought was to swerve and hit him.

I decided to ignore both urges and just drive past with a friendly wave to Evan. I glanced in the rearview mirror to see if he recognized me. The mirror was tilted toward me, and I noticed that my hair was a complete frizzone. Naturally.

At the store, Eddie was busy helping another customer, so I picked up this big flip-book from the counter that showed hundreds of colors and tints of paint. I went through all of the blues, but none of them sounded familiar.

I kept flipping through colors, hoping I'd recognize it when I saw it. Then I gave up and wandered down the paint aisle. I was surprised I didn't see Betty McGonagle there, stocking up on a few gallons of Atlantic Ocean Blue and Sunset Sea Foam. She must buy her paint by the gallon.

"Colleen? What are you doing here?" Eddie asked when I drifted past the counter for the third or fourth time.

"I need paint. Do you remember the paint my mom bought? For the master bedroom?"

"Hm." Eddie scratched his head. "No, can't say as I do."

"You don't? Because I don't, either. And I've got to buy some more because I need to repaint."

"No sense painting in this weather," Eddie said.

The little bell above the entrance jingled, and I turned to see Evan walking into the store. He was sopping wet. Rain dripped from his hair to his shirt, from his shirt to the floor. His shoes made a squishy sound as he approached the counter.

"What did you need today, young man?" Eddie asked. "Besides a raincoat, an umbrella, and more sense than God gave a lobster."

Two points for Eddie, I thought with a smile.

Evan ran his hands through his hair. "Uh . . . ants." He pointed to the boxes stacked in the display rack beside the counter. "I mean, ant traps."

"Ant traps," I repeated. "You ran here in the rain for ant traps."

"The man's got a problem," Eddie said as he rang up the sale.

Man? No. Problem? Yes.

"All of a sudden, they're everywhere. My cousin's panicking," Evan said. "I told him I'd pick these up when I was out on my morning run."

"Right." I nodded as he pulled a ten-dollar bill from his shorts pocket.

"It might stop raining, you know," Eddie said. "I suspect we'll be done with this front in . . . oh, two, three days at most." He chuckled. His telephone rang, so he picked it up with a polite wave to both of us. So much for getting paint.

Evan and I walked to the doorway and stood there for a second, watching the rain come down even harder now.

"Do you want a ride back to your house or anything?" I offered.

For a second he looked flustered, which was nice, because so far I felt like I was doing all the flustering. "Yeah. I'd better not get these traps wet," he said.

"You wouldn't want wet ant traps," I agreed. "Anything but that."

"Shut up," Evan said, and we both sprinted to the car, which was silly, considering he was already drenched and I was about to be. I slammed the door behind me and started the engine. A Volvo was a good thing to have in a flood.

"So. You still owe me for the sandals, you know," Evan said as we started down the road.

"What? I *gave* you money," I reminded him.

"No, you gave me half."

"Evan!" I slapped the steering wheel. "Come on. Do you really want to be like that?"

"Like what? Cheap? Like you're being?"

I ignored his "cheap" shot and drummed my thumbs against the steering wheel as I drove. "So, I have a question."

"Yes?" Evan asked.

"Why did you come back this year?"

"Where else would I want to be in the summer? This place is paradise," he replied.

"Paradise." I rolled down the window a little bit, and raindrops pelted my arm. Evan must have run pretty far. He didn't exactly smell . . . paradisiacal. Then, too, there was that Ultimate Endurance deodorant scent sort of hanging in the air. "Are you training for anything right now?" I asked. He'd run a few marathons already. I'd never even made it the whole way around the island, though some busy nights at work, I could have sworn I'd walked five miles—unfortunately, all of them back and forth from the dining room to the kitchen.

"No, not really. Well, I want to make the cross-country team at BU, so I guess I'm training for that. But if I don't make it . . . you know. I'll just transfer to Bates or something."

I laughed. "Yeah, right." I looked over at him. "You wouldn't."

"I wouldn't?" he said.

"Come on. Really. Would you?" I asked.

"I doubt it, Coll. Aren't Maine winters brutal?"

"They're cold, but they're not horrible," I said. "At least, I don't think so."

"Yeah, but you love sweaters. I don't do sweaters."

I smiled, because it was almost sweet of him to remember my stacks of sweaters in the hall closet.

Then I really remembered how he knew about them.

We'd been in my house; he had come over for dinner so he could finally meet Mom and Dad, and I'd brought him upstairs as part of the house tour.

"We keep this door open because Hutch likes to sleep on the sweaters," I had explained. And Evan had gently pushed me inside the closet and closed the accordion-style door behind us and started kissing me. I was thinking, Good idea, Mom, getting this walk-in closet added during the big home renovation! And we were still kissing in the dark when I stepped on Hutch and there was a loud cat "Yowl!"

We all jumped, and Evan flung open the door so quickly that it sprang back shut again—on Hutch's tail. "Yowl!" Hutch cried while we were laughing and kissing.

"Everything okay up there?" Mom called up the stairs.

"Fine! Everything's fine, Mom!" I yelled. "Hutch is just being funny."

Evan wiped a smudge of my lip gloss off his mouth while Hutch hissed at him as he finally bolted out of the closet to safety. That was one of the times we'd very nearly gotten caught. It wasn't the only one.

"Colleen?" Evan coughed. "The house is back there."

"What?" I suddenly snapped out of the memory. "Oh. Right. *Right.*"

"Were you thinking what I was thinking?" he asked as I did a U-turn.

"Um. What was that?" If he said anything about the closet incident, or asked how Hutch was doing, or said he wanted to visit the cats, I didn't know what I would do. I was still mad at him. But I also might jump him and head for the nearest closet.

I am such a bad person.

"With this weather? Work's going to be so dead tonight," Evan said. "Don't you think?"

"Oh, yeah. Really, incredibly dead."

The way I should be for thinking such disgusting things about an ex-boyfriend.

When I got home, Sam and Erica were huddled in front of the TV, watching a movie.

"Where've you been?" Sam asked when I walked in.

"Oh. Ah. The hardware store."

"What did you get?" Erica asked.

I looked around the living room for a minute, trying to remember. "Nothing. I guess."

Erica stared at me with a confused expression. "Oh."

"You seem kind of down," Sam commented. "Is everything okay?"

"Yeah, everything's fine," I said, but I was talking as if I were a prerecorded message.

"Coll. Really?" Erica pressed.

"Yeah." I didn't want to admit, not even to Sam and

Erica, that I had no idea (a) what I was doing, (b) how I was feeling, (c) what I should do next, and (d) what it all meant.

I told myself I should call Ben. It was almost four and he'd be home from work, so we could talk before I went in at four thirty. But it was like I didn't even know what to talk to him about right now. I definitely wouldn't tell him how I spent my afternoon.

So I told Erica and Sam about the purple lupine paint job Blair had done on my parents' bedroom, and we all ran upstairs to check it out.

"No wonder you were in such a bad mood," Sam commented.

"Don't worry—we'll fix it. My grandparents have tons of painting supplies," Erica said. "Masking tape, rollers, pans, all of it."

"What was she *thinking*?"

Blair walked out of the bathroom with a towel wrapped around her head. I'd had no idea she was home, and I don't think anyone else did, either.

"I was thinking I needed a change. I don't see what's so criminal in that. My parents always let me paint my room whatever color I choose."

"But . . . that's your house. Not her parents' actual bedroom," Sam pointed out.

"Look, it's okay—we'll just have to repaint before they get back. It's fine for now," I said.

As long as Aunt Sue and Uncle Frank didn't see it. I could just see Aunt Sue placing a panicked, late-night phone call to Spain—about paint.

Chapter 12

"Colleen, there's someone at the takeout window who wants to see you," Maggie said the next day as lunch was winding down.

Maggie was a fourteen-year-old girl with braces, here for the summer and getting her big break at the takeout window the same way that I had.

"Who is it?" I asked. For some reason I glanced over my shoulder to see where Evan was. As if he'd run outside to the takeout window or something to try to trick me. He was devious like that.

"A very cute guy," Maggie said. "So I'm really bummed that he wouldn't let me take his order. Now *go*. I'll do this."

She took over my salad prep work while I wiped my hands on my apron and crossed the kitchen, toward the windows. I looked through the screen and saw Ben standing there, arms folded in front of him.

"Hey," I said. "What are you doing here?"

"I came to see you?" Ben smiled.

It was so nice to see him smile like that. And at me, no less. He must not be angry anymore, but I wasn't going to push my luck. "Thanks," I said. "But what about work?"

"I'm done for the day," he said.

"Oh, my gosh, is it three already?"

"It's three thirty, actually," Ben said.

I couldn't believe it. We hadn't stopped being busy long enough for me to even take a short break, never mind look at the clock more than a few times.

"So could I get a lobster roll and fries?"

"To go or to eat here?" I asked.

"Coll, I was kind of hoping you could come outside for a break and eat with me," Ben said.

"You know what? That's a great idea," I said, smiling. "Hold on one second—grab a table and I'll be out with your food." I went back into the kitchen, placed an order for the two of us, and went to find Trudy so I could tell her I was taking my half-hour break. It was a good time, because the between-shifts lull was actually, finally, happening. An hour and a half later than usual.

By the time I found Trudy our food was ready, so I carried it out the back door. I set the plates down on the picnic table where Ben was already sitting. "Oops—I forgot drinks. What do you want?"

"Lemonade or iced tea—whatever," Ben said.

"Be right back," I promised as I headed back inside. When I came back out, I realized I'd forgotten ketchup for Ben's fries, so I ran in to grab a couple of packets and some extra tartar sauce for my fried fish sandwich.

You might think I was doing all this because I was stalling. And probably I was, just a little bit. Ben and I hadn't talked much since the ferry incident two days ago, since I confessed to not telling him everything about my past. (Which sounds a lot more dramatic and soap opera–like than the actual situation. It wasn't as if I'd killed someone, or been married.)

"Why do they call it tartar sauce?" I asked as I spread a spoonful onto the bun. I knew that was harmful to my health, because tartar sauce must be higher in cholesterol than, say, fried fish pieces, which were also stacked high on my sandwich. "I mean, what is tartar about it? What is a tartar, anyway?"

"I don't know, but my toothpaste says it removes tartar." Ben grinned at me as he ripped open a straw and poked it into his lemonade.

"Gross!" I cracked open my little carton of milk. A child's portion. So unfair. I sipped my milk and looked across the picnic table at Ben. I tried to smile a little. I felt so vulnerable, sitting there. And it wasn't because seagulls were circling overhead, just hoping I was going to drop a crumb. It was the feeling that I had no idea what was going to happen next. Ben seemed to be okay with me now. If he was angry two days ago—and he was—then he'd somehow gotten past that. Or was he just being nice because he wanted to break up with me, and eating lunch together was the easiest and kindest way he could think of?

But no, Ben wouldn't be that heartless. He'd never tell me something difficult in public, least of all at my workplace. He'd come and find me, alone, or suggest we take a walk, or—

Wait a second. Why am I thinking of ways he could break up with me? I thought as I dabbed tartar sauce off the corner of my mouth. I had this tendency to think things through a little *too* much, envisioning things in the future while I completely missed the present.

Or, as my first grade report card said, "Prone to daydreaming."

"So, busy today?" Ben asked.

"Ridiculously busy, yeah. I think I had a snack at like

eleven, and I haven't had a chance to sit down since," I said. "This is nice."

"Yeah, it is." Ben paused. "Sorry I've been kind of—"

"No, it's okay," I said quickly.

"Not really," he said. "I kind of acted like a jerk about it. It was just—it really came out of left field. I wasn't expecting it. I mean, I guess I remember you or Haley talking about someone from last summer . . ."

"You do?" I asked.

"Vaguely."

Phew. Vaguely *was* the best way to remember Evan, especially if you were Ben.

"But why didn't you tell me?" he asked.

"I really thought I'd never see him again. Maybe that was stupid, but that's what I thought. Trudy said he wasn't coming back this year. And I hadn't heard from him since last fall, so—"

"Yeah, but why didn't you tell me, like, the day he showed up? You waited a week," Ben said.

"I was nervous?" I said. In fact, I'm still nervous? And couldn't we have this conversation a *little* farther away from the building? And couldn't I get a few more shifts that weren't the same as Evan's? It was like a Trudy conspiracy.

"Yeah. Well, I can understand that, I guess. I was just really surprised. But I'm over it now. I realized that I probably haven't told you every single thing about my exes, either," Ben said.

"You haven't?" I asked. *Hold on a second,* I thought. What exes was he talking about? And why was it plural, as if there had been a lot of them?

"No. And I'm probably not going to, unless there's a

point, unless there's some reason why I need to, because that's all in the past," Ben said. "Like you and that Evan guy. And I understand you had to tell me, since he showed up here unexpectedly."

Is Ben the greatest guy on the planet or what? Well, maybe not the planet, but definitely this one little self-enclosed subplanet.

"Thanks for understanding." I stood up and leaned across the table so I could kiss him on the cheek.

"You're welcome," he said.

I sat back down and started eating my sandwich again, this time with a little more appetite for it. So I had nothing to worry about. Ben knew now; case closed.

"So." Ben popped another French fry into his mouth. "Is he here?"

"Is who here?"

"Colleen."

"Oh, *him*. You mean . . . him him," I said.

Ben smiled. "I don't know. What does that mean?"

I had to laugh. I really was being slightly psycho about this, I knew that. "Well, he's inside still, I guess."

"Is he one of those guys?" Ben pointed with a French fry at the restaurant.

I looked over my shoulder as I heard the back door close. A group of co-workers had just come out of the restaurant, and they were walking over to take another picnic table. "Yeah. He's over there," I said.

"Well, which one *is* he?" Ben asked, laughing. "Or is this supposed to stay a secret? Well, hold on, I know Rick . . . and Chad—"

"He's the one with the . . . um . . ." Nice ankles? Somewhat handsome stubble? Triathlete body? How did you describe one boyfriend to another? "Birkenstocks."

"Colleen. I can't see *shoes* from here," Ben said. "They're all sitting down."

"Well, he's kind of . . ." I was about to mention the brown hair, green-blue eyes, and short sideburns when Evan noticed we were both staring at him. He popped a straw into his mouth and waved at us. "He's the one waving at us," I said as I quickly waved at him, then turned back around with a nervous feeling in my stomach.

Oh, God. This was the most uncomfortable situation I had ever been in, the most awkward minute of my entire life. Evan, waving at Ben. What next? Were they going to talk? Shake hands? Sit at the same table with me?

"Maybe I'd better head back inside to work," I said. "Since they're all taking breaks now, Trudy probably needs me."

"Okay, but what about tonight? Can we get together tonight?" Ben asked.

"Of—of course," I said. "I'd love that. I'll be home at ten—or do you want to pick me up here?"

"That sounds like a good idea. Maybe we can go down to the beach for a little while."

"See you then!"

I knew Ben wanted me to kiss him good-bye, but I just couldn't. I felt so awkward, like I didn't want Evan to see me with Ben, and I didn't want Ben to see me with Evan. But that was ridiculous, because I wasn't doing anything wrong, I wasn't cheating on anyone. It *felt* like it, though.

Even though everything was supposedly out in the open now, I still felt like I was keeping things from both of them. I was acting like someone in a cheesy love song, the kind my mom would play loudly while she was doing housework, the kind I usually said "ick" to.

Now I was living an ick life.

The rest of the day was just as crazy at work, which was okay with me. Keeping busy was a good thing—and I was making more money than I could count.

I bumped into Evan at around eight, when I was refilling my water and iced tea pitchers.

"Is this the busiest Saturday you can remember?" he asked. "My feet are killing me."

I glanced down at his sandals—a new pair, a different kind—and decided not to comment this time on the fact that he should wear running shoes, that he might be more comfortable, that sandals were banned. If he wanted to be in pain, fine, good, that was his business, not mine. Not this year.

"So, who was that guy you were eating lunch with?" Evan asked as he filled a couple of pitchers with ice.

Oh, no. Here it came. More ick. "That was Ben," I said.

"Ben," Evan repeated. "Ben . . . who?"

"Ben . . . my boyfriend Ben. My boyfriend," I stammered.

Evan stopped mid–ice shovel. "Oh. You have a boyfriend?"

"Well, yeah. I do." I dropped a couple of lemon slices into the pitcher of water, and realized I'd meant to drop them into the iced tea. So, the water would have a nice crisp taste now. I dropped lemon slices into the iced tea and was about to bring the pitchers out to my tables when Evan said, "Interesting. Very interesting."

I stopped and turned around. "Would you stop saying that about everything? What's interesting about it, anyway?"

"Aha! Are you saying he's not interesting? Or maybe you're not interested in him?"

"No." I shook my head. "Don't flatter yourself."

"I was flattering myself? I didn't realize. Usually I'm a lot more demonstrative when I do that. As in, Evan, you have the best—"

Ankles, I thought, but thankfully my mouth didn't open. *Stop that, brain. Stop that right now.*

The swinging doors flew open and Trudy stood there with a stack of menus in her arms. "Evan, Colleen, come on—you've got three new tables apiece."

"Aren't we supposed to get a break at some point?" Evan asked. "I mean, a lobster takes breaks, Trude. A lobster can't keep going and going and going. Not even with eight legs."

"Yeah, every now and then a lobster has to stop and smell the roe," I said, quoting a T-shirt joke Evan had come up with last summer, along with one that said "Dip Into Something More Comfortable," with a picture of a butter dish. He had even gotten a few fake T-shirts printed up with that slogan, to try to convince Trudy to use them, but the T-shirt shop had messed up and spelled Bobb's as "Boob's." So Trudy wasn't convinced, but he kept them and wore them for running.

We smiled at each other and then started laughing.

"You two." Trudy shook her head. "Same as always."

No, we're not, I wanted to say. We're not the same—things aren't the same! We weren't back here together because we were trying to sneak in a moment alone, so we could kiss by the fluorescent glow from the food-warming lamps.

Yeah, that *is* as tacky as it sounds, and we'd done it last year. How embarrassing.

"Come on,. Trude. Cut us a break. Has anyone else been working since ten A.M. straight?" Evan asked.

"Well, I have," Trudy said. "Now run—your tables are waiting."

"I can't believe we're still seating people, and it's almost nine o'clock," Evan complained.

"We're not getting out of here at ten, are we?" I muttered.

I'd have to call Ben and cancel our plans. The way this summer was going so far, I was spending more time at work than I was with Ben. Which meant, in a way, that I was spending more time with Evan than with Ben, even if I was only constantly bumping into him in the kitchen.

This was a trend that had to change. Soon. But how?

That night, Haley borrowed her family's pickup truck and drove down to Bobb's to get us when we were finally released. She knew that if we weren't home yet, we'd all be too tired to walk when we finally did get out of work. Erica called her grandparents and told them she would be sleeping over at our house. Then she sat up front with Haley, while Sam, Blair, and I all piled into the back of the truck. When we got home, it turned out Haley had bought ice cream and cookies for all of us, and the five of us sat on the porch and ate and talked and laughed until long after midnight.

Chapter 13

Sunday afternoon I was exactly where I wanted to be: lying on a giant towel on the beach, right next to Ben. It was pretty warm, and very sunny, and we'd just eaten a late breakfast together over at his house. I hadn't seen Ben's family in a while because I'd been so busy. It was cool to catch up with everyone and remember how nice things used to be before the summer started and we both got overworked and overtired.

We don't have a big sandy beach on the island, because most of the land at the water's edge is very rocky and covered with trees, pine and otherwise (Maine *is* the Pine Tree State). But there's a small sandy beach where you can lie comfortably and watch the surf roll in—and swim if you're feeling either very very hot or very brave. The water temperature never gets all that warm.

We were enjoying having the time to ourselves to snuggle against each other. Everything was finally okay again, and it felt so perfect to be close to Ben like that. Nobody cuddled better than Ben. We fit together perfectly. He was gently moving strands of my hair off my face, and kissing me as he did that. I didn't know what I wanted more: to fall asleep with him holding me or to run off this beach and go somewhere more private together, like to a small cove, the way we did last summer when we ended up taking off our clothes and—

And then I stopped myself from thinking about it.

Because that hadn't been Ben. That wasn't something Ben would do. It was too risky, too dangerous—what if somebody saw us? He'd never go for that idea.

That had been Evan.

A second later a shadow fell over us as someone stopped beside our towel.

Don't be Evan, I thought. *Please don't be Evan going for a jog and stopping by to say hello.* It would be just like him to do that, now that he knew I had a boyfriend, and now that I was lying here next to Ben—thinking about Evan. He'd be able to tell I was daydreaming about him; he'd see it in my eyes somehow. He was devious and horrible like that.

"You guys mind if I join you?"

I squinted up into the sun and saw Haley standing over us. "Hey!"

She lifted the beach towel that she'd been carrying on her shoulders and shook it out. "Is it okay?"

"No, we want you to go sit over there," Ben said, sitting up and resting on his elbows. He gestured to John and Molly Hyland, who were sitting underneath an umbrella where they'd both been reading and not speaking to each other since we got there. "With the Hylands."

"Shut up." Haley pretended to kick sand into his face. "How long have you guys been here?" She peeled off her T-shirt and shorts, revealing an orange floral bikini.

"Not long. Hey, is that suit new?" I asked. "It's nice."

"Looking good, lass," Ben teased her in a bad Scottish accent, for some reason.

"Again. Shut up." Haley grinned at Ben as she lay down on her towel beside me.

"Man, what a nice afternoon." Ben turned onto his

side, looking at both of us.

"I feel like this is the part of summer we kept talking about all winter, when we were freezing our butts off on the ferry every morning," Haley said. "This was what kept us going."

"That and the thermos of hot chocolate my mom kept packing for me every day." Ben shook his head, embarrassed.

"Hey. At least she finally let you stop carrying that Superman lunchbox," Haley said.

Ben laughed and collapsed on his towel. "Oh, man. What'll she pack when I go to college?"

Neither of us said anything for a minute. Thinking about the three of us splitting up to go to different schools was a little daunting. We'd gotten so inseparable senior year. The three of us had even gone to the prom together.

"Maybe it's not too late to change our minds and transfer. What do you guys say? We'll do one of those Internet schools so we can all stay on the island." Haley rolled her T-shirt into a ball to use as a pillow.

Ben reached for my hand and squeezed it tightly. "Maybe we should. That way things could stay like this."

I turned toward him and smiled, but as fond as I was of the island—and there's no place on Earth I like more— I was looking forward to the changes ahead. If only that being away made me realize that I wanted to come back here to live, and to be with Ben. But I didn't want to just stop looking at other options yet.

I knew they probably didn't, either—it was just this building fear we all had of leaving, of possibly being so homesick for this place that we wouldn't be able to stand it.

I was working on a new collage on Monday when I heard a loud laugh coming from the front porch.

A very familiar laugh.

And then I heard Blair's voice saying, "I'll be right back."

I got up and peered out the window, but I knew I couldn't really see the porch, since it was below my window. That *laugh*, though. Had he come over to see me?

I heard Blair come upstairs and I opened my door, expecting Blair to be about to knock. But she wasn't. Instead, her bedroom door was just closing.

I went downstairs anyway. He had to be here to see me. Right?

The screen door closed behind me, and Evan asked, "So, you ready?"

"Ready for what?" I asked.

Evan looked up from the magazine he'd been reading. He had a baseball cap on and was wearing a pair of old, beat-up running sneakers without socks, khaki shorts, and an old Bobb's T-shirt that had a hole by the neck.

"Oh, sorry. I thought you were going to be Blair," he said.

"No. Not quite." I smiled. "A little shorter, a little less . . . blond."

We both looked at each other and did these awkward sort of nods. As in, Ahem, isn't *this* uncomfortable? At least I was uncomfortable.

Evan leaned back in his chair and stretched his arms over his head. He didn't seem uneasy at all. In fact, he almost looked like he was happy to be here.

"So this is the bachelorette house," he said. "Funny,

it looks the same as it did when your parents were here."

"Yes, but have you been *inside*?" I asked. "We've painted the entire place pink." Or at least late-afternoon lupine.

"I've been inside," Evan said.

Before I could respond or even process that, Blair flounced through the door. "Ready!" she proclaimed. She was wearing a white polo shirt, blue shorts, and what looked like a brand-new pair of tennis sneakers. "Hey, Colleen. When did you get home?" she asked.

"I was . . . home," I said slowly.

How she could come out of that messy, dirty room where the floor was covered with clothes and old coffee mugs sitting on the dresser and look so neat and put together was beyond me. Of course, looking like Blair was beyond me, period.

And then they announced they were off to play tennis. Tennis, of all things. I hadn't noticed the racket propped against Evan's chair, probably because I was trying very hard not to look at him.

"You don't play tennis," I said to Evan.

"Sure I do," he replied with a laugh. "I've been playing since I was a kid."

"You have? But you never—"

"The thing is, *you* don't play tennis, Coll. That's the part you forgot."

I could have picked up his racket and overhead-smashed him, right then and there. Did he have to be so smug? When he was here picking up another girl—my housemate, no less? Did he have no respect for me?

"She does play a mean game of cribbage, though," Evan told Blair as she pulled her hair back into a ponytail and secured it with an elastic.

"Cribbage?" Blair scoffed.

"You know, fifteen-two, fifteen-four," Evan said, standing up.

"No. The only fifteens I know about are in tennis," she said.

"Then I'll teach you how to play cribbage. Come on, let's go. See you, Colleen."

"Yeah. Bye," I said. Good riddance. Have fun. Don't trip over the net. No, do.

And then they took off, just like that. Oh, wasn't that nice; he was going to teach her to play cribbage. He only knew how to play because of me, because I taught him!

Now he was the expert?

I hated him. I loathed him.

And Blair was definitely not one of my favorite people right now, either. She knew I'd gone out with Evan, so why did she have to flaunt the fact that they were hanging out by bringing him here?

Of course, I didn't have any dibs on Evan. I knew that. It was still really incredibly awkward, though.

It's not about Evan, I told myself. *It's about me and Ben. Just forget Evan.*

Still, I felt that I needed to blow off some steam, and also, Ben would be getting out of work soon.

I ran upstairs and cleared up my worktable. I put all my art materials away, closing the tubes and jars.

Then I got my bike out of the garage and started riding down toward the Landing.

On the way, I went past Betty McGonagle's house. Mr. McGonagle had died about five years ago, leaving

Betty on her own. The house was at the top of a little bluff, and it had a gorgeous view of the water and the smaller islands in the distance. Betty was standing on her deck in front of an easel. Why did she even need to look at the ocean when she painted? I wondered. Didn't she have it memorized by now?

Blue here, white here, green here. This one would be called *Early Morning Sea Foam*, would be 5"x7", and would sell for $45. No, wait—$39.99.

Stop being such a snob, I told myself just as Betty looked up and noticed me approaching.

"Hello, Colleen!" she called to me. "How's your summer going?" Betty was in her mid-seventies. She tended to wear big denim shirts that invariably had paint drops on them, and she wore a scarf over her short, completely white hair. When she worked, anyway—I hardly ever saw her when she *wasn't* working, except maybe at public suppers and the post office occasionally.

"Great!" I called back.

"Any new pieces to show?" she asked. "Anything I can see?"

"Not yet—maybe soon!" I yelled. Then I coasted down the hill, feeling terrible. *She* was supportive and nice and interested in my artwork; I was mean, judgmental, and cruel about hers. She was a real artist who'd actually made good money selling her paintings; I displayed my stuff at an elementary school—and only because both my parents *worked* there. I was really awful.

On my way to the Landing I had to ride past the tennis courts. I had to. Really. And . . . ick.

Blair was standing at the net, practicing her volleys.

Evan was hitting shots to her, and Blair laughed as she smashed a tennis ball that hit Evan's leg and nearly knocked him down.

I rang the little bell on my bike's handlebars in approval. "Go, Blair!" I yelled. Keep that up, would you? She waved at me and smiled. Evan didn't look nearly as happy to see me. I was tempted to hang out for a while, because I had a feeling Evan was going to get beaten, slightly badly. That would be fun to watch.

But the ferry was coming in soon, and I wanted to be there to see Ben when it did. So I continued on my way, regretfully.

When I reached the Landing, the ferry had already docked. I saw Ben walking off, talking to the tall red-headed girl again.

Why did he have to get his stupid sea legs, so he could flirt with that girl every day? What was her deal, anyway? She didn't even have a frizzone. It was ninety-five percent humidity, and she showed no signs of it. Come to think of it, she'd *never* had a frizzone.

Which could only mean one thing: She was wearing a wig. Extensions—that had to be it. I had to cling to *something*.

"Who is that girl?" I asked Ben after I gave him a kiss hello.

"That's Holly," Ben said.

"And, uh, why does she seem to be on the ferry every afternoon?" I asked, trying to sound casual.

"Because she works on the mainland. She's doing an internship in a law office there, from eight to two every day."

"Hm. Really," I mused.

"Yes, really." Ben laughed as he put his arm around my shoulder. "Why is that so fascinating?"

"It's just . . . why did we never see her before?" I asked.

"She's older than us. She's in college, home for the summer. You know."

Yes, I did know. All about this painful pang of jealousy I was having, anyway.

First Evan with Blair, and now Ben and this . . . Holly. I was having a very jealous day. I didn't like feeling that way, especially on my day off, when I should be enjoying all things and not stressing about anything. It seemed shallow, and petty, of me.

But maybe that was how I was.

Chapter 14

Saturday night, Sam and I were walking home, both completely tired out. Blair wasn't with us because Erica had worked for her. Blair had said she had an urgent personal matter to attend to. That had us all curious, but we hadn't asked for details.

"This isn't how Saturday nights are supposed to be," Sam said. "We're supposed to be at the movies, or the mall, or out to dinner, or—"

"Asleep," I interrupted. "That sounds good, too, doesn't it?"

I heard a loud bass beat as we got closer to our house—the kind you usually hear coming from someone's car stereo.

"Where's that coming from?" Sam asked.

"Probably the Browns'. But they usually invite us to all their parties. Oh, well, maybe because Mom and Dad are away." Our neighbors were famous for their summer bashes.

"Coll? I don't think that's the Browns'," Sam said as we passed by their front hedge and the music got even louder.

"What do you mean? That's *our* house?"

"I think so. Yup."

I cringed as we turned into the driveway and I saw a sign hanging from our birch tree: PARTY HERE.

"Okay, so this is an urgent personal matter? She

wanted to throw a party without telling us about it?" I complained.

"It's very personal, all right," Sam said.

Dance music was blaring from the living room stereo, and someone had put a speaker in the window that pointed directly at the driveway. There were about two dozen people on the front porch—I recognized about half of them, but the other half? I'd never seen them before. Wasn't there a rule about "small gatherings only" and "not annoying the neighbors"?

In the kitchen, I waved to a few people I knew, then I peeked around the living room, looking for a sign of Blair—or Haley. Did Haley know about this, too?

The downstairs bathroom's bathtub was filled with ice and cans of soda—and beer, and some other bottled drinks.

Wasn't Rule 1 "No drugs or alcohol allowed"? How hard was that to understand?

Was it possible to break all of the house rules in one night?

I ran into Blair as I closed the bathroom door behind me. "What are you—I—we—we can't have a party like—" I was so angry that I couldn't complete my sentences.

"Hey, how's it going?" she replied with a smile. "I kind of invited some people over. What's the big deal?"

"I—we—can't do this."

"Colleen, relax. We *are* doing this." Blair grinned. "Isn't it great? Can you believe how many people showed?"

"No. *You're* doing this," I said.

"I did it for all of us. It's a surprise party! Come on, aren't you surprised?"

I stepped back as a couple of guys I'd never seen before pushed past us to get to the bathtub cooler. "Very," I said. "Why didn't you just tell me you wanted to have a party? Blair, my parents don't want anything like this happening here. They wrote it down for us, so we wouldn't forget."

"Come on. It's just one party. It's a couple of hours of your life. Did you know today is the summer solstice? The longest day of the year. I celebrate it every year with a big party."

"Well, I don't. Why didn't you tell me you wanted to do this?"

"It was a spur-of-the-moment-type deal."

I frowned. If she planned it to celebrate the summer solstice, then how could it be spontaneous? Did she just find out that today was the summer solstice? I thought it was on the calendar. "You shouldn't have done it," I said.

"Look, do you *really* want me to ask everyone to leave? Or do you want to just try and have a good time, like everyone else is?" she asked.

I didn't like the way Blair had done this at all. But she was right—I had two choices: (1) Tell everyone to get out, and (a) be hated by a crowd and (b) be considered extremely uncool, or (2) get myself some potato chips and a Coke and just try to have fun while it lasted.

So. In other words, there really wasn't much of a choice at all.

"Okay. But could we turn down the music a little?" I asked.

"No problem!" she said breezily.

I grabbed a soda for myself and went outside to sit on the porch with Sam. That's when I saw Evan walking up to the house with his cousin Jake.

Oh, great. Of course. Of course Evan would be here.

Just as I was saying hello to him and Jake, Ben cruised up on his mountain bike. "Apparently we're having a party," I told him when he walked over to the porch steps where Sam and I were perched.

"I know—Blair called to invite me. But that was *after* I heard about it from Eddie down at the hardware store," Ben said.

"Eddie? She invited *Eddie*?"

"I guess she walked in and invited everyone." Ben laughed.

"Oh, my God. This is a nightmare," Sam said. "Well, except for the fact I like parties. And there are some cute guys here. But I mean, come on—we just got off work and we can't even shower and change for a party at our very own house." She smiled. "*Your* very own house, actually."

"Same difference," I told her.

"What's he doing here?" Ben gestured toward Evan, standing at the other end of the porch and talking with Blair.

"I don't know. She invited everyone, you said. They know each other from work," I said.

"Right." Ben shook his head. "You know, if your parents could see this place right now . . . They didn't even let you have a big graduation party."

"Tell me about it," I said. "I'm just hoping things wrap up before any real damage gets done. Do you think that's possible?"

"If you start kicking people out at midnight," Ben said. "Good luck with that." He patted my back and went into the house to talk to some friends.

Haley drove her family's rattling old pickup truck into the crowded driveway, saw there were no spots available, and went out to the road to park.

When she slammed the door and walked back to the house, she just stared at me and Sam with wide eyes. "What the . . . ?"

"Blair," Sam and I said in unison.

At about midnight, I went upstairs to get a couple of sweaters for me, Haley, and Sam. The night was getting chilly. The party had thinned out, but there were still about thirty people milling around, dancing, talking, singing, laughing.

When I got to the top of the stairs, I nearly bumped right into Evan. I hadn't even realized he was still around; I thought he and Jake had left.

"What are you doing up here?" I asked.

"Well, I was playing a chasing game with Starsky, and he ran up here, so I followed him. And then I had to visit Hutch, so . . ." Evan leaned against the closet door and gave me a small smile.

He hadn't been in the house—with me—since last year. And he was leaning against the closet. That walk-in closet.

"Actually, I wanted to see what you've been working on. Some pretty good stuff. Really good, actually."

One thing I always loved about Evan was that he was interested in my collage work. He didn't have to know there were a few I'd made about him. First, the romantic one. Then, the one with angry black brushstrokes all over the top of it. Those were, thankfully, safely stashed in a box in the closet—the Evan/last summer box. To be opened in the event of nuclear war only.

"I probably shouldn't have gone into your room without asking," he said as I just stood there, momentarily speechless as I thought about that box and whether it was hidden well enough under a pile of winter hats, scarves, and mittens.

"No, you probably shouldn't have," I finally said.

"Too late," Evan said. "What are you doing up here?"

"I live here?" I said. Then I laughed. "Actually, I came up to get some sweaters."

"You and your sweaters." Evan stepped aside so that I could open up the closet door.

"Actually, I think, ah, sweatshirts," I said, going into Haley's room and then Sam's to grab the sweatshirts they'd said they had hanging on the backs of their doors. Then I pulled my Bates sweatshirt off my bed, where I'd thrown it that morning.

When I came back out, I glanced awkwardly at Evan, who was now standing at the top of the stairs, apparently waiting for me. I didn't want to be alone with him, not like this. "We should get back," I said, starting down the stairs.

"Right behind you," Evan said.

When we walked into the kitchen, Haley was turning around from the sink, holding a bowl of freshly washed green grapes. She looked over my shoulder at Evan, then glared at me. "What are you doing?" she whispered after he went into the living room. "Why were you upstairs with him?"

"I wasn't . . . *with* him," I said. "We both ended up there at the same time."

"Whatever. Here, these are for Ben. Take them." She shoved the glass bowl at me.

I handed her the sweatshirt. "You're welcome," I said, annoyed by her tone. As if I were sneaking off with Evan while Ben was there. As if I'd *do* something like that. She was really selling me short if she thought that about me.

I went outside and handed Sam her sweatshirt, then held the bowl out to Ben. "Grape?"

"Look! Grapes!" Blair cried, stumbling over with a couple of slightly drunk friends of hers.

"It's going to be a long night," Ben murmured to me. "Or . . . morning."

I leaned against him and put my arm around his waist. "Please don't leave," I said.

"I can stay until one, but that's it," he said. "My parents are waiting up for me, you know."

"Maybe we should go to *your* house, then." I smiled up at him.

"Helloooooo! Colleen? Colleen!"

I blinked my eyes a few times and peered at the alarm clock beside my bed. Ten twenty A.M. Who was that yelling my name?

"Colleen! You up there?" my uncle Frank's voice echoed over the stairwell.

"Oh no. Oh no." I remembered falling asleep with Ben sitting on my bed, stroking my hair. *Please let him be gone, please,* I thought. Ben and I had never had a sleepover, and I really didn't want today to be the first time he ended up in my bed in the morning.

I opened my eyes and slowly turned over and saw that he was gone. "Phew," I said out loud. I quickly threw on some shorts and a fresh T-shirt and called out the bedroom door, "Be right down!" I brushed my hair, slipped on some flip-flops, and hurried downstairs.

"Hey, you guys—what a surprise!" I said with a big smile. Which was the understatement of the year. I cringed at the pile of dishes in the sink and the trash can overflowing with plastic cups.

"We brought you some breakfast." Aunt Sue held up a straw basket filled with blueberry muffins. "Hot, too! Well, they were."

"Thanks so much—those look awesome," I said. "So, what brings you by?"

"Good morning!" Haley said as she walked into the kitchen, looking as sleepy as I felt. I couldn't believe we'd all slept so late—then again, we'd been up pretty late.

"Hello, Haley," Uncle Frank said.

No sooner had he said hello than there were thundering footsteps coming down the stairs. A guy I vaguely remembered seeing at the party bolted past us with an awkward wave and ran outside.

Aunt Sue couldn't have looked more shocked than I felt. Was that guy coming out of Haley's room? The house rule was: no sleepovers. Haley's rule had always been: no dumb, one-night things with guys. What was going on?

"Who was that?" Aunt Sue asked.

Uncle Frank was already out on the porch, watching whoever it was sprint down the road. If my uncle chased someone away from the house, I would feel very, very embarrassed. For both of them. And anyone who happened to see them.

"Oh, that was . . ." I hesitated. Who *was* that?

"That was Chuck," Haley quickly said.

Aunt Sue looked suspiciously at her. "Chuck who, Haley?"

I was wondering the same thing myself.

"Chuck, ah . . . Chuck Jacobs," Haley stammered.

I just stared at Haley. Had she really been with this Chuck Jacobs guy? And who was he?

"And what was he doing here at ten thirty in the morning, upstairs?" Aunt Sue asked.

"Well, uh, he came over to help clear the drains," Haley said. "In the upstairs bathroom. You know Blair, who lives here? She's got really long, thick hair, and it completely clogs the drains."

This was all starting to sound vaguely credible. I couldn't believe it.

Haley stretched her arms over her head. "So when I tried to take a shower this morning, everything was overflowing. I called Chuck."

"Well, why didn't you call us?" Aunt Sue complained. "We would have come right over. Frank is an excellent handyman," she said as my uncle walked back into the house, apparently having decided not to run down the mystery man.

Uncle Frank nodded proudly. "I like to think I have a knack."

"And where was this Chuck's van? And why wouldn't you just call your parents, instead?" My aunt can really grill a person when she wants to. I'd forgotten about that quality of hers.

"He's sort of a handyman type guy," Haley said with a shrug. "My family always calls him when there are plumbing emergencies."

"Chuck Jacobs, Chuck Jacobs," my uncle repeated,

like a mantra. "Funny, I've never head that name. And we pretty much know everyone on the island."

"Not everyone," I said.

"Well, maybe not everyone, but . . . how did he get here? And where was his toolbox?"

"Oh, we've got all the tools he needed right here. We just weren't sure how to actually use them," I said, nervously looking around at the kitchen. The place was totally sloppy. The only good thing I could say was that there wasn't a bunch of beer bottles or cans lying around. Some people had been drinking last night, but I hadn't. I wasn't sure about Haley. I couldn't see her sleeping with someone, sober, just because she was so dead set against it.

Please don't let anyone else wake up and come downstairs, I thought. Especially not any boys. Or men. Or boy-men. Or book club targets.

"Well. The house is a mess, and a few things don't look quite right," Aunt Sue commented as she turned to my uncle. "Do they?"

He shook his head. "No. Your parents would be a little disappointed right now. No, check that. A *lot* disappointed."

"Aunt Sue, Uncle Frank? You just caught us on a bad day," I said. "This isn't what the place usually looks like, honestly. Sunday's our day off, so that's when we clean the house," I explained.

Aunt Sue gave the kitchen a look of disapproval. I glanced at the black cat clock on the wall. Its tail was switching back and forth, counting the seconds until she grabbed the phone and called my parents, dragging them out of a museum to let them know we were all living like heathens. "Girls, you'll have to do better," Aunt Sue said sternly.

I figured I had to do something to prove to them that we really were taking good care of the house. "Why don't you both come over for dinner tomorrow night?" I asked.

Aunt Sue and Uncle Frank agreed to the plan, and the second they walked out of the house, I jumped all over Haley.

"So who was that guy? That guy who almost got us in trouble by running out of your room and downstairs?"

"What? He wasn't with me!" Haley cried. "Are you serious?"

"Oh." Sam snapped her fingers. "Darn. I was hoping for some really good dirt on you."

"Forget it, I'm boring," Haley said with a sigh.

"So. The question remains. Who was that guy? And if he was running downstairs, why wasn't Blair? And what about the no sleepovers rule?" I groaned.

My parents would find out about this from my aunt and uncle. They'd be on the first plane out of Milan, or whatever the city du jour was. I'd have to check the itinerary on the fridge.

They'd no doubt hear about the party, too. The downside of living on an island is that everything gets back to everyone eventually. We're not very good at keeping secrets here.

Chapter 15

"What do you think I should get?" I asked Ben as we pulled into the Bobb's parking lot. I'd picked him up at his house five minutes before. Since he was coming over for dinner, it would be fun to hang out for a while together before Aunt Sue and Uncle Frank descended.

I'd tried to make something at home, but it hadn't exactly worked out. All those cooking lessons my mom had given me. She'd tried so hard. And I had no talent at all.

Erica was working all day to cover for Blair, who needed the day off so she could go to the mainland for something. (She'd never explained about the guy who slept over. She claimed to not even know who he was.) That left me holding the potholders.

It was one of those times when I really wished that I didn't live on an island. If I could just drive to some restaurant, or takeout deli, and get some pasta and salads. If there were a McDonald's or Wendy's anywhere in sight. Yes, I could buy grinders at the general store, and cheeseburgers at the Landing. But that didn't exactly say "Meal home-cooked by Colleen with care."

Neither did takeout from Bobb's, but it was the only option left.

"You know, I can cook. I'm not bad, either," Ben said. "I make a mean mac and cheese. Or we could just throw some burgers and hot dogs on the grill."

"I know, but I feel like I need to do something a little more special for them," I said.

"But don't your aunt and uncle eat at Bobb's all the time?" Ben asked.

I shook my head. "Not really, no. They think it's overpriced. My uncle once went on a ten-minute tirade about how the side salad was too small to cost a dollar ninety-nine. Then he insisted Trudy take the dessert off the check because the ice cream melted a little before it got to the table."

Ben laughed. "Yeah, that sounds like him."

"So this will be kind of a treat for them. And I really appreciate that you're doing this with me." I reached over and squeezed Ben's knee as I parked in front of the restaurant.

All of a sudden I remembered that Evan was working. Okay, so I'd known that, but I suddenly realized that I didn't really want Ben to come in with me and see Evan and wonder if that was why I'd come up with this plan to stop by Bobb's for food. Because it wasn't. Because I'm the world's worst cook, and if I didn't buy food here I'd be serving shredded wheat cereal to my aunt and uncle. That wouldn't get me back on their good side. I needed to be on their good side.

"I'll just run in and get a container of clam chowder and some other things," I said to Ben. "Okay?"

"You need help?"

"Nah. It'll only take me a sec." I grabbed my wallet from on top of the dashboard and leaned over to give Ben a quick kiss. "Thanks."

"Wait," Ben said as I closed the door. "Coll, hold up."

Please don't come with me, please don't say you want to

come with me, I thought. I leaned back in through the window. "Yeah? Do you want me to get something for you, too?"

"No. I just want the keys," he said. "That way I can listen to the Sox game while I wait."

"Right. Sorry!" I tossed the keys to him and hurried down the sidewalk into the restaurant.

When I walked into Bobb's, I waved to Erica, then Trudy. Samantha was busy waiting on a table. In the kitchen, Evan was sitting on the freezer, eating a basket of fried clams.

"Hey. Did you start missing the place?" he asked.

"I need to buy some food for dinner," I said. "I'm having my aunt and uncle over." I cleared my throat. "I mean, ah, we are."

"We?" Evan repeated.

"Me and Ben," I mumbled.

"Is he a glutton for punishment or something?" Evan laughed. "Why don't you just bring them here for dinner? It'd be fun. I'll get your table, and I can make them laugh so that they cheer up and get off your back. Or if I don't make them laugh, then I'll give them something to complain about instead of the food prices."

"I know. How about they come here for dinner and I stay home?" I suggested.

"Come on, they're not so bad," Evan said. "I mean, besides being ridiculously judgmental, and the fact they wish you'd never gotten older than nine." He slid off the freezer and dropped the empty plastic basket into the dishwasher. "Why *are* you having them over for dinner?"

"Well, you know how we had that party on Saturday night," I said. *Because you were there and you kept talking*

with Ben, and then looking at me, and then putting your arm
around Blair?

"Yeah?" Evan asked.

"Well, they sort of heard about it. I guess the Browns called them when things got loud, and they called but I didn't hear the phone. Which is sort of bad, I guess. But they decided it was no big deal, that the Browns were just exaggerating, so they went to bed. So instead they showed up on Sunday morning, really early, to check on me," I said.

"You're kidding. How early?" Evan asked.

"Okay, not that early. Ten thirty. But that's early on a Sunday, when it's your day off." I felt my face turn red. "The place was trashed, and then some guy came running downstairs while they were *standing* there, so they're convinced we're like heathens. Haley tried to cover by saying he came over to fix the sink."

"Haley should never be the one to cover," Evan said. "She's a terrible liar."

"I know," I said.

"So. What guy?" Evan asked. "Wait a second. Not Ben, was it?"

There was this weird look we exchanged when he said that. Because if I said yes, Ben was the one who spent the night, it would somehow change things between us. I don't know what it was.

Finally I just smiled. "Don't you think my aunt and uncle know what Ben looks like? It'd be kind of hard to make up a story about that."

"Right." Evan nodded. "Of course."

"Anyway, I don't know who the guy was. Since Haley

and Samantha insist he wasn't with them, and I know he wasn't with me, I have to assume he either passed out in the hallway or spent the night with Blair."

"Really." Evan nodded.

I watched his face for any sign of surprise or disappointment. He and Blair had been spending a lot of time together. Were they an item or weren't they? I really wanted to find out without asking.

"Yeah," I said. "We actually didn't hear one way or the other yet."

"Interesting. Was the guy anyone we know?"

I shook my head. "Not that *I* know, anyway. Oh, well, if it's important we'll meet him, I guess. Anyway, I have to convince my aunt and uncle that I'm doing just fine on my own and that the house is doing just fine, too. I've been cleaning since dawn, I think."

"You? You hate cleaning."

"Not as much as I hate cooking," I complained.

"You are so domestic. It's frightening," Evan said.

"I know."

"So after you got busted . . . did your parents call to tell you they're canceling their French château tour and coming home tomorrow?"

"No." I laughed.

"So forget about it," Evan said with a wave of his hand. "It'll blow over. These things always do. Everyone panics, and then a week later no one even remembers."

What a refreshing attitude. Of course, Evan didn't care much what other people thought of him, and he wasn't the one who'd get a parental lecture. I'd never met his parents, in fact. I had no idea what they were like.

"All I think of when I remember your aunt is how she threw a fit last year when she caught us drinking," Evan said. "Remember?"

I laughed, "Oh, my god. She was ready to send us to jail and a rehab clinic just because we sneaked one glass of wine at that end-of-summer party. One glass! And we split it."

"And she ran and told your dad, and he was like, well, it's a holiday, and they're walking home, and it was only one glass, and they're leaving now," Evan said. "Your dad is so cool."

"Yeah. But of course, when we left . . ." That was the night of the lighthouse incident. Why did I have to bring that up?

"Well, yeah. But nobody knows about that. Right?"

"Right," I said quickly. I might have confided in a friend or two, but *he* didn't need to know about that. In fact, sometimes I wished that I couldn't remember that. It made me feel sort of stupid. That I'd misinterpreted the way we acted toward each other as something serious and lasting, instead of just a . . . what? A "fling"? But it wasn't.

"So," Evan said, glancing over my shoulder. "What are you picking up to eat?" he asked quietly.

I followed his gaze and saw Ben walking into the kitchen. Oh, no. I'd been in here too long, and now I didn't even have what I'd come in for. "Food. Right!"

"Let me check if your order's ready," Evan said. "Hey, Ben. How's it going?"

"Hi," Ben replied, a little stiffly. "What's going on?"

"All the cooks decided to go on break at the same time. Should be just a second," I added.

I smiled at Ben, thinking this was terrible. Evan and I were lying to him over something as stupid as why it took me so long to pick up some takeout dishes. Why did we have to lie? But we'd already done it, instead of just saying that we'd gotten caught up in talking. That meant we felt like we had something to hide from him. But nothing was going on, so what were we hiding?

"I am so sorry. I am like the slowest shopper in the world." I grabbed Ben's hand and squeezed it tightly. "So what sounds good to you?"

Ben looked confused. "Didn't you already order?"

"Well, yeah—a few things. But if there's something special you want . . . ?"

"No, just you." While Evan went around collecting various containers for us—I had no idea what he would pick out—Ben put his arms around my waist and nuzzled my neck. He was usually physically affectionate with me, but not *this* affectionate, not in public. It was almost as if he was looking for some kind of reassurance that he was the one now, and Evan wasn't. And I was supposed to prove it to him, right now, in front of both of them.

"You know what I was thinking? I was listening to the radio and I heard an ad for this inn up on Mount Desert. We should both ask for a couple of days off at the same time," Ben said. "So we can go away on a trip together. Before summer's over and we go off to college. You know?"

"That sounds nice," I said, still distracted by the thought of what had just happened. I felt like I'd gotten caught cheating on Ben. Just because I was having such a good time with Evan that I literally could not tear myself away. I was in Bobb's, on my day off, *lingering*. Usually I didn't come within a half-mile radius on my day off. Not that I hated the job—I didn't, at all. I just enjoyed my time away from it.

"We could go to Acadia, spend a couple of nights camping."

"Yeah, sure."

"You don't sound that excited about it. Is it because camping requires cooking?" Ben teased.

Normally I would have made several jokes about my cooking and envisioning the disaster that taking me camping could turn into. But I just didn't feel like even playing along. Going off with Ben, by ourselves, didn't sound that good to me. That was crazy. A couple of months ago I spent days begging my parents to let us do just that. I'd even managed to convince them to let us go to Portland for a couple of days; we stayed at Erica's house—in separate rooms, of course, and under the supervision of Erica's parents. Still, it had been a romantic type of getaway because we'd never done anything like that by ourselves before.

But now? I didn't want to leave the island. Not really. Not at all. And not with Ben.

I should have heard alarm bells ringing as loud as a foghorn. Or at least I should have done everything in reverse and started the day over. The last place I wanted to be was standing in the kitchen at Bobb's with both Evan and Ben.

"Let's go outside and wait," I said, backing out of Ben's embrace. "Come on."

"I'll find you, you know!" Evan called after us. "You can run, but you can't hide."

I turned around and gave him a quizzical look. So did Ben.

Evan held up a brown paper bag. "When your food's ready."

"Riiiiiight," I said. "When the food's ready."

Chapter 16

"Guess what? Trudy just called," Samantha said when I walked downstairs for breakfast. "We get a catering gig next week, and guess who it's for!"

I sleepily rubbed my eyes. "Orlando Bloom?"

"Close. Remember that guy we saw get off the ferry a couple of days ago—with the blond hair and the goatee and the white T-shirt and the khaki cargo shorts, and he asked us where he could rent a mountain bike?"

"Um . . . sort of," I said.

"You remember. We said he was the first actual book club sighting of the year," Sam said. "Actually, that was what I said."

"The party's at the Hamiltons' house, and I saw Mr. Hamilton coming to pick him up at the ferry," Haley said.

"You mean . . . *the* Hamiltons?" I asked. "The ones with the little cottage on the hill?"

Haley laughed. We both knew how really wealthy people referred to their summer homes around here. "I have a cottage," they'd say, and that was our clue that it was at least a five-bedroom, six-bathroom house. "Exactly," she said.

"You really cleaned up the kitchen nicely last night," Sam commented as she put a filter into the coffeemaker.

"Yeah, well, it's easy when you don't actually cook anything. I mean, it's not too hard to rinse out plastic containers for recycling." I smiled, thinking of how much my aunt had teased me for picking up carryout food the night before. For some reason she thought it was the most amusing thing she'd ever heard of, and she couldn't wait to E-mail my parents and tell them how I'd had them over for takeout.

The whole time I was trying not to laugh because I kept thinking of how I had no more idea what we were going to eat than she did. I hadn't bothered to open up the containers before she and my uncle came over. I'd expected the clam chowder and lobster salad on a bed of lettuce. I hadn't expected the cold French fries—and so many of them—that Evan had picked out for us.

"So what was the verdict?" Haley asked. "Did they decide we're not such horrible people after all?"

"Yeah. They inspected everything," I said. "Well, everything downstairs. I didn't let them see the upstairs. I didn't want them finding out about the new paint job in my parents' room."

"Good plan," Sam said as she took out three mugs from the cabinet.

"Yeah. Besides, I didn't exactly clean my room or scrub the upstairs bathroom, either." I smiled. "So what are you going to do with your day off?" I asked Haley, who was busy making herself a slice of toast.

"Absolutely nothing," she said. Then she laughed. "Yeah, right. I'll be at my mom and dad's, and they'll rope me into helping out, as usual."

"You should just get out of here and go to a movie or something," I said.

"Yeah, but it's no fun doing that by yourself." She

wrinkled her nose. "You know?"

"You wouldn't be totally by yourself. At least not on the ferry," I said.

"True. Maybe I could convince Ben to—"

Samantha held up her hand for Haley to be silent. We all sat and listened to a car pulling up in the driveway. "What's that sound?" Sam asked.

I got up and looked out the screen door. A car was very definitely pulling up in the driveway. And it was the old Volvo—*my* old Volvo. Which meant that I was definitely not the one driving it, because I was standing in the kitchen. And it couldn't really drive itself, which meant . . .

I watched as Blair climbed out of the driver's seat and slammed the door shut. *Easy!* I wanted to say. If you close the door too hard, rusted pieces of the car fall off!

As I stepped back and watched her walk from the car to the steps, I wondered: Didn't I leave the keys on top of my dresser last night, where I always left them? So had she really come into my bedroom and taken them off the dresser? And now what? Did I have to hide the keys somewhere whenever I wasn't going to be around or awake? Should I sleep with them tied around my ankle?

I mean, who sneaks into someone's room when they're asleep and takes something?

"Hi, guys," Blair said as she strolled into the kitchen carrying a small plastic bag.

"Where were you?" Haley asked.

"I had some errands to run," Blair said.

Blair picked up a mug from the ones we'd gotten out for ourselves and poured herself some coffee.

"Funny, I was just about to have some," Sam muttered

under her breath.

"Errands? Really important errands, I hope. Extremely urgent errands," Haley said. "Like, someone on the other side of the island needed CPR."

"I was out of conditioner." Blair held up the ends of her hair. "It's hard to figure out what kind to use out here because it's so humid. You know?"

Haley cleared her throat. "So I'm wondering, Blair. Did you not *read* the list?"

"What list?" Blair asked.

"The rules. The ones posted right there." I pointed to the poster board on the wall. "The ones I gave you to look over the day you came to visit the house for the first time, and you said okay to, that you said were like something your parents would make you do."

Samantha removed the pushpin and pulled the list off the wall. "Here. Read and review." She put it on the kitchen table, next to Blair's freshly poured mug of coffee. "It says that only Colleen drives her car. It also says no big parties."

"God, you guys are so uptight sometimes," Blair said as she shook her head. "I mean, really. What's the big deal? It's not like anyone can check on us."

Except my ever-present relatives, I thought. Not that Blair would know about them, because she hadn't been around that Sunday morning, even though her overnight guest still had been.

"Yeah, maybe not, but it's still cheating," Sam said. "It still means breaking the rules."

"Anyway, it's not just about the list. It's about respecting the basic principles of the house and being a good housemate," Haley said. "You left like four wet towels on the bathroom floor yesterday. You left your laundry in the washer for three days straight."

"So?" Blair asked. "Just put it in the dryer."

"And fold it when it's dry? Like the last three times I did laundry?" Haley scoffed. "No thanks. When I want to do my laundry—okay, maybe *need* is a better word than *want*—I don't want to do yours, too."

"I'm sorry," Blair said. "I've been really busy."

"And we're not?" I asked.

There was a very awkward silence for a minute or so. Then Samantha picked up the jar on the counter that we used to collect and store "house money." It was empty. We each contributed twenty-five dollars every two weeks. Now it was time for everyone to refill the jar. Haley passed it around the table, and everyone contributed—except when the jar was passed to Blair.

"I don't have it, but I'll get it to you later today," she said.

"Didn't you make some tips last night?"

"Yeah, but I had to pay back Evan," Blair said.

"You too?" I blurted. "For what? I mean, um, did you ruin something of his?" Why was I asking? Maybe I didn't want to know the answer.

"No. He loaned me money when we took the ferry the day before. We went into town and had lunch and bought some stuff, and I didn't have enough cash on me."

I nearly choked on my coffee. Since when was Evan so flush—or generous? And why hadn't Ben told me he saw them together on the ferry?

Then again, it probably wasn't important to Ben. Probably he'd been glad to see the two of them hanging out together, because it might mean that Evan was attached to someone else now. Or had he been too busy flirting with Boat-and-Tote-Bag Girl to notice Blair and Evan?

This was turning into a semi–soap opera—without the international intrigue, romantic sex, and extreme close-ups.

"So, is that okay?" Blair asked.

The fact you're broke? Or the fact you're totally going after the guy I used to be in love with? No—and . . . no.

"Sure," I said, forcing a polite smile. "That's fine."

"You know what? I'll put money into the jar—I'm always over here." Erica handed me two twenty-dollar bills. "Here, Colleen."

"You don't have to," I said.

"I know, but I want to," Erica said.

I handed her back one of the twenties. "This will be great," I said as I stuffed the other twenty into the jar. "Thanks."

"You know what took me so long?" Blair said. "Some old lady fell and broke her arm and wrist or something. Everyone was talking about it at the store. She had to go in to the hospital last night on someone's boat and get it set. There was this really long line because everyone was talking about it."

"Yeah, you can't even sneeze around here without people talking about it," Samantha said.

Which was sometimes a very annoying thing, but it meant that if Blair ever took the car again without asking, at least I'd find out about it.

"Who was it? Did you get a name?" Haley asked.

"No. Well, Betty something."

"You're kidding. Betty McGonagle?" I asked. "Was that it?"

"Yeah, that sounds right." Blair refilled her coffee mug, draining the last drops left in the pot.

Poor Betty, I thought. But maybe it wasn't her painting hand. Then again, maybe it was.

"Hello, Mrs. McGonagle?" I knocked again and called into the house. "Can I come in?"

"Only if you call me Betty!" an irritated voice called back.

"Okay. Betty." I smiled and opened the screen door. "How are you?" I asked as I walked into her living room. She was sitting on the sofa with her right arm propped up on the side of it. She set down the book she had been reading when I walked in, and looked up at me. She was thin, with short, bright white hair that almost looked dyed that color, as if it were one shade short of platinum.

"Well, I've got a claw now," she said, holding up her right arm, which was wrapped and bandaged and partially in a cast. "Other than that, perfectly fine, same as always."

"Sorry to hear about your accident," I said. I hadn't been to her house since the last time I trick-or-treated, which must have been five years ago. I didn't remember all the abstract paintings on the walls. "Did you do those?" I asked.

"Most of them. Now, what can I get you? How about a cup of tea?" Betty said, starting to get to her feet.

"But I'm here to help you—to see what *you* need," I said.

"Nonsense. Don't need a thing," she said. "Now, what have you been up to this summer?"

"Well, you know. My parents are in Europe. I'm working at Bobb's."

"Well, I know all *that*, I'm not living in a cave," Betty said. "Honestly, Colleen. I'm old, not dead," she snapped.

"Sorry," I said.

"Oh, it's not you. It's my idiot son. Wants me to leave the island, move in with him, in Bangor. Told him I'm not leaving this place. Just because I hurt myself, he thinks I'm helpless."

"You're not," I said. "Obviously."

"It's not as if I can't get help when I need it. Which I don't," she insisted. "Except last night when I had to call Cap and get him to take me in to the hospital in his boat. But that worked. That worked just fine."

One thing I really like about our island is that everyone takes care of one another. They might grumble about it, but they'll do it. And we might talk about each other too much, but at least we keep up with each other's lives.

"So how did you hurt your arm?" I asked as I followed Betty into the kitchen. "How long will it take to heal?"

"Six weeks or so." She groaned as she filled the tea kettle with water from the tap. "An eternity, in other words."

"Well, you'll tell me. If there's anything I can do to help, I mean," I said.

"You could come by now and then," she said. "Bring me some of your work. If I can't paint, then I can live vicariously through you. Right?" She smiled as she took mugs from the cabinet above the counter.

I wonder if Evan's working tonight. I stirred my spaghetti around my plate, and stared off into space, picturing Evan working with Blair, wondering whether there was anything going on between them, or if it already had. I should never have asked Blair to live with us. Not just because of the Evan thing, although that was awkward, too.

Suddenly I remembered a big fight Evan and I had had last summer, when I thought we were going out exclusively, and he had spent an entire day sailing with this girl named . . . Kelley.

Wait a second. No wonder she'd left Bobb's for the summer to work at the Spindrift B&B. Somehow, she'd gotten the heads-up that he was coming back for the summer. It wasn't about wanting to make muffins or beds. No, she was the *smart* one on the island.

I am a horrible, terrible person, I thought. I was sitting with Ben's family, having dinner, and I was thinking about Evan.

I was pathetic. It seemed as if I couldn't stop having these thoughts. What was wrong with me? Had I repressed all these things for months, and now they were taking their revenge? But did it have to happen mid-spaghetti? One strand went down the wrong way, and Ben nearly had to give me the Heimlich maneuver to save me from choking.

"Are you all right?" Ben asked.

"S-sure," I said. "Sorry. Don't know what I was doing. I just spaced out there for a second."

"You're tired, that's all," Ben's mother said. "In fact, you two are both working too hard this summer. I don't see how you've had time to just have fun together."

"It's been hard," I agreed. Not to mention complicated.

"How *is* your job going?" Ben's father asked.

"Good." I nodded.

"Busy?"

"Very. Well, not every night," I said. "But most of them."

"So you're making some good money?" he asked.

"Definitely." Unless you counted the expensive-Birkenstock-sandals deduction. Or maybe it was more of a Colleen-impulsive-act-of-stupidity deduction. If he'd gotten mad or upset, the ninety dollars would be well worth it. But no, he'd enjoyed being tossed into the drink.

I looked up from my salad bowl and smiled at Ben's mother, who was watching me for some reason. Could *she* tell, somehow?

Meanwhile, Ben reached over under the table and put his hand on my leg. I was so surprised that I nearly kicked their dog, who was lying at my feet. Ben hardly ever did anything like that—not in front of (or under the table of) his parents and family.

I glanced at him and gave him a small, questioning smile.

After dinner, we had planned on watching a movie together, but I just wasn't in the mood. I felt too restless to sit still—like I needed to be out on a walk or something.

Hanging out with Ben like this, sitting around and listening to music . . . it was all fun and good and wonderful, when Evan wasn't here. But he *was* here now. And I was sitting on the sofa with Ben, wondering what Evan was doing that night. Not the *whole* time, but wasn't even part of the time bad enough?

Suddenly I couldn't take it anymore. I just needed some time to think, some time to breathe.

"You know what? I know we planned on watching a movie and everything, but I think I need go check on Betty and see how she's doing," I said, standing up.

"What?" Ben asked. "Check on Betty? McGonagle?"

"Yeah. I was over there yesterday, and she just . . . she needs some help," I said. "I promised I'd stop by, so I'd better do that before it gets too late."

"But . . . you always made fun of her," Ben said, getting up to follow me outside.

"I know. And that was really horrible of me. She's actually very nice," I said. "And she showed me a lot of her other paintings yesterday. I mean, she paints so much more than just . . . oceans. The stuff she sells at the gift shop, you know, that's just to support herself. She does abstract stuff; some of it's really incredible." I'd spent more than an hour at her house, looking at her work. I'd had no idea she was more than just . . . rolling surf.

"Yeah." Ben had never really been that interested in art—mine or anyone else's. "So . . . wait. Are you serious? You're going over there right now?"

"Just to check on her on my way home," I said. "Why? Is that okay?"

"It just seems strange, that's all." Ben stood in the open doorway. "Are you sure that's where you're going?"

What was he trying to say? Oh, no. He thought I was leaving because I was going to see Evan. I could see why he'd think that, but it wasn't true. I might be confused at times, but I wasn't a liar.

"Yes, I'm sure," I said, trying to keep things simple. I didn't really want to go into it right now. "Do you want to come with me?"

He shook his head. "No. Not really."

"Okay, well, I'll see you tomorrow?" I walked back and gave him a quick kiss on the lips.

"You want a ride?" Ben offered as I started down the driveway.

"No, it's okay—I want to walk," I said.

After a quick visit to Betty, who looked at me like I was crazy for coming by twice in one day, and assured me she was still fine, I went home, walking the long way. I just felt like I couldn't be home tonight, I couldn't be with Ben. I dropped by to say hello to Haley's parents when I went past their place. I stopped in to say hello to my aunt and uncle. I even had a semi-okay thirty-second visit with the grumpy John and Molly Hyland, who were out for their evening stroll.

I'd never done so much socializing in my life, but mostly it was because I wanted to keep moving and I didn't want to stop. I didn't know why I had so much energy or what, exactly, I was looking for.

When I finally gave up and went home, Hutch was lying on the end of my bed, curled up on my red sweatshirt. I changed into my pajamas and lay down beside him. I scratched him behind the ears, and he turned over and stretched out on his back. Then I rubbed his belly. It was a good five minutes of cat therapy before Hutch turned and looked right at me. He stood up and rubbed his face against mine.

"I know, Hutch," I said softly. "I don't know what I'm doing, either."

Chapter 17

Saturday morning, when I went downstairs to make myself breakfast, I saw a body stretched out on the sofa. I almost didn't want to look—did we need any more unidentified overnight guests in this house? But then I quickly realized that it was my big brother lying there, curled up under a blanket.

"Richard! When did you get here?" I squealed. I ran over to give him a big hug. I hadn't seen him in a few months, and hadn't even realized how much I missed him until, suddenly, there he was.

"I caught the last ferry last night. I thought for sure I'd wake you guys up when I came in, but—well, I guess I perfected the art of sneaking into this house late at night a long time ago." He sat up and rubbed his head. "Though I did hit my head coming in the window." His short, wavy blond hair was a floppy, curly mess, as if it had absorbed half of the ocean on the way over on the ferry, as if he'd been at sea for weeks. If my hair became a frizzone, Richard's turned into a curlizone. He nearly had *ringlets*. Which could have been embarrassing if he didn't have such good cheekbones.

"Why didn't you call or E-mail before you came?" I asked. "I would have come to pick you up, if I knew when to."

"I wasn't sure I was going to make it. Then a guy I work with rented a car, and I drove up with him. He's in Machias now. Anyway, don't worry about it." He stretched his arms over his head and yawned. He was wearing a white T-shirt and shorts. "I met this girl on the ferry last night—"

"Oh, no," I groaned. "Here we go again."

He grinned. "She gave me a ride. She's staying at the Ludlows' this weekend. Do we know the Ludlows?"

"Richard." I picked up a pillow and bashed him on the head with it.

"'Cause we should, I think," he said, laughing. "That name sounds familiar. Where's the phone book?"

"You are horrible. You're so horrible," I told him. "Don't you have like a serious girlfriend in New York?"

"Correction. Had," Richard said.

I rolled my eyes. That was Richard for you. Every girl was perfect, every girl was the one he'd been waiting for, the one he wanted to marry. And then . . . he'd be on the ferry and there'd be someone cute and his old relationship would be history.

At least he was nice to them while he dated them. The problem was that they weren't prepared for how short an attention span Richard had for relationships. It was like everyone came with an expiration date. "I don't know where he gets it from," Mom would say, "but it's not from me."

And then Dad would get sort of red and flustered and mumble something about "skipping a generation," but I'd always start wondering what exactly happened when they met in college. Dad was so mild-mannered and sweet and . . . well, goofy . . . that I couldn't picture this cloud of women around him, fighting over him. No, not in a million years.

Richard, on the other hand? That I could see. I *had* seen it. He'd dated so many girls on the island that he'd run *out* of them. And he didn't even have a bad reputation. If a girl ever did what he did? Well, never mind. He was here now, and I was very excited to see him. "This is going to be so cool. I'm working tonight, so you should come in and eat for free. Bring . . . whoever. Then we can all go to the fireworks together. You, me, Evan—I mean, Ben—"

"Whoa. What's up with that?" Richard sat up a little on the sofa. "Now we're getting to the good stuff."

"There's no . . . stuff," I said. I was about to tell Richard the situation when Blair came downstairs.

"Hello. Who are you?" she asked Richard. The thing that killed me about Blair—okay, one of the things—was that she could look good no matter what time of day it was. Sure, she spent tons of time in front of the mirror to do it, but the thing was that it paid off. Me? The more time I spent, the worse I looked, it seemed. I'd make too many second guesses about my makeup and end up ruining my face, or hair. Or both.

"This is Richard. You know, the guy in all the pictures?" I pointed to the living room wall, where the photos of Colleen and Richard Through the Ages—from the cute to the embarrassing to the okay to the good— were displayed.

"Oh, my god. Of course you are. And Colleen said you might be coming for the weekend. That's great!" She walked over and held out her hand. "Hi, I'm Blair."

"Nice to meet you, Blair," Richard said as he slowly shook her hand.

"Hey, would you like some coffee?" Blair offered.

"Sure. Sounds great." Richard smiled at her. "Thanks." Then he turned to me. "It's really strange being in our house and being waited on by someone I don't know. Not to mention sleeping on the sofa."

I didn't mention that it was also really strange, because Blair never made coffee. Or did anything around the house, actually. Except occasionally borrow the car without asking and use up groceries she didn't pay for.

"Did you see Haley?" I asked. "She would have had to be at work already."

"Horrible Haley? No, I didn't," Richard said.

"She's staying in your room this summer," I said.

"Yeah, you told me that. Your E-mails have kind of dropped off lately, though. Anything I need to know about?"

"Ah . . . Betty McGonagle broke her arm?" I said.

Richard sighed and snuggled back under the blanket. "Slow news day on the island, as usual."

"No, but I feel really bad for her," I said. "I've been visiting her."

"Huh?"

"Come on, get up—let's have breakfast. Then maybe you can get to work. We've been saving up some stuff around the house for you to do. The hinge on the screen door is busted, for one."

"Oh, great. That's what I want to do on my long weekend," Richard complained. "It better be *good* coffee."

"Don't count on it," I told him.

"How about a Bobb's bib?"

Richard looked up at me with his eyebrow raised. He was having lunch at Bobb's with a couple of his old high school friends. "How about no?" he said.

"Come on, you have to wear a bib," I said. "If you order the lobster, you get a bib. Free of charge. No, really."

Carl leaned over to Richard. "I know I asked you this before, but is that gorgeous girl your sister?"

I'd had such a crush on Carl when I was ten and he was eighteen. He always teased me like that, whenever I saw him. Now he was already starting to lose his hair at twenty-five. It made me feel old.

"No, that's not my sister, that's an annoying waitress," Richard said. "Colleen, when is the last time you saw me wear a bib? Never."

I shook the plastic bib in front of him, the way you'd shake a towel that had sand on it. "Come on. For me?"

"No. I think I can eat a lobster without ruining my shirt."

"And I had my camera ready and everything," I complained. "I was going to take a picture of you in the bib and E-mail it to Mom and Dad."

"Well, forget it. So that's your boyfriend, right?" Richard pointed at Evan with a lobster leg. "I remember him from last summer."

"No, it's not," I said. "I'm with Ben. You know Ben—you met him at Christmas."

"Oh, right. Ben." He stared at me and gestured for me to come closer. He lowered his voice and said, "Coll, reality check time. That guy is either your boyfriend or he's going to be—"

"No!" I interrupted. "He's my *ex*-boyfriend. Evan. Remember how upset I was last fall? How I was crying and miserable?"

"No." Richard shook his head. "Sorry, but I don't."

"Oh. Well, that was all *his* fault." I glared at Evan, who was cheerfully greeting a large table of twelve guests.

"Uh-huh. Well, I don't know what happened back then, but he seems to kind of like you now. I saw the way you guys made sure you got in each other's way? Just to get through the door?"

"We did not," I said, remembering how I'd had to squeeze past Evan. Wait! *Was* one of us going out through the in door? On purpose? And was that one of us . . . me?

"It's not like that," I said, but I was wondering. Was it like that? Evan had never given me a reason to think he wasn't still maybe interested in me. We were just not seeing each other now.

"Well, why don't you bring me another lobster?" Richard said as he cracked a claw.

"Are you serious?" I asked. "Two lobsters?"

"Yeah. Completely serious. And when you get it for me, try not to touch that guy," Richard whispered. "I want to see if you can pull it off."

"Richard!" I whispered, slapping his shoulder. "Quiet."

"Don't hit me," Richard said.

"Yeah, hit me instead," Carl said. "And you can bring me another lobster while you're in there, okay, Colleen?"

Luke was busy chewing, but he held up his hand and signaled for another for himself, too. Richard and his friends always ate *so much*, I thought as I walked into the kitchen. They hadn't changed at all since last summer, or the summer before that, or . . .

"Did you see him?" Samantha asked when I nearly crashed into her. She was standing right by the door, peeking through the window in it. "Did you see how cute he is?"

"Who?" I asked.

"That blond guy at table seventeen. I'm waiting on him," she said. "Remember, the guy Mr. Hamilton picked up from the ferry?"

"Oh, yeah. Now I remember," I said as I checked him out.

"His name's Troy Hamilton." Samantha nodded. "And guess what? They're here to evaluate the catering menu because they hired Bobb's for his cousin's engagement luncheon next week. And I was right—we're totally invited. As caterers, that is."

"Sounds fun," I said.

"Well, sort of. Does walking around offering trays of mini crab cakes count?" she joked.

When I got back to Richard's table with the tray of three lobsters, Richard was on the other side of the restaurant, talking to someone at another table. I glanced over just as a woman's arm shot out and she doused him with a glass of water, right in the face.

Richard stepped back, looked shocked, and then came walking back over to his table. The front of his faded navy polo shirt was drenched.

"You should have gone with the bib," I teased as he sank into his chair.

Carl and Luke were laughing at him. "What happened?" Carl asked.

"I was trying to talk to that girl from the ferry last night. The one staying with the Ludlows?" Richard dabbed his face with a napkin. "Ludlow, Ludlow . . . what Ludlow do I know who would want to throw water at me?"

Carl snapped his fingers. "Emily Ludlow, you idiot. You went out junior year."

"Right! Right. But that was like ten years ago." He rubbed his neck. "Why is she still holding that against me?"

"You stood her up for the prom," Luke said. "Does that ring a bell?"

"Oh, crap. This place *is* small," Richard complained.

"You know what?" I said, thinking of my own predicament, being stuck on an island with my current and my ex. "We should live in Montana or California. Even Rhode Island would be bigger."

"Why do you think I moved to Manhattan?" Richard replied, casting a nervous glance over his shoulder at Emily Ludlow's table.

"Wait a second, wait a second. I know all about Richard, but why do *you* say that?" Carl asked me.

"Oh. Uh, looks like another table needs me." I escaped before they could ask any more questions. I could just see those guys having a field day with my situation. Before they left Bobb's, they'd probably harass Evan to no end. I didn't want them doing that.

That was *my* job.

Richard was catching a ride back to the city on Monday morning with Luke, who was driving down to Portland, where Richard could get the train.

I hadn't seen him too much the night before, when everyone on the island had gone to watch the fireworks. Ben and I hung out together, while Richard ran around with his friends. They'd stayed out until at least two in the morning. I wasn't surprised that Richard was looking a little the worse for wear as he got out of the car and we walked slowly toward the ferry. We both waved at Luke, who was already on the boat, waiting for him.

"I know I should be a better big brother. I don't really set a good example." Richard took a sip from the can of ginger ale he'd grabbed on the way out the door, and made a face. "But I do have to give you some advice."

"Don't drink heavily the night before you have to get on a ferry and then be in a car and then on a train?" I said.

"Ha ha, very funny. I'm *fine*." He scratched the blond stubble on his cheek. "It's just—look, Colleen. About you and that guy at the restaurant."

"There is no 'about' us," I said.

"Just think about what you really want. Because if you don't *know* what you want, you're just screwing around with other people's feelings."

This would have to be ironic, coming from him.

"No offense, Richard. But I just don't know how much you know about real relationships."

"Ooh. Ouch." Richard pretended to dab his face, as if I'd punched it and given him a bloody nose.

I laughed. "Well, sorry, but it's true."

"It might be true, but I do know no one likes being lied to. I mean, once it's over . . ." He shrugged. "It's over."

"Yes, but it's not over until it's over," I said.

"That makes no sense." Richard leaned over to give me a hug. "But whatever works for you, Coll. I'm off to make my fortune."

"That's what you said last time. Send me some *checks* already."

"I'll come visit you at Bates in the fall!" Richard called as the ferry started to pull away. "Make some cute friends, okay?"

"You're horrible!" I yelled.

That was all I needed, Richard, Mr. Short Relationship Attention Span, hitting on my college roommates and breaking their hearts. And being way, way too old for them—only he wouldn't think so.

But as I watched him go, I had to wonder: Did Evan and I really act that obviously toward each other that even my brother had to comment on it? Was I still as attracted to him as I used to be? And if I was . . . then what was I doing with Ben?

Chapter 18

"Rich much?" Blair asked as we climbed out of the Bobb's catering van. I stood next to her and looked up at the "cottage" in front of us. It was a large, white house overlooking the ocean, with green shutters, a wide porch that wrapped around the entire house, a gorgeous rose garden, a shuffleboard court, and a three-car garage and a little carriage house. The Hamiltons probably put more money into mowing their lawn than my parents put into our entire house.

"So this is how the other half lives," Evan said, getting out of the backseat of the van.

Samantha walked around from the driver's seat. "Wow. The Hamiltons do all right, don't they? I'm so jealous, I almost hate them."

"As long as they keep inviting cute grandnephews here, who cares?" I whispered to Sam.

"No doubt. So I've been thinking about what this year's excursion should be," she said as we started to unload the van, carrying trays of food into the house. "You know, last year we did the sailboat cruising thing. What should we do this year?"

"I haven't really thought about it," I said. The memory of Ben asking me to go to Acadia with him flitted through my brain. That was a summer getaway excursion plan, and for some reason it didn't make me want to . . . excurse. It made me want to *excuse* myself.

"I have two ideas," Sam said. "One, we take a road trip somewhere we've never been before. It could be Maine, it could be Canada—Nova Scotia, maybe. Or two, *we* have a party catered by Bobb's. And Trudy has to wait on *us*."

"That sounds good," Evan said. "Am I invited?" He pulled open the back door we'd been instructed to use, and held the door open with his foot for the rest of us.

"No," Sam said bluntly.

"Come on. I got to go last year," Evan complained as I walked past him.

"That was then—" I began.

"This is now," Evan said. "Why was *then* so much better than now?"

Don't, I thought. *Don't do that.* He was really turning it up a notch with the flirting lately. As I bumped into him in the kitchen, struggling to set down the tray I was carrying, I thought about what Richard had said, how we couldn't get through a shift at Bobb's without touching each other. Was that true?

I tried to keep my distance while we got ready for and then worked the party, which was held on a large deck overlooking the ocean. Everyone was very nice to us, except for one grumpy older man who kept insisting the shrimp were no good, that he expected *prawns*, not "itty bitty shrimp."

"But jumbo shrimp is an oxymoron," Evan said. "Sir."

He grunted at both of us and then turned away to get another glass of champagne, or whatever he was drinking. They'd hired a bartender from somewhere else, since (a) all of us were underage, and (b) Trudy's selection of liquor was limited to Geary's Ale and a few domestic beers.

I saw Blair laughing with Troy Hamilton, and Sam gently interrupting to tell her to go to the kitchen for the cheese puffs. Then Sam and Troy leaned against the deck railing for a couple of minutes, talking. *Good for her,* I thought. *Go, Sam, go.*

"Hey, Sam? Could you drop me off here?" I asked as we drove past the Landing on our way back to Bobb's. I was thinking that I could see Ben when he finished work, and in the meantime I could visit with Haley.

"Sure thing," Sam said, pulling over and stopping. "Tell Haley I said hi!"

"Yeah, for me, too," Blair added.

I climbed out of the van and was about to close the sliding door behind me when Evan stopped me. He hopped out of the van. "I could really go for an ice cream. All that small talk and politeness gave me a sore throat," he said, as if that explained why he was following me.

"Yeah. Sure," I said as Sam drove off in the van with Blair. I felt kind of bad that they'd have to unload everything without us now. But most of it was empty trays and dirty silverware.

"Sure what?" Evan laughed as he fell into step beside me. "You sound like you don't believe me."

"Should I?" I asked.

"I have no idea what you're talking about."

"Never mind," I said. "It just seems like a coincidence, that's all. I get out of the van, so you do?"

"Okay, so. In your . . . fantasy world . . . a person wants a little mocha chip and suddenly it's a plot?"

I started laughing, despite myself. Okay, so maybe my ego was getting a little out of control. Evan was allowed to crave mocha chip. It didn't have anything to do with me. Although . . . if he really wanted the ice cream, why hadn't he jumped out of the van first?

We walked over to the Landing's takeout window. Haley was leaning on the wooden shelf with her elbows and staring out at the water.

"Pretty boring between ferries, huh?" I asked.

"Hey, Coll!" she said, her face lighting up when she saw me. Then her expression changed a bit. "Oh. Hi, Evan," she said coldly.

"Haley. What's up?" Evan asked.

"Not much." She sighed. "Pretty slow. How was the catering thing?" she asked me.

"Fabulous," I said.

"Yeah, fabulous for them, because all the chicks were lusting after this guy at the party," Evan said.

"No, we all weren't," I said. "Sam likes him, and he likes her—"

"Same old, same old," Evan said.

"Yeah. It is getting old," Haley said. She stared at Evan. "Really old."

She was acting very standoffish toward him. I realized she probably hadn't seen him much at all this summer. She was no doubt still angry with him for making me cry last fall. She can hold a grudge longer than you'd think it's humanly possible.

"Anyway, aren't you guys supposed to be at work?" she asked.

"We get a break before dinner," I said. "So I thought I'd come see you."

"I think I'd go home and chill by myself for a while," Haley said with a pointed look at me. "If it were me."

"Uh, maybe you're right," I said as I heard the ferry horn. "Maybe we should get back to work."

Evan shrugged. "Okay, but I want the mocha chip first."

"Cone or dish?" Haley asked. She quickly got Evan a double cone, and me a single dish of praline pecan. I wanted to get out of there before Ben showed up. I felt this nervous energy, like I was doing something wrong.

Relax, Colleen. It's only ice cream. And you're not even sharing a spoon.

"We'd better get going," I said, heading for the road.

"Yeah, we'd better," Evan said. "It's a bit of a walk from here. Want to call a cab? Or, wait. Even better—let's hitch."

"I don't hitch rides," I said.

"Don't worry. You'll be safe with me," Evan said.

Somehow I doubted that, as he hailed an old station wagon that was driving past. It felt like we were running away together—except for the fact that we were carrying ice cream and wearing black-and-white catering uniforms. Which kind of took some of the thrill of adventure out of it.

We got into the backseat of the station wagon against my better judgment. Two guys I'd never seen before, a skinny one with long straggly hair and a large-ish one with a crew cut, both (sadly) bare-chested, turned around and nodded at us. "Right on," they said in unison.

"Where are you headed?" the straggly-haired guy asked.

"Bobb's restaurant," Evan said.

"Right on." The crew cut guy nodded in approval.

Evan and I glanced at each other. "Is there any other answer?" I whispered.

"Right on," he replied, and we both grinned.

We were halfway through the dinner shift at Bobb's when Trudy said she wanted to talk to me in the kitchen. I had no idea what it was about. I'd brought out the wrong salad dressing a couple of times that night, but it wasn't like her to get on my case about small mistakes.

"The Hamiltons just called," she said. "Olivia Hamilton, to be exact."

"And?" I asked. I was expecting praise, expecting her to have said she wanted to hire us for another event. "The party went really smoothly—did she say that?"

Trudy wiped down one of the prep tables while she spoke. "Not exactly. She has a problem."

"Problem? What kind?" I asked.

"Some of her jewelry's missing. An entire box, I guess."

I put my hand to my throat. "You're kidding!"

"I wish that I were." Trudy frowned at me. "This is very serious."

"Okay. So who do they think is responsible?"

"Well, that's just it, Colleen. And believe me, I hate to say this. But I've talked to everyone else already—Sam, Blair, Evan. And you were the last one in the house, and—"

"What? But I didn't—I wouldn't—"

"I didn't think you did, either. But there are witnesses."

"Witnesses?" Why was this turning into an episode of *Law & Order*? I was being accused of a crime. What next—I was supposed to hire a lawyer, wasn't I? *Were* there any lawyers on the island? "Trudy, the only reason I was the last person in the house is that I was the last person in the van, because Blair forgot a tray on the deck and I ran back in to get it."

"Well. The fact remains that you were in the house after everyone else—"

"But the entire family was still in the house!" I protested. "So how would I even know where to look or what to steal? I don't think like that. I've never stolen anything."

"I promise I'll check into this. I'm not letting you go right away," Trudy said. "No one's going to press any charges until there's some more facts. But this is the story right now, so far. We'll see what develops in the next few days."

"Trudy! How can you even *think* I'd do something like that? You've known me for *four* years. Have I ever—"

"I'm sorry, Colleen. But—"

"You know what? Never mind. I can't believe this. I didn't take *anything*, and I can't believe I even have to tell you that!" I stormed out through the back doors and ran to the end of the dock. I was so upset that I started crying.

I heard footsteps clomping down the dock toward me. I turned around and there was Evan, reaching out for me, putting his arms around me, holding me close. I didn't bother to resist. I didn't have the strength to—besides, I needed him.

"She thinks . . . she thinks . . ." I sputtered.

"Don't worry." Evan stroked my hair. "I know you didn't do anything. Trudy will find that out."

"But why would she . . . ?"

"She had some woman call up and yell at her,"

178

Evan said. "Ten to one, Mrs. Hamilton finds her jewelry tonight."

I kept sniffling, and he kept running his hand over my head, and then he kissed my cheek.

"And you know what? The stuff she was wearing today was so gaudy that I'm surprised it could even *go* missing. I mean, it could light up an entire town."

I smiled. "True." I brushed his T-shirt sleeve against my face to dab away the tears, and it was so soft, and smelled just like I remembered him.

Suddenly, out of the corner of my eye, I saw someone else on the docks.

My eyes widened in horror. That figure in the dark was *Ben*.

And as soon as I recognized him, he turned and ran.

Chapter 19

"Ben! Ben, wait!" I called.

Evan was still holding my arms, not letting me go right away. I twisted my way out of his grasp just as I heard a car peeling out of the parking lot. I teetered on the dock, nearly tipping over. Evan caught my arm to keep me from falling into the water, but I shook him off. "Let me go!" I said.

I ran inside and found Trudy as quickly as I could. She was at the host stand with Erica, inserting the sheet with tomorrow's lunch specials printed on it into the menu.

"Trudy, I—I have to go," I said. "I can't work the rest of my shift."

"Colleen? You can't just leave," she said.

"I have to!" I said.

"Colleen. We still have to talk about this missing jewelry issue. And you've got a shift to finish. I really don't think this is the time for you to be taking off—"

"But I have to. Trudy, you know me, you know I'd never do anything like steal—anything to break the law—come on!" I insisted. "And this is a really important personal issue and I have to deal with it now. You always say that we can have time off for personal days. Well, I need some personal hours—now."

"Colleen! It's too short notice. What are we going to

180

do if you just take up and leave because you feel like it?" Trudy said.

"Trudy, I'll work for her," Erica said.

"But you're hosting," Trudy argued.

"That doesn't take all of my time—anyway, the evening's winding down, and we're only seating tables for another hour. I can handle it," Erica said.

I loved her for sticking up for me.

"We'll split her tables," Samantha said, walking up. "Go, Colleen. Do what you have to do."

"You guys are the best."

"Colleen? Consider yourself suspended," Trudy said. "I don't want to see you here tomorrow. Is that understood?"

"Yes, ma'am," I grumbled. I could care less about my job right then, and besides, I was still mad at Trudy for not trusting me. I wished she'd suspended me about two hours ago.

I pulled off my apron and handed it to Erica, then I quickly went over with her and Sam which tables I had and what they still needed. Then I was on my way. I had to catch Ben before any more time went by. He was thinking terrible, horrible things, and they weren't true.

"Hey, Coll! Where are you going?" Evan called as I hurried past him, out the door.

"Where do you think?" I said, still moving, going down the dock beside the building. I didn't want to talk to him right now. Maybe he hadn't meant to, but he'd ruined things for me—again. Just like he was always ruining things for me.

"Look, maybe you shouldn't go over there right now."

"I have to," I said.

"I know you *want* to, and you think you have to," Evan said. "But give the guy a second to deal with it. If it were me, I'd be really angry—"

"But it wouldn't be you, would it?" I said. "You don't understand. You don't know what it's like—Ben's a nice person, too nice to do stuff like what we just did to him."

"I didn't mean anything by it. I was only trying to make you feel better—"

"I know. I *know*. But look—not right now." I started jogging toward Ben's house, which was about a mile and a half from Bobb's. Good thing I always wore running sneakers to work.

"Colleen?" Ben's mother stared at my outfit, at the flush in my cheeks. She stepped aside to let me walk past her into the house. "Have you been exercising?"

"I—I was in a hurry," I said. I didn't want to get into the details with her.

"Did you get out of work early?" She smiled at me. So, she didn't hate me yet. That must mean Ben hadn't told her anything. Of course, why would he? It wasn't the sort of thing you went around bragging about. *I saw my girlfriend with another guy.*

"Um, yes," I said. Not in the way she thought, but the fact was I *had* gotten out early. "It was sort of a slow night." Except when it came to me messing up—in that respect, it was a very busy night.

"Well, I'll run upstairs and tell Ben you're here. He just got home," she said.

While she was gone, I paced around the living room. Through the doorway to the den, I could see Ben's father sitting in front of the TV, watching a Red Sox game. I waved to him, and he smiled and waved back. It was about nine o'clock, and Ben's younger brothers, Colin and Philip, were no doubt already asleep, or at least in bed.

I was checking out the crystal figurines in their hutch display when I heard footsteps coming down the stairs. My hand shook and I nearly knocked over a crystal swan. That was all I needed—to break the collectibles on top of everything else.

I took a deep breath and turned around.

"I'm sorry, Colleen. He's already gone to bed," Ben's mother said.

I bit my lip, trying to decide what to do next. Maybe Ben was just angry, and he needed some time to recover—the way he had when I'd first told him about Evan that day on the ferry. (Which felt like months ago, instead of weeks.) It had taken him two days to talk to me about it. Maybe I should let the whole thing blow over this time, too.

Then again, if I just left, I'd have no chance of explaining what had happened. Ben would assume the worst. Like he already apparently had.

"I hate to ask you to do this. But do you think you could wake him up?" I asked. "It's really, really important."

"Is it an emergency? Is everything okay?"

"Well, no. It's not. I have to talk to him," I said. "Tonight."

I guess she could see how desperate I was, because she nodded and said, "All right. I'll try again."

Try again. That meant he wasn't sleeping, that she'd asked if he could come down and see me, and he'd said to *tell* me that he was asleep. Wow. He'd never done that to me—never lied. At least, not that I knew of.

When he finally came downstairs, I could tell he hadn't been sleeping at all.

"Hey," I said.

He ran his hands through his hair and just looked at me.

"Can we . . . can we go for a walk or something?" I asked, thinking about his father in the den, and his mother somewhere else nearby—and she knew something was up.

"Sure."

We went down to this really big rock beside the road, where we often sat and talked. I was walking slightly behind Ben, and as I looked at his back, I felt like I was about to start crying.

I remembered one of the first nights we went out on a date, to the winter dance, how Ben had been sitting on this rock, waiting for me when I pulled up in the car, and how he was carrying flowers in the dead of winter, how he had mittens on with his dark suit, and how I was wearing my mother's thick wool coat over my dress and attempting to drive—and walk—on the ice in heels, and how Ben had picked me up and carried me into the school.

Ben leaned against the rock, and I tried to stand next to him.

"I saw you run off tonight," I said. "I know you saw me and Evan and you thought we were . . . I don't know what you thought, actually, which is why I came over to explain. It was just a quick hug. Really."

Ben didn't say anything for a minute. I bit my lip, wanting him to understand, wishing tonight had never happened. "It lasted five minutes," he finally said, his tone cold.

"What? No, that's impossible." I shook my head. "Look, what happened was—"

"I don't care what happened or whatever spin you're going to put on what happened," Ben said. "I know what I saw, and it wasn't some ten-second hug. Five minutes, Coll."

"But . . . it's important," I said. "Please, listen. See, we had this catering job—you remember, at the Hamilton house? And they reported some jewelry missing, and someone actually said *I* was responsible. Me."

Ben crossed his arms in front of him. "Well. Were you?"

"Ben! Come on. I'd never steal," I said. "Do you really think so poorly of me?"

"I shouldn't have said that. I'm sorry," Ben said.

"No, *I'm* sorry. I was just—I was upset when the whole thing came up and Trudy accused me—and I—I went outside. Evan followed me and I just—I turned to him because I was so upset. I mean, Trudy . . . of all people. You know?"

"You could have turned to Samantha. Or Erica," Ben said. "Couldn't you?"

"Well, yeah, of course, but they weren't right there—"

"Or you could have just called me. That's sort of what I'd expect you to do," Ben said. "If you were upset. I wouldn't expect you to be all over your ex-boyfriend, in front of me, in front of everyone eating at Bobb's—"

"I didn't know you were there," I said.

That sounded terrible, as if I were going around hugging Evan whenever I knew Ben wouldn't be there. "I mean, I wasn't thinking! It wasn't a *plan*. It was a gut reaction. I would have hugged Cap, or John Hyland, or Eddie from the hardware store . . . if he'd been out there. I would have hugged a seagull, if it was possible."

"You're not being honest. I know what I saw, and I know it didn't mean . . . I know it meant *something*," Ben stammered. "And in a way, it wasn't even surprising. I mean, it was so . . . obvious what was going on. What's been going on all summer."

"Nothing!" I said. "Nothing's going on now, nothing's *been* going on—"

"Yeah. It is," Ben said.

"But . . . no. It isn't," I insisted. "And Evan—and I— we're not. That's the only time we ever hugged—there's nothing between us."

"There's something," Ben said slowly. "Which really sucks. Because this was supposed to be such a great summer for us. You know? Yeah. Turned out really great."

"Hasn't it?" I asked.

"No. You've changed, Colleen."

"What? I haven't *changed*," I said.

"Yeah, you have. You used to be so . . . reliable. Stable. Now you're all over the place. You can't even commit to going on a trip together because you can't make up your mind what—I'm sorry, who—you want from one day to the next."

"That's not true," I said. Reliable and stable? As if I were a car or something. That sounded boring. Maybe that was how I acted, or how he perceived me, but that didn't sound like the way I *felt*.

"Look, we're not going to be together next year

anyway," Ben went on, as if he'd made up his mind. "Let's stop kidding ourselves—this isn't going to work out then. It's not working out now. Let's just forget about it. Stop seeing each other."

"No. No!" I said. "Don't say that." I reached for his arms and tried to pull him toward me, but he wouldn't budge.

He just glared at me. "You can't hold on to me while you decide which of us you like more. I don't want to be the backup boyfriend. You know, for whenever this year's summer fling—which was exactly the same as last year's fling—is over," he said bitterly.

"It's not like that!" I said, starting to cry.

"No. Actually, it's worse than that. Because the fact that you guys are still spending time together after the way things ended between you means you still have feelings for him, even though he treated you like—like an afterthought for months. So you want someone like Evan, who's here today, gone tomorrow. Okay. Whatever. I'm not that person."

I was sobbing while he said this. "No, that's *not* what I want. It's . . ." What was it? Did I need to prove to myself that I *could* get Evan back? That he had tried to reject me, but it wouldn't work because I was too irresistible? What was my problem?

But if I couldn't, right then and there, say that I didn't want Evan, and that I wanted Ben . . .

I couldn't do it.

Ben was the completely good and logical choice for so many reasons.

Evan was not.

And I was giving up on Ben when I didn't even have anything with Evan.

"Bye," Ben said as he started walking up his driveway.

I couldn't say anything. I wanted to ramble on, explain myself ten times over, tell Ben how much I loved him—because, despite everything, I did love him. But maybe I wasn't *in* love with him. Maybe he knew more about how I felt than I did.

When I got home, Haley was sitting on the porch. I was so glad to see her, because I wanted to tell her what happened, but I didn't know if I could. I'd spent the entire walk home crying. It was embarrassing, really.

"What are you doing up so late?" I asked.

"Just thinking about things." Her legs were propped on the porch railing, and she was holding a glass of lemonade. "Where have you been? Wait—why aren't you at work?"

I started crying all over again. I sat down in a chair next to hers and buried my face in my hands.

"Colleen! What is it?" She shook the arm of my chair. "Come on, tell me—what happened?"

I took a tissue out of my pocket and dabbed the tears from my cheeks. Then I told her about how I was a suspect now, and how Ben had seen me hug Evan, and how Ben and I had broken up. When I finished the story—the short version—I looked over at her. I couldn't wait to hear what she had to say. She was always so supportive of me, especially when I messed up.

She shook her head as if she couldn't believe what she'd heard.

"I know, I know," I said. "Isn't it awful?"

"Yeah." She nodded. "God, Colleen. You really have been acting like a royal jerk."

"What?"

"You deserve to feel this bad." She tossed my crumpled tissue onto the porch. "You deserve everything that's happened tonight. If I were Ben, I'd hate you, too."

"What?" How could she talk to me like that? I knew she could be mean, and stubborn, with other people, but she'd never been this way to me. Never.

"As soon as Evan got here, you acted like Ben was just . . . runner-up. You know that?" she asked. "As if you had a contest: Who can date the great and wonderful Colleen—"

"There was no contest," I said, her words stinging me. "That's a terrible thing to say to me."

"Well, you treated Ben terribly. You completely dropped him. Like, summer boyfriend, winter boyfriend. Like you can just shut off feelings, like—like—like it's as easy as closing all the outdoor taps over the winter. Ben really, really cared about you—"

"And I cared about him!" I cried. "I *still* care."

"Obviously *not*," she said. "You know what? You're just like Richard."

"What? I am not."

"No, you are. I didn't see it before, but now I do."

Haley stood up and walked into the house, the screen door slamming loudly behind her. I'd forgotten to make Richard help me repair that loose hinge.

Me—just like Richard? Since when? And where did Haley get off, telling me I was holding a contest and that

I didn't care about Ben? I wasn't, and I did.

I sat on the porch for a while, thinking about everything that had happened that night, listening to the crickets, watching moths fly around the porch light. I was glad nobody else would be home for a while. I needed time to recover.

Chapter 20

The next morning I was in my room, lazing about in bed, enjoying my dictated day off. I had no reason to get up early because I had the whole day ahead of me. And I hadn't slept well the night before, so if I dozed back to sleep, who cared?

"Suspended." Who gets suspended from a waitress job? I'd made it through high school with no suspensions, but apparently I couldn't make it through the summer without one.

As if my life weren't bad enough right now, with Ben hating me, Haley disapproving of me, and Evan . . . hugging me. Okay, so that last one wasn't bad. In fact, it had felt pretty good at the time.

But it was horrible that it came about because Trudy suspected me of stealing. As if I would. I'd worked for her for four years now, and suddenly I couldn't be trusted? What kind of sense did that make?

If Trudy wanted to think I was a thief, after everything I'd done for her, after the countless Bobb's bibs I'd fastened, the silverware I'd bundled, the onions I'd chopped until tears streamed down my face—to say nothing of the way I pushed the cups of chowder (not that I needed to, really) to customers and the fried seafood Fisherman's Platter—well, I wasn't so sure I wanted to go back to work tomorrow, even if she said it was okay. Maybe I'd just take the rest of the summer off.

And do what, exactly? I thought as I stared at my drafting table and work area. I'd go crazy after a couple of days without working.

Okay, *more* crazy.

There was a knock at the door, and I sat up on the bed, not wanting to be seen looking as hopeless as I felt. "Yeah?"

Samantha strode into the room and put her hands on her hips. "Are you *ever* going to get up?"

"Eventually," I said with a yawn as Erica walked in behind her. "Why?"

"We have great news!" Erica said.

"What?"

"Blair's gone!" Erica cried.

It was funny to hear someone as nice as Erica say something that catty. "What do you mean, she's gone?" I asked. "I can't believe it. She *left*?"

"Her room's cleared out," Erica said. "In fact, I think I could even move in right now."

"Would you please?" Sam asked her. "Because one lying, cheating, deadbeat housemate is enough for one summer."

I raised my eyebrows. "What?"

"You won't believe this," Erica said, sitting in my desk chair.

Sam grabbed a pillow off my bed and sat on it on the floor. "Yeah, she will," she predicted.

"You know that whole thing yesterday . . . about the catering? And the missing jewelry?" Erica asked.

I nodded. "How could I not know? I took it, remember?" I rolled my eyes. "Trudy. How could she—"

"Blair was the so-called witness," Erica said.

"No. You're kidding," I said.

Erica shook her head. "Not only that, she's the one who stole the stuff. And Sam's the one who busted her."

"How?" I asked. "Come on, I haven't seen you guys in like twelve hours. And all this happened?"

"I just had a feeling about her, you know?" Sam said. "A very, very *bad* feeling. I mean, first I considered the whole theft story could be made up, or a setup or something. You never know when someone's going to have a grudge against someone on this island."

I thought about Mrs. Boudreau's feud with Trudy. There were numerous long-standing disagreements like that around here.

"Then I thought about the group of us who went on the job. You, me, Evan, Blair. Who else would be a witness?" Sam asked. "That cranky old guy who insisted on *prawns*? And it just didn't make sense to me. And remember how we didn't see Blair for like ten minutes at one point, and when we did, she said she had to use the bathroom and she went on and on about the house and how rich they were? So I had Erica distract her with some bogus credit card mistake, and I snooped in her backpack at work. I know I shouldn't have, that it was *completely* wrong. That stuff never holds up in court or whatever. But I just couldn't stand her anymore. I couldn't stand that she was accusing *you*, of all people."

"So you found the missing things?" I asked.

Samantha nodded. "Oh, yeah. Plus three CDs of mine and a shirt I think is yours."

"So . . . what happened?" This was sounding too good to be true. I still couldn't believe it, though. I had invited her into my house, and she'd framed me?

193

"I confronted her with it as soon as the restaurant closed. She had to confess. She apologized to Trudy for everything, and then Trudy fired her," Erica said. "We all just stood there, totally speechless for a second. Then after she walked out everyone was all buzzing about how you should never have been suspended and I don't know what happened, but I think Trudy gave Blair a serious earful."

"Why didn't you guys wake me up last night to tell me all this?" I cried.

Erica and Samantha looked at each other. "I didn't think you were home, actually," Sam said. "I thought you were with Ben."

I shook my head. "Nope."

"And I don't know where Blair went last night—I never heard her come home—but she's gone now."

"Do you think she left the island?" I asked.

"It would have been too late last night to get a boat out. But we can easily find out if she left this morning. We'll just go ask Ben."

"Um . . ." I murmured. "Maybe not."

"Uh-oh." Sam shifted on the pillow and leaned back against the bookcase. "This doesn't sound good. Tell us what happened."

I gave them a brief description of our talk, skipping over the really painful parts. Which made it extremely brief, actually. I explained what Ben had seen, and what he had said. They knew part of the story already, because of last night.

"You really broke up with Ben?" Erica asked. "You're kidding."

"No. Actually, he really broke up with *me*," I said.

"And now Haley's mad at me because she thinks I was mean to Ben. She's like . . . furious, in fact. She was sort of mean about it."

"Well, she and Ben are really good friends, too," Erica said. "I mean, you guys did everything together. Right?"

"Yeah." I nodded.

"She's sort of stuck in the middle," Sam said.

I sighed, thinking about how much damage Blair had done with her stupid, unfounded allegation. "I can't believe Blair got me in trouble, which is why I was hugging Evan, which is why Ben broke up with me, which is why Haley hates me. That all happened for nothing—for no reason!" I said.

Erica and Samantha glanced at each other.

"What?" I said.

"Maybe she did cause things to speed up," Sam said tentatively. "But it did happen for a reason. I mean, that's what prompted you and Evan to hug . . . but maybe that was going to happen anyway."

"What are you saying? That I *wanted* to hug Evan?"

"Well . . . yeah," Erica said. "It seems like you did."

If even Erica, the nicest person in the world, thought that about me, then it must be close to true.

"Didn't you?" she asked when I didn't respond.

"I don't know. In some ways, yes." I thought about how attracted I felt to Evan, how I'd been sort of fighting that feeling ever since he came back. But then I thought about how I didn't approve of the way he treated me, and how he was about as reliable as his friend's car that had broken down on the highway. When Ben said he'd be somewhere, he was there—early. When Evan said that, I knew I couldn't believe him. He might be there, and he might not. And he wouldn't pick a time.

So the question was, how important was that to me?

"And in some ways, no?" Erica pressed, sounding a little hopeful that I wasn't being completely sucked into the Evan phenomenon again.

The telephone rang just then, and I reached over to grab it. "Templeton residence," I said.

"Templeton? As in Colleen Templeton?"

"Mom!" I felt a huge smile spread across my face. I'd E-mailed her last night, just before I went to bed, that I hoped she could call me today.

"Everything all right?"

"Sure, everything's fine." I waved at Erica and Sam, who were leaving my bedroom so that Mom and I could talk in private. I wanted to celebrate being unsuspended with them as soon as I got off the phone. Of course, that meant I'd be going in to work, and I'd kind of been excited by the prospect of spending the day by myself, gluing, pasting, maybe visiting Betty again.

"Are you sure?" Mom asked. "Because you don't sound fine, and neither did your E-mail."

"I'm all right," I assured her. "It's just . . . certain things aren't going all that well, actually, Mom." I didn't want her to worry, and I didn't want to ruin any fun they were having. I didn't want them to come home, either. I could handle this, but I just needed to talk to her. I definitely wasn't going into the whole evil housemate/ Colleen's-nearly-getting-fired-and-jailed story. She didn't need to know that until she got home. And maybe not even then.

"Oh, no. Why not?" She sounded immediately concerned.

"Ben and I . . . well, we broke up," I said. "Last night."

"What?" Mom sounded completely shocked, as if all the breath had gone out of her. "You and Ben? Are you joking? I'm sorry—I take that back. Of course you wouldn't joke about something like that. Oh, honey. I'm sorry. What happened?"

How could I possibly explain long-distance? And did I even want to? "It's a long story," I said. That sounded ridiculously vague, though, so I went on. "But remember Evan? Of course you remember him. Well, he's around again this summer."

"Evan." I could hear the disapproval in her voice, coming all the way from overseas. Across an ocean, after a year, Evan was still doubted. "That Evan?"

"Yeah. That Evan," I said.

"Ah. That must be awkward."

She's always had a great gift for understatement.

"Actually, in retrospect? The awkward part was the easy part," I said. "Once we got past that was when things got complicated and weird."

My mother cleared her throat. "So . . . I almost hate to ask. But are you and Evan . . . ?"

"No, we're not—not at all. But maybe . . . we could be . . . I don't know. I don't even know what I want." I sighed. "That's okay, right?"

"Of course that's okay," she said. "You know, Colleen, they both care about you. They're both probably confused, that's all—just like you are. Love is confusing."

"I'll say," I muttered.

"You know what, honey? Just relax. Let things take their course," Mom said. "You're moving in a month, and you might as well *not* be serious with anyone right now."

That was so logical. It sounded right, easy, fair. But it didn't sound fun. Did it?

"Hey, Coll. Look what a nice afternoon it is!" Sam said cheerfully, walking into the kitchen.

"How was work?" I asked. Trudy had given me the day off, with pay, after all. She'd actually come by to apologize in person and bring me my favorite, the fried fish sandwich, and an entire strawberry-rhubarb pie. Which I wasn't sharing, at least not yet.

I'd spent the day lounging, painting, collaging, and visiting Betty, while keeping a very low profile around the island. Extremely low. I was glad I didn't have to go to work, because I didn't want to see Evan yet. And I wasn't going near the post office, the general store, or anywhere anyone else might be.

"Nothing too exciting," Sam said. "Come on, Erica's waiting outside for us. We've got to hurry to make the three o'clock."

"The three o'clock?" I repeated.

"Hello, it's Friday. There's someplace we need to be," Sam said.

I shook my head. "No thanks. I don't want to see Ben."

"So you won't," she said. "We can be busy talking when he gets off the boat. Heck, we can even be gone by then. We just have to stick around long enough to see if Orlando Bloom's on the boat."

"He's not coming!" I laughed. "Doesn't he live in New Zealand or something?"

"Hey. We *saw* him last year," she insisted.

"Sam, I'm sorry. I just—I don't care who gets off the

ferry today. I'm not looking for anyone else to date."

"Who cares about you? You've *had* your share. This is about us—me and Erica," Sam declared.

"But you found your dream date," I said. "Troy."

"Yes, but—come on, it's a tradition. Book club. Your contributions are vital to the discussion." She grabbed my arm and started pulling me toward the door. "Come on."

"So, let's talk about the worst thing a guy ever did to each of us," Sam declared when we sat down on our designated book club bench. They should add a plaque to it, after we leave, if any of us ever became famous or known for anything. COLLEEN TEMPLETON SAT HERE. REPEATEDLY.

"That'll make you feel better," Sam said. "Trust me."

"They didn't do anything," I mumbled. "It was me."

"So you're indecisive. So what?" Sam said. "That isn't a crime. Unless you're sitting at one of my tables and you can't choose from the menu and you take like twenty minutes to order." She laughed.

Erica went over to see if Haley could come join us, but she said no. That didn't surprise me. If she had been mad at me last night, she was still going to be angry today. In fact, it might take her a week or more to forgive me. The whole thought of that was just depressing.

"Does she know about Blair yet?" I asked Erica as she sat down beside me.

"Yeah, we told her," Erica said.

I thought about what Betty said when I told her about the situation. "She's lucky she left. I'd have taken her out myself with this claw." Betty had waved her broken wrist in the air like a weapon. "What an ungrateful wretch."

"What am I doing here?" I asked now. "Haley doesn't

199

want to see me, and I don't want to see Ben when his shift ends."

"You're here because if he does want to see you, well, you're making it easy for him," Sam declared.

"Okay, but doesn't it make me look sort of pathetic? Like I'm hoping he'll talk to me?"

"Well, aren't you? Pathetic or not?" Sam asked.

I wasn't sure. I knew that a lot of the things that Ben had said to me last night were true. That my heart really wasn't in it anymore. That I was stringing Ben along while I sort of waited to see whether Evan and I got back together again.

Which made me a real cretin.

I didn't necessarily know what a cretin was, but it sounded despicable, and I felt that I deserved that sort of insult right about now.

I stirred my chocolate shake halfheartedly as I heard the ferry's warning horn. It was approaching the landing. Then it was turning and backing up to the ramp. I knew the routine by heart, which was good, because I didn't want to watch. I was *afraid* to look over there. What sort of look would Ben give me if our eyes met? Or would he just stay on the ferry when he saw me, and wait for me to get the message and get lost? Or would he walk past holding up a life preserver in front of his face so I wouldn't see him?

"Hey, who's that with Ben?" Erica asked.

I rolled my eyes as I saw the red-haired college student with the white-and-blue boat-and-tote bag striding off the boat beside Ben. They were talking and laughing like they did every other day.

"Oh, God," I groaned. "It's that beautiful girl on the

boat with him every single day. Great, now she can move in, if she hasn't already."

"Colleen. She's holding hands with the guy next to her," Samantha said.

"She and Ben are holding hands?" I blurted.

"*No*. She's holding hands with the guy on her left. The guy in the business suit?" Sam said. "I don't think you need to worry about her and Ben."

"Oh." What a relief. On the other hand, it would have been nice to have something to be angry about. I'd feel less guilty if I knew that Ben had already moved on to someone else.

I watched Ben and Haley say hi to each other, and I felt this huge pang of regret. Why did I have to go and ruin everything?

It was killing me. What was really sad was that I was hiding behind my sunglasses. Yes, the same ones that I got cat food on. They didn't smell like cat food anymore, because I'd run them through the dishwasher to get rid of the smell. Unfortunately, they'd melted into a strange, wavy shape, but I didn't have new ones yet, so I was wearing them anyway.

They were the official bad-luck sunglasses of the summer.

Of course, there are those who believe in making your own luck. And if you're running around in stinky, melted sunglasses, you're not exactly a recipe for success.

But at least they still sort of hid the tears welling in my eyes.

"Well, *she's* definitely thrilled to be here," Sam commented as a woman with short black hair spotted someone on the dock and started jumping up and down, waving wildly.

There could not have been a bigger contrast between the way *she* felt and the way *I* felt. "Ever seen her before?" I asked Erica.

Erica shook her head. "No." She glanced around, looking slightly uncomfortable. "So, you guys want to get going?"

Samantha coughed. "Maybe we should go see Haley. I could use a cup of ice water."

They both sort of tried to herd me from the bench where we were sitting.

"Hold on, hold on," I said as I spotted a pair of familiar-looking legs on the dock. They weren't Ben's. "Is that Evan over there?"

He was wearing a baseball cap and a T-shirt that was too big for him. It was like he was intentionally trying not to be seen.

I watched as the excited woman with short black hair dropped her red duffel bag and shrieked and sprinted into his waiting arms.

Chapter 21

"So, I hear we've got an AWOL co-worker." Evan arranged some butter pats into a small white bowl, then put the bowl onto his tray next to a plastic lobster trap full of dinner rolls. "What made her do it, anyway?"

I just kept putting salads into bowls. I couldn't talk to him and pretend everything was the same. I couldn't do the flirting thing or the weird looks. I wasn't going to act like a freak anymore.

"Is anything missing from your house?" Evan asked. "You know . . . have you checked for Starsky and Hutch? Or wait. They were probably on the case. Right? They busted her."

"Ha ha, very funny. She owes me money and a repainted bedroom," I said.

"So. There's an extra bedroom. Is that what you're saying? 'Cause Jake's place *is* getting a little cramped." He left his tray on the counter and walked over to me.

Don't get any closer to me, I thought. *Any closer and these salad tongs go right in your . . . face.* "Yeah, I can see why it would feel cramped," I said.

"Why's that?" Evan asked.

"With an extra person," I said.

"Meaning . . . me."

"And," I muttered. *Her,* I thought.

He just stared at me for a second as if he were trying to figure out what I was talking about. "Hey, do you think

203

you could make up a side salad for me? I've got to make a couple of cappuccinos. Who wants cappuccino with fried clams? That's disgusting, but okay."

"No, actually, I can't." I put the tongs back into the large bowl of premixed salad.

"You can't?" Evan turned around from the espresso machine. "Or you won't?"

"That's not my table," I said. I knew I was being juvenile, but I just couldn't help it. I was sick of the whole game. Him taking stuff to my tables, me making salads for him—it was so fake. Especially when you considered how he'd spent his weekend.

"I'm totally swamped, Coll. Could you just give me a break?" Evan asked.

"Why should I?" I replied.

"You know, a lobster has big claws, but that doesn't mean it actually has to *use* them constantly," Evan said. He stared at me, waiting for some sort of reaction, or explanation, for why I was acting so difficult.

"I can't believe you," I suddenly blurted. "Why didn't you just tell me she was coming?"

"Tell you who was coming?" Evan looked sort of confused, but I knew it was an act. He might only come here in the summer, but he had to know that we lived for gossiping about who gets on and off the ferry—with whom. Did he really think he could just hide her, that he could bring someone to the island without *someone* finding out? And we'd been there and seen it happen. And I'd seen how he was trying not to be recognized, because he *knew* it would get back to me, but he wanted me to think he wasn't seeing anyone. Why?

"You know. That woman with the short black hair

carrying a red duffel who practically tackled you on the dock?" I said. "Does that ring a bell? The reason you took the entire weekend off, so you could be with her?"

Evan took a step back. "God. Why are you so angry?"

"Because you're such a liar!" I said. "Why couldn't you just tell me about her? Why didn't you just say, Hey, I have a friend coming for the weekend. A *girl*friend."

"I didn't lie about it," Evan said.

"No, you just chose not to tell me," I replied. "Just like you chose not to tell me why you suddenly dropped off the face of the Earth and stopped E-mailing. I mean, I'm sure some other girl was involved then, too, but you didn't tell me about it, either."

"We were living in separate states, Coll. Did it matter? Did you really want to know?" Evan asked.

"I wanted to know *some*thing. Some reason for why you vanished."

"Hey, I didn't vanish. You did!" Evan said.

I'd heard of revisionist history, but this was ridiculous. "I vanished? Since when?"

"You said you were coming to visit, but you didn't," Evan said.

"Are you serious? I never visited because you never told me when, or how. You quit E-mailing. Obviously because you had a girlfriend."

There was a long pause. Evan focused on finishing making the cappuccino, and I was about to go back over to pick up my tray—I'd been in here way too long already—when Evan put his hand on my arm. "Look, Colleen. I only started seeing her—Dahlia—in May."

Dahlia? What kind of name was Dahlia? I thought. (Okay, so it's a very nice name actually, I was just feeling

205

a little jealous at the time, especially since she was as pretty as her name.) "And then you left town in June, to come here? Hm. Sounds familiar."

"Colleen, come on. We went out a few weeks—she wanted to see the island," Evan said. "It's not *serious*. It's not like you—"

"No, of course not," I said. "Nothing's ever serious with you."

"What did you expect? Did you think I was going to move to the island so we could be together?"

"No. Of course not. I know. I know you had to go home. But . . . look, never mind." It was already the end of July. We'd all be leaving in a month, or less than that. "It's just—" Part of me wished we could go outside and keep talking until we got this straightened out for good. And part of me wished we could go outside so that I could push him into the harbor again. I looked down at his stupid new pair of Birks. When had he gotten them? I couldn't risk his losing those sandals again. It wasn't about the money, although I definitely didn't want to shell out any more where Evan was concerned. But I couldn't take the risk of being in contact with Evan like that again.

"I don't really get where you're coming from. We're not together," Evan said. "Do you want to be? Because you've been dating someone else all summer—hey, all year, even—"

"Yeah, well. Ben and I aren't together anymore. Thanks to you," I said.

"Oh, no. No way." Evan shook his head. "I'm not taking the blame. Coll, I'm not responsible for that."

"Yeah, you are. Because you came back here," I said.

"Well, I didn't come back here for you," Evan said.

Ugh. Did he have to be so brutal? I was going to say "brutally honest," but I wasn't sure he *was* being honest. If he didn't come back here for me, then why was he here?

I was starting to wonder why *I* was here, as I picked up the tray of salads and went out into the dining room, plastering a phony smile on my face. Maybe I could meet my parents in Italy. Why not?

Because you invited your friends to live with you, and you can't just bail on them, even though one of them isn't talking to you right now. And you can't just bail on Trudy, the way Blair did, because you're not like her. And you can't just bail on Betty, because she needs you.

Why was my life being dictated by older women with old-fashioned-sounding names?

In the morning I got up early and rode my bike to the Landing. Haley hadn't been staying at the house since last week, since our fight. Having both her and Blair leave at the same time had been strange. I didn't like the fact that it had been nearly a week and we still weren't talking. I was determined to make things up to her. Whatever she needed me to say, I'd say it, but I wasn't ending the summer like this.

As soon as I got to the Landing, though, I felt almost panicky. Why was I even down here? Ben hated me. Haley wasn't talking to me. I couldn't have felt *less* welcome.

There was Haley's old green pickup truck. I rode over to it and leaned my bike against the truck before I walked up to the window.

"Haley. Where've you been?" I asked.

She was in the middle of making a pot of coffee, and she didn't answer me right away. "I've been here," she said when she finally turned around. "Why—were you here earlier?"

"No. I mean . . . I haven't seen you around the house for a few days," I said. *Obviously.*

"Yeah. Well." She just kept going about her business while I stood there, stupidly, stubbornly, waiting for her to talk to me. If she could be stubborn, so could I. She should know that by now. She wasn't going to get off the hook by just making herself busy behind the counter. I'd stand here and repeatedly order stuff if I had to.

Which I would probably have to, because I could see people heading off the ferry toward the window for their morning cup of coffee. Come to think of it, I was feeling pretty hungry after my bike ride. Maybe I'd pick up some breakfast pastries for me and Sam, drop off a couple of muffins with Betty.

"So, is there anything I can do to fix things?" I asked. "I mean, you have to tell me what I did wrong. Because I can't apologize if I don't know. Is it the Ben thing, still? Because I apologize if I acted badly. But you said a lot of other things that night, too."

"It's not that," she said.

"Then what?" I asked. "You can't be mad at me for the Blair thing."

"It's nothing," she said.

"Really," I said.

"I just wanted to spend some time with my mother the past few days. She hasn't been feeling well, so . . ."

"Really. I'm sorry to hear that. I hope she feels better

soon." Now I knew she was lying. I mean, you might think that was cold of me, that I should have asked how her mother was feeling—and it wasn't that I didn't care. But I could tell she was making the whole thing up, because I'd seen her mother at the store yesterday when I went by with Erica to rent a video. And she was completely fine. She didn't even complain about a sniffle or a headache.

Haley was the one who hadn't been feeling well. About me, her former best friend. Man, could she hold a grudge. So I'd made a mistake. How long was she going to hold it against me?

I wanted to tell her that the house wasn't the same without her, that she should come home and celebrate the fact that Blair was gone, that it was just me, her, and Sam. But she'd been gone as long as Blair had. The house felt empty with just me and Sam rattling around inside.

For the benefit of sleepy customers, I stepped aside and waited a few minutes, alternately watching Haley pour coffee for them, and staring out at the ocean.

"So. Will you be at the house later?" I asked once she got through the line.

Haley shrugged. "I don't know."

"Don't you need some clothes or something? You practically moved all your stuff in there," I said.

"Yeah, well, maybe I'll see you later, maybe I won't," she said. "Next!" she called over my shoulder to another customer.

So much for conversation. I walked over to the dock and stared out at the ferry, rocking gently on the waves. Moby looked sort of sad today. Or maybe it was me.

I loved the sound of the ropes and bells clinking and

knocking against the boat as it floated, nestled against the dock. I wondered if Ben was working this morning. I took a few steps closer to the ferry, then stopped. What would I say to him if I saw him? Hello? How are you? That would sound stupid. But I did want to know how he was doing. I missed him. We'd spent all our time together for the past eight months or so. Now there was this hole. Ben wasn't there to ask me how I felt, or to tell me I looked great, or to listen to me complain or worry about Haley and how she was acting. I needed Ben to confide in, but I was completely on my own in this. It had been a while since I was on my own, I realized. And I didn't mind *being* alone . . . but I didn't like *feeling* alone. Especially now that Haley wasn't speaking to me, too.

When I heard a male voice saying "Hi" behind me, I nearly jumped. I turned around and saw Troy Hamilton standing there.

"Oh, hey," I said.

"Hi. Again." He smiled sort of cutely.

"How are you?" I asked. (See, I knew it would sound stupid—whether I said it to Ben or to someone else.) If there were a way I could have instantly summoned Samantha down to the Landing, I would have.

"Good." He nodded. "You're Colleen, right?"

I nodded.

"So, sorry about that crazy stuff with my grandmother. The theft thing. That was a huge mistake," he said.

"Yeah, it was. But it's okay now," I assured him. "Don't worry about it."

"Okay, but I'm sorry. So, I heard you live here year-round?"

I nodded. "Yeah."

"What about your friend—you know, not the rude one. The, um . . . ?"

"Beautiful one?" I suggested.

His ears turned slightly red. "Was her name Samantha?"

I nodded.

"Does she live here year-round, too?" Troy asked.

"No, she only comes for the summers. She lives in Richmond the rest of the year."

"Richmond, Maine?"

"Is there one?" I laughed. "I have no idea. But she lives in Virginia. She's going to college at UVA."

"Oh, yeah? Cool. I'm going to UNC. I guess it's not all that close, but it's in the same time zone anyway."

This definitely sounded promising. He was interested in Sam, even if he was trying to be casual about it. There had to be some way I could get them together again without suggesting his family host another catered event or telling him to come into Bobb's. That would be tacky, and besides, he wouldn't really get to spend any time with her.

I knew what I'd do—I'd have the party this time. Not a loud beer bash, like last time. A dinner party— something simple we could do, like a barbecue. And I'd invite him, on Sam's behalf. Only . . . who else could I invite, so he wouldn't be the only guy there?

Not Evan.

Not Ben.

Definitely not Uncle Frank.

Maybe we ought to make it a huge, raging party, so that it wouldn't seem like such a formal setup. I could invite everyone from Bobb's, plus other island friends. A Sunday barbecue. I'd made a killing at work that week and could afford to be generous—we were hitting peak tourist weeks. And I'd make it such a big deal that Haley would have to be there, too. She wouldn't be able to say no or not show up. I'd have Sam invite her and stress that it was a group event. I'd be killing—or uniting—several birds with one stone. (Not that I'd decided on barbecued chicken yet.)

"So, you're here for a while yet?" I asked Troy.

"One more week," he said.

"Cool. Well, how'd you like to come to a party?"

I chose the date off the top of my head—that Sunday night. I wrote down the house address and handed it to him. "Six o'clock. Be there, okay?"

When I walked back over past Haley's takeout window to get my bike, Haley called out, "Two guys weren't enough for one summer?"

"What?" I couldn't believe her. "No. He's not— Look, I'm trying to fix up . . . Oh, never mind." I didn't want to bother saying it. What was the use explaining when she was so mad, so ready to see the worst in me?

Chapter 22

"So, how many people are coming?" Sam asked as she set out a column of plastic cups next to a stack of paper plates. We'd learned from our first party—well, Blair's first party—not to use the good stuff. One, it created a lot of dishes for us to wash; and two, we'd lost a glass or two that night—cheap ones, fortunately, that we had several others of. I didn't think my parents would miss a couple. At least, I hoped not.

"Well, besides the guest of honor—" I began.

"Troy, you mean?" Sam interrupted.

"Yes," I said, smiling at her. "Besides him, probably about ten or fifteen people, some from work and some Haley and I know from school. You're not mad, are you? That I sort of set this up?"

"As long as there are a few more people than Troy here, it's not a setup, or at least it won't look like one," Erica said.

"Uh-huh. I hope not," Sam said.

"Look, we already know you guys like each other," I said. "Everyone knows that, including you and him. So just relax."

"Right. No problem." Sam gave a nervous smile, then went into the house.

Meanwhile, I went over to the black kettle barbecue to check on the coals. They were almost ready, so I went inside to get a plate of burgers and a package of hot dogs.

People started wandering up as I was cooking, and Erica helped everyone to lemonade and iced tea and soda. After a while, Haley showed up. It was good to see her, even though she was still angry with me.

"This is going to be a lot nicer—and quieter—than the last party here," I predicted as she and Erica came to check on the food and see if I needed help.

"I wonder where she is now," Haley said. That was typical, that she'd talk to me when someone else was around.

"Blair?" Erica said.

Haley nodded. "Yeah."

"Probably moved into someone else's beach house, working at some other summer place," I said.

"She *was* good to work with," Erica said.

"Yeah, it was her best quality. Too bad we met her there, so we didn't realize she wasn't like that at home." I laughed.

"I'm sorry. It's my fault," Erica said.

"Shut up, it's not your fault," Haley said.

Erica nodded as she set her cup of lemonade on the porch railing. "Yes, it is! You said we didn't know her at all, that we shouldn't have asked her—remember, the first time she came over?"

"Yeah. But she seemed all right," Haley said. "Except when we realized she wouldn't do a thing around the house but use things up and not pay us back. She's just lucky she didn't steal anything from us. I mean, I would have tracked her down, you know?" Haley's face suddenly lit up, and she smiled.

I looked over my shoulder and saw Ben walking up. Haley went over to say hello to him, and the two of them headed into the house together.

"What's he doing here? Who invited him?" I asked.

"I did," Erica said. "I thought maybe you guys wanted to make up."

"No, we don't," I snapped. When I saw the hurt look on Erica's face as she turned to leave, I reached out and grabbed her arm with my hand, which was covered with a potholder. "I'm sorry," I said. "I shouldn't have said that."

She shrugged. "It's okay."

"No, it's not. I'm sorry," I said. "I just—I got really stressed when I saw him. But I appreciate what you were trying to do."

I looked up at the porch as Ben walked back outside by himself. He headed to the table and started helping himself to some chips and dip. He looked really cute in his black T-shirt, long khaki shorts, and unlaced tennis sneakers. *Go talk to him,* I told myself. But I couldn't.

"Coll? I think something's burning." Erica waved her hand in front of my face and pointed down.

I looked down at the grill, where a hot dog had just fallen victim to a raging inferno of hamburger drippings. "Why am I doing this? I'm horrible at this!" I said as Erica and I laughed at the charred food.

"We've got salad," she said, taking the tongs and potholder from me. "Don't worry."

A couple of hours later everyone had eaten, and they were either sitting on the porch and talking, roasting marshmallows for S'mores over the dying glowing coals, or playing croquet in the backyard. Troy and Samantha seemed to be getting along great. They'd been together ever since he arrived.

And me? I was sitting next to Ben, chatting about things. Nothing serious, mind you. I'd mingled with everyone else and it was just time for me to talk to him. We discussed this and that—what his little brothers were up to, what country my parents were in, and, you know, the weather. When all else fails, you can talk about the water temperature and the tide.

We weren't about to have a reunion or anything, but it was nice to just be civil, even if it felt awkward. But then, just before dark, Evan showed up.

Ben's eyes narrowed as he watched Evan stop and talk to some friends from Bobb's at the grill. "What's *he* doing here?" he asked. He sounded exactly like I had when Evan had shown up at Bobb's that first day.

"I didn't invite him," I said to Ben. "Honest."

"That's what you said at your last party," Ben complained.

"I didn't invite him then, either! Blair did," I reminded him. "And come to think of it, I didn't even invite you to that party—it was Blair who invited the entire town."

"Yeah, but that was different. This is private," Ben said.

I could tell it was hurting him, seeing Evan here. But I had nothing to do with it, not really.

"So. He's just the type of guy to crash parties?" Ben asked. From the tone in his voice, I could tell that he hated Evan. And I could understand why. But it made me not like Ben, because he wasn't giving Evan a chance.

"Yes. That's the kind of person he is," I said.

"And Haley said he made you hitch a ride back to Bobb's the other day. Is that true?"

"He didn't *make* me," I said. "It was his idea. Spontaneous, you know." Actually, Ben wouldn't know.

"Colleen, he could have put you in a dangerous situation," Ben said.

"Maybe," I said.

"And you went out with him for *how* long?"

I stared at Ben. I didn't like the way he was acting. I knew he had every right to be that way, but it still made me mad because (a) he didn't know Evan, and (b) he wasn't like Evan.

That was what had drawn me to Ben in the first place—the fact that he was the opposite of Evan. Now, I didn't find that quality all that attractive.

"I'll see you later," I said as I got up. I knew that I'd hurt him and maybe he felt the need to hurt me back. But I didn't have to sit there and take it any longer than I already had. I glanced around the yard, where Erica was laughing with some other friends of ours from Bobb's, then I went out back to say hi to Samantha and Troy. Samantha had just knocked her croquet ball through a hoop and Troy was congratulating her with a high-five. After they slapped hands, they held on for a while, looking at each other. Well, I definitely wasn't needed back there, I thought with a smile as I headed in the back door.

Evan was standing in the kitchen, helping himself to a cup of water. "Hey, Coll."

"Oh. Hey," I said.

"Nice party," he said.

I walked over to the trash can and dropped my empty plastic cup into it. "Yeah. It is, isn't it? I should probably clean up or something."

"Yeah, but people are still hanging out," Evan said.

I leaned back against the counter and sighed.

"Hey, you want a S'more?" Evan offered. "I'll make one for you."

I shook my head. "Nah. But thanks. I already had two."

Evan smiled, walking over to me. "I think you have a little marshmallow. Right there." He reached out his finger and dabbed at my upper lip.

I grabbed his hand. "Don't do that."

"Why not?" he asked.

"Because," I said. A little lame, considering I could give him a thousand reasons why not. Because the last time we really talked, we were fighting. Because you just had a girl visiting last weekend. Because of Dahlia. Because you said you didn't come back here this summer for me.

And because Ben was still out on the porch and I wouldn't throw this in his face.

"You—you know what?" I stammered, getting completely flustered by how close Evan was standing to me, how he nearly had me pressed up against the counter, how he'd just touched my mouth.

"No. What?" Evan asked.

"I think I'm going to go upstairs and get a sweater. Sam's cold," I said. "I told her I'd get her something warm to wear."

"Is that your second job this summer?" Evan joked as I edged away from him. "Getting sweaters and sweatshirts for other people?"

"What?" I turned around at the bottom of the stairs.

"Well, it's just that's what you were doing the last time I was over here for a party," Evan said.

"So I'm predictable!" I called over my shoulder as I started walking up the stairs. I opened the walk-in closet door in the upstairs hallway.

"What are you really doing up here?" Evan asked as he came up the stairs behind me.

"Sweaters. I'm getting sweaters." I reached out and petted Hutch, who was lying on top of my favorite black V-neck. He'd left a layer of golden-tan fur that was about a quarter of an inch thick.

I heard the closet door close behind me. And then Evan was behind me, his arms around my waist, kissing the back of my neck. "So, which sweaters are you going to get?" he whispered.

For a second, I panicked. I didn't know what I should do, whether to run out the door or turn around and start kissing him back.

"No, actually, I'm . . . hiding up here," I said as a shiver of pleasure went down my back. "I just . . . I kind of couldn't take it down there."

"Why not?" Evan asked.

"Because I just—I don't know," I said. "I don't know what to do anymore."

"I do," Evan said, gently turning me to face him. "Look, about what I said the other day. When I said I didn't come back to the island because of you. I mean, not *just* because of you. But when I thought about you and us? It did make me want to come back. It was the reason I changed my plans."

"So, why . . . why couldn't you just say that when you got here?" I asked.

"Are you joking? You hated me. You loathed the sight of me," Evan said. "And I couldn't even blame you. But then you were with Ben, and . . ."

"I guess it was kind of complicated," I said.

Evan traced the edge of my face. "You're even more beautiful than you were last summer. You know that, don't you? That you've been torturing me?"

I laughed. "I have? I don't think I've ever tortured anybody before. Is it a good thing? Am I good at it? Just like that, right off the bat?"

"You could practice some. Like, if you tell me you want me to leave right now, and you insist on it. That would be perfect torture." He leaned down and kissed my neck, first on one side, and then the other, and then my shoulders.

"Yeah. I agree," I said softly, enjoying every second that his lips were on my skin. "For both of us."

Evan looked into my eyes. "Is this okay?"

"Very okay," I whispered, and our lips met in a passionate kiss, our bodies were pressed together, and we were moving backward, toward the shelving where Hutch lay innocently sleeping.

"Hutch," I murmured between kisses. "Hutch needs his privacy. We don't want to wake up Hutch."

Evan took his hands off my hips and reached for my hand. "How about we go to your room this time?"

I nodded, unable to speak, not wanting to discuss anything anymore, just wanting to stay in the moment. As we walked into my bedroom I felt excited and scared, as if I were taking a risk I wasn't sure that I wanted to take.

And then Evan was closing the door and kissing me, and I knew that yes, I was completely sure I wanted to.

Chapter 23

When I got up the next morning, I sneaked out of the house.

Afterward, after . . . Evan . . . I hadn't gone back downstairs. I wondered if everyone knew. I wondered if anyone had seen Evan leave, and if they had, what time it was. I wasn't sure when he'd gone. I'd woken up in the middle of the night, around three A.M., and I was alone. I hadn't been able to get back to sleep. I was happy, I was worried, I was excited, I was a thousand different things.

One thing I didn't feel was guilty about what I'd done. But I didn't necessarily want to talk about it, or analyze what had happened or why. Not even with Sam, and especially not with Haley.

So at dawn I tiptoed out of the house. I took my bike instead of the car. It was a misty, cloudy, humid morning, and I could feel my clothes becoming damp as I rode.

I wanted to bring Betty something to eat—I'd promised I'd drop by with something for breakfast. But I couldn't cook, I hadn't baked, and I couldn't go to the Landing and see Haley—I was too embarrassed. Also, I didn't want to be yelled at by her for being with Evan.

I dropped by the general store and browsed through the rack of Drake's baked products. Hm. Would Betty like Devil Dogs or Ring Dings for breakfast?

"Colleen!" Aunt Sue's voice rang out behind me. "What are you doing up and about so early?"

"I'm going to visit Betty," I said.

"Well, isn't that sweet of you. I'd heard you two had become buddies," she said.

I couldn't quite picture Betty ever referring to herself as anyone's "buddy." She was a bit too curmudgeonly for that.

"I actually was hoping to pick up something to eat. She always makes tea for me, so—"

"Why don't you take her a couple of muffins? No, wait. I'm out of muffins." Aunt Sue tapped her chin as she thought. "How about a lemon-blueberry pound cake?"

"Yum. That sounds great. But did you have plans for it?" I asked.

"No, don't be silly. Now come on." She paid for her half gallon of milk and we walked down the road to her house, which was only a quarter mile away or so. I walked my bike beside her.

"So, anything new?" she asked.

"Not really." I shrugged.

"Have you been riding a lot this morning?"

"No, why?"

"Your cheeks are awfully pink," she commented.

"Oh. Well, I think I got a little too much sun yesterday," I said as we approached her house.

"Really? What were you doing yesterday?" she asked.

Again, I could feel myself blushing, so I glanced at my watch and said, "You know, I really should get going. Betty's expecting me, so . . ." That wasn't the truth, but I didn't see how that little white lie could hurt anyone.

"Well, just wait a second and I'll get you that cake!"

Aunt Sue hurried inside her house and came out

222

carrying a loaf shape wrapped in aluminum foil. I put it into the wicker basket on the bike's handlebars. Maybe that was why my grandmother had put this basket on her bike—to carry Aunt Sue's pound cakes home. It fit perfectly in the basket.

"Thanks—see you later!" I called as I rode away.

I'd escaped two things: (1) Telling my aunt about sleeping with Evan, not that I would ever do that, unless someone was sticking pins into my skin, and (2) Telling my uncle I was going to see Betty, and hearing "You should paint, Colleen, why don't you paint!" for the thousandth time.

"How many blueberry recipes does your aunt know, do you think?" Betty asked as I unwrapped the aluminum foil and started to cut us some slices of pound cake.

"Twenty? Fifty? A hundred?" I guessed.

"Oh, no. Got to be at least a thousand," she said. "She should open a bakery instead of handing it out for free all over the island. How does she even find enough berries?"

"I think she has Cap buy flats of them for her at the farmer's market near the wharf. I'm not totally sure, though."

"Hm. Well, at least she's good at it. Everyone should be good at something. And baking is an art, just like cooking's an art. You've got to be creative."

"Yeah, I guess you're right. I never looked at it that way," I said.

"What, did you think you were the only one who inherited some of your grandmother's talent?" Betty asked.

I hated to admit it, but I guessed I did.

She took another bite of pound cake. "Do you know that you're sort of glowing? You look so happy today. What's new? And don't tell me it's this pound cake."

How did these women know that I'd had sex? Was it the way my skin looked? The way my hair looked? This was not sex, this was humidity, people. A frizzone. I pulled my hair back into a ponytail. "Nothing's new," I said.

"Has something old changed, then?"

"Uh. Um." I didn't know what to say, or whether to say anything. I didn't confide in Betty about my love life, or at least I hadn't yet. I didn't necessarily want to start. I liked that we talked about a couple of subjects—like art, and independence, and her annoying son. Couldn't we just keep it at that? Then again, I enjoyed her take on things. Maybe it would be worth asking what she thought.

"Colleen." She refilled my mug of tea. "I don't subscribe to a satellite dish or to the island grapevine. You know that. You could tell me you were madly in love with Pastor Cuddy and I wouldn't tell a soul."

I burst out laughing. "It's not Pastor Cuddy!"

"Then who?"

Was it Evan? Was I in love with him? Or was it just that I'd done something I'd really wanted to do? "I don't know. Does it have to be someone? Can't it just be me?"

Betty nodded. "Sure it can."

But I still couldn't get Evan out of my head. On my way home, I stopped by his cousin's to see if he was around.

"Hey, Colleen, nice party last night," Jake said when he opened the door.

"Um, thanks," I said, suddenly feeling ridiculous. Evan had come to the party with Jake. He definitely hadn't left with him. If anyone knew what went on between us, it was Jake.

"Looking for Evan? He actually went to town today," Jake said.

"Oh. Really?" What was he doing there? Why hadn't he mentioned it to me earlier?

"Yeah. Should I tell him you were here?"

"No, that's okay." I thought it over for a second. Didn't I want him to know I was looking for him, that I expected him to be around? "Well, yeah. Tell him I came by."

Samantha, Erica, and I spent the afternoon at the beach. It was one of the few times we'd all been able to do that on our own. I kind of liked not spending all of my day off with Ben. I had a lot more options.

I was still feeling a little guilty, though, about the way I'd acted, about how I'd slowly but steadily pushed Ben away. On our way home, when we had to drive past his house, I mentioned it to Erica and Sam.

"Coll, look. You know as well as I know that there's no point staying with someone just because he's *nice*," Samantha said. "Nice only gets you so far."

"Same with charm," I commented.

"Yeah, okay. But you and Evan had this . . . I don't know. Fire. Passion."

"Which also only goes so far," I mused.

"Unless you're not careful," Sam added. "If you know what I mean."

We all started laughing, and I glanced at Erica and Sam as I turned into our driveway. Did they know about me and Evan and last night? If they did, they were acting as if they didn't. I hadn't told them yet. It felt like something so private, and so strange, that I had to hold on to it myself for a while yet.

And then, as we got out of the car, we all saw it. This giant bouquet of red roses sitting in a glass vase on the porch. There must have been at least two dozen—maybe three.

That's why he went to the mainland, I thought. To get flowers. I ran over to the bouquet and plucked out the little white card.

"Are they from Ben?" Erica asked excitedly as I read the card. "Are they from Evan?"

I felt my heart sink and shook my head. "No. They're for you." I smiled and held the vase out to Sam.

"*Me?* No way!" She read the card out loud. "'Dear Samantha, thanks for a great vacation. I'll be thinking of you, Troy.'"

I was so happy for Sam and so overemotional myself that I felt tears filling my eyes.

Why was I hoping for something from Evan that I knew he absolutely refused to deliver? Not just flowers. A whole, intact relationship. Evan wasn't about romance, though, not in the sweet, present-giving, thoughtful way.

I went upstairs to my room and stared at the bed. Hutch was curled up at the end of the bed, on top of the blanket. I sat down next to him and petted his fur. Maybe I felt confused, I thought with a smile, but what about Hutch? How much had he seen in his lifetime, how many things had he witnessed that he didn't want to see? No wonder he'd stopped sleeping in the closet.

Maybe I should *start* sleeping in there.

I pictured Evan's body, his shoulders, his chest, the little hollow where his shoulders met his chest. . . .

I was hopeless.

I couldn't fall asleep that night. I was too revved up. The air outside was thick with humidity, the kind of humidity where towels don't dry and everything is just heavy with dew. The sheets were sticking to me. I'd turned off the light at eleven, and it was midnight now.

I hadn't heard from Evan all day, and it was killing me. I couldn't stop thinking about him and about last night. How was he feeling about it? Had he taken off for Philadelphia on the first ferry? Or was he lying in bed at his house, feeling like this?

I wanted him to be here. And wanting that as much as I did terrified me. I didn't want to feel like this, as if my life were on hold until I saw him again. I'd thought I was past this, somehow. And yet it was more physical than emotional. I didn't need him, I realized, as much as I just wanted him.

But it was still frightening to want someone so badly. Especially Evan. Especially after last year.

I turned on my light and read for a while to make myself sleepy, to stop myself from thinking about my life. It worked. I switched off the light and was about to drift off when I heard a creaking sound. Like a hinge that wasn't quite working right. The screen porch door, I realized, sitting up in bed. We never locked our doors on the island.

I heard a cat meow outside in the hallway. And then my bedroom door opened.

In the dark, Evan made his way toward the bed.

"Hey." He sat on the edge and leaned down to kiss me. He ran his fingers down the side of my cheek.

"Hey," I said.

"Did I wake you up?" he asked.

I shook my head. "I couldn't sleep."

"Yeah. Me either. You know what? I really can't stay away from you," he said.

I smiled, glad that he felt the same way I did. "Where were you?"

"Running," he said. "I've actually been trying to stay away from you all day."

"So, you succeeded," I said as I pointed to the alarm clock beside my bed. It was 1:15 A.M. "It's tomorrow now."

"*Finally.*" Evan kicked off his sandals and climbed into bed beside me.

Chapter 24

It seemed like I had been asleep for only a few minutes when I woke up again, but I guess it had been a little longer.

The weather had changed. Now the wind was blowing fiercely, and a branch kept scraping against the window. The leaves of the trees around the house were rustling in the wind, and when I glanced out the window I saw a flash of lightning in the distance. There was a low rumble of thunder.

Somehow Evan could sleep through this. Neither he nor Hutch had moved yet. Hutch was curled up at the foot of the bed—lying right on Evan's ankles, if I wasn't mistaken. So. Even Hutch was drawn to those ankles.

I gently pulled off the top sheet and quietly walked to the door. I closed it behind me and went downstairs.

Starsky hated thunderstorms. He was sitting on the kitchen counter, where he knew he wasn't supposed to be, his pupils completely black and dilated as I switched on the overhead light. "It's okay," I whispered, rubbing his head.

I poured myself a glass of milk and stirred in a spoonful of chocolate syrup. When I sat down, I found that I was face-to-face with the infamous poster board of house rules.

I felt this nervous gnawing in my stomach that the milk wouldn't help. I was *really* breaking the rules here.

My parents trusted me *so much*. They'd felt okay leaving me here for ten weeks because they did trust me, because I was almost always responsible. And now, what? My boyfriend, or whatever Evan was to me, was asleep upstairs.

All I could say in my defense? Sticking to the rules wasn't nearly as easy as it looked. I went down the list.

1. No drugs or alcohol allowed.

Well, okay, I'd had a beer or two, but nothing that harmful. And it had only been because Blair had brought it into the house.

2. No sleepovers. Especially of the boyfriend variety.

Ahem.

3. The house will be kept clean. To that end, the house will be cleaned once weekly.

Also ahem, but we were doing a lot better since Blair moved out.

4. No loud parties. Small gatherings are fine, but do not annoy the neighbors.

We'd broken this one once.

5. Each girl will be responsible for her own long-distance phone calls made on the house

phone, as well as for excessive Internet connection charges.

No problem.

6. Any damage done to the house—not that there will be any—will be repaired by the time we get home.

Which meant I needed to get started really soon.

Maybe my parents thought that writing things down would make me stick to them. They were expecting a lot. And how could I let them down this way? I didn't think any of the rules were as important, to them, as number 2. As far as they knew, when they left, Ben and I were dating. Maybe they trusted me so much because they knew Ben and I weren't going to have "sleepovers." Ben and I cuddled, we snuggled—but we never got carried away by our feelings, we never fought, we never had to make up, we never felt like doing anything outrageous.

It was all really sweet and romantic with Ben, but it was also really safe.

That's who my parents thought they were leaving me with. Not Evan. Would they have gone away if they'd known we'd be together again? Because I'd told my mom, anyway, that I'd had sex with Evan, so I'm sure she told my dad. We'd talked about it and I'd told her that I'd learned I wasn't ready for that, that I'd gotten too close to Evan too fast. So I'd held off with Ben. I'd waited.

And now?

I unclipped their printed itinerary from the fridge.

They were in London for a week now. That was five hours ahead, timewise, and it was three-thirty here, which meant they should be eating breakfast there, or in their hotel room getting dressed.

I took a deep breath and dialed. "Mom?" I said when she answered the phone.

"Colleen?" Her voice sounded bright and cheerful. "Hi!"

"Hey, how's it going?" Now that I had her on the phone, I didn't know what exactly I planned to say.

There was a bright flash of lightning—and a second later a loud crack of thunder. A branch fell somewhere close by, and suddenly the overhead light went out. The fridge switched off, the microwave clock went dark. Starsky let out a long, plaintive yowl.

"Mom? We're having a huge storm here," I said into the telephone as I went to pick up Starsky, but I couldn't find him in the dark. "Mom? Hello?"

The line was dead. She was gone.

We'd lost both our power and our phone line. I stood at the window looking out at the rain that was building in intensity, hammering against the house.

I saw a flicker of light reflected in the window and turned around. It was Haley, carrying a candle. I was so glad to see her, so glad to know she'd come back to stay. Sam was right behind her. "I'm freaking out!" Sam said.

"Don't worry," I said. "We're going to be fine."

I watched as Hutch strolled sleepily into the kitchen and went right up to Starsky, who was huddled against a cabinet, trying to get inside to hide. They touched noses, then Hutch gave Starsky a lick on the head.

Hold on. If Hutch was downstairs, that meant . . .

Evan walked into the kitchen wearing a T-shirt and shorts, his hair sticking up on the back of his head. "What's going on?" he asked.

Haley and Samantha both turned to me. Even in the semi-darkness, I could see their shocked expressions. "Yes. What is going on?" Sam asked, raising an eyebrow.

"The storm—it knocked out the phone lines and electricity. I'm glad you knew where a candle was," I told Haley.

"I didn't think I'd ever say this, but I'm really glad you're here," Haley told Evan.

The four of us all gathered by the living room window, watching lightning flash across the sky.

"I wonder how high the water's going to get," Haley said. "I hope my parents are ready."

When the heavy rain paused for a few minutes, Evan stepped out onto the porch. "Come on!" he called back to us. "It's wild!"

We watched as he grabbed one of the heavy Adirondack chairs to get his balance. The wind had nearly knocked him down. The little white folding table had already blown off the porch and was lying on its side on the driveway. Plastic cups we'd left outside were flying around like kites. The trees were bowing and swaying in the wind. The barbecue kettle was rolling around and spinning on the ground like a top.

"I'm staying inside," Sam said. "Funny, I didn't hear anything about a hurricane coming."

"This isn't one," Haley said.

"You're kidding."

"No. This is just a storm. A severe one, but no hurricane."

I stood and watched Evan step out from under the porch into the falling rain. He turned around and waved at us, laughing and making a motion as if he were about to dive into the water on the lawn.

"Coll?" Sam said.

"Yeah?"

"You have weird taste," she said.

"Agreed," Haley said as we watched Evan skip through a puddle.

I couldn't believe they weren't going to give me more of a hard time about Evan's being here than that. But they didn't.

"Agreed," I said.

I woke up on the living room couch, alone, to sun streaming through the window. Sam was crouched beside me, holding a mug of coffee under my nose. "Come on, sleepyhead."

I rubbed my eyes and struggled to sit up. "How long have you been up?" I asked.

"Since last night. Maybe you can sleep through a tornado, but down in Richmond we don't have those kinds of storms."

"Is the electricity back on?" I asked, taking the coffee from her.

"Nope. But since your stove runs on propane, I heated the water and made you a modified French press coffee."

I took a sip. "Does French press mean bitterly strong?"

"Hey, as long as it gets you up, what are you complaining about?"

I took another sip and rubbed my eyes. I must have slept about two hours total. "You know what? I don't think we're even going to have to work today. It's like a snow day."

"How come?" Samantha asked.

"No electricity? No Bobb's," I declared. "So, ah, where's everyone else? Still asleep?"

"Heck no. Evan went home after you fell asleep. Haley went to check on her parents and the pier and stuff. I think we should go find her, see if we can help. I already did some cleaning up around the yard, but I'm sure there's more we can do."

"Okay—I want to check in on Betty, too, make sure she's okay."

"Sounds good," Sam said. "And on the way? Maybe you can tell me when you started sleeping with Evan."

We both started laughing. "Yeah, okay," I said. "I'll tell you all about it."

"Then let's get going," Sam said. "I'm dying for a good story."

The road was littered with branches that we cleared as we walked. It seemed as if every resident was outside, clearing their property, repairing docks, collecting debris, and talking about the storm—where they'd been and what they'd seen.

The sun was out, and there was a stark blue sky. There was almost no wind, which was very strange. It felt eerie, almost, looking around at all the damage on such a gorgeous sunny morning.

Only the ocean still looked angry and violent. All of the storm remained in the water, which was riled up—the waves were high, and water pounded against the dock pilings and splashed onto the rocky coast. I remembered something my grandfather used to say: "The sea has a longer memory than an elephant."

Down at the Landing, Haley wasn't behind the window, working. There was a sign on the window that said CLOSED FOR REPAIRS.

Over at the commercial dock, the ferry was still tied up, rocking in the rough waves. "Hasn't made its first trip of the day yet. Too rough," someone commented behind us.

I pictured Ben trying to work with such massive waves and getting seasick. And then I saw them. They were tying up beside the dock, in an old aluminum boat that belonged to Haley's family. Ben had his arms on Haley's waist. He was helping her out of the boat, and when he helped her up to the dock, they held on to each other a second too long for friends.

Ben and Haley. Haley and Ben. It sounded right. I didn't think they'd been having an affair or anything, I knew neither one of them would ever do that. It just seemed like there was more to them than friendship. And that was a good thing.

That night, Evan and I were sitting on the porch, playing cribbage by the light of a lantern. It reminded me of when I was little, and I would come here to visit and my grandfather taught me by candlelight one night when a storm knocked out the power.

At the table beside us, Sam and Erica were playing backgammon. After each game, we'd switch and play a different game and/or opponent.

I nearly jumped when the telephone rang inside the house. "Well, sounds like the phone's back," I said as I reluctantly got up from the table.

Evan gave my arm a squeeze as I went past. "Whoever it is, get rid of them," he said.

I picked up the phone. "Hello?"

"Colleen! Oh, thank goodness. I'm so glad to hear your voice. Is everything okay? I was so worried when the phone went dead," Mom said. "We've been trying to call all day!"

"Everything's fine—just a storm." I glanced over at Evan. *And a few other stormy things.* "We didn't have phone service until just now. We still don't have electricity, so we're all sitting outside, playing games by lantern."

"But everything's okay?" she asked.

"Sure. Everything's great." Through the screen door, I could hear Evan giving Sam a hard time about the way she was playing. "How's London?" I asked.

"Well, it's lovely, but we've made a decision. We had to tell you right away."

"A decision?" I asked.

"Yes. We miss you too much, so we're cutting our trip short. We'll be home the day after tomorrow."

"You'll be home the—the day after tomorrow?" I repeated loudly, through the screen door. "Really?"

Evan, Sam, and Erica all stared at me, then looked at each other with widened eyes.

The day after tomorrow?

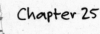

Chapter 25

"Don't worry, we'll get it all done."

That was the first thing Erica said the next morning. It was good to have such a positive person around; otherwise, I'd probably give up and throw in the towel. Especially the dirty ones.

The four of us were sitting at the kitchen table drinking coffee at six A.M. (Fortunately, the electric power was back, and the coffee was a lot better.) I didn't get up at six A.M., unless school was involved. But this was almost more important than school.

Haley had to be at work at seven; the rest of us had to be at work from eleven to two. Then we'd have two free hours to get the house completely ready before the dinner shift.

How could we possibly get it all done?

Erica had called her grandparents last night and they'd come over with supplies so we could prepare my parents' bedroom for painting. We'd stayed up late taping around the windows and the doors—I noticed Blair hadn't done such a neat job—and putting down the drop cloths. I would paint; Erica would clean and scrub other parts of the house; Sam would do laundry and help me paint.

As soon as the hardware store opened, I drove down to pick up a couple of gallons of paint. I still couldn't remember the right color, but it turned out that Eddie had found a record of it in his customer file. "You have a file on us?" I'd asked. I didn't want to think of the implications of that, but it was a lifesaver right now.

"Here it is," Eddie said, showing me a chip. "So Blue Over You."

"Seriously? My mother picked out a color called So Blue Over You?" It sounded like a country-western song, not a color for my happy-go-lucky parents.

"That exact color isn't available anymore," Eddie said. My heart started to sink, but then he smiled and said, "They just changed the name to Bluebird On My Shoulder. I'll mix some up right away."

When I walked in the front door, excited to share the good paint news with Sam and Erica, I saw my aunt and uncle working in the kitchen.

"What are you doing here?"

"Just baking a few things to welcome them home," Aunt Sue said. "The blueberry loaf will be out in a jif, and I'm working on a cobbler or two. And I think I'll make some muffins for everyone who's working so hard."

"I'm on cleanup duty." Uncle Frank held up a spray bottle and a sponge. "You really haven't wiped down the cabinets in a while, have you?"

"Um . . ."

The telephone rang, so I set down the paint on the kitchen table and picked it up. It felt like everything was happening all at once.

"Colleen. I heard your parents are coming home tomorrow." It was Betty McGonagle.

"Ah yes, the good old island grapevine," I said, laughing.

"Yes. It's still got a few grapes on it. But next time you

create gossip, make it a little more exciting, would you? My TV went out in the storm and I'm bored to tears over here," Betty said.

"I'll try," I said. I could tell her about yesterday and Evan, but I probably wouldn't. Especially not with my aunt and uncle in the same room.

"Now, what can I do to help?" Betty asked.

"Oh, nothing, Betty. Really."

"Colleen. You are a wonderful person and a fine artist, but you're the worst caretaker I've ever seen." Betty cleared her throat. "Why don't I come over and fix up the garden for you?"

"You don't have to do that," I said.

"Yes, I think I do. I was going by yesterday and I saw weeds that are taller than I am. I'll be there in an hour," Betty said.

"Okay. See you soon." I hung up the phone and smiled.

"Who was that?" my aunt asked. "Ben?"

"Ah . . . no," I said. "That was Betty. She's coming over to help with the garden."

"Betty McGonagle? You know, she really cleans up at that gift shop. Boy, does she make a good living. You ought to think about doing some paintings," my uncle said as he spritzed the window over the sink. "Colleen, have you thought about painting some nice seascapes?"

But I was already on my way up the stairs. I'd be painting, all right.

"So I finally figured out what our excursion should be this year," Sam said. We were halfway through applying our first coat of paint. Because the lupine color was darker, we'd have to put two coats over it—one now, and one in the afternoon.

"What?" I asked, putting the roller into the pan to pick up some more paint.

"Tell me if we can pull this off," Samantha said. "We go to Portland to the museums, and then we take the train to Boston and go to the Museum of Fine Art. We'd have to stay over, probably—either we get a hotel in Boston or we rack our brains and think of someone we know there."

"Are you serious? I'd love to do that," I said. "But do we have time?"

"You would have to be practical." Samantha stopped to dab the brush into the gallon she was working from. "Okay. I know. How about if we just have a showing of your work here? The Colleen Templeton Gallery. No— we'll sell your stuff at Bobb's! Trudy would definitely have an art show for you."

"That's not much of an excursion. I mean, it doesn't sound like fun for anyone else," I commented.

"What are you talking about? We organize it, we have an opening—make it a major end-of-summer island event," Samantha declared. "We circulate with crab cakes. You just stand there, mingle, and make *money*. People would buy your stuff for souvenirs of the island. You know, quaint native art."

"You know what?" I smiled. "That's brilliant. But do I have enough pieces to show?"

"You have a closet full," Sam said.

"Yes, but is any of it *quaint*?" As I turned around to dip the paint roller again, I saw Starsky on top of their dresser, walking back and forth. He was swishing his tail against the wall. "Starsky—no!" I cried.

But it was too late. His gray-black tail was now streaked with blue paint, and the wall had a swirled, marbled effect—with cat fur mixed in.

"Starsky's helping. That's cute." Sam laughed.

Starsky knocked a pen off the dresser, then jumped down to play with it, waving his light-blue tail behind him. I grabbed a wet rag and tried to clean his tail, but he thought it was a game and kept running under the bed.

"We could sell Starsky at the art show. He's quaint *and* native," Sam suggested.

"No, let's sell cat paintings," I said. "Tourists would be all over that. Maine coon cat paintings! He's not a coon, but you know, it sounds good."

"Anyway, it's not going to be a meet-and-greet-the-artist type event," Sam said. "They won't know. We'll take a picture of him and then we can alter it to make him look bigger and furrier."

I pictured Starsky presiding over a show of his art, wandering around and playing with women's (and maybe men's) earrings and jewelry. Lapping a glass of milk and signing autographs with his paw.

Sam and I both started giggling so hard that we ended up lying down on the plastic drop cloths, laughing until we started to cry. Maybe it was the stress of trying to get the house ready, I don't know. But every time I thought about Starsky, the painting Maine coon cat, with a little black beret on his head, doing a meet-the-artist event, I started laughing all over again.

"Don't do that to me."

I was slicing pieces of a banana cream pie at lunchtime

when Evan came up behind me and started kissing the back of my neck. "Please don't do that to me," I said as I tried to correct the jagged cut I'd just made.

"Don't?" Evan asked.

"No, do. Just . . . not right now." I served a new, more cleanly cut slice of pie onto a plate, and put the pie back into the refrigerated case. "Not today." I turned around to face him.

"You know, we won't have a chance to see each other that much when your parents get home," Evan said. "How about we go swimming between shifts today?"

"Swimming?" I asked. "But I'd have to go get my suit."

"No, you wouldn't," Evan said. "I was running last week and I went down this abandoned trail—I found a new cove. Total privacy."

That sounded tempting. And freezing. And impossible, in broad daylight. And not likely, given the work I had left to do at the house. "No, I can't," I said as I hurried over to the coffee machine to fill a carafe.

"Why not?" Evan followed me.

"Because I have to paint some more," I said, placing a small white bowl of creamers and sugar on my tray.

"But . . . can't you do that tonight?" Evan asked.

"No, not really. I'm working, and then—"

Erica was in the kitchen to fill some glasses with water, and she came up beside me. "It's okay—Sam and I will finish the painting. If you guys want to go do something this afternoon, we'll do the second coat."

"No, I can do it," I said. "I'll just have to go really fast."

"Which will ruin everything!" Erica said, laughing. "Come on, Coll, it's the least we can do. You invited us to stay in your house for the entire summer."

"But you didn't live there," I pointed out.

Erica waved my comment away. "Technicalities. Go do whatever, and we'll see you back here at five. Oh, and did you hear? Sam talked to Trudy about selling your art. She's totally psyched to do it."

"Really?" I asked as I hurried past both her and Evan with the pie and coffee.

Erica nodded.

"You're the best!" I told her.

"Thank you!" Evan replied. "I know!"

Evan and I spent so much time hanging out at the private beach together that we barely had time to stop by his cousin's to pick up some fresh clothes before work. I'd used my T-shirt to dry myself off after swimming, and it was soaked.

I pulled on the T-shirt Evan tossed to me, and we nearly sprinted side by side to Bobb's so we wouldn't be late. My hair was still slightly wet when we walked into the kitchen.

"You're so lucky you got here in time!" Sam greeted me when I walked into the kitchen. "It's not Orlando Bloom, but it's close."

"Who is it?" I asked, wrapping an apron around my waist and checking over the specials for the night.

"Graeme Helman," she said. "The guy from the movie with—"

"The really incredible body?" I interrupted.

"Hey," Evan said. "Keep it down over there."

"He's in *your* section, too," Sam said. "You can thank Erica later. Plus, my section was full, or I would have killed her." She shoved an order pad into my hand. "Now, go. He's got water already and I'm sure he's ready to order."

"Thanks!" I said, laughing as I headed for the swinging doors to the dining room.

"But—wait—Colleen—" Sam said. "Hold on. You can't go in there like that!"

I turned around, shaking my head. "No way, I'm not giving you his table. He's in *my* section, and I'll wait on him."

"Should we tell her?" Evan asked.

"Tell her what?" I said. I peered through the little peephole window. "He's alone? Oh, wow. Here's my chance."

I walked out into the restaurant and went straight to Graeme's table. (I was already calling him "Graeme," as if we were close.) He looked even better in person than he did in the movies and on TV. He had wide shoulders, a face with perfect-looking-enough-to-be-sculpted features, and dark brown eyes. Why on earth was he dining *alone*? Why on earth was he at our little island?

"Welcome to Bobb's," I said. "Have you heard about our specials?"

"Yes, thanks," he replied in a deep voice. "But I think I'll go with my standard. The Fisherman's Platter."

"Your . . . standard?" I asked. "You've been here before?"

"Sure. Not for a few years, though." He grinned. "You probably weren't here then. Hey, nice T-shirt."

"Oh, uh, thanks," I said, glancing down at the shirt. Something about it looked weird, but I couldn't place it.

"Anything to drink?"

"Iced tea," he said. "Extra lemon. Oh, and extra tartar sauce and extra lemon slices for the platter, too."

"No problem! Be right back with your iced tea," I promised.

When I turned around and headed for the kitchen, I saw Erica and Samantha huddled by the host stand. Sam was laughing so hard that she couldn't stand up; she put her hand on the wooden counter to balance herself.

Erica's face was bright pink as I walked over to them, and she was trying not to smile.

"What's so funny?" I asked. "Does my hair look that bad? Oh, no, it's a frizzone day, isn't it? I shouldn't have gone swimming."

Erica burst out laughing. "Colleen, you might, ah, you might . . ." She reached into the glass counter next to the host stand. She rifled through a stack of Bobb's T-shirts and pulled one out. "Go to the bathroom and put this on."

"Why? Did I spill?" I asked, peering at my T-shirt. This time I actually looked at it long enough to read the upside-down script: "Dip Into Something More Comfortable," it said, with a butter dish.

Oh no, don't tell me. Then I twisted the shirt around so that I could read the back. There it was, in large blue letters: "Boob's." Not Bobb's.

Evan had given me one of his mock "funny" T-shirts to wear to work. No wonder Graeme had said "Nice T-shirt." No wonder everyone was laughing at me.

I hated him. With every fiber of my being.

And then some.

* * *

I tried to say good-night to Evan outside the restaurant, but it took us so long that Erica and Sam went home without me. "Evan, I just can't break the rule about no sleepovers tonight, not when I'm going to see my parents tomorrow," I said as we walked down the road toward my house.

"Do you really think they'd care?" he asked.

"Um, *yeah*?" I said.

Evan laughed. "Yeah, probably they would. Sorry. I just . . . I can't stand that they're gonna be here, and we have two weeks left, and I . . ." He leaned closer to me and whispered in my ear, "I want to spend every night with you."

I didn't say anything. I wanted that, too, but I knew it was impossible.

"So let's go somewhere tonight," Evan said. "If we spend the night together somewhere else, that isn't technically breaking the rule, you know."

"But I can't!" I laughed. "And anyway, the house is mostly fixed up and neat and perfect, but I have to make sure it stays perfect because I have to go pick them up tomorrow morning . . ."

Evan put his arm around my shoulders as we walked. Then he started gently pushing me in the direction of the path to the beach. "The house is in great shape. It's never been in better shape. Don't worry."

"Yeah. But I have to worry," I said as we stepped off the road onto the path. It was like trying to resist the tide, or the undertow maybe. An impossible thing to do, but I felt like I should at least try to resist, as if giving in right away was not really playing the game. "Plus I'm still mad at you for giving me that stupid shirt and letting me wear it in public for ten minutes, so I could embarrass myself."

"You're *mad* at me? Come on. I think it made Graeme *like* you," Evan said.

I wrinkled my nose. "I actually don't think he noticed."

"Oh, he noticed." Evan nodded. "He noticed, all right."

"I hate you," I said.

"I know. You really hate me. You can't *stand* me." Evan slipped off his sandals and ran straight toward the ocean.

"Pretty much!" I called as I sprinted to catch up with him and push him into the water.

Chapter 26

"So. This is what it's like down here at seven in the morning," I said. "I kind of forgot." The days of catching the ferry to school at seven seemed like a long time ago. In fact, had that even been me?

"It's usually a lot colder and foggier," Haley said.

"Uh-huh," I said.

"No, really!" Haley insisted.

"Yeah, I'm sure it's really awful." I grinned at her.

"What are you doing here?" Haley asked. "Oh, right. How could I forget? You're picking up the kids in Portland."

"Yup." I stretched my arms over my head, then reached down to touch my toes. "Is Ben working today?" I asked when I straightened up.

"Um . . . I don't know," she said.

I just stood there and waited for a second for her to answer me.

"Okay, I think I do know. He has today off," she said. "But why did you want to know?" She sounded suspicious.

"Oh, I just wondered if he'd be on the ferry," I said. "That's all."

"Right. Of course." She seemed a little relieved, as if she'd been afraid I was down here to find Ben and try to win him back or something. That was the last thing on my mind. Maybe it was a little bizarre to think about the two of them as a couple, but I'd get past that. I was already halfway past it.

"You know, Haley? It's okay if you and Ben . . . you know," I said.

"What?" Haley asked, a little flustered.

"I saw you guys the other day. I noticed the way you just sort of *fit*." I'd thought that before of me and Ben, but it wasn't true. He and Haley fit. I loved him, but it was as a friend. And I loved him for being with Haley, because I knew what a great person she was and that deep down they made a better match, they were more alike. It had so often been the three of us. And maybe it still could be, sometimes, but things were rearranged now.

"I could never do that to you," Haley said. "Ever. I'd never—"

"No, it's okay."

"But . . . come on, Coll. He doesn't even like me that way—"

"Sure he does. Just ask him." I couldn't believe I was saying that. I felt like I was standing on this tiny island of my own, only it was about as sturdy as a lily pad or a piece of paper. I was giving up the sure thing, or what used to be the sure thing, anyway. Everyone had always assumed Ben and I should and would get married some-day, after we finished college. And I had no guarantee of anything permanent, or safe, with Evan.

In fact, it was almost guaranteed we *wouldn't* stay together. Evan wasn't in it for the long haul—not now, anyway, and maybe not ever. He was sort of like my brother, in fact.

And maybe I was more like them than I wanted to believe.

But I had to be okay with that. And surprisingly—to myself, more than anyone else—I was.

My life wouldn't be as predictable in the future as it had been in the past. None of our lives would be. It was scary, terrifying, and exciting. Like being with Evan.

"Well, I'm not like rushing into anything," Haley said. "I mean . . . wouldn't it be really awkward if me and Ben were . . . you know, together?"

"Yeah, kind of," I said. "But we'd get over it. If things got weird, I could always give him a hard time about almost puking on us a year ago."

"I can't believe that was a year ago," Haley said. She took a sip of coffee. "And now this summer's almost over. It went so fast. I mean, here you are, going to get your parents, and it seems like they only left last week—"

"Of course, they did decide to come home two weeks early," I said.

"Yeah, that does make the summer seem a little shorter," she said, laughing. "Especially since I had to move back in with my mother yesterday."

"Sorry," I said.

"No, I was just kidding. It'll be good for me to be at home for a week or two before college. It'll make me appreciate college even more, right?" she asked. "With my luck, I'll get a roommate who's just like my mother. She'll probably tell me to clean all the time."

"Can you believe there's only a few weeks before we leave?" I said. As the day I was required to be at Bates got closer and closer, I seemed to be having a harder and harder time fathoming it.

"I can't believe it. I don't want to, I don't think, in a way. But I'm excited about getting to Dartmouth. I can't

251

wait, actually. I'm just doing a good impression of some-one waiting patiently."

"It's going to be hard. Saying good-bye to . . . every-one. You know?" I felt my eyes fill with tears. I was feeling really emotional about leaving the island. About leaving our life here behind—if not for good, at least for a while. Nothing would be the same in a few weeks. And Haley had always been there for me, from that very first day of school, when I felt scared and alone, in third grade.

She'd been there that day on the ferry when we both met Ben. She was the one who'd pulled out the Tums after the cinnamon-raisin bagel didn't really help. How could I forget? Now we'd be nowhere near each other, and neither would she and Ben. I wondered how much things would change and how we'd all deal with that, whether this time next year we'd all be here again—or somewhere else completely.

Me? For now, I was planning on being back here. Maybe someday working at Bobb's Lobster would get old, and I'd be even more aggravated by having to deliver dinner rolls in quaint trap-shaped baskets and serve "chowdah" and tie Bobb's plastic bibs onto complete strangers. But until then, I'd be happy to live on the island whenever I could.

I sort of felt like today was dress rehearsal, as if I were getting a chance to practice leaving home. I glanced at my watch. It was ten minutes before the ferry would leave.

Last night Evan had said he'd meet me down here, to see me off—he'd promised, in fact, to buy me a cup of coffee and a couple of doughnuts and sit and hang out with me, but at the time, I hadn't really believed him, even as he said it and even as I said, "That would be so nice." Evan had a habit of vanishing just when things mattered to me.

But at five minutes to seven, I saw him jogging down the hill toward me. I smiled, even though I couldn't help feeling a little disappointed that he was so late.

"You missed the coffee," I said as he stopped in front of me. "And the doughnuts."

"Yeah, well. I'm trying to cut back on doughnuts." He patted his extremely lean stomach.

"Yeah, you need to do that." I reached out to pat his stomach, too.

He grabbed my hand and pulled me toward him. "What time do you think you'll be back?"

"I don't know—late afternoon, I guess?" I snuggled against his chest. "But you know my parents—we'll probably hang out by ourselves tonight, just the three of us. I know you want to see them, but it'll have to wait a couple of days."

Evan stepped back. "Don't tell me. Slide show. World War I battle sites. Castles. Cathedrals."

I laughed. My parents had bored Evan a few times last summer with slide shows, one set from a visit to the Museum of Fine Art in Boston, and one from their colonial inns tour. How they could be so fun sometimes, and so dull at others, never ceased to amaze me. I hoped I wasn't anything like that, that it wasn't written into our genetic code like the lack of good timing.

Speaking of which, the ferry was leaving in a couple of minutes, and I really needed to get on board.

"But I really do want to see your parents. Tell them that, okay?" Evan said.

"I know, I know. And you will, just not tonight."

"Okay." Evan leaned forward and whispered in my ear, "But I might sneak over later."

"You wouldn't," I said.

"Coll."

"Okay, you would, but don't. Not tonight, anyway. We'll see about later."

"All right." He sighed loudly. "Now, if you're on your way to pick them up and that old car of yours breaks down—"

"What," I interrupted. "You'll come get us?"

"No. But I know a couple of nuns in New Hampshire."

"Yeah. I bet you do." I shook my head, laughing at him.

He put his hands on my waist and pulled me toward him. He ran his fingers down the side of my cheek, and we kissed just as the ferry horn blew three times, warning me there was a minute left before she sailed. I'd already driven the car onto it, so I didn't have to worry about that. I had a space and my ticket, and all I had to do was jump on.

But I didn't want to stop kissing him. This wasn't our big, sad good-bye scene—that was coming in a few weeks. But somehow I knew I would be ready for it this time. This wasn't *Casablanca*, and we weren't Humphrey Bogart and Ingrid Bergman.

And I wouldn't fall apart this time.

"You'd better go," Evan said now.

"I know," I said. "I really should."

There was one more—the final—blast of the ferry horn, and I wriggled out of Evan's arms. I sprinted toward the boat, losing a sandal on the way. I turned around, ran back to slip the sandal back on, and saw Evan grinning at me. Then I took off my sandals and dashed barefoot toward the boat. I dodged a couple of kittens roaming around the docks, nearly falling facefirst onto the gangplank as a big calico cat got in my way. I waved at the guy collecting tickets that morning as I hopped on board. Half a minute later, we were untied from the mooring and starting to pull away from the dock.

I climbed up the stairs to the upper deck, which wasn't that crowded—it was a Tuesday morning, post-early-rush.

"Colleen! You almost didn't make it," Cap Green said, leaning out from the cabin.

"Yeah. I know!" I sat down in the back and gazed out at the water, and at the island disappearing behind us. The way the sun was shining on the ocean reminded me of something. Maybe one of Betty's paintings.

All of a sudden I thought I heard a baby crying. That was weird, because I hadn't seen anyone with a baby. I listened again for the crying.

It wasn't crying, I realized as I turned around and saw a cat crouched under one of the bench seats across from me. It was *mewing*.

I crept over to look more closely. It was the calico cat I'd almost fallen onto a minute ago, right near the gangplank. It had sneaked onto the ferry. But that didn't make sense. What did a cat want on the mainland?

The cat came out and rubbed against my legs. It had black-colored fur around its eye that almost looked like a pirate eye patch.

How did the cats get to the island? One took the ferry; one came from a pirate ship.

I smiled. I couldn't wait to see Dad and Mom.

Banana Splitsville

How hurt do you have to be to sue for emotional distress?

Do you have to be completely devastated? Or can you just be extremely mad?

What about "really, really pissed off"? Does that hold up in court? I need to call *Judge Judy*. I need to be *on Judge Judy*. She'd rule in my favor. She would. After I made a devastating case against him. Which I think would be easy, even though I haven't exactly gotten into law school yet.

Is it bad form to drink a diet Squirt at 9 in the morning?

Well, I don't know, and I don't care. I don't even know why I'm writing this down—I don't keep a diary. But I have to jot this down—for history's sake. The History of Jerks.

Nothing I do could be in as bad form as what Dave did last night. I haven't even slept. Well, except from 4–8.

I can't believe I'm about to write this down. Dave actually broke *up* with me.

Broke up with *me*!

Sorry if I'm writing in really bad form, what Mr. Arnold calls "choppy" in my essays. But I feel a bit chopped up.

What was even worse than the fact he dumped me was how he did it. So tacky. Over the BBQ, while I watched my veggie burger burn, tempeh breaking down into flames like my life. I invite him over for a cookout, so we can plan how we're going to move all his stuff to Boulder next weekend. And he has a soda and some chips and then proceeds to tell me he's going to move on with his life now, thank you very much. Like I'll ever be able to eat again.

He comes to my house and does this. Doesn't he know anything about how to break up with someone?

Oscar was running around the yard, yelping, like he does before a big thunderstorm and during fireworks every July 4th. Animals can *sense* these kinds of things coming—why didn't I?

What follows is actually what he said. I'm not making this up. I wish I were.

"We'd probably break up in October anyway, so we might as well do it now, start the year free and clear."

Free and clear—that's like a *deodorant*, right? No, wait—that's a cell phone plan. Are you listening to the words coming out of your mouth, I wanted to say. Do you realize you are rhyming really offensive words, like "year" and "clear"?

"Yeah, and we'll probably die one day, so we might as well kill ourselves now," I said, following his brilliant logic.

"Courtney. Don't be like that," he said.

"Me? You're going to tell me how to be now?" That was when I got a little hysterical. Like he had the right to stand there and calmly eat barbecue-flavor potato chips and tell me my personality needed work. He's about as sensitive as a day-old hamburger bun. Which I wish I had served him. Maybe with nails inside the bun. He had orange-red powder on his lips from the chips and a speck or two on his soul patch. I was going to make fun of him, but I started thinking really depressing things like how I'd never kiss him again.

Then he thought he was getting through to me, because I was crying. So he went into his "this is really for *your* benefit" speech. "It'll be so different, with me away at college, I don't want to burden you or hold you back—"

"You're the one who doesn't want to be held back!" I said. "You don't want a high-school girlfriend. You want to go to frat parties and pick up girls—"

"I do not!" he said. "That's not why I'm doing this at all."

"Then why *are* you breaking up with me?" I said.

Ha. He didn't have a comeback for that.

But unfortunately I got caught up in staring at him while I waited for his comeback and I realized he was wearing that T-shirt I bought him when we went on that trip to Phoenix and Taos last spring and it's all faded now and looks really good on him because the washed-out blue kind of matches his eyes. And I got so furious at him for being able to look good while being such a jerk that I told him to leave.

"I'll call you," he said.

"Don't," I said, indignantly, like you're supposed to. Then he drove off, just like that, and I started bawling like a two-year-old. Okay, like *Bryan* when he was two years old.

People warned me about this. Said it might happen. Alison (supportive big sister as always) said we *should* break up, because "that kind of relationship never works."

"What *kind*?" I said.

"Long-distance," she said.

"He'll be in the next town," I said. "It's a half hour *drive*. When the traffic's bad." From Denver to Boulder is nothing, people do it every day as a commute. They have buses on the half *hour*. Crowded ones. And we even live slightly on the west side of the city, which is that much closer. He could get here by bike, even.

"Same thing. You're not in school together anymore.

It wouldn't work."

Well, sure, it definitely wouldn't work *now*. After all the stupid things he said, about how we needed to grow and how we might find out we wanted to get back together, but we'd cross that bridge when we came to it.

I'm not crossing that bridge. I'm not even looking for it on a map. As far as I'm concerned, I was on that bridge, and he cut the rope on the other side, and now I'm hanging over a raging river, and people are going by in their kayaks and laughing at me. You know, those people who are really good at kayaking and never take off their sandals, not even in the winter. I hate those people. I think kayaks should be banned, except that extremely buff guys seem to paddle them bare-chested a lot.

I have to go back to school in a week. Ugh. Everyone's going to ask how my summer was, and I'm going to have to tell them me and Dave are over. That's so humiliating. Couldn't he have waited until October break or something? His timing sucks. Just like everything else about him. I can't believe what he did, I can't believe him. I'm never going out with another guy again. At least not for a long long long time. Mom doesn't care about men. Why should I?

Anyway, Dave's whole position is just so absurd. Alison, college girl, actually tried to *explain* his viewpoint. What does Alison know about relationships? She hasn't even had one since first grade with Timmy What's-His-Name.

Of course, she did sit up talking with me and Beth until 2 A.M., and she did go out and buy Ben & Jerry's Chocolate Fudge Brownie for us (which I technically don't eat anymore) (yum). We asked her to go, since Beth was so upset she was afraid if she went, she'd buy a pack of cigarettes. (She never gets asked for an ID. She's looked 20 for the last 3 years. Must be nice.)

Jane kept calling and we put her on speaker phone so she could join in the Dave-bash. Dave and I have been together for over a year. A whole year. Twelve months. We met last summer, and we were like John Travolta and Olivia Newton-John in *Grease*, only I have straight reddish hair and would never wear Spandex pants. Plus we fell in love in the summer and we didn't break up when school started. (At least, not *last* year.) And we didn't sing.

Anyway, now he wants to forget the whole thing and "move on" and "grow," like a transplanted house plant in fresh soil. Mom tries that all the time. Each one *dies*. That's why she has the world's largest rock garden. Rocks, she can grow—or steal from national forests.

I hate plants.

I hope he gets replanted in that expansive soil that houses sink into and disappear. I hope he gets . . . what's that thing where you try to save water in your garden? Zeroscoped . . . xeriscaped . . . whatever. No water for Dave.

Mom and Alison left for Oregon today. I am supposed to be taking care of Bryan.

Like I'm not depressed enough.

Why is it so easy to write the first entry in a diary— and so hard to write the second? Is it because you read over what you wrote the day before and realize how dumb you sound? You tell yourself that you should never write in a journal when you're upset, because it ends up being so embarrassing to read it over. But the only time you really want to write in a journal . . . is when you're upset.

It's like a trick that blank book companies came up with. We keep grabbing for them, spilling out our guts, then getting embarrassed and throwing them out because we can't go on with page 2. Then we get upset three weeks later and buy another blank book and do the same thing. Total conspiracy. So forget it, journal industry. I'm not giving in, no matter how dumb-looking and dumb-sounding this is.

I could just . . . rip *out* the embarrassing pages, maybe. But that would probably ruin the binding. I'd really like to tear off the cover, except it's great camouflage because no one would ever guess this is mine. It's this disgusting pink-and-blue floral rose corduroy thing. *So* not me. It was a gift from Grandma Callahan (a Von Dragen by birth), who's still trying to feminine-ize me after all these years—like a pierced belly button with a small silver hoop isn't feminine.

Anyway, this book has about ten lines per page. Like I write that big anymore, like I'm a seven-year-old. I've already run over seven days with the first entry. That's okay; last night felt like it lasted a week.

Of course this style comes in handy on days when I don't want to write anything. Like, today.

Panicking about school. Contemplating calling in sick to Bugling Elk. For the entire year.

Home schooling works, right? People get into college from home schools.

Dropping out. Is the stigma really that bad? I mean, tons of kids do it, right?

I didn't tell Mom the whole story. She hates men enough already. I told her breaking up was a "mutual decision."

That wouldn't explain why I was bawling while I watched *The Serengeti Scene* tonight. Lions, tigers, Dave. Oh my.

Oh crap.

Okay, I've figured out what I need. A new diary = a new attitude. Will throw this one out as soon as I get through this. Which, as much as I'm writing lately, won't be long.

Whatever I just said doesn't make any sense. Another reason to throw this out soon.

I'll buy a cool sketch book with a black cover so it looks like I am drawing or only writing brilliant thoughts that don't require lines because they come so fast and furiously.

Alison called me tonight. She's settled into her new dorm room at Stafford and she likes everything and Mom is on her way back.

There was this really loud music and high-pitched screaming in the background. I kept asking her what was going on and she said, "Oh, nothing."

???

Since when does Alison hang out listening to loud alternative music with screaming girls? She hates them. She's supposed to be in like the conservatory or something. Playing concertos. Duets. In like . . . adagio. With a candle burning on top of the grand piano.

Then Dad called. Same old story from Phoenix. He's loving life and loving Sophia. Then he said he was very excited about becoming a grandfather soon.

"Don't push it, Dad," I said. "I just told you that Dave and I broke up. Alison's perennially single, and Bryan is *so* not ready."

He laughed and said he wasn't talking about *us*, he was talking about his stepdaughter, Angelina, who's having a baby in December, didn't he tell us?

Dad never tells us stuff and always thinks he has. It's chronic. Like when he was moving out.

(Sorry, but that still makes me mad.)

Angelina is only 17! And I'm not being judgmental, but I just can't imagine being a parent right now. I can barely take care of a dog. Do you give babies their pills in hot dogs, too?

Three days until school starts. Back to Bugling Elk High. Or, as I like to call it, Bulging Elk. I keep staring into my closet, as if there are answers in there, as if there are clothes I like in there. As if Dave's hiding in there.

I can't walk down the same bulging halls, sit at the same table we always sat at, listen to the same stupid bells ringing between classes. Also, after considering every item in my closet, my outfits suck. I'll need to focus more on outfits this year. Apparently I'm *single* now. I need to find dates and stuff.

Or not.

Beth and I had the same shift at Truth or Dairy this afternoon, masterfully mixing smoothies. Today was my day to be dairy and her day to be truth. I hate those days, because I guess you could say I'm pretty lactose intolerant. Or just sort of generally intolerant.

I want to be truth every day, but let's face it. Sometimes I'm dairy.

Anyway, I was stuck wearing the vinyl black-and-white Holstein apron; she got to wear the natural hemp one. I made 4 sundaes, 6 cones, and 3 milk shakes; she made 6 fruit smoothies, a soy shake, and she scooped up a dish of rice ice cream. Then she could tell I was depressed enough, and so she switched aprons with me. I thought that would cheer me up, but it didn't. Nothing could.

"Dave wasn't going to be here this year anyway, right?" Beth said while we were at T or D and she caught me staring at my reflection in the chrome base of the blender. The smoothie I was making got pulverized into tiny atoms, so thin and runny you could see through it, and I had to start over with another Sunrise Strawberry Supreme.

"You were going to miss him anyway. So now you'll just miss him . . . more."

"Beth," I said, "I'm never going to cheer up if you keep talking about stuff like that."

"But you should be sad," she said. "You need to be sad. You have to go through the phases of grief. See, first there's denial, then anger, then—" Blah blah blah.

She kicked into self-help mode. When she wanted to quit smoking, she went out and read every book and watched every show on getting over just about anything. She could probably be a psychologist with like two weeks of additional college courses, or at the very least give Oprah a run for her money.

Of course she only smoked for like three months, but she was really into it. Personally I think she just liked the boxes.

And she hasn't done too much about her addiction to boys, but I guess it's more important to quit smoking. For her, anyway.

"What you have to do, Courtney, is go for some sort of closure."

I flipped the sign on the front door of T or D before we locked up. "Like this? Closed?"

"See, that's what I'm talking about. Denial," Beth said.

Has he called? Like he said he would? No. I half expected to see him at Truth or Dairy today. He's sort of addicted to Coconut Fantasy Dreams. We both are. It was like . . . our drink.

Half expected. Whole-not-surprised when he wasn't there. I was all ready to give him the cold shoulder, easy to do when working around ice cream at Truth or Dairy all day. I could give him a really bad ice-cream headache, maybe, mix in extra ice in his smoothie and freeze his brain.

Like he could be any colder.

Dave moves to Boulder today.

I hate him.

The thing about breaking up with someone (okay, the thing about being *dumped*) is that your whole life just sort of . . . sucks. No, actually I was going to say that it *stops*. Dead end. (Don't worry, I'm not getting morbid here. Not much, anyway.) It's just . . . you thought you were going one way. And then the road just sort of ends, and you're staring at one of those yellow signs with a big arrow pointing in two directions and you have no idea which way to go.

The way I drive, I'd probably flatten the arrow. Head off into some farmer's field. Crush a few rows of corn. Maim a prairie dog.

How did I ever get started on this? Oh yeah. The breaking-up thing.

Like I really want to write more about *that*.

I think *I'll* start smoking.

It's true: life *can* get weirder.

There's this woman who comes in every day at 3:40. Well, every day I work, anyway. Even on Sundays. She does a shot of wheatgrass juice while she stands by the window looking outside, like she's either running from the law and wants to take off when she sees the police cruiser coming—or waiting for a bus that's really late, like maybe the route was discontinued a few years ago and nobody told her. She has wild, long frizzy brownish white hair. She wears really long skirts. And she has this bag. It's purple velveteen with silver swirls. Like something Merlin should have.

I call her Witchy Wheatgrass Woman. Not to her face, of course—just to Beth. I also abbreviate that to "WWW," as in "www.insane.com." She's the one who got Gerry to start giving out punch cards for one free wheatgrass with every ten purchases. Bluck. If you can drink ten ounces of wheatgrass, you should get a free *car*.

At least making wheatgrass juice is sort of satisfying, putting it in the little grinder thing and smushing it down. Something you'd like to do to a certain person named Dave.

After she does her ounce of green juice, she crushes the cup with her left hand and comes over to the counter for a water chaser. Everyone else says "water back," but she has her own term. Most regulars *don't* get water back, but then she's more like an "irregular," or maybe a factory second.

Then she talks. And talks. "A blue streak," Gerry says, although for her it should really be a green streak.

Today she felt like giving me advice on my love life. I guess I was saying something about missing Dave, and Beth was telling me the only way to get over him was to see someone new. Like how when she quit smoking she started chewing gum. Etc. Anyway, I think WWW only stands by the window so she can pretend she isn't listening to our conversations. I'm telling Beth—no more talking while she's in the store.

"To tell you the truth." She always starts off this way. Then sometimes she kind of laughs and says, "I'll get to the dairy later," only she never does. I don't know what the dairy would be—lies?—but. There you have it.

"To tell you the truth, I was never one for relationships."

Oh. Really. I dropped my scoop. Not in shock, but in shock that she felt the need to state the obvious.

"But if you have to have one . . . Courtney . . . " She always peers at my name tag, as if it changes on a daily basis. "Please. Practice safe sex. *Promise* me."

Oh my God. Why do all these people feel like they can give me advice all of a sudden? So she's health-conscious. So am I! Ice cream hasn't touched my lips in months. Well, okay, weeks. A week and a half, definitely.

But she annoyed me so much that I did a shot of hot fudge in retaliation. Don't tell me how to live my no-sex-life. Celibacy. Whatever. Free and clear of sex.

Came home and did yoga to relax. Didn't relax. Instead I stayed up late watching this *Our Mammals, Our Selves* program. Was starting to feel warm and fuzzy seeing all that video of baby animals, then made the mistake of switching to Animal Planet. That vet show was on. Surgery. Blood everywhere.

School in August? Does this make sense to anyone else? It's 90 degrees. We're sweating. My cool new sweater is wasting away on the shelf.

Made it to homeroom. Nobody seems to know about the breakup yet. Which might explain why everyone keeps asking me how Dave is. "Dead," I wanted to say. "With any luck." Maybe that was a bit harsh. I don't want him dead. Just temporarily maimed. Maybe by a wolf, or possibly a bear or mountain lion. If they can roam into the outskirts of Boulder, lounge in people's trees, and knock down their fridges, they can find Dave. It'll happen eventually. I just have to have faith.

I figure if I keep my head down and keep writing all day, no one will bother me. They'll think I'm psycho, but they won't bother me. Not sure which is the better way to kick off the school year. Reputation for being psycho, or fielding questions about my relationship. Or lack thereof.

I realize I may be psycho and also boyfriendless. And if so, I'm at risk of being a stereotype.

LATER THAT SAME DAY . . .

The word is out. Apparently Dave felt like telling all his friends before he left town that it was time for him to be Free 'n' Clear (maybe not a deodorant—maybe a zit cream). They must have helped him with his brilliant lines.

So I went to the caffy for lunch (why? You may ask. Well, I figured it's that old story about getting back on the bike after you crash, or was that the horse? But mentioning horses and cafeteria food in the same sentence is a little scary), because Beth and Jane talked me into it, and because I was almost sort of hungry for the first time in a few days. I was trying to decide between the veggie taco and the peanut butter sandwich when it started. This murmur behind me. Like a wave of water. I thought maybe it was because I had picked up a taco shell to smell it, and it was kind of close to my ear, so I listened to it for a while as if it were a seashell, but all I could hear was grease soaking into my hand. I put it on my tray and grabbed a sandwich. But I could still hear the rushing sound.

I turned around and saw Grant Superior, one of Dave's best friends, who I used to think was nice, in this semihuddle with a bunch of other guys. All seniors. These guys huddle a lot, like they're attached. Three of them glanced over their shoulders at me at the same time. They are so unsubtle, it's scary.

I tossed my sandwich back onto the tray, and it glommed back onto the pile. "Excuse me?" I said, walking toward them. "Was there a question?"

"Oh, uh, hi, Courtney," Grant said nervously. "We were just talking about . . . uh . . . "

"You and Dave. Splitting up. He says you hate him. Is

that true?" Tom Delaney asked. He's so sleazy we call him "the Tom," as in "the tomcat." Constantly on the prowl. "'Cause if you guys aren't together anymore, I would really love to take you out sometime." He tried to put his arm around my shoulder.

"Yeah. Right," I said. "That'll happen."

Then I put my tray back. The idea of lunch after that was really rude.

Grant came up to me at the end of the day in Life Issues—this dumb new elective we have to take as seniors, it's supposed to teach us stuff that's not taught at school— hello, does anyone see the contradiction here? We're taking it *in school*.

Mr. Antero passed out the curriculum. It has things on it like "Coping" and "Moving On" and "Deal with It." Totally useless.

Anyway, Grant said he was sorry about the Tom being a jerk. I said, "We're *all* sorry about the Tom."

Grant laughed and started telling me how he'd talked to Dave and how it was too bad we split up. I cut him off. The last thing I want is sympathy from some good-looking guy about some other really good-looking guy.

After school Jane, Beth, and I went for our yearly first-day-of-school splurge. Well, okay, so it only started two years ago when Jane moved here from LA.

New lipstick, new nail polish (not tested on animals, naturally) and mega mochas. I picked out Better Red Than Dead, New Money Green, and extra nondairy whipped topping on my soy mocha.

It feels really good to keep my standards up.

"You're going to do so much better than Dave," Jane said as she tried on her twenty-third pair of identical black platform loafers. Easy for her to say.

"We'll find you someone to go out with. Not that you need help," Beth said as she checked out the socks.

I saw this pair of suede boarder sneakers on a display. They were the ones I helped Dave pick out a couple of weeks ago. It killed me.

Phone just rang. I ran to answer it, but first checked the Caller ID. There was Dave's parents' name, same as always. I reached for the phone. Then I stopped, wondering if I should answer it. Then it stopped ringing. I waited to see if he'd leave a message. He didn't. Then I thought since he'd probably already moved, maybe it was *his* mom calling *my* mom. Not very likely, but still. They could be commiserating. No, definitely Dave, home to get more of his stuff or a free meal, I told myself.

Plus I told myself to quit standing in the hallway by the phone having private conversations with myself about who's calling from now on.

I picked up the phone to call Dave back and tell him to quit calling and not leaving a message. But I wouldn't give him the satisfaction.

Then as soon as I put it back, the phone rang again. Mom grabbed it in the kitchen. I could hear her yelling, "What are you trying to sell?" and "How did you get this number?" and "Please take me off your call list!"

So much negative energy here, or at least phone calls. I think I'll drive up I-70 to the buffalo overlook. Gazing at the herd always make me feel better. They're so incredibly huge, and majestic, they always make my problems seem really small. They suffered for so many years—well, not those particular ones, but their people. Their buffalo. Whatever. Slaughtered. By the thousands. And now they have this huge piece of land that's theirs and they don't have to do anything except try to have baby buffaloes. Buffets and Buffettes.

There are better places to see buffalo, like the zoo,

and buffalo ranches, where you can see them up close. But at the zoo they're fenced in and look depressed, and at ranches they're waiting to become steaks and burgers.

What's so unbelievable to me now is that the first time Dave and I went out, he ordered a buffalo burger and I asked him to change his order, and he *did*. And he asked a billion questions about why I don't eat meat, and I told him why not buffalo, and how ordering cheese on top just compounds the problem, how our whole meat-eating culture is basically wrong, we use way too much water—he didn't even fall asleep or take off for the bathroom. He just listened. And he also said I should use all that stuff on my college entrance essays.

But then we got to know each other better, and I admitted I slipped up sometimes—I actually felt close enough to him that I could admit that I liked Taco Bell. I told him it was okay for him to order whatever he wanted, that I had no right to preach when I was still sneaking ice cream at work now and then. But he still wouldn't.

Everybody else gets sick of me watching *National Geographic* and *Wild Discovery* over and over. "Not the polar bears again," Bryan's always complaining. "You've seen this like thirteen times!" Beth yells.

But Dave understood. He wouldn't watch them with me, but he understood. Sort of. I thought so, anyway.

He's a Buffalo now. I mean, he's a CU Buff. Not sure if he deserves to be.

8/28 3:42 A.M.

Just woke up from really horrible dream about Dave. Have
to write it down before I forget it.

Damn. Forgot it already while I was writing that.

Mom is wacko. More than before.

She announced at dinner that we're all going to this big family Thanksgiving reunion at Grandma and Grandpa Callahan's in Nebraska. She's planning it three months ahead of time because the whole Von Dragen side of our clan will be there. Also because she lives for planning, right next to cleanliness and budgetliness. Like I want to see the Von Dragens after they gave me obnoxious middle initials that I have to leave off forms unless I want to be rejected from college due to my infectious nature. Repulsive middle name, boring last name. Smith.

Why can't I have a cool last name like Jane? Nakamura. Courtney Nakamura. Okay, so it doesn't really match, and I'm not Japanese, but so what?

You can't fit Von Dragen on a form. I've tried. The closest you can get is "Von Drag," and that is definitely not the impression I want to give. It's been my mission in life to keep anyone from finding out my middle name. I think the only person who knows it is Beth. Well, Beth and Dave. Of course he's already forgotten it, like he's forgotten me and my phone number.

"I thought we arranged this," I said to Mom. "I want to stay here for Thanksgiving. There's the football game, and the parade, and the *fun*." Besides, Dave might come home for a few days. It might turn out that we both grew enough in 3 months that we're ready to get back together. You know, like that fast-grow fertilizer Mom uses on the lawn. Not that it works for *her*, but that's because she buys the no-name brand left over from last year.

I shouldn't be so harsh about Mom. She really only

does all this because she's a single mom now, and the three of us probably are expensive to keep up. But come on, where's all that child-support money from Dad going?

Back to reuniting with Dave. I know I've changed in the past month. For instance, I'm about a hundred times more better—oops, meant to write "bitter."

"But Courtney, your grandmother will be so hurt if you don't go," Mom said, as the phone started ringing. The phone rang like six times while we were trying to eat, and each time it was a telemarketer. Mom gets really mad. I tell her to unplug the phone, but she's made it this personal mission to yell at each and every telemarketer.

"Mom, we got Caller ID so you don't have to take those calls," I said.

"If they can disturb me? I can disturb them," she said. But the problem is she gets in this really nasty mood and all of a sudden normal topics become battles.

"Courtney, you're going, and that's final. We all have to be together," she said. "It means a lot to me. Don't you care how I feel?"

Then Bryan starts talking about how if I don't have to go, he can stay home with me—

"Okay, okay, I'll go," I said. I don't eat turkey, but does she care about that? About how it makes *me* feel—nauseous? Thanksgiving is like poultry worship. I'm not into that.

Besides, baby-sit Bryan all weekend? No thanks. I'd rather get salmonella poisoning, which is very possible at Grandpa's. He likes a moist bird—i.e., still breathing.

The only positive thing I can say about my little brother is that he has a crush on Beth. That is his *only* saving grace. Other than that, his personality is as distinctive as the dozens of crumpled tube socks scattered on his bedroom floor. "You don't get it," is his favorite expression. "I have to live with three women and no guys. Nobody gets it."

No, we don't. And we don't want to.

Deep Late-Night Reflection (a/k/a Insomnia):

Maybe this thing with Dave bothers me so much because of Dad. How he took off to be "free," but now he's married again. (Speaking of jerks.)

Then again he and Mom are happier apart; they used to fight a lot. About money, about her working as a temp accountant instead of having her own business, about the rock garden and lawn care, about everything. So him leaving and the divorce wasn't an all-bad thing, except at the time.

I wonder if Mom ever thinks about getting remarried. Of course she'd actually have to date someone first, and she hasn't done that in a long time. I told her once that she should hook up with this guy from her book club, and she told me she was against hooking up on principle. I think she thought I was talking about drugs.

Anyway, if I don't date this year and Mom doesn't . . . does that mean I'm turning into her?

Let's see. Do I wear panty hose until they're so sheer they're transparent and held together by 8 swabs of clear nail polish? No.

Do I wash out plastic bread bags and reuse them, even when they've had tuna-onion salad sandwiches in them and make peaches taste like dead skunks? No.

Do I sit with my three best friends every Saturday morning and gossip and drink too much cheap coffee? No. Well, sometimes. But I only have two friends.

I'll have to check this list from time to time—make sure I don't slip into Momdom.

Dreamt I was driving to Nebraska. I was going too slowly and horses pulling covered wagons kept passing me. This little girl with a white bonnet stuck out her tongue at me as her pa's wagon dusted me. Pioneer road rage.

Then a buffalo came out of nowhere and ran out right in front of the car. I swerved so I wouldn't hit it. Only I swerved the wrong way and plowed right into the buffalo. And all the wagon people started shaking their fists at me, like I was the one responsible for slaughtering all the Plains bison.

The movie could be: *Buff Meets Bull* (our car or at least the one I'm allowed to drive is an old maroon Taurus, so I decided to go astrological and call it what it is) (anyway, I love hoofed animals, just not eating them).

Buff was now roadkill.

Bull was now totaled.

Then Jaws of Life approached to pull me from the wreckage (the pioneer wagons took off for Kansas), and I discovered Dave was sitting in the backseat.

"You could have missed her," he said. "If you just hit the brakes a little quicker." *Her!* Did he have to call the buffalo a her? Why did he care more about what happened to her than to me?

This dream was the pits. I was jealous of a BUFFALO.

We argued about my driving until I started feeling really guilty: the car was totaled, a buffalo was dead . . . and Dave hated me. Then the gigantic metal Jaws of Life dropped me onto the pavement, rejecting me like a too-small fish. It was awful.

Today's Truth or Dairy trivia question:

"Who holds the record for being the most annoying person ever?" (Actually it was something about the number of Coloradans who've won Olympic medals—nobody got it.)

There is nothing worse than a failed, frustrated guidance counselor who ended up starting a business making ice cream and smoothies instead of counseling, because there was more "potential" in it. Gerry's favorite word. "Potential." I'd potentially like to whack him with the ice-cream scoop every time he says it.

We never knew him when he was a counselor at Bugling Elk—I don't think he lasted more than a year or two, tops. But it seems like he always has kids from BE working at T or D—he keeps getting people referred to him, and so he never has to work hard at hiring. It was Beth's idea we go work there. On days like today, I do so want to remind her of that. When she quit smoking, she decided a job here would be a "healthy outlet" for her. Me, I just needed some CASH. (Jane won't do it because she won't work in fast food because she's against uniforms on principle because of bad fashion. We told her it's not fast food and it's not a uni, it's an apron. She still won't even consider it.)

But anyway, the thing about Gerry is that it also seems like he never really quit counseling. It's in his blood or something.

Today at work, he said, "Courtney, I have an observation. Would you like to hear it?"

I restrained myself. I need this job. Plus it's fun,

working with Beth. "Sure, Gerry!"

"I couldn't help noticing that over the past few days . . . well, don't take this the wrong way. But you're not making the sundaes and smoothies with your usual flair."

Flair? Like I'd won awards or something.

Then Gerry leaned in with his patented look of concern. "Is everything all right?" he asked me.

I had just made three Banana Splitsvilles in a row. They were works of art, as far as I was concerned. You have to stick flags with toothpicks through banana wheels and then into each scoop of ice cream, and arrange coconut and chocolate flakes in perfect symmetry with chopped pecans and walnuts, and then there's the whipped cream. I mean, it could take some people three or four minutes. I've got it down to two and a half.

"Everything's fine," I said.

"Really." He gazed into my eyes as if he were about to tell my fortune. "Everything's fine at home."

I nodded.

"At school," he said.

I nodded again.

"With Dave."

I tried to nod, but my neck got stuck in this cramp all of a sudden, and I couldn't get it to move. So instead I smiled, showing him all my teeth.

"You've been snacking on the pecans again," he said.

Busted.

I did see Grant on the way home from work, out in the parking lot. Avoided him. He'd only try to tell me something about Dave. I'm not ready.

Besides, any of Dave's friends are former friends of mine—i.e., enemies.

Oscar got a new prescription today. He looked like the world's most pathetic mutt when I got home from school. He was fritzing out—his tongue was hanging out (more than usual) and his legs were twitching and there was this trail of frothy drool around his bed. Another grand mal seizure. I hate when Oscar has seizures, it really scares me.

I called Mom at work. She said to call Dr. Wolper right away. It's cool because Dr. Wolper makes house calls and you never have to wait that long, unless she's in the middle of a surgery. She came right over when I told her about Oscar's latest seizure.

"I see this in a lot of patients like Oscar," she said as she pressed the stethoscope to Oscar's chest. "Probably needs to have his dose upped a little."

How she can find a heartbeat through all that gray fur is a mystery to me.

The funniest thing about Oscar's prescription bottle of phenobarbital is the sticker warning him not to drive after taking the medication.

"He's a dog," I told the lady at Walgreens when I went to pick up the new 'scrip.

"Then he really shouldn't be driving, should he?" she replied. Not even cracking a smile.

"Actually, he's fine during the day. He just shouldn't drive at night," I said.

I heard someone behind me laughing. So I turned around and saw Grant "Lake" Superior standing behind me in line for a prescription. Why? I feel like I keep seeing him everywhere. His face turned red when our eyes met.

Don't look at what he's picking up, I told myself. Just in case it's condoms or something private.

Who gets prescription condoms, though? I mean, that would be pretty weird.

"Um, hi," I said, stepping aside to make room for him.

"Hey." He signed the form, and the pharmacist handed him a little bag.

Grant doesn't think he's superior to anyone—you know, casting against type and all that. I remember when he used to be this really scrawny guy, the kind everyone pushes around in the lunch line back when that stuff was funny. Then last year he got taller and wider and turned into a hotty. And he still has the scrawny-guy personality, so he's like this perfect hybrid, something nature designed over time like the way certain snake species look like leaves so they can be camouflaged under a pile of leaves and then kill anything that comes close.

Not that Grant's a killer. Or a snake. In fact, if Beth were smart she would have held on to him after their little tryst last year. (Is tryst the right word? Or do I mean rendezvous?) Except for *that* disaster (remember how hurt he looked when she blew him off that day at lunch? He thought they were a couple—she was already checking out someone else), I can't think of anyone he's gone out with.

"So, um, this isn't for me," I said, pointing at the bag. I didn't want rumors floating around that I was dumped because of some . . . infection or something. When your middle initials are V.D., you can't be too careful. "My dog has seizures unless he takes this stuff."

"Really? How come?"

"He has this head-trauma-induced epilepsy thing condition. I think that's the official term. Ever hear of it?"

"Sort of," he said.

"Basically, he got hit by a car, and it sort of scrambled his brain. For instance, sometimes he forgets where he is and he gets freaked out really easily and then he runs away and can't find his way home."

We exchanged awkward nods. I was talking too much but for some reason couldn't stop. I was about to ask him if he'd heard from Dave when he made a bolt for the door.

"Sorry about your dog. Well, gotta go," he said. "Hope . . . "

"Oscar," I said.

"Hope Oscar feels better." Then he tapped me with the crinkly white bag on his way out—on the arm, kind of intimate-like. He wouldn't do that if there was something really gross in the bag. Would he? Outside I saw him getting into this car in the blue zone—for the disabled. And he was driving it! Here I thought Grant was a nice guy. Instead he's picking up prescription condoms and parking illegally.

When I got home, after stopping at Safeway for a gigantic box of cheap hot dogs for him, Oscar was missing. Typical. I run around getting his new drugs and hot dogs to put them in, and he can't even wait for me? Bryan and I found him at the park about half an hour later. He was pawing through a trash can, and he had a bunch of spaghetti in his mouth. He does this so we look like bad owners, I swear. He's into pasta. Maybe we should put his pills in manicotti.

When we cornered Oscar and got a leash attached to his collar, this guy with a billion plastic grocery bags hanging all around his belt came up to us. He had a big button on his fishing vest that said, "Leash Be Friends."

He told us we shouldn't let Oscar off his leash and that people not respecting the leash law led to death and destruction blah blah blah.

"Did you know that unleashed dogs are responsible for all of the goat killings in the Denver area?" he asked.

He was so crazy! We ran away before he leashed *us*.

When we got home we told Mom about it. She said that some goats had been brought in to control weeds in the city parks, something about a natural alternative to pesticides. So they spent the summer eating a bunch of noxious weeds and then got offed by some vicious dogs. Nice. Excellent plan. So much for natural.

Next year I bet they use those crop duster planes and just spray the hell out of the parks.

When I walk down the hallway, everyone looks at me like I have the plague. Just because I'm no longer half of a couple! As if there's a problem with that, as if it's not my ultimate *goal* right now.

I hate when people have an attitude about me. Like they've worked on it, like it matters to them. And I've never even spoken to them.

Sometimes I wish I went to an alternative school, in another country. One where there were only hardened criminals and nobody spoke to each other except in some language I couldn't understand.

Maybe everyone's looking at me weird because Grant told them about seeing me at Walgreens. Saying a prescription is for your dog is probably a really common excuse. I should have been more original. There's probably a rumor going around that I have seizures, or else there's one that I'm addicted to phenobarbital or something worse, and that's why Dave dumped me. Which would make him *so* much less of a person. If that's possible.

I can't believe he hasn't called yet. So I told him not to, he has to know that wasn't what I meant. I hate when people say they'll do something, and they don't.

I should have broken up with him first. I wanted to, you know. It crossed my mind several times. But I'm a bigger person than that, I don't break up with someone over petty things like moving to another town or living separate lives. I'm a middle child, I'm used to making sacrifices just to make things work out. But not Dave. He has to be free. And clear.

I hope he gets a really big zit on the first day of

classes, from all the stress.

He won't even be able to handle college classes. And the sad thing is, he doesn't realize that.

Everywhere I go, there's this chorus of "You and Dave were such a good couple!" and "I can't believe he wants to see other people when he had you!"

I know they *mean* well.

No, actually, maybe they don't. But some of them do. I think.

In gym class today Ms. Ramstein announced that we were going to learn Tae-Bo. Jane gave me this look, like, "She can't be serious." First of all Ms. Ramstein has no idea what it is, second of all she's like a year behind the times, third of all she teaches gym but we don't know why, because she can't lift her leg higher than a foot off the floor—in any event. When she tried to teach gymnastics sophomore year, she ran into the vault at least eight times a day.

Anyway, so she's all excited because she got a video on sale at Target. "Girls, we're going to kick butt today!" she cried. Her purple cotton sweatshirt and gray sweatpants hanging off her like a 70s soft rock tune.

It was so obvious she'd only watched the video once, and maybe in slow motion. She kept calling it Tai Chi by mistake and getting all meditative, not understanding that the point of this was to kick things. With force.

"Ms. Ramstein? I think we're supposed to be like . . . madder. Or something," I finally said.

"Take a deep breath," she kept telling us. "Let it go. Let it all . . . go."

So ridiculous. Let it go. Beth's always saying that, part of her psychobabble. Where's "it" going to go? You can't expect bad things to fall off like old skin or run away once you "let go" of the leash (Oscar, anyone?). You have to push them off. That's all I was thinking. That and how much I hated Dave for ruining my senior year. How I had to forget about him or I was never going to have fun. How I needed something else, like Tae-Bo, to focus on, because I was sounding shallow even to myself.

"Ha! Ha! Ha!" I chanted with each kick.

I was so into it I didn't even notice that Jane was waving her hands in front of me to get my attention. I thought she was just personalizing the workout for herself, doing her own moves.

"Hold on, girls—I think Courtney's got the hang of it. Everyone stop and watch Courtney!"

"You've got to punch him out!" I told Ms. Ramstein. Oops. "I mean, punch it out. Your, um, anger," I said. "I mean, to get the full aerobic benefit." The music suddenly went off. I stopped kicking and started panting, totally out of breath.

When I looked up I saw this entire line of guys standing there staring at me. They had just jogged into the gym from outside.

"Hey, Courtney!" the Tom yelled from across the gym. "Nice moves!"

The other guys were all grinning, like something I did or said was funny. Which might be nice if I weren't exercising and doing Ms. Ramstein's job for her and demonstrating the stupid moves. Or what I thought were the moves, anyway. Like I know.

"What's the matter, haven't you ever seen someone do Tae-Bo before?" I yelled back.

"Yeah—and that wasn't it!" someone yelled back.

"Ignore them," Jane said. She hadn't even broken a sweat.

I'll never get a date now. Not that I want one with any of *them*.

Ms. Ramstein stopped me after class. She was squeezing sweat out of her red-white-and-blue headband. "You're a bit young to be so jaded, Courtney."

I hate when adults come up with these adjectives for me. As if they know more about me than I do. Like they *could*.

Here are my adjectives for Ms. Ramstein:

sloppy

no fashion sense

bad dresser

also, not very limber

Jane and Beth dragged me out tonight. I hate when people ambush me into going out.

"It's Friday night and we're going to have *fun*," Jane declared when she picked up me and Beth from Truth or Dairy. She had these new green glasses on, the latest from her Glasses of the Month club for extremely hip people; they get a new pair every month for a reduced price as long as they stay hip enough to sort of advertise for the place. It goes along with her haircut contract; Jane's got more contracts than the jocks at school. And better, glossier hair. She has some shoe deal, too. Must be nice.

"We're going to a concert at Juiced and Java'ed," she said. I just have one problem with that place—it's a total ripoff of T or D!!!

Except they substitute coffee for ice cream. And they book good bands and you can smoke in this tiny section and drink all the coffee you want. Which is why the line to the bathroom is always at least five people long.

"I don't know," I said. "Do we have to go out? Couldn't we just stay home and turn up our stereo really, really loud?"

Beth punched my arm. "Shut up. You know how much I love concerts. You're not going to deprive me."

That's when I remembered. My dream—I mean, nightmare—from a week or so ago. In it, I was at a concert. The formal kind, like the ones Alison gives with her chamber orchestra. I was all happy because I was there, sitting next to Dave. But then I realized I was there by myself—and he was there with *Beth*!!!

Also it was a really bad concert. Sting wearing a tux

and playing with a full orchestra.

I can't believe Beth would steal Dave, even if it's only in my subconscious. Is it in hers? You know how sometimes your dreams tell you something you're trying not to know in real life?

I stared at her all night. Watched her every move. She seemed to be flirting with a dozen other guys that weren't named Dave, but maybe I just *wanted* to see that. We meet lots of guys when we go out, because Jane's so beautiful.

"What's wrong with you? Why do you keep looking at me instead of the band?" Beth finally asked.

"Oh. No reason." I smiled at her. "I was just afraid that you might want to smoke." *And go out with my ex-boyfriend.* "Being around all these smokers."

She shook her head. "I have so much else to live for, you know?"

Like stealing my ex-boyfriend.

"There's no way I'm ever going back to smoking." She and Jane clinked their glass mugs and drank more decaf. I started looking at the dessert menu. It was really hard to avoid the chocolate eclairs that kept going by on trays.

Got home and the Caller ID was flashing. I thought it might be Dave, but all it said for the caller's name was UNAVAILABLE. Yeah, no kidding, I wanted to say. It started with 440, which is Boulder, so I know it was Dave. (Hey, I've read *Nancy Drew*, okay? Or actually I think what I read was Sue Grafton, Mom keeps buying used copies at yard sales.)

But Dave didn't leave a message. What kind of call is that? He wants me to know he's thinking of me, but he doesn't want to actually talk to me or have me call him back?

I actually slept with him. Like, more than once.

Why? When he's going to be such a jerk, leaving no messages and sleeping with my best friend?

Actually I didn't sleep with him that many times. Maybe that's why he dumped me. Well, too bad. He *said* it was okay, that we had plenty of time for that in the future.

What a liar!

I called Beth. "I just wanted to make sure you got home okay," I said when she answered.

"Courtney. Jane dropped me off first," Beth said. "You saw me walk into my house!"

"Yeah. I know. I'm just sort of . . . paranoid lately," I said. "So, did you get any phone calls while you were out?"

"A couple," she said. "Nothing good. Just this guy named Rand who I met at work last week, I thought he was cute so I gave him my number, but then I realized I can't go out with someone named *Rand*. And this other guy, Bill? Remember me talking about him?"

Beth doesn't have a "little black book" for all the guys she goes out with occasionally. She practically has a zip drive.

Which only makes me more suspicious.

I just looked over the last 3 entries. Every other sentence starts with "I hate when."

I have to stop hating so incessantly. I need to be more positive, or no one will want to be around me. Like last night when I kept saying how I hated when other people cut in front in line, and I hated when there was no toilet paper in the bathroom stall and nobody reported it, and I hated when bands played for only 45 minutes after I waited 2 hours in line to buy the tickets to see them—

Well, anyway. You get the point. I get the point. I can't Tae-Bo my way through life. It's a great workout, but a little hostile.

And that stuff about Beth going out with Dave? That would never happen. Paranoid, jealous, hateful. I resolve not to go through life like that. Beth would never go out with Dave; she doesn't like being more than 10 seconds away from the guys she's seeing, for one thing. For another, he's so annoying—and she isn't. I love Beth. I trust Beth.

And I want to embrace life. Not kick its ass.

I hate when I'm self-critical. Like in what I wrote yesterday. So what if I hate things? I can't like everything. Not even close.

So I might as well not hate myself, right?

And Beth is acting suspicious. She hasn't made a move on anyone in the past month that I know about. Which must mean *something*.

Okay, so I sort of formalized this pledge today and I guess I should write it in here. It's going to sound so predictable when I write it down because it's something I've believed for a really long time.

So here it comes: I am not going to get involved with anyone my senior year. No guys. No girls, either. Don't get me wrong. I'm not giving up on guys *completely*. I just don't want to get involved with anyone senior year because we'll have to break up at the end of the year, apparently that's the way it's done and I was a fool not to realize it earlier.

"Just do what I do! Don't get serious with anyone," Beth said.

"But I don't work like that," I told her. "I'm a very serious person."

"You're serious," she said. "About being serious?"

"How can you doubt me so much?" I asked her. It's okay for me to doubt her. She's the one showing up in my dreams.

So once I made this decision, I had to tell Jane, too. We were sitting in French class. Jane actually looked *un peu* French with her new glasses and haircut. I scribbled her my decision and asked her to sign the piece of paper, as a witness. She signed it and wrote, "This is so perfect!"

"*En français*," I wrote back, as a joke. But then I realized what she'd just said. My life being ruined for an entire year, sitting home alone, night after night, was "perfect"?

"Were you jealous of me being with Dave or something?" I asked her after class.

Jane was so excited about her idea, she didn't even

hear me. "If you are absolutely sure you're not going out with *anyone* this year, it means *you* can run for vice president! You can make our senior year great."

There's this sudden vacancy in the student council spot because the vice prez, Jennifer Scher, used to go out with the prez, Tom Delaney, last year before they were elected. The Tom is very good-looking and has gone out with at least half the girls in this school. Including Beth, naturally. He has this irresistible quality, according to Beth, you don't know when it's going to hit you but it does. He's the kind of guy who uses flowers and jewelry as weapons, if you know what I mean. He also dresses really well, like, all the time. He wears all this Tommy Hilfiger stuff as if he's the Tommy who designed it.

Anyway, it looked like he had sort of settled down with Jennifer, they went out for like 6 months. Then as soon as they started student council this year, Tom had a fling with the secretary and totally upset Jennifer. Does he quit? Resign? No. He makes Jennifer's life so miserable that *she* does.

Just like a guy. Just like a president.

So all of a sudden our class projects are going nowhere, because Jennifer was like the driving force behind everything.

"Okay. I'll think about it," I told Jane. It's not like I have anything else to do with my time. Besides, being on student council would look good for my law school applications.

What am I going to do next year, anyway? Go to college, duh. But where? Should I try to go where Alison went, make it a Smith Family Tradition? The Stafford brochure said something about "producing great men and women for over a century." Like it's a factory, like we're shoes.

My wish list for the future:

go to a good school

make sure Dave is not at that school

make sure Beth and Jane are within driving distance

unless it's an incredibly long drive

then I'll fly

get into law school—Ivy League

sue Dave for emotional distress

become a righteous prosecutor in tradition of Marcia Clark, only win cases

then go on to become CNN commentator like her

but with better makeovers

Talked with Grant after Life Issues today. We spent half an hour learning ways of coping with change and making lists to help us cope. It all boiled down to the fact that you basically just have to change, you won't like it, and you can forget about coping with it. Anyway, after spending all that time listening to people talk about their big life changes (switching cell phone companies, dealing with new hairstyles, etc.), I was suddenly desperate for that info on Dave that Grant kept trying to tell me. I had to know if he's as miserable as I am. But at first Grant just said he had a "great" roommate and really liked his "great" dorm and his classes were all "great."

Excuse me, but that's a little too perfect. It has to mean Dave's lying. He probably *told* Grant to say all that stuff.

So then Grant asked how I was doing. I started telling him. I wanted to give him a perfect story for Dave. About how fabulously I was doing, about how I had a fabulous new boyfriend and had actually been recruited by three fabulous colleges. All of them in Boston—no, Europe.

But the next thing I knew I was pouring out my guts to Grant, telling him gruesome details that no boy should know, like about how I couldn't sleep at night and how I had started watching *90210* reruns instead of nature shows, and right now the only ones on were from back when David was nerdy and short and Kelly slept around.

"God, why am I telling you all this? I'm sorry," I finally said. "I should go."

"No, don't," Grant said. "I mean, it's okay. I understand."

"You do?" Somehow I doubted that. Had he gone out

with Dave for a year? And if he had, did I want to know that?

"Sure. I haven't been there, but it has to be really hard, breaking up with someone after so long. I bet, actually, that it really sucks," he said.

For some reason that made me laugh. "Yeah. It does. But I guess it's not the end of the world or anything."

"So . . . have you guys talked to each other at all?" Grant asked. "Since then?"

"No. He said he'd call," I told him. "And he does call. But he doesn't leave messages. And he always calls when he knows I'm not home."

"I don't know, that's probably just a coincidence. Why don't you call him?" Grant asked.

"Because he said *he'd* call. And the one who gets broken up with can't call the breaker upper," I explained.

"Oh." He nodded. "I guess you're right."

"He said we were meant for each other. What did he *mean* by that? People don't just say things like that and not mean them."

Grant's face turned sort of red. "Well . . . yeah, Courtney. They do. A lot of guys do, anyway."

"They do?" It was like I was doing an interview with a scientist about another species. Tonight on *Wild Discovery*: Males.

That's it. I'm through with boys. Until college, and that'll be far from here. I'll show *him* long-distance. "So when they say something serious to you . . . they really don't mean it. At all."

He looked very thoughtful for a few seconds. "Some of them do. I do. Anyway, it's not just guys that lie. Girls do, too—a lot of the time."

All of a sudden I got this very clear idea he was thinking about Beth when he said that. Like when they were making out and dancing that night, he'd said he really liked her, and he meant it. And she didn't. I was kind of shocked that it still bothered him.

"Yeah." I cleared my throat. I was kind of uncomfortable about this conversation going any further, because then I'd have to defend Beth, and I didn't necessarily know if I could. "Well, I didn't mean to um . . . say that all guys were evil—"

"And I didn't mean to say anything about—"

"It's okay," I interrupted him. "So, um, see you around."

"Right. Sure," Grant said. "And don't worry about Dave, because, you know, you're going to be okay."

"I'll just use some of my new *coping* skills," I told him.

Grant laughed, and I noticed he has this chip out of his front tooth. Either it's from ice hockey or it's from the getting-pummeled years. That's one thing I really like about him, you never know. "Go home tonight and make some lists," he said. "I'm sure you'll feel a lot better."

So here's my list based on the brilliant concept that "change is inevitable." (Hold on, I thought that was "death.")

Mr. Antero told us to ask ourselves: What can I do to deal with this inevitable change?

1. Hate Dave.

2. Try to move on by getting involved with other things. Which I am already doing by joining student council.

3. Stop obsessing about Dave. Which I will do this instant.

307

The Tom endorsed me today.

No, that's not new lingo for "hit on me," although with the Tom you really never know.

He literally endorsed me, for vice president of the student council. Like, he put up these signs and posters advertising me as Tom Delaney's Choice.

Then again, I don't know why I'm surprised. I mean, of course he's going to endorse me, I'm a *girl*, and I'm the only girl running for the office, and I'm a girl he hasn't scored with yet. Big challenge there, winning him over.

But he's actually trying to be nice or something. He cornered me at lunch and said how I'm the best person for the job, and how I shouldn't listen to anything negative Jennifer says—if I get the job, I should take it.

Naturally I went and found Jennifer right away.

"I don't want to talk about *him*," Jennifer said. "I'm moving on with my life." She was cleaning out her locker at the time. Perhaps that should have given me a clue.

I begged her for details, so I'd know what to be prepared for. I told her I knew what it was like to have your heart broken, that I was going through the same thing.

But before we could really bond, her parents walked up and said, "Ready to go, then?"

Turns out she's transferring to another school—a private one, in another state. That's how much she hates the Tom. She started walking away, but then she stopped and came back to me.

"There are things you really need to know about him," she said.

"Like never to say yes when he offers me a back rub?"

I asked. (Beth told me that was Move 1.)

"Yeah. But it goes way beyond that," Jennifer said. "You have to really watch him, keep track of everything he does—"

"Jennifer? Come on, we're double-parked," her mother said. "And talking about that boy is just a waste of your time." She pulled Jennifer away.

"Thanks!" I called. "For the warning!"

Like I needed one.

I wrote Alison an e-mail and thought it was so good I'd print it and paste it in here instead of writing:

Dear Alison,

Sure, you can laugh. You're living it up, going to frat parties every night. Me, I'm stuck here, bored out of my skull. When exactly am I coming for my prospective student visit? Let's make it October. No, wait—how about tomorrow?

Mom won't even notice I'm gone. She's too busy planning our Thanksgiving family reunion wagon train to Nebraska. *Already.* She told me you decided to go to a friend's house nearby instead of making the trek to the Von Dragens of Ogallala. How could you do that to me? Mom told me I'm in charge of "all the breads" for the meal. What does that mean?

If that isn't enough to make me crazy, then how about sharing a car with Mom, Bryan, and Oscar for 4 hours? Don't you love me anymore?

Courtney

The frat party thing was a joke. Alison's not really the kegger type. She has a bunch of friends from the music department, and they sit around practicing together. It would be annoying if she weren't so good. But then her being so good is annoying, too, in its own way. "Don't you have an instrument, Courtney?" all the teachers would ask when I came into their classes. After a while I just started holding up my pen.

Oops—she wrote back already! Here's her reply.

Dear Courtney,

You didn't mention anything about Dave. What's going on? Are you okay? Have you heard from him?

Love, Alison

Dear Alison,

No! God, no. Do you think that's my whole life or something? Dave?

Wonder what Dave's new e-mail address is. I wonder if I could find him on Yahoo?

"Phase three," Beth told me when I was reminiscing about Dave at work today. "Acceptance."

"Phase four," I said. "You quit observing my phases. I feel like the moon."

"Interesting metaphor, Courtney." Gerry nodded. "You feel like the moon. You see yourself as a celestial body. Out there in your own private world, in outer space."

"She could be feeling independent," Beth said. "That would be good. Because she broke the chain, she completed the cycle."

Excuse me while I go into the ladies' room and get my period. All this stupid talk about moons and cycles. It sort of made me want to forget about being a lawyer and sign up for the NASA shuttle. Just to get away from the psychological profiles.

Talk about having a bad weekend. I disgust myself sometimes.

I was giving Oscar his pill tonight—phenobarbital in a budget value hot dog, delish—and all of a sudden I wanted a hot dog.

I cooked 2 in the toaster oven and ate them right away.

I melted *cheese* on top of them. Not even good cheese, but those watery American slices Mom buys in 5 pound blocks. Then I put on ketchup, mustard, relish, and even some Frank's Hot Sauce.

I feel so gross now. I should have eaten Oscar's pills instead of his hot dogs. They're not even good hot dogs, they're the kind you buy 40 at a time because they're for a dog. Dogs for a dog. I wish I was one of those people who could make herself throw up.

I called Beth and told her I'd slipped up. "You mean, you broke your dumb no-dating law? You went *out* with someone?" She sounded really excited.

"*No*, of course not," I said. "I ate a hot dog. Okay, two."

"Ewww," she said. "Courtney, are you all right? Do you want me to come over? You know, that reminds me of the time that I was really upset about not getting into the arts school and I chain-smoked all night. Which wasn't that long after you didn't get the summer internship at that law firm and I took you out for dinner and you had a big fat steak and a crème brulée—remember?"

At this rate we might as well have eating disorders, except we lack the discipline. Maybe Beth and I need to be hospitalized, though. We should be. Maybe instead of going to college. Could save a lot of money on red meat, fat, and cigarettes.

"Courtney Smith. *You're* running?"

Suzanne Stupemeier stopped me in the hallway this morning.

I hate when people my age talk to me like that. It's like, get out of your minivan, take off your soccer-mom sunglasses and your cardigan sweater, put down your Tupperware container and just *talk* to me.

This student council vice-president thing wasn't my idea, okay? My friends made me do it because I'm the only one who can stand up to the Tom's hormones, or hormone, actually—testosterone. The one element I can remember from Health Issues, the junior year class to teach you things you don't learn in school but that you take at school.

And I wasn't sure I was *going* to do it until I had a precollege-application meeting with my guidance counselor yesterday and she pointed out although my grades were excellent, except for that incident in Driver's Ed, the extracurricular section of my college apps was a little blank.

"You might want to add a few things here," she said. "They like . . . active applicants."

Sexually active? I thought. Really? Because right now I don't have a shot in hell—

Mrs. Greene must have seen me blushing. "You know, well-rounded people, who get involved at school, play sports, and have interests outside of school."

"Oh. Right." I sighed. That kind of active. "Well, I do have a job," I said.

"Yes." Mrs. Greene nodded. "You do have that." She

made it sound like a disease. What's so bad about working at Truth or Dairy?

"And I adopted that highway," I reminded her.

"You and a group of a hundred others," Mrs. Greene reminded *me*.

When it came to sports, I had nothing to say. I was just sort of average at everything. But hey, not everyone can be on varsity teams. Especially not Jane, because she hates uniforms, though we talked about it once and both agreed it would be cool to have a number.

Okay, back to my campaign.

"Well, what *are* your ideas?" Suzanne asked me.

"I'm working on my platform," I said. Does anyone in student council do anything but organize parties anyway? Is it that important?

"I heard you were antigay. Is that true?" She picked a pill off her sweater. "Because that's really wrong. I guess."

"Not anti*gay*, anti*guy*," I said.

That sort of stumped her. "Well, how do you differ from your opponents?"

"Uh . . . they're all guys?" I said. Because Tom's gone out with too many girls and been too mean to them for any other girl to run. Talk about a gender gap.

How he got elected in the first place, I have no idea. Maybe we were all voting for the couple, Jennifer and Tom. They would have been prom king and queen, if they'd lasted.

"But anyway, Suzanne, I'm really devoted to the cause," I went on. "Our school's the best. We need to leave a legacy." Of truth, justice, and the American way, I should have said next. Family values! Suzanne was a bit of a Primster.

314

"Exactly," she said. "And our legacy is . . . ?"

"Growing every day," I told her. Like a freaking house-plant. "Like our . . . futures." Or maybe our waistlines. Or maybe the waiting lists at the colleges we want to get into but don't have a chance at.

"Exactly!" she said. "That's exactly how I look at it, Courtney. You have my vote. But I don't have to hate guys. Or gays. Right?"

"Of course not. Freedom of choice," I said. "That's what it's all about. Being . . . you know. Free and clear."

"God." She gazed at me for a second. "You're so *smart*."

Okay, this is really bizarre. You know how I've been seeing Grant everywhere lately? A few times when I leave work, and at Walgreens, etc. Like, everywhere I turn? Mind you, it's not a bad *view*. When you get right down to it, I probably think he's the most underrated senior guy in terms of looks, but he's always hiding in these standard plaid shirts and nondescript jeans, half the time he blends into the crowd. But not today.

I got off of work and he was *right* behind me in the parking lot when I went to get my car. I felt like I was on the Monday night TV movie, *The Acquaintance Beside Her, Constantly, Dogging Her Heels*. There was *his* car. Next to mine.

"Hi, Grant." I waved, all friendly-like. (It's supposed to be the best way to throw off intruders.) He waved back. "So, um, Grant," I said, trying to be casual. I was glad to see he wasn't parking in the disabled zone anymore. "Why do you keep following me?"

He gave me this weird look. Well, sure, who wouldn't after they'd been busted. *Get over me*, I wanted to say. You talked to me—don't you know? I'm unavailable this year. For dating, for fun, for like . . . life.

"What? Oh, no. I wasn't following you, Courtney," he said. "I was—"

"Look, never mind," I said. "I'm in a hurry."

"So am I!" He made this face at me, as if I was being a real jerk. And suddenly I realized what was going on.

"Are you keeping tabs on me or something? For Dave?" I asked.

His face got all red. "Are you serious?" he scoffed.

"Well, *are* you?" I asked.

"*No,*" he said. "You know, not everything's about you and Dave!"

Oh, how I wish that were true. "Look, Grant, you're nice and all, and I appreciate you talking to me the other day. But you can't go around following people just because your friends ask you to—it's not cool."

"You're going to tell me about cool?" He stared at my black-and-white cow apron. I was in such a hurry to get home that I'd forgotten to take it off.

"I have a job, okay?" I muttered.

"So do I," Grant said. He was about to go on when I jumped into my car and slammed the door. I know it was rude, but he was acting so weird, I had to get out of there. He was practically picking a fight with me.

Lighten up, Lake Superior. I think I'll copy my class and work schedules and put them in his locker just to make this easier for him. Like he doesn't know my work schedule already. I mean, how much shopping can one person do at the Canyon Boulevard stores? You've got your pet shop, your dry cleaner's, your pizza place, a fabric store, some tax place that's only open from January to April, and an insurance office. And Truth or Dairy. The only original place in the bunch.

Can't believe I've been working there over a year already. Time flies when you're separating frozen banana chunks.

The Over-the-Hill-and-through-the-Woods-to-Grandma's-House Campaign continued at dinner tonight.

"We'll leave at twelve that Wednesday," Mom said. "It's a five-hour drive, so we'll get there just in time to help with the pies." She had a stack of index cards in front of her. Turkey leftover recipes she's already excited about making and storing in plastic bags.

"Mom, it's two months *away*," Bryan said. "And it's not five hours, it's four. And what's the big deal?"

"The big deal is that this is a long trip, and we need to plan ahead, and we need to factor in an extra hour in case of bad weather," Mom said. She started her lecture on the virtues of planning.

Bryan took another helping of pasta. Oscar gazed up at him with intense love in his eyes, dying to get a mouthful of rotini.

I tuned them out and started thinking about the reasons I need to stay here. Index cards, please.

1—Don't want to spend multiple hours in a car with family.

2—Hate turkey. Grandpa won't even consider free range. Grandma won't even consider me not eating everything on my plate, which will be approx. 2 lbs of turkey.

3—Don't want to spend multiple days at Grandma and Grandpa's with family.

4—Could see Dave, back in town to visit his family for weekend, could get together, share a passionate night of romance, rediscover lost love for each other—

"Courtney, you and Grandma are sharing the guest room," Mom said. "You can both sleep in the queen bed—"

"What?" I asked. Was she joking? "She and Grandpa—"

"Are not getting along that well these days," Mom said.

"They don't share the same room?" I asked.

"Oh, not for a while."

Whoa. The secrets this family is hiding. What next?

"In fact, they have what you might call an 'open' relationship," Mom said.

"What? Mom, what are you saying?" I demanded.

"Your grandmother's gone on a few dates lately. Nothing serious, but—"

"Are they getting a divorce?" Bryan asked. "They're like . . . seventy. Can't they sort of stick it out at this point?"

"They might. But they have some . . . problems. You know."

Bryan and I looked at each other. I think we both knew what she was getting at, but I shut up right then. I didn't want to know what the "you know" was referring to.

My parents are divorced . . . my grandparents are having sex problems . . . my grandparents are having affairs. . . . Doesn't *anyone* in this family know how to have a relationship?

It's good to have something else to focus on, but not something that makes me this nervous. I have to give a speech for my vice-president gig, in front of the entire school. So here goes. I'll use the rest of this page—make it short but sweet. I'll write it *now*, get it out of the way, no procrastinating.

"Hi. My name is Courtney Smith. I see a lot of familiar faces out there."

And they're all scowling at me. Laughing hysterically. I've probably got a scrap of toilet paper stuck to my shoe. And my face is as red as my hair, the way my skin gets when I'm nervous, all the blood rushing to the surface in fight-or-flight mode. But I must go on. This is for . . . history. This is for . . . my entrance applications.

I have to get in somewhere really good. Dave and I were going to both go to CU, but that plan is definitely off. The school might have over 20,000 students, but that's not enough. Besides, he'd probably think I was following him there, chasing him, refusing to believe it's over.

Like I *would*.

"Thanks for taking time to listen to me today. If elected, I will . . . ban dating between seniors and juniors. Nobody will be allowed to break up with someone on the eve of the new school year. Labor Day will become the new Valentine's Day . . . a time to show your love instead of your really rotten and mean side."

"Also, we need more vegetarian lunch choices."

No. I'm going to push the school to be even better. "We need more vegan lunch choices."

Grandma just called to see how I was doing. I thought

she wanted to sympathize with me about the Dave situation. They met Dave; they know Dave; they love Dave. I hoped she wouldn't be rubbing it in, how perfect we seemed together.

Not to worry. I had just begun to tell her how much my life sucked when she launched into this long story about Grandpa and did I know how hard it was to live with a man for 50 years blah blah blah. Please don't go into details, I thought. Please don't tell me about the guy from the bingo palace you're dating now.

I rushed her off the phone but not before she got in the phrase "my needs are not being met."

Like *mine* are?

Football game tonight. Could not have been weirder. Kept seeing all these people from last year's senior class, and they kept asking me how Dave was. I told them I couldn't talk because I had to get to my student council booth.

Mrs. Martinez, the faculty advisor, thought it would be good if the candidates mingled with the public, and what better time than during a football game when Bugling Elk is so busy losing by 50 points that everyone has lots of time to chat. Everyone still goes to the games, because it's fun anyway.

So me and three guys were hanging around this table over by the hot dog stand. Two of them were telling everyone that if they got elected they'd make sure Bugling Elk hires a better coach. The other guy told everyone he would disband the football team and put the money into chess club competitions.

Then there was me. Saying how the important thing about sports was to stay involved and participate, and not every team could win—even the Broncos had bad seasons sometimes, right?

"Courtney has a point." The Tom strolled up and stood beside me. Then he kept telling everyone who stopped by that I'd do a good job.

The other candidates kept glaring at me.

"You're just supporting her because she's a girl," they accused the Tom.

"She's not a girl," the Tom said. "Not like *that*."

"Hello! I'm right here, you don't have to talk about me in the third person. And what does that mean?" I asked, poking him in the chest.

"Nothing! It's just . . . you're different. Unique!" Tom said like he'd had a brainstorm.

In that I haven't made out with you yet—yes. "So are we done campaigning?" I asked. "Can I go?" Because I'd said "hi" so many times my face was getting a cramp.

The 3 guys looked at me and shrugged. The Tom shrugged.

"Okay then, *I'm* going," I said. "And I'm still a girl."

I rushed off looking for Jane and Beth. I didn't see Jane anywhere, but I spotted Beth in the smoking area, which has a new location this year: right next to one end zone of the football field. It can't be next to the school, so it's next to the sports area. *That* makes sense. Bring on the oxygen tanks. Anyway, I could see Beth over there visiting her old smoker friends. No doubt showing them those wallet-sized photos she has of blackened lungs.

Saw Grant pull up and park in disabled spot again. I was running over to tell him how wrong that was—didn't he know there were plenty of BEHS students and parents who needed those spots?

Then he helped this older lady out of the car. She had a cane and walked unevenly, like she'd broken her hip. Oops. Must be his grandmother. Instead of being a creep, he is the type of guy who drives his grandmother to football games and picks up her prescriptions. I completely misjudged him. Or rather I'm back to my original judgment.

"Courtney?" he said.

"Oh, um hi. I was just looking to see if Jane's here yet. Have you seen a white Acura?"

"Jane's in the bleachers. She's waving at you." Grant pointed behind me.

"Oh. Okay. Well, bye!" I started to run off.

I was halfway up the bleachers when the Bulging Elk mascot grabbed me in a bear hug. (Idea: if I become VP, outlaw mascots.) He has these furry antlers, and they kept poking me in the eye.

"Get away from me!" I said.

He picked up his bullhorn and made this horrible bugling noise. I nearly lost my hearing. He bugled again, because our team was for once about to score. Then the crowd went wild, everyone was bugling and yelling and screaming so loudly that the quarterback couldn't get anyone on the team to hear him. They got a delay-of-game penalty and then there was an interception in the end zone and the other team ran it all the way back down the field and scored. Oops.

Ditched the mascot with bad timing and found Beth and Jane sitting on the top bleacher because it's the best place to scope the boys. Bryan was up there, too, with his sophomore friends. All really pimply and angry about not having driver's licenses or facial hair. No doubt they were up there because it must also be the best place to scope girls, like cheerleaders. Bryan's not really the cheerleader type. He's making it his life's mission to find someone as perfect as Beth.

When I got to the top bleacher, Beth and Bryan were laughing about something, completely violating the sophomores/seniors boundary line up there. I immediately sat in between them and then moved us over, away from Bryan. I'll never get elected if I let this sort of stuff happen.

Tonight was definitely not your normal football game. But on the plus side, I think I am finally getting over

Dave. I didn't really miss him tonight. Not *much*.

Anyway, to celebrate, and also because I'm now writing on the inside back cover, I'm starting my new journal tomorrow. New journal, new life. Plus I can carry it around and look cool, plus it won't have anything about Dave in it. It's been over a month since we split. That's history now. He's history.

Still can't believe this! Not that this is a fresh cool sketch-book, but *THIS*, which was waiting for me in the mail drop when I got home from work.

Dear Courtney,

Hi! How are you? I know you're probably wonder-ing why it took me so long to write. I've been thinking about you a lot. But it seemed like we needed some time apart. I hope you're not still mad at me. I didn't mean to hurt your feelings. It just seemed like the only thing to do at the time.

How is school going? How's Beth? How's Jane? I hope you guys are having fun.

School is okay. The classes are pretty intense, especially this Intro to Geology one. I thought I knew a lot about geology, but I'm really bad at memorizing stuff. My roommate, Chad, and I get along fine. He has a monster stereo, so we're always getting in trouble for playing it too loudly. He's really into rap, so I call him Puff Chaddy.

I should probably go now. I have class in twenty minutes and it's on the other side of campus. I'm so glad I got that new bike last spring. I use it every day. Thanks for helping me pick it out. When I ride, I think a lot about our trip to Taos and how much fun it was exploring the bike trails together (after we finally ditched my parents).

I hope you're doing well. I miss you.

Dave

I'm still in too much of a state of a shock to write. Plus this new journal is sort of intimidating. Too many wide-open spaces. Tomorrow.

I know I should be sleeping, but I have been up all night analyzing Dave's letter, like at a crime lab. Boyfriend Forensics. Or I guess it would be Ex-Boyfriend Forensics.

Several lines bear repeated reading. It seems to me there are 4 important items:

(1) Actually the first one is that he didn't mention any girls. Not a single one.

(2) "I've been thinking about you a lot" and "I think a lot about our trip to Taos." Clearly having remorse. Obsessing. I am constantly on his mind.

(3) "It just seemed like the only thing to do at the time." "At the time" implies there are other options now. Also implies he made a big mistake and realizes that now.

(4) "I miss you."

I don't know how he could have made it any plainer. There's only one thing to do. He *wants* me to do this.

Does car insurance cover natural disasters? And how much does that make the premium go up when you're 17 and it already takes all your allowance plus a part-time job to pay for?

And why do these things always have to happen to me? Why? Just when everything seemed so clear, so obvious . . . so easy.

I set out for Boulder to see Dave at about 3. Didn't want to look too eager, besides, had to be in school all day. But I figured if I got there on a Friday we could patch things up and then spend the weekend together. Beth tried to talk me out of it, but then I showed her The Letter. She gave me a coupon she won for a free Big Gulp and told me to hit the road. I brought all my favorite CDs and I was blasting them on the stereo as I cruised down the highway. Everything seemed perfect. My life felt like a movie for some reason. *Thelma and Louise*. Without Brad Pitt in the backseat. And not in a cool convertible.

When I started heading west on 36, the sky had a sort of black section, over the Flatirons. It wasn't that unusual, really—typical Colorado 3:00 thunderstorm. But this one was like . . . superthunder. Extra loud. All of a sudden I heard this big boom, and it shook the highway pavement, I swear. Then hail—giant ice balls—started thwacking against the windshield. I couldn't see anything! The hail was actually the size of golf balls. I felt like each one was going to smash the glass, and I kept cringing with each one, until my shoulders were even with my ears. I was so crouched over I could barely see over the steering wheel. I was driving like my grandmother.

I pulled over at the next exit and stopped at the first gas station I saw, my heart pounding in my throat. I ran into the Complete station. (Complete station. So badly named. So *completely* lacking.)

A whole bunch of Dave's friends were in there. Grant (still following me apparently), the Tom, Pete and Paul Desaulnier, Gary Matthews. What did they do, drive a minivan?

"Courtney?" The Tom was gazing out the window. "You're supposed to park *under* something."

"Oh." I'd kind of forgotten to save the car in my panic to save myself.

"Hello, Dent Clinic," Paul joked. "Can we make an appointment for tomorrow? Yes, it's a maroon Ford Taurus with a bunch of vegetarian bumper stickers—"

"Save the Tofu? Is *that* what that says?" Pete laughed. "More like save the Taurus. For my *grand*parents."

The thing about being identical twins is that you have identically bad jokes. And it's not a Taurus, it's the Bull.

"Where are you going?" Grant asked, having the decency to seem concerned.

"Um . . . shopping," I said. "You?"

"We're going to see Dave." Tom said it like it was the most natural thing in the world. He knew it bugged me, and he smiled when he said it. Do I *want* to be on student council with this jerk? Who's so devoted to Dave that he's basically a clone?

I'd rather be outside in the raging hailstorm. It would have been less painful.

"He planned this killer weekend for us, including a big party tonight at his dorm, meeting tons of college girls, then we're going to the CU football game tomorrow, and—" Blah blah blah. If he didn't kill me by going on, I was going to grab a plastic knife off the Snack Station and start stabbing myself.

All of a sudden Grant stepped in front of Tom holding a stack of napkins from the Snack Station. Then he reached up and put his hand in my hair. I felt this shivering sensation from him standing so close. It went all the way down my back, and it was cold. "What are you . . . doing?" I asked.

He pulled a couple of ice hunks out of my hair. "Your hair's kind of . . . full of ice," he said.

I reached up and felt malted-milk-ball-size hail in my hair. It was melting hail sliding down the back of my coat that was making me shiver—not stupid Grant Superior and his CU-bound buddies.

"Excuse me," I muttered, and I ran into the bathroom. The last thing I want is for them all to go to Boulder and tell Dave how horrible I looked. So I turned on the hand dryer and bent over, sticking my head underneath, until I smelled something burning. All the blood had rushed to my face, and now I had flyaway hair. Disaster two for the day.

When I came out, the guys were still there, but the hailstorm had ended, so I rushed past them, bought a fruit juice, and waved good-bye. No, really. See ya. It's been real.

The roads were covered in icy hail, and I kept sliding all over the road, it was like driving on gumballs or jawbreakers must be. But I had to get out of there. I drove up to see the buffalo herd, to make sure they were okay. And to think about other things for a while. The hail was a couple inches deep on the ground, so I was worried when

I didn't see them right off. Then I realized the buffalos were all standing on the downslope, under trees. Their brown hides looked drier and better than my matted hair. "Hi, guys!" I called. They wouldn't come over to the fence, which is cool, they hardly ever do, and their hoofs might slip on the ice anyway. But it made me sad, for some reason. Like I had nothing, and no one.

I drove home going about 5 miles an hour. There was killer rush-hour traffic. As I sat there, waiting to merge, the sun came out, and I realized the hood had dozens of dents. Large ones. The car looks like it has acne pit scars. I told Mom when I got home, but she seemed curiously unconcerned, too busy yelling at a telemarketer who was calling to offer a special deal on hail-damaged car repair. "I won't give him the satisfaction!" she seethed.

"You might," I said. "I mean, maybe you should take their number—"

"That's it!" She slammed down the phone. "Is there no privacy in American society today? I'm ordering continuous call blocker."

"But my friends—Mom, you can't do that!" Bryan protested.

"They'll get special codes to punch in," Mom said. "Their calls will go through. But no one else's!"

I could almost see her not giving Dad the special code for a few weeks. She can be so vindictive.

Mom saw the Bull in direct sunlight. My car privileges have been revoked for the next week. Will have to ride my bike to school, work, etc., and also beg Beth for rides. As if it's my fault that a cold front raced across the foothills. The weather guy on Channel 9 didn't know it was coming—but somehow I was supposed to? "It's hard enough for me to afford two cars," she said. "And now this?"

"I'm sorry, Mom," I said, over and over. I did really feel bad about it.

Mom has zero sympathy for the fact I did it all out of love. She said I shouldn't be driving to Boulder to see Dave; he should be driving here to see *me*. He has to make the first move, she said. I pointed out the letter. She said anyone can write a letter; but it's when they show in person that you know they mean it.

She went into this long, detailed story about how one time this guy wanted her back and drove across the country to apologize and beg her to move to DC and marry him. She got this really dreamy look on her face. I thought about the pictures of Mom in college with her friends, dressed up for parties, laughing, and how pretty she was. She's still pretty, don't get me wrong. She just wears all these clothes that work against her; they're all called Princeton Harbor or Sage Garden Grove or something like that. They're her country-club-wanna-be outfits. Actually she looks good in them, I just wish she'd meet some guy who was *in* the club. She could quit worrying about money and I could have a new car.

"So he drove all the way out to Ogallala from

Washington—this was right after college, and I was home for the summer. And his car was full of roses," Mom went on. "It was so romantic. My parents were so shocked, my father told him he could have my hand in marriage before he even *asked*—"

"And . . . was that Dad?" I said.

"Oh, no. Heavens, no." Mom's face got all red. It's the first time I've seen her blush in a long time. "This guy was a complete phony. He said he loved me, but." She shook her head. "He didn't mean it."

I could practically hear birds singing. It was this magic moment where I realized Mom and I might actually have something in common.

Then the phone rang. I grabbed it. It was Beth, calling to ask how my visit went. She said she'd been waiting to call, that she was on pins and needles. I explained the hailstorm, the Complete disaster.

"Wow. I hate to say this, but in a way it's a relief," Beth said.

"What is?"

"Well, what happened yesterday . . . it's like a sign. It means you guys aren't meant for each other," Beth said. "If you were, the heavens wouldn't have opened and thrown golf balls at you."

"It's called a weather system," I said. "It has nothing to do with fate."

"Oh, *really*. And that's why it happened at the *exact* moment you needed the roads to be clear," Beth said. "You ran into those guys at the gas station—"

"Because we left school at the same time and traveled at the same speed," I said. "It's like an algebra word problem. It's not a *sign*."

334

"Just accept it, Courtney. Don't fight it," Beth said. "You have to try giving up on Dave again, and it might feel even harder this time, but it'll be easier, I promise."

"Beth? I love you to death. But don't talk to me about quitting Dave like it's quitting a really bad nicotine habit," I said. "Because cigarettes don't write letters begging you to come back."

"Is that what his letter said?" Beth asked.

I reread the letter. Maybe he didn't beg me, but he was definitely hinting at a reunion. Just . . . not that strongly, maybe. Because his phone number isn't in the letter.

I called Directory Assistance, but there's no phone in his name. "Do you have a listing for a . . . Chad?" I said. The operator laughed at me. It's not a sound you want to hear.

I'll write him instead. Just because Beth, Mom, and now the heavens are against me, not to mention the phone company, I'm not giving up.

Maybe I will give up. I cannot write this letter. I've tried 8 times and each time I sound more stupid.

> Dear Dave,
> I hated you a couple of weeks ago. Actually, it wasn't until a couple of days ago that I stopped.
> So why am I writing you now? Am I a complete hypocrite?
> Don't I have any self-respect left?

I'm going to just send him something . . . a message . . . without a long, sappy letter. I'll tear off a boxtop from his favorite cereal. I'll send him my most prized South Dakota buffalo postcard from the bulletin board over my desk. No, he doesn't deserve that.

> Dear Dave,
> You don't deserve this postcard. You realize that.
> But I just wanted to let you know I miss you, too.
> Love,
> Courtney

Can't believe I just wrote on the back of this postcard. Now I have to put it back on my bulletin board and I'll have to look at it and remember how stupid I sounded. Must try again. Must wait a few more days, though, so I don't look overly eager. Guys like that.

Have you ever wanted to take a day back and just call a "do over"? Today was Courtney the Candidate Day.

"Do over! Do over! Do over!"

It was like a battle I read about once. Where the army gets beaten down and broken and has to summon every ounce of courage it has just to get out of the foxhole.

My Own Private Waterloo? Saving Private Courtney?

It started out nicely. Mom has this real gift for making theme food when we have big events. Cello-shaped Jell-O the day of Alison's recitals. Sneaker-shaped cookies for Bryan's track meets. So this morning she put this hammer-shaped pastry in front of me. I kept staring at it. I had no idea what it was, but I couldn't tell her that. So I just ate it and said thanks. Then she asked if I wanted another gavel.

"Mom, I'm not going to be a judge!" I laughed.

She laughed, too. "I know, but do you have any idea how hard it is to bake a vice-presidential seal?" She held up this flat, round, semiburned, semifrosted pancake. I tried not to take it as an omen.

First thing at the assembly, we all had to state what we wanted to do for the school and what we were all about. I told everyone that I would be a really good vice president because I'm the middle child and am used to getting along with everyone. (I stole a bunch of psychological-profile lines from Beth.) And I mentioned all the things I wanted to see happen. No more dissecting animals in science class, no more using the leftover animals from science class in the cafeteria, etc. (Okay, just kidding.) Anyway, I think my speech pretty much rocked.

After each of our speeches, we had to take questions from the audience. The first one was asked by Mrs. Martinez—I guess it was supposed to be a warm-up question: "Please state your full name."

So I stated my name. Courtney Smith. That's full enough, right? I mean, you don't hear Al Gore or George W. Bush running around dishing out *their* middle names. It's just a "W."

So then we had these questions from the audience; there were mikes set up, like this was a TV talk show. One of the Desaulnier twins stepped up to the mike, and asked: "Courtney, I heard a rumor about you, and I want to verify it."

"Sure thing," I said politely. As I recall, I even *smiled* at him. There was no dirt on me. I'd been completely celibate lately. I wasn't worried.

"Okay, um . . . is it true your middle name is V.D.?"

Everyone started laughing, like it was the most hilarious thing they'd ever heard. My face got hot, I could feel it. This was so dumb, this was the last thing anyone needed to know or talk about, it was just this attempt to find something to laugh at me about. And how did he know this? Was it from Dave? I could feel this onion ring I ate for lunch expanding into a giant circle in my stomach, strangling me like a big squid. Hanging me out to dry.

"V.D. is not my middle name," I said.

Oh my God. I sounded like a public service announcement! "Don't identify me by my sexually transmitted disease, I'm a person deep down inside."

It was *awful*. Everyone started laughing really hard. Mrs. Martinez called for quiet—when it finally happened, it didn't last long.

"Is it true you put the *vice* in vice president?" the other Desaulnier shouted.

All of a sudden the Tom came up behind me, I guess to support me. He put his hand on my back. I was kind of glad, if you want to know the truth, because I felt really stranded out there. Then he put his *other* hand on my back. I waited for him to offer me a backrub. Here we go, I thought. The beginning of the end.

But he didn't do anything except press once and let go. Then he stepped forward and said, "If everyone would just give Courtney a chance to talk, we could wrap this up."

I was so shocked I nearly fell down. The Tom being nice? With nothing in it for him?

I cleared my throat. "My middle name *is* Von Dragen," I said. "And I realize these are very unfortunate middle initials. But I can't help it, it's an old family name. And I don't think anyone should be punished for their name, or for anything else they can't control, like their background, or their skin color, or their sexual preference." Oh my God. I was on quite the tirade.

But somehow it worked. Everyone totally cheered me, and started shouting "Courtney for V.P.," "Courtney V.P. Smith!" instead of V.D. I was convinced everyone was going to vote for me. A landslide victory, or, more to the point, a rockslide victory. People get killed by rockslides.

Maybe they were just applauding because they felt sorry for me. I mean, I applauded for the other guys, and there's no way I'm voting for them.

Hmmmmm.

Of course when I walked through the halls today, I heard it all. "Hey, it's Courtney STD." "Look, here comes Courtney the Dragon." "Yo, Dragon Lady, what's up?"

Like you can rise from the ashes and all, and everyone will applaud that, and everyone pretends to believe in being so open and supportive of people who are middle-name-challenged. But when it comes right down to it? You'll get teased. Humiliated. If anyone can find fault with anything about you, they'll point it out.

Beth and I went to the girls' soccer game with Jane after school to watch her superstar little sister play. Jane kept going on and on about what great hair accessories she found at Miser Mart. Beth and I kept looking at each other in amazement. What is Miser Mart and why in the world is Jane shopping there? She was sort of slipping on her pledge to never be caught dead or alive in anything nondesigner and nonexpensive.

I waited for them to shower me with sympathy. They stole a cup of Gatorade from the team's table for me, but that was about it.

"Von Dragen, huh? Well, *that* sucks," Jane said, clipping and unclipping her new barrettes.

"Your face was so red," Beth said. "I've never seen it like that."

I think I need more supportive friends.

P.S. I'm calling in sick tomorrow. Someone just called and asked if I would be willing to give a health services speech on sexually transmitted diseases, since I'm out of the closet on having one.

I'm sitting at my computer and I have a paper due in 12 hours that I haven't started yet. So I got up and put on my favorite Steve Maddens with my pajamas.

I'm like the "before" picture. In a computer magazine. I need a makeover and also a memory upgrade.

Time for another pledge: I will never leave a paper until this late again.

Would it be so awful if I didn't go to college? I'd save Mom and Dad a lot of money, for one thing. I'd start working at an interesting place sooner—get out of the food service industry. If smoothies and shakes qualify me for anything.

SLIGHTLY LATER...

Took a short break to do some reading. I just threw down my fashion mags in disgust.

Why is everything "bubble gum" color this year?

Nail polish. Perfume. T-shirts. Etc.

We are a Bazooka Bubble Yum Society.

Was there ever a spearmint year? Sugar-free cinnamon?

Don't they realize that for those of us with reddish hair, this is a complete and utter disaster? I have enough problems without trying to wear baby *pink*, okay? Like, for instance, freckles. Not getting completely fried when I step out the door. My lips are chapped beyond recognition. And what do I get to put on them? What is selling at every stupid gas station and convenience store? PINK LIP BALM.

Where is the "balm" in that?

Realize I am going slightly insane over worrying about election results.

Whoa. Just got off the telephone. First the Tom called to say he thinks we will win. "You already won," I told him. "It's me that's running."

"We all win if you win," the Tom said. Being disgustingly nice. Then he had to go back to his date.

Then Alison called. She is so homesick or something it's scary. She started crying the second she heard my voice. "Is Mom there?" she sniffled.

"No, she's at her book club," I said. "What's wrong? Didn't you make first chair? Did you have a bad recital—"

"My whole life isn't music!" Alison yelled. Funny. Then how come she spent all her free time reading sheet music and risque biographies of famous composers? Why was she even at this college that specialized in having a great Music Dept?

"So what else is going on?" I asked sort of awkwardly.

"I can't . . . it's just . . ." She was totally fumbling.

So I told her about my Life Skills course and how dumb it was so I had nothing to offer her, but I could tell her what an idiot I was during my speech, and she could relate, what with the Von Dragens being her ancestors, too.

"But who's Tom Delaney?" she asked.

I forgot how totally out of it Alison could be. Her social circle was more like a semicircle. Shaped exactly like an orchestra.

By the time we hung up she seemed much better. I guess she just misses us.

8:45 A.M.

I WON!!!

10:01 A.M.

The euphoria has worn off. The reality has set in.

I have to be vice president with Tom Delaney, the boy who has scored with every single member of the senior class. Or at least everyone on the student council. And probably some of them in the student council office. On the student council desk. Gross.

Should I wear garlic around my neck? Or pepper spray?

"Don't you see what's so perfect about this? You're the only one who can resist him," Beth said. (I'm in study hall now. Studying. Just look at me go.) "Because you're not even into good-looking guys. You have, like, no effect on them."

"Excuse me?" This was my best friend talking?

"I mean—they don't affect you," Beth said, laughing.

"No. Not nearly as much as I'd like them to," I said.

"Shut up. You could go out with any guy you wanted," Beth said. "Forget about Dave. Start looking!"

"I told you, Beth—I'm not dating anyone this year," I said.

"Okay, okay. How about just . . . you know. A *fling*?"

I raised my right eyebrow. "And those always work out so well for you."

"They do," she argued. "At the time, anyway." Then we both laughed.

Okay, so: Beth and I were at Truth or Dairy for our dreaded/favorite Saturday shift. We like it because we work together. We hate it because everyone from school comes in, and Gerry's always there, hovering, telling us to "scoop now and chat later."

Then all of a sudden at about five o'clock she dropped her scoop and said, "Oh my God. Courtney. Look who just walked in."

I figured it was her Crush Du Jour. But it was Dave. Walking through the door with that saunter of his. Wearing jeans and a new T-shirt.

"What is he doing here?" she asked, as he made his way toward the counter. "Don't they make smoothies in Boulder? So why does he come here?"

"Because we're the best," I said. "We use organic fruit and—"

"Shut up with that promotional crap!" Beth practically screamed at me. "It's because of you, stupid."

When he looked at me, I ran into the storeroom to get a fresh tub of frozen yogurt out of the freezer. But after I picked it up, I didn't feel like going back out there. What would I say? What would he say? My hands were getting all sweaty. What if I dropped his smoothie? What if—

"Courtney, what are you doing back here? We have a *line*." Gerry had his hands on his hips, doing his outraged stance. He's big on not having lines.

"We needed more nonfat plain."

"We did?"

"There's going to be a run on it," I said.

He shook his head. "Never mind predicting what

people want, Courtney. Go take their actual *orders*."

I shuffled back out to the front. Beth was standing right under the giant arrow that said, PLACE ORDER HERE. And Dave was standing across from her, gazing up at the menu on the chalkboard. Like he doesn't know all the drinks already. He came here a hundred times to pick me up or hang out with me.

I tried to step in front of Beth and take his order. She wouldn't let me. She's only 5'1" but when she gets her stance going, you can't move her. I guess she thought she was protecting me. "What can I get you?" she mumbled in this sort of angry voice.

"Hi, Beth." He smiled at her. My knees kind of buckled. It could have been the giant tub of yogurt, so I set it down on the counter by the minifridge we have up front. Dave was all by himself. That was weird. I tried not to read too much into it as I rearranged spoons in all the fixins' bins.

"Hey. I got your letter," he said, looking at me.

"You wrote him a *letter*?" Beth almost shrieked.

"So, do you want the usual?" I took the opportunity to move in front of Beth. I tried to smile at Dave, but I was having a really hard time looking him in the eye. It was impossible. I was afraid I'd see something in there I didn't want to see.

"Um. Yeah. Coconut Fantasy Dream," he said. "Extra—"

"Fantasy?" I asked.

He laughed. "Coconut." Like I didn't know.

"I'll make it," Beth said.

"No, I'll *make* it," I said, pushing her aside by the fruit bin. Did she really think she could step in and steal my

345

ex-boyfriend just like that? Just because I *dreamt* it?

"It's a smoothie. I'm Truth today," Beth said, very self-importantly. "See this apron?"

"But the Coconut Fantasy Dream has yogurt in it, so technically, it's Dairy." We have arguments like this a lot. Usually only when good-looking guys come in. "It's both, and in case of a tie we look to the possession arrow." I stared at the dangling arrow above our heads. "Oh, look at that—it's pointing at me."

"Courtney. *Don't* make him a drink—after the way he treated you?" Beth said. "Unless you're going to make it really bad—" We sort of started shoving each other. It was like we were seven years old again and fighting over who got to ride the teeter-totter.

"Girls? Is there a problem?" Gerry materialized at my elbow like a housefly. "Does it really take two of you to make one smoothie? Courtney—help the next person in line."

I mindlessly scooped pralines and cream into sugar cones for an older couple. Dave hovered in front of the ice-cream tubs.

"So I heard you got caught in that hailstorm." He sipped his Beth-made CFD. "Where were you going?"

"Um . . . that new mall complex thing. In Broomfield? With the new shoe pavilion wing?"

"Oh." He seemed sort of disappointed.

"Yeah. Got some great deals," I told him.

"Grant says you're the new vice president. Is that true?" Dave asked.

I nodded as I started putting together a Hot Fudge Fudgorama. "True. I just started a couple of days ago."

"*Why?*" he said in this really snotty tone. "You never

cared about that stuff before."

I ladled about an extra pint of hot fudge sauce onto the sundae. "Why are you even *here*?" I said.

"Courtney. Don't be like that," he said with this soulful soul-patch look. Wait a second. Isn't that what he said the last time we spoke? "I came to apologize. I came to talk to you. I came—"

"To get a Coconut Fantasy Dream. And in case you haven't noticed, they do make smoothies in Boulder. Maybe not as good as ours, because they're all chains. But there's a place on the Hill, I think, and they have bagels, too, I went there once with my dad when he visited—"

"Courtney! I came here today because of your letter," Dave said. "Didn't you *want* me to?"

"Courtney? Is there a problem?" Gerry asked, pausing in front of me, holding a wet dishrag in his hand. "I need you to clear some tables." He shoved the clammy dishrag at me.

Just then Bryan walked in. He said he was there to catch a ride home with me and Beth. When he saw Dave standing there talking to me, he started glaring at him. As if he was creating this force field or something.

"So I should probably go. I have a lot of studying to do," Dave said, backing away. "Hey, Bryan."

"Yeah. You should go," Bryan said angrily.

My little brother had never stood up for me before. And I hated him for it. Instantly.

I ran over to the window and pretended to be cleaning off tables as I watched Dave get into his cute red Jeep and drive away.

"Hey, Bryan, what you did just now? That was really nice," Beth told him.

"Nice? You were totally rude!" I said.

"Give me a break. You've been moping around the house for almost two months. You've been completely miserable. And now when you're starting to feel better? He shows up here for a smoothie? Come on!" Bryan scoffed. "He probably didn't even pay."

"He did, too," I said.

"Okay. But did he *tip*?" Bryan asked. "I bet he didn't appreciate the service. Just like he didn't appreciate you." He dropped a dollar in the tip jar. "Thanks, Beth. This is great." Then he turned to me. "That's how it's done, okay?"

"What do you know?" I said. As if Bryan knows anything about romance.

So we were all standing in the parking lot, about to get into Beth's car, when Dave drove up again. He pulled into the spot beside us and looked at me. I could tell it was time for The Talk. Or *a* talk, anyway.

"Beth?" I said. "Go ahead and give Bryan a ride home. This might sort of take a while."

I'll write the rest later. My fingers are starting to cramp.

THE BIG TALK CONTINUED . . .

So Dave drove us to my house and we sat in the parked car, beside the curb. I didn't think I should ask him to come in. That would be like revisiting a major crime scene. Mr. Novotny was outside his house raking leaves—or, rather, "leaf." He's completely obsessive about his lawn. When a leaf falls, he runs outside to rake it— unless there's a Broncos game on.

So Dave started out by saying *again* how ridiculous it was that I was on student council.

Finally, he admitted that it was all about the Tom. "I can't think about you and Tom," he said. Is that why he drove down to Truth or Dairy? Because he's jealous?

"What are you talking about? You don't have to," I said. "There is no me and Tom. It's not like we'll be dating."

"I *know* Tom. You guys will be dating within a week."

"No way," I said. Anyway, weren't we sitting there having this Talk so that *we* could get back together? Or what was the point?

"Look at all the other girls he's gone out with," Dave said.

"I don't have time. And anyway, I'm not *other girls*," I said. "I'm me."

He considered that for a second. Like perhaps it was true? But it wasn't necessarily a good thing.

Maybe I don't love Dave. Maybe I hate him.

"So anyway," I said. "What did you want to talk about?"

"You know. Stuff. Like maybe us getting back together."

My heart pounding, my palms sweating, etc. Panic attack.

Then he went on. "I mean, I don't think we should get back together right now. But I think three or four months from now—"

I couldn't believe it. He's *obsessed* with time lines!

"You have these really warped ideas about time and space, you know that? You should be in like a science fiction movie—not my life."

Was that a great line or what?

I got out and slammed the door. My coat got caught on the window, so I tugged at it. The zipper ripped the Jeep's plastic window like it was a worn-out reused Ziploc bag.

Why did I do that?

Why did he drive down to *say* that? Am I supposed to start planning? Counting down the next four months? He took off down the street. Mr. Novotny was shaking his rake at me, so I ran into the house, lay on the bed, and started crying.

I hate this!

Naturally I called Beth instantaneously. She had the nerve to not even be home yet. Of course Bryan wasn't either so I figured they must have stopped at Safeway or Blockbuster or something. So I called Jane; her mother said she was out shopping for some more new hair accessories to match her new eyeglasses. I wish I had her life. I wish I had anyone else's life right now. Even Oscar's.

Had my first student council meeting today. Since I'm new, I'm supposed to have all the new ideas. I couldn't believe how slowly it was going. Also, the Tom *has* no ideas, unless they're about sex. Mrs. Martinez said how wonderful it was to have me on board and asked what my first issues would be.

I casually mentioned how we should assume a leadership role, for the middle school. The closest one in our district is called Goat Mountain Canyon. Don't ask me how they came up with these names. The area is growing too fast and they ran out of cool names about thirty years ago.

"I like the mentor concept," I said. "We should help build their futures." Because with the name Goat Mountain Canyon, they're going to need help building self-esteem.

It sounded good, really. I didn't have much of an idea where I was going with the whole thing when I started, but then I remembered this article I'd read about how a teacher challenged his students to read a certain number of books. If they did, then he vowed to kiss a pig on the lips.

Do pigs have lips? Maybe this teacher kissed the snout. Anyway, there was a picture of him in the paper, because the kids read even more than he challenged them to, and I thought it was great.

So I suggested we challenge the Goats. A peer pressure sort of thing to see if they could read as much as we did.

Nobody cared about the kids reading the books, but

they got really excited about some dare that we'd have to pull off or be subjected to. All of a sudden there was a vote and now if the middle-school kids read 3 books on average each by November 15, we all have to spend a night sleeping on the roof of their school—Principal "the Duck" LeDucque, too. Wonder if she knows yet.

After the meeting the Tom wanted to talk to me. "We need to go over some details," he said.

I bet, I thought. "Like what?"

"Well, you and I have to go over to the middle school and run this by the principal," he said. "What time is good for you?"

I couldn't believe it. He was so not putting the moves on me. Of course, it was only my first day.

When I got home I told Mom there was no way I could go to Nebraska because I was on student council and was too busy planning stuff like Homecoming and now I had this book-challenge thing going.

She did this paper-rock-scissors thing, only it involved school-politics-family. Family won.

Crap.

This diary has been certified by the FDA to be dairy-free***. Wheat-free. Gluten-free. Whine-free. (Okay, maybe not, but definitely wine-free. Alcohol-free in general.)

What the heck is a gluten, anyway?

What I really need to focus on is staying boy-free.

This is a Boy-Free Zone. Imagine signs like that at school. Perhaps I could institute this as my first official vice-presidential act.

*** Not to be confused with free and clear.

You could say I'm throwing myself into my work lately. Beth called in sick, so I was bored and got really into making up new drinks. I made one for Gerry called the Wheatgrass Whirl when he dropped by. "I love it!" he cried.

"You do?" I couldn't believe it.

He poured himself a large glass of water and downed it. "Oh. Well, the drink is *horrible*, yes. But what I love is your initiative! Keep inventing drinks, Courtney, and I'll keep trying them until you get it right. You're such an asset to this place."

What a boss. "Okay then," I said. "I've been thinking we should take the Coconut Fantasy Dream"—my voice nearly choked on the name—"off the menu. And put this on instead."

See? I'm trying to move on, I really am.

I put orange juice, coconut, and frozen strawberries in the blender, then raspberry sherbet. But that was too much like a Sunrise Strawberry Supreme. So I tossed in some pineapple and a little plain yogurt.

"I'll keep this under review," Gerry said. "But Courtney, don't even think of getting rid of the CFD. It's our most popular drink. A business survives—no, thrives—on *hits*. So . . . hit me again." Gerry laughed. "Get it? Hit me? Hey, speaking of gambling. Did I tell you I went to Central City and played the nickel slots last night?" The man lives *so* dangerously.

When I'm old enough to gamble, I'm starting with the quarter slots. Minimum.

For some reason this whole experience led me to the

Taco Bell drive-through on the way home at 9:00. I got all the change from the tip jar and pooled it into a value meal (people are so generous). Only I ordered the wrong kind of gordita. I don't eat meat often enough to know the difference between gorditas. Ended up with way too many vegetables. Not the point at all.

No wonder I can't sleep.

Why didn't I drive up to see buffalo instead? Much healthier alternative. But probably too dark to see them.

Agh! Nightmare. Just went downstairs to grab some toast and juice. Still in my PJ's. Mom and her gang are all sitting at the kitchen table, drinking coffee, laughing, telling stories, talking about their kids. It's her Saturday routine.

I heard them on the stairs and paused as I heard my name mentioned. By Mom.

"Courtney says she'll never date anyone again. No, wait—she says she won't this entire school year," she told her pals.

Everyone started laughing. What is so *funny* about having a little integrity?

"We'll see how long that lasts," Mrs. Brell snickered.

"Even if she won't date them, they'll want to date her," Mom said.

"Well, of course, I mean, look at her," Mrs. Lebeau said. "Her skin is so lovely. And her figure, and that copper red hair . . . I wish Mark would ask her out."

Gross! So much for wanting breakfast. Mark Lebeau? Is she insane? He's a sophomore, and he's skinnier than I am. He's also incredibly rich; they have a mansion practically, the biggest house in the neighborhood, and they have parties where they actually valet-park cars (but Mom makes us walk because it's so close).

Anyway, why do Mom and her friends want to talk about us? Why don't they talk about themselves and their own dates or husbands or whatever? Probably it would be boring, but at least it would be about them.

I'm going back to bed.

So Mom got us all digital pagers. She and her friends went out shopping Saturday after their coffee fest and had technological breakthroughs. There was a big special; buy 2 get 1 free. She was acting like she was doing this for us, but it's her thing. She's obsessed with phones, or not answering phones. She said the pagers are part of our new call block program. More like cell block—we're only allowed to receive one call a day, if we're lucky. I *want* to get calls.

It's almost like she used to date a telemarketer and that's why she hates them so much. They're just people with fast, annoying voices and a habit of mispronouncing names. What's the big deal?

Anyway, besides the pagers there are all these codes we have to use. And we have to punch in about 100 numbers to even reach her at work.

So there I was in the middle of math class, watching Rick Young at the blackboard. All of a sudden I started to get sort of hot. You know. Like I was attracted to him. There was this sort of buzzing sound under the desk, and I felt palpitations.

I never really liked Rick Young, but you know how your body sometimes has this will of its own, genetic needs, looking for the best mate, just like species in the wild, etc.

Then I realized it was my pager. I had set it to vibrate by mistake, instead of turning it off like I usually do in class.

It wasn't Rick Young, it was Grandma. She was checking to see if I got her Halloween card yet.

Damn. I thought in this weird way it meant I was ready to think about dating again, that I could be attracted to someone besides Dave. Apparently not.

I can, however, receive messages with up to 50 characters.

Hi, it's me. Courtney's Beth friend. (She used to say that when she was little, because she had a slight lisp. It became my nickname. That's the history, okay?) We're waiting for Courtney, who's only taking the longest shower in history. We commandeered her journal as punishment. We're going out tonight to celebrate her new role as vice president. I think it would be great if there was a coo and she took over Tom's job. But he'll never go for that, because he has to be the center of attention.

I guess I don't have much to say, so here's Jane. I hear music. I'm going to see what Bryan's up to.

This is Jane. And it's "coup," as in taking over something, not "coo" as in lovebirds whispering sweet nothings.

I kept a diary once. My mom found it and read it and got all worried because I had all this stuff written about *horses*. I loved horses. Not in that way, just—you know, I was 7. And she made me go to this kiddie psychologist and act all this stuff out with a My Pretty Pony and a Fisher-Price Barnyard and a Barbie. I swear, I'm not making this up. Ever since then I've been very reluctant to write stuff down.

All I wanted was a horse. To take lessons, wear those tan jodhpurs, carry a whip crop (which I'd never actually use). They thought that was twisted. So why did they rent me all those horse movies and buy me all those horse books?

Anyway. Now that I have a chance and a place to write in that my mother will never ever find, I can make a confession.

I still have my plastic Secretariat stashed in a shoe box under the bed.

So *ha ha*, Mom.

Courtney, back to you. By the way, I'm really glad you and

Dave broke up. You might not be, now. But you will be.

Cannot believe my journal was like . . . violated.
But the Jane thing explains why she keeps insisting senior class trip in spring be to a dude ranch.

Oprah did a show today on dealing with the mother-daughter relationship. Mom was unfortunately home with the flu and saw it. She put on a coat and rushed down to the bookstore and nearly bought out the mother-daughter section (is there such a thing?). She tried to give me a reading assignment when I got home.

"Mom. We get along *fine*," I said. Except when you're going ballistic about phone calls and insisting I just *try* the veal cutlet.

"What?" she said. "I can tell you're thinking something about me."

"I wasn't," I lied.

"Tell me," she said.

"Okay, well, I was just thinking how sometimes you don't understand why I don't want to eat meat. I mean, you understand, but you think it's just a temporary thing. And it isn't."

She nodded. "I did think it was a phase—at first. But I can see you're dedicated. Most of the time. I was just wondering whether your decision to not eat the lamb shanks I cooked that night last year . . . was a rejection of me."

"No," I said, thinking back to that momentous night when I decided to give up meat. Should I tell her that the mint jelly didn't help matters? "I just don't want to eat lambs. Or sheep. Or other things that walk around on legs."

She smiled faintly. "I wish you wouldn't phrase it like that. But okay. So what other issues do you have with me?"

"I don't have any issues. Period," I said.

"Are you sure?" she asked, like she *wanted* me to hate her for something. I don't. I wish she spent more money on herself and that she would lighten up sometimes, and that she'd go out on a date once more in her life, but I couldn't help her with that.

"I'm sure, Mom," I said. "Just relax. You're doing great." I gave her a little hug and then ran upstairs to my room. Escape!

So now she and Alison have been on the phone for like an *hour*, and I can't call anyone.

It's unlikely I'll have a breakthrough. A complete breakout, maybe. I'm sitting here staring at a stack of college catalogs and applications. They should come with complimentary tubes of zit cream.

"My most meaningful life experience was . . . (a) filling out this application, (b) taking the SATs, (c) getting my first computer, (d) deciding I'd rather manage a Truth or Dairy for eternity than fill this out."

Gerry keeps talking about expanding. And Beth and I have to not laugh, because the fact is that since he opened the shop a couple of years ago, he has to have gained about 30 pounds. He has this belly, the kind guys get when they drink a lot of beer. But with him, it's from coconut and kiwi and strawberry. The other day he said he could really see himself growing. We started to laugh, but then he added, "as a businessman and a pillar of the community."

"Do you want to be a chain?" Beth asked him. "Do you want to be all over the country?"

"Well . . . define *chain*," Gerry said.

"More than one," Beth said. "Linked together? With standardized napkins and recipes."

"I'd like to be a Colorado chain. Yes. I see that," Gerry said, as if he'd just called the psychic hot line. "But I want to grow in a healthy way. You two will help me, won't you?"

Afterward Beth and I went into the storeroom and just cracked up. "Sure we will," Beth said. "We'll put *diet coconut* in your smoothie."

"Don't forget the sugar-free strawberries," I said.

"He thinks fat-free is like . . . all there is to it," Beth said. "He's so wrong."

Most people are.

This is too embarrassing to write down. But so is almost everything lately, so here goes:

Mom asked me to pick up food for Oscar on the way home. So you know there's this pet shop at the other end of the strip mall from T or D—it's called Pet Me, which has all these weird connotations, so I used to think it was a sex-toy shop. I went in there after work and found the chow Oscar eats. I picked up this humongous bag—Mom only buys it forty pounds at a time. I was dragging it up to the cash register, clutching it like I would a small toddler, when I heard this familiar voice.

"Need some help carrying that? Hey, how's your dog?"

It was Grant. He had a Pet Me Staff shirt on, plus one of those weight lifter's belts. An interesting look. I'd forgotten I ran into him that day at Walgreens and told him about Oscar.

Well, okay, so I guess he wasn't *following* me. He works here. That's why I kept seeing him in the parking lot after work. I am such an idiot.

And that's why he has such big shoulders, it's not from sports or dietary supplements. It's from hauling forty-pound bags of pet food and cat litter.

"You know, we offer free delivery," Grant said. Now he tells me. "But I can help you with that now, if you want."

I was tempted, but sweat was running down the front of my shirt, about to mix in with the kibbles and make my own gravy.

I was so embarrassed I paid and ran out to the car. I realized my Grant-as-stalker theory was a bit off the mark. It isn't all about me and Dave. It's all about me being self-centered and oblivious and stupid.

Had to sprint into T or D today from parking lot. I'm so embarrassed about what I said to Grant. I skipped my class with him, my major life issue today being to avoid Grant. So humiliating. Thinking someone is stalking you when they work in the same strip mall. Not only that, but I've droned on and on to him about Dave, I'm sure he thinks I'm completely unbalanced, crazy, deluded. No wonder Dave would break up with me. All I could think about last night when I was trying to fall asleep was how Grant probably called Dave and told him what happened. Instead of giving him this cool image of me going on with my life, no problem, Dave has a new image: me thinking I am the bomb, that everyone wants to go out with me . . .

Okay, enough about that. Gerry wants to send me to some management class being held in a few weeks. He says he's following up on his idea of branching out, the store being a very successful concept, smoothies being trendy and all, while ice cream never goes out of style.

"Don't tell Beth," he whispered to me by the supplements. "She doesn't have management-quality potential."

She'll be crushed. I'm sure.

I'm calling her tonight to tell her, so she can deal with the pain privately.

I asked Gerry if it could wait until next summer—when I'll quit. He launched into some speech about the ideal smoothie shop, how the serving of cold fruit drinks side by side with rocky road is the yin/yang feng/shui harmony of food service. Completely off his rocky road.

"I'll pay for the class, and I'll pay you overtime for the hours you attend the class," he finally said.

Yes!

Something weird is going on with the Tom. I think he has ADD or something, well, especially when it comes to girls. Like he can't *focus* on which one he likes. Today he had three different gifts on his desk and couldn't remember which one he was supposed to give to whom. He kept pushing them around on his desk like he was doing that trick with 3 shells and a nut underneath. I don't know where he gets the money for all this; I guess he comes from money, because I know he doesn't work. I was waiting for my gift. Shouldn't he be giving me presents right about now?

We went over to Goat Mountain last week and issued our book-reading challenge in person (the principal already told them about it). They have two more weeks (plus) to get it done. The kids had a lot of funny questions, like: "What roof are you going to sleep on?" "Can we watch?" "Can we sleep on the roof?" and "Can't we throw cream pies at you guys instead?"

Then someone pointed out we'd be sleeping up there in November and how that's usually one of the coldest months and what if it snowed, wouldn't *that* be funny? I think they started reading as soon as we left the auditorium.

Dave called tonight. He said he just wanted to know how I was doing.

Did he mean that?

I can't believe it's been over two weeks since the last time I saw him. I'm starting not to miss him everywhere. It's nice. He asked if Tom had made a move on me yet. I told him not to insult me. Of course he hasn't, and of course he won't. He's too busy planning whose sleeping bag to sneak into after we lose the Goat Mountain challenge.

Goat Mountain Challenge. Isn't that a Disney movie?

Just woke up. Dreamt that I was sleeping on roof of Dave's house. Kept sliding off.

That was a dream within a dream. Woke up from that one into another one. Turned out I was trying to sleep on Flatirons, rocks with sharp angles, mountains above Boulder. I was up there to spy on Dave, had binoculars and was trying to find his dorm. Strap on binocs nearly strangled me.

Then I realized I was naked.

Oh yeah. I am really over him.

Had a last-minute emergency meeting today to talk about
Halloween party at school. A group of students submit-
ted a petition asking us to ban costumes. We can't *cancel*
Halloween. I'm sorry. It has these . . . themes. Scary ones.

In the meantime it is only 3 days away, and I have no
idea what I can go as. Last year Dave and I went to the
party together as Sonny and Cher—and there's no way I
can top that. I could be Cher, I guess. But that would be
really pathetic, even if in real life she was the one who
dumped him.

Maybe I can be a witch. Or wait—a dragon. Since my
secret is out. I could go as Princess Von Dragen. Sounds
good, but who is it?

The theme of the party at school is Trick or Treat. I
have to consider reassigning the head of the social committee. Her name is Laura, and she has no ideas. Period.

Called Alison to see if she has any costume ideas. She
was out. She's *always* out lately. So frustrating. She must
be practicing for a big concert.

I called Beth. I could have sworn I heard a guy talking
in the background, but she kept saying it was the TV and
she had to go because she was in the middle of watching
a show for a paper.

Jane picked out her costume last spring and wouldn't
understand leaving it to the last minute.

I was so desperate I even went to Bryan's room to ask
him for help. He wasn't home.

Oscar ran away. He got spooked by all the kids coming to the door and ringing the bell and screaming "Trick or Treat!" at Mom, who was wearing a belly dancer costume. A bit skimpy in my opinion, but she and her friends all went to this Act Your Shoe Size, Not Your Age party this afternoon, so Mom's feeling 8 1/2.

Since I got home from the party at school, we've been looking for Oscar all night—me, Mom, and Bryan. Probably the most time we've spent together since the summer. Mom drove; I ran alongside the car; Bryan kept yelling Oscar's name out the window until he was hoarse.

First we cursed the neighborhood—I mean coursed— on foot, then we drove to all his favorite places: the park, various Dumpsters, the grocery store, even Pet Me. No Oscar.

All the funny things that happened at the party seem kind of insignificant now. But still funny. I found this old costume of Alison's in the attic. She went as a cat a few years ago. Slight problem, I'm a size bigger than Alison, but the leopard material was stretchy and besides, it perfectly matched my new leopard print fuzzy slippers. I looked hot, maybe a little too hot though, sort of like a stripper.

Anyway, Jane was a figure skater, with a dress that had a billion sequins so she sparkled even more than usual and she had awesome four-inch-heel shoes that looked like skates. Beth was dressed as Smokey the Bear, which was really weird because Bryan was a firefighter so we kept asking if they had talked about using a fire *theme*. They kept swearing they hadn't. Bryan kept picking up Beth and pretending to carry her out of a burning building. It was hilarious.

I danced once with the Tom, but people kept grabbing my tail when I spun around and he got annoyed because I was getting more attention than him. Naturally he wasn't in costume. He's too cool for that. Right.

Beth, Jane, and I ran into Grant at the punch vat. He was dressed as a cowboy, he even had those leather chaps.

"You should be on a calendar," Jane told him as she looked him up and down.

"Courtney—I didn't recognize you," Grant said. "You look sort of . . . curvy."

Jane and Beth started laughing. Then Grant was smiling, too, like he was really enjoying embarrassing me for my Feline Stripper outfit.

It's really cold tonight. Seems like it always is on Halloween. Or maybe it's because I was wearing too-thin, stretchy material.

I hope Oscar finds a warm place. I hope he doesn't get caught by that leash guy, either. Crazy guy. Would probably jail Oscar for killing goats, like Oscar's ever killed anything. His food even scares him.

Oscar's never been gone this long before. I was a total mess at school today. I shut my hand in the door when I was leaving Mr. Arnold's classroom, then I almost started crying in the hallway. I think I might have even whimpered. So embarrassing.

Grant was right behind me and grabbed my arm. "What's wrong?"

"It's Oscar. He ran away." I pulled this old crinkly photo of Oscar out of my backpack and nearly started bawling. I took the picture when we brought Oscar home from the hospital after he got hit by the car.

"Oh? Oh no." Grant looked really worried. "Do you have any idea where he went? I mean, can I help you look for him?"

"Why, do you know all the dog hangouts?" I snapped.

He looked sort of hurt. I realized I must have sounded a little harsh and insensitive. Which is sort of typical for me these days.

"I'm sorry, I didn't mean *you* would know. Because you're a dog or something. Because you're not, at all, believe me, I wasn't implying—I just thought, well, you work at that pet shop—"

"It's okay, Courtney." He put his hand on my arm again. "I know you're upset. Do you want to look for Oscar after school together?"

"I can't—I have to work," I said. So he promised he'd look around his neighborhood and call some people and see if they'd heard anything about a sort of gray and brown and black mutt.

I was making a Silly Sherbet for a kid today (I hate when people order it and say "Sherbert", like "sure, Bert!") when there was a slobbery thing on the glass in front of me. You know, like spit, smeared back and forth over the sherbet tub? I hate when people let their kids actually drool while they're deciding what to order.

"Listen, kid, do you mind?" I started to say.

Then I saw this gigantic tongue. Something gray—fur— OSCAR!

I leapt over the counter and hugged him before Gerry could tell me it was all a giant health code violation waiting to happen, and before Oscar could lunge for this little boy's strawberry sugar cone he was eyeing, mouth open.

Grant followed me outside. I was so grateful I thought about hugging him, too, but he didn't exactly have that huggable look. "Where did you find him?" I asked.

"By the pasta factory. Apparently he got sort of mesmerized by the flashing red ziti-shaped lights. You know what? I think maybe he needs a new diet."

"More pasta?" I asked.

Grant shrugged. "Maybe. It couldn't hurt."

I played with Oscar's frayed green collar. I didn't really see how new food could clip years of brain fur off his life, so I didn't say anything.

Funny. Dave never knew where to find Oscar.

Grant just drove around, block after block, for like *hours*.

I opened the door tonight to Mr. Novotny from across the street. The yard/Broncos-obsessed man is about 60, bald, with big square glasses. And very, very single as a direct result, as far as I can see.

"I don't know who Dave is," he said, "but would you tell him to stop calling?"

How embarrassing. Not only is Dave calling me (*why?*) but he's getting Mr. Novotny.

"Is Dave the guy with the red Jeep? Who used to be over here all the time?" he asked.

"Um . . . yeah," I said. Thanks for reminding me. "We broke up, but—"

"Good. And I don't want you to get back together with him!"

"Um . . . really? Why not?"

"His driving is frightening. I've star CSP'ed him at least twice."

*CSP is this cellular direct connection to the state police. But it's not a *verb*.

Mr. Novotny has a cell phone? Mr. Novotny has road rage? I've never even seen him leave the perimeter of his yard. He mostly mows his lawn on a riding mower that he's painted in Bronco colors. Except in winter when he shovels snow with a Broncos snowblower. And puts up his orange-and-blue Broncos season lights on the front porch.

"Well, um, what did he do, exactly?" I asked.

"His parking is atrocious. But that's not the point," Mr. Novotny said. "He shouldn't drive so fast. He nearly hit me on the Field Captain."

"Mom?" I called over my shoulder. Save me!!!

She came out and explained how she'd asked for this new phone feature to block out calls. When MegaPhone installed it, they must have crossed the lines or something. It's called call control plus. Which to me sounds like queen-sized panty hose.

"More like control minus," Mr. Novotny grumbled.

"No wonder we haven't heard the phone ring in a few days!" Mom laughed. "But I kind of enjoyed the vacation from the telemarketers. Sorry for the inconvenience—we'll get it taken care of tomorrow," she told Mr. Novotny.

It's weird we didn't notice, but I guess I've been busy. Plus, I always call Beth—it just works that way between us.

That wasn't good enough for him. He wants us to run a really long extension cord across the street so the phone will ring in our house instead of his. Mom pointed out it might get run over. She apologized over and over.

Mr. Novotny finally said he'd ignore his "land line" and instead use the cell phone he carries on his mower. And uses mostly to report bad drivers.

I called Dave to see why he kept calling. He sounded very annoyed. I asked if I was bothering him or interrupting him—maybe he was studying for an exam or something. He said no. Then he asked why I was calling him now, why I was bothering to take the time out of my busy schedule as vice president. Huffy like a bike.

I told him maybe if MegaPhone fixed our line, his calls wouldn't keep going to Mr. Novotny's house and maybe I'd have a clue he called.

"What are you talking about?"

"Our phone. It's been broken, and we didn't know. And um . . . this is really funny. Do you want to hear it?"

I started laughing.

"Wait a second. Mr. Novotny?" Dave laughed. "The Broncos mower guy? *He* heard my messages? No. Please tell me that isn't true."

"Why? What did you say?"

"Never mind, what did *he* say?"

"He's called the police about your driving. You went too fast and it somehow messed up his lawn ornaments, sent all the whirligig things into a whirl."

We kept laughing and talking about how weird Mr. Novotny was, how he was the kind of person who might flip out one day. But instead of everyone saying afterward that "he was such a nice neighbor," they'd probably say, "the signs were there all along."

Then Dave said, "So do you want to come up here or not?"

I do. So I am. Tomorrow.

But why is he always calling and writing just when I really am *not* thinking about him? Like, at all? He has this sixth sense or something.

Room 314. Welcome to *My* World.

I'm sitting outside in the hall, thank you very much. Dave's not here. If I sit outside and wait, I'll miss him—too many entrances and exits.

I look ridiculous.

People are playing hacky-sack around me.

I know, I'll call him and tell him I'm waiting outside . . . in the car . . .

Hold on, I hear laughs in the stairwell. Sounds like Dave.

It isn't. There's a guy with pink hair approaching Room 314. I think he just said my name.

It's Chad.

LATER . . .

Still can't believe what happened. Puff Chaddy knew me because Dave told him I was coming plus he has a photo of me over his desk. (!) (Dave, not Chad, that is.) Chad said he'd been looking forward to meeting me. Then he put on some really loud music, a rapper I didn't recognize, so loud the walls were shaking. He got out his lighter. I thought he was going to smoke something, but he lit this patchouli incense and lay on his bed and said he had to unwind after organic chemistry.

"What's organic about that?" I tried to joke.

He didn't get it. Or he wasn't in the mood to laugh. Dave came back about ten minutes later, and he tiptoed into the room, took my hand, and we tiptoed out. I asked him what was going on with the Puffster. Dave said he's incredibly driven to be a doctor.

"Dr. Puff?" I said. We laughed really hard. Dave showed me around the campus and when we ran into Alicia from our school, she didn't even blink, she was just totally excited to see us together.

It all seemed normal, except when the afternoon was over and Dave said something about studying and it was clear I was supposed to leave and clear we were still just friends. I tried not to make a crack about his 6-month plan. I failed.

I left in a huff. I was halfway out of town when I realized I was the one being rigid, sophomoric, etc. So I went back to apologize.

Stood in hallway outside his room, staring in at Dave and some girl. He was laughing and having the time of his life.

Unreal! I am so unbelievably hurt. I can't even write any more. I can't even call Beth or Jane and tell them. It's humiliating. Was I the 3 P.M.–6 P.M. date?

Is that part of the New Plan?

I cornered Grant after class again. I needed more insight. A guy's perspective. Plus, I was hoping he could identify the suspicious laughing girl in Dave's dorm room.

"So why would he ask me to come up, say he missed me, etc. and then be with some other girl?"

"Maybe she's just a friend?" Grant could tell he sounded lame, so he didn't go on. He didn't even put any heart into the comment.

"Do guys like torturing us or something?" I asked. "I mean, is it sort of *fun* deep down?"

"No, of course not," Grant said. "But people get, um, conflicted I guess. You know, when they want two things at once?"

No, I don't know. You either want something, or you don't. Like me and *dating*.

Speaking of conflict: the Tom keeps buying stuff for our office: plants, pens, posters. Things Beginning With "P" For $100, Alex. I think this must be out of frustration that he hasn't scored with me yet, or else he's really into interior design and can't admit it.

Still really mad at Dave. Jane and Beth and I are going shopping tonight; screw sitting around and waiting for the phone calls.

No messages? What is his *problem*? Too busy laughing with his 6 P.M.–overnight girlfriend?

The Tom continues to amaze. Today we had this table in the cafeteria set up so that people could sign up for Homecoming activities and buy tickets for the party, etc. While we're sitting there (after he eats 4 cheeseburgers in 5 minutes) he's working on his college apps. And every single (pretty) girl that comes up gets the same question, as he bats his so-long-I'm-jealous-of-them eyelashes. "Hey, could you help me with this section? What do *you* think are my three best qualities?"

The girls take it really seriously and crouch down by the table and offer suggestions like, "You have a strong leadership quality," and "You take charge," and "You're responsible," etc. etc. blah blah blah. Then after a while he switches to asking what his three best features are, whether it's his eyes, or his perfect nose, or his amazingly huge . . . ego.

He offers the really pretty girls back rubs for helping him, and our student council table turns into one of those 5-minute back rub carts at the mall. And I have to listen to him say, "Well, you know this works a lot better skin-on-skin" about a dozen times while *I* do all the work, sell tickets, make change, etc.

Finally, the bell rang. I thought we'd get out of there but then remembered there was one more lunch period to go.

"So I could probably help you with your applications," I finally offered. "You don't need to give me a back rub."

"Oh. Yeah?" He actually looked sort of interested for a second.

"Sure. I mean, if you want to thank me, you could just go straight to the full-body massage," I suggested.

The Tom stared at me, beyond shocked. "Oh. Well, actually, my applications are sort of like . . . done. But, um, thanks, Court." Then he ran off for a glass of chocolate milk.

What? After all these years I decide to flirt with him, and he has the nerve to not flirt back?

I complained to Beth and Jane about it after school.

"He probably doesn't want to mess up your . . ." Beth stopped, not able to think of the right word.

"Presidential relationship," Jane said. "Like he messed it up with Jennifer. If you leave, then he'll have to find another VP, and he's already had two—"

"He hasn't *had* me yet," I said. "And we're not going out, I don't want to go out with him. I just think it's ridiculous that he doesn't even try."

"Maybe he's not attracted to you," Jane said. "It happens."

"We're talking about the Tom," I reminded her.

"Oh."

Nobody said anything else. It was too awful to suggest Tom wasn't attracted to me. That would be like saying I was dead. But I bet he's into that, too. He's attracted to everyone, alive or dead, except me.

Then I realized I was being ridiculous. My whole life I'd wanted the Tom to avoid me. So he was. So what? He's a ridiculous person who looks good, and that's it. It's time to focus on something besides boys.

Got in the car and drove to see the buffalo. Stared over the fence at them. Life would be better if I were a buffalo. They all look alike, more or less, and even if they don't, they mate regardless of looks. Of course I'd have to wear the same hooves every day.

Finally talked to Dave today. As it turns out . . . that girl he was laughing with is his resident adviser in his dorm. She came up to talk to him because everyone is getting kind of concerned about Chad. He's been experimenting in his chemistry class a little too much, making things that aren't on the lab assignment, etc. Everyone was worried he was stressed out and making something dangerous. So they did an Organic Intervention.

Turned out he was trying to invent a new line of organic hair coloring. He's so stressed because he doesn't want to be a doctor, he wants to be a stylist. His parents won't accept that he wants to be a hair doctor, not a surgeon.

"Does CU offer a cosmetology degree? Or is he going to drop out?" I asked. And did you have to laugh so hard with her, when I was standing in the hallway? We used to be able to *sense* each other's presence.

"Come up tomorrow," Dave said.

"I can't," I said. I told him about the Smoothie Seminar I'm attending tomorrow night. Then we laughed again.

It's 7:30 P.M. and I'm sitting in the Matterhorn Conference Room at the Rockies Swiss Alps Inn (does that strike anyone else as redundant?). There are about 26 other people here for the smoothie management course. We're going around the room bonding over questions like: "If you could be one additive, what would you be and why?"

I tried really hard not to laugh. One guy said he'd be creatine. I said I'd be ginseng—no, wait—bee pollen. Because more people are allergic to that.

"If you had to classify yourself as a drink, are you milky, tart, smooth, or citrus?"

"I'm a milky tart," I said. Because you know. I can't really be *defined* by these *limited* terms.

Claude (a/k/a Clod), the director of this panel (a/k/a Claude the Fraud) is giving me these looks, like I'm dissing the juicing phenomenon and ought to be run through the blender myself.

We're moving on to motivational skills now. I'd better pay attention. I can't even motivate myself, much less someone else.

We all went out to eat tonight—student council "we," I mean. The Tom insisted on going to this place near Golden because they serve Rocky Mountain Oysters, i.e., bull you-know-whats. He probably thinks they'll make him more virile, like he needs help in that department.

Maybe he does. Maybe that's what all this is about. A desperate attempt to—

Nah.

Anyway, it was sort of fun. I told him it was a horrible thing to eat. Did he know how tortured a bull had to feel when he had them cut off? Did he think that was right? I asked how he'd feel if someone cut off *his* major organ.

The menu consisted of things that turned my stomach. Chicken fingers. I always picture a poor chicken's pathetic little claw being fried up. Who wants to order fingers, anyway? Are we all cannibals at heart? At least they call a wing a wing, except for Buffalo Wings. I bet buffaloes wish they had wings. They could fly away and not become burgers.

I ordered a salad. Oil and vinegar. Very boring, shredded carrots and a radish the only saving graces. "You've got to loosen up," Tom said as he glanced over at my meal. "Live a little."

"Oh, yeah? What do you suggest?" I asked.

He held his plate toward me.

"No. Thanks. Really," I said.

We made final arrangements for Homecoming and Tom said not to worry about cost. This should be the biggest, best ever. There's plenty of money in the budget, so we can go ahead and have a parade, a rally, a dance, etc.

"The theme will be . . . coming home," Laura actually said. She needs a brain infusion.

I wonder if Dave is coming home for it. I want to know, but I don't want to ask. Of course he *should*. He's close by. But it might be too much of a commitment for him, making that long drive.

Grant asked if I wanted to eat lunch today. Of course I did. I mean, why wouldn't I eat lunch, I practically live for the meal. But with him? Just us? The concept sort of freaked me out, so I ended up saying something really stupid. "What section would we sit in?" I asked.

"Do you really care?" He sort of laughed at me.

"No. *No*," I said.

"We'll sit outside," Grant said. All cool about it, like it was no big deal. So it wasn't, I told myself. It's not a date or anything—just a sort of calorie-sharing plan. "I'll go get some sandwiches and then meet you by the fountain, okay?" he said. "Ham and cheese okay?"

Not okay! The fountain is where Dave and I used to eat lunch. I know where every bird dropping is. But what could I do? I went outside and waited. Looking pathetic. All the still-together couples stared at me like I was clinging to the past like bird crap to granite.

Grant came out with our lunch. I took out the cheese and then the ham. I basically had a mustard sandwich going. On white. I tried not to let him see me toss the ham and cheese part, but he noticed.

"Oh, I forgot," Grant said. "Dave told me you don't eat that. Sorry."

"It's okay," I told him. "Don't worry about it."

"So when did you quit eating meat and cheese?" Grant asked. He kept looking at his sandwich like he shouldn't eat it. "After a really bad sub?"

"*No*," I said, laughing. I loved the way he made a joke out of it.

We talked about Oscar. Grant asked how we named

him, and if it was from my intense love of the Academy Awards.

"I don't love any awards show," I said. "What are you talking about?"

"And the Oscar goes to . . ." he kept saying in this really deep fake announcer voice, and we both kept laughing really hard.

Every time he lifted up his straw to use as a microphone, and did this silly pose, the muscle in his dog-food-lifting arm rippled.

Did I just use the word rippled to describe something other than a potato chip?

What is happening to me? Maybe I need to get out more.

Afterward he told me he has a golden retriever and two cats and one of them belongs to his grandmother who lives with them now and the two cats don't get along blah blah blah. It wasn't boring, it was just that I stopped listening at some point because I had to focus on myself. I was starting to feel like (a) I was on a date, and (b) I really wanted to be on this date and (c) I was attracted to Grant and (d) I would be breaking my rule really soon if I kept this up.

Wrong! No pledge broken. This wasn't a date. This was a lunch that didn't taste very good. This was a discussion about pets. Animals, my real passion. And I'm not interested in Grant.

But then why did the phrase "Pet Me" keep going through my head?

Stupid Question of the Day:

"There's this long-distance company that offers free ice cream when you sign up. Are you guys in on that deal?"

Beth and I looked at each other and then back at the guy asking. "No. But there's a pay phone outside the fabric store over there."

He went outside and nearly got run over by one of the Guccheez Pizza (they were Gucci's but they got sued) delivery guys. He leapt to the sidewalk, fell, and scraped up his hands. I went out to see if he was okay, and I saw Grant in the parking lot, so I waved to him. He smiled and waved back. I started thinking how I feel about Grant. (Pet me! Pet me!)

But there's no point. I'll go away to college. He won't. Or maybe he will, but not to the same place. And then what? Forget it. I'd probably just end up blowing him off like Beth did, and he doesn't need to get rejected by both best friends.

"Could I get a Band-Aid or something from you people?" the guy yelled up at me. "Or does your store offer nothing to the public?"

Whoa. Talk about an unhappy customer. I brought him back to the store, made him a Mind Soother (with antianxiety herb additives), put extra ice on his hands, and let him use Beth's cell phone. And stopped thinking about Grant.

Those stupid kids at Goat Mtn. read all the books by November 15. Now I have to sleep on the roof with the Tom. All night.

We were supposed to do it on Friday night, but this Friday is Homecoming (duh) and next Friday is Thanksgiving (duh). So much for using a calendar. They said we could do it now, or wait for a Friday in December, which sounds like a really bad idea. So we're camping on the Goat Mountain school roof tomorrow night, and we'll get to miss our early Wednesday morning classes and our teachers will supposedly understand.

But will they understand the hell I've gone through, sleeping outside with the Tom? I can't imagine. I don't want to imagine.

"I have one of those sleeping bags that wraps around you like a burrito," he said to Laura, our social committee director, after our meeting broke up today. (Still need to fire her, by the way.) "It's big enough for two."

"Really?" Laura asked. "What do you mean? It's a tortilla? That's kind of gross."

"No, it's just that style. We can roll up together," he said.

"Oh." She shrugged. "We can?"

Yeah, and then we can all vomit over the edge of the roof.

There's going to be Mrs. Martinez, Principal LeDucque, and the rest of the student council up there. Does he seriously think he's going to score, on a roof, surrounded by people, as part of an "increased literacy" program?

Sexual literacy, *maybe*.

"Up on the roof . . ."

Someone keeps singing that annoying tune. I'm going to kill him, whoever he is, even though he has a good voice and can pull it off.

The Tom is pretending we're camping. He's telling ghost stories. The scariest part of the story is how bad he is at telling it.

It's so cold out here. And the air has that smell, like snow is coming. Bitter and sort of damp. Whose idea was this, anyway?

Oh. Right.

From this school high atop Goat Mountain (which is in reality a small hill, on top of which is this rectangular building and a bronze goat sculpture), I am looking down at a billion identical subdivision houses. A sea of lights. They're not very attractive, but the fact they have lights makes them look really warm and inviting on a night like this.

I just looked at my watch. It's only seven o'clock.

I think I should have worn more clothes. Why was I trying to look good? Should have worn 3 pairs of long underwear.

Have to stop writing. Hand is becoming frostbitten.

The first snowflakes just started falling.

THE NEXT MORNING, BACK HOME . . . FINALLY THAWED

"So Courtney. This was *your* idea." That's how Principal LeDucque greeted me. She was wearing a big knit Avalanche hat. While she was glaring at me, snowflakes started hitting her eyelashes. She had a megamug of coffee in her mittened hands.

"At least we're getting good publicity," I said. A few reporters had shown up. We'd been photographed earlier, when it was still light out. Cars full of Goat Mtn. Canyon students kept pulling up to check on us—and laugh. Their parents even laughed.

"Yes, I guess so," she said. Then she smiled. "And it is a good cause." She put down her mug and started rubbing her hands together as she gazed up at the snowy night sky. "I'm afraid we won't get much sleep tonight."

"No, probably not." So I suggested we go ahead and have our next student council meeting now—after all, the entire student council was up there. We huddled by the big square heater vent and talked about how not to dare the middle school again.

"So I suppose it's time to turn in," Mrs. Martinez said. "If anyone is too chilly, let me know. We can call for additional supplies."

Everyone seemed okay. I couldn't admit to her that *I* was the unprepared one. I looked around for my sleeping bag. Turned out that it was right next to Tom's. He had me on one side and Laura on the other. He was explaining his sleeping bag to her. Actually she needed some help with her own. She's a bit slow on the uptake. On any uptake.

"You guys might want to, you know, *move*," I suggested. Because I didn't want to be around when they wrapped their burrito.

"We have a great spot," Tom said. "What's the problem?"

"N—nothing," I said. My teeth were already chattering. I got into my sleeping bag and zipped it up. They were talking for a while, but then they both drifted off to sleep.

Snow was still coming down. I pulled my hat tighter on my head and scrunched into a ball. That didn't help. Mom bought budget sleeping bags for us, and I swear, this one was only rated to 60 degrees. It was designed for sleeping on the floor of a well-heated family room. In front of a roaring fire in the fireplace.

I heard snoring and looked over at the Tom. I didn't have a choice. I told myself that if he woke up, I'd have to deal with whatever happened. And maybe it wouldn't be so awful. If anything happened, it would be meaningless and vapid, not like anything real.

I really slowly and carefully (hands frozen, didn't work very well) unzipped my sleeping bag. Then I unzipped his. Sleeping bag, that is. Then I tried to zip them together but my shirt sleeve got caught in the zipper and I couldn't get it out. I must have spent half an hour struggling with that cheap icy zipper. I was muttering and swearing and Tom still didn't wake up. So I moved a little closer to him.

And then the next thing I knew I woke up with snow on my face and I was spooning right next to Tom.

I heard him say, "Good morning." I quickly checked to see if my clothes were on. They were. I said, "Good morning" back, and he turned around like the devil had spoken.

"Oh! I thought you were Laura," he said.

"Sorry," I said. "My sleeping bag is so thin. I sort of . . . had to."

"Oh. Well, whatever." He got out of the sleeping bag and stretched his arms over his head. The sun was coming out, and the air felt a lot warmer already.

"This is so *cool*," Tom said. We sat on the edge of the roof, ate donated donuts that were dropped off by someone's parents, and looked out at the sunrise.

I kind of felt like we were in that IMAX *Everest* movie. Only we didn't have to hike up more than Goat Hill, there was plenty of oxygen, and nobody died.

"This was harder than I thought," I told Tom. "I didn't really think about the fact it would be November."

"Yeah. But we made it. And you know why? You're a survivor, Courtney. Just like me." Tom slapped me on the back. "Don't worry. I won't tell anyone how you came on to me last night."

"I didn't come on to you," I said. "I was trying to avoid hypothermia."

"Okay, fine, whatever you say." Tom took another donut. "*We* know what really happened."

I have to run to school now—I'm late late late!

Beth and I were at work today. She kept disappearing on me. Like she'd start to go outside, sneaking through the supply room, and then she'd stop. And come back. But finally she did go outside, so once I had a free second I went to find her.

She was standing outside, with her back pressed against the wall like she was trying to hide. And she was SMOKING.

"Have you ever done something that you thought maybe you shouldn't be doing?" she asked me.

"Hel-lo. Like *smoking?*" I almost screamed. What were we, Truth, Dairy, and Nicotine now?

"I'm sorry," she said. "I can't help myself."

"Are you serious?" I said. "That's all you've been talking about lately, how much you *can* help yourself and control your life."

She just took another drag.

"Beth! Snap out of it," I said. "You don't need to smoke. Remember all that junk you said about steps and addiction? And those disgusting black grilled-lung photos and—I mean, do you realize how many *hours* you spent lecturing on the evils of smoking?" I tried to grab the cigarette from her hand, but it was impossible.

"I still believe in that," Beth said. "But sometimes you have to be yourself."

"Yeah. Whatever." I can't believe her!

Beth again. Courtney tries to hide this now, but we found it under her computer keyboard. This needs to be documented: we're all going to a big party shortly, at Keith's house. Homecoming! Whoo-hoo. Like I care. I can think of many things I'd rather be doing. (Not smoking. Not smoking. I slipped up, but I've confronted my feelings and faced my problems head-on and that won't happen again.)

Tom made this point of personally asking Courtney and then repeating himself like 6 times. So we're all calling it a date. Except Courtney. She's claiming to be only going because we are and because it's good for the student council for her to be seen in public. And because Dave might be there, and she only saw him for about 5 minutes today, and he said he'd "see us tonight," but I could tell he wasn't coming.

Anyway, come on, if Tom asked me 6 times? I'd know he was interested in me. Especially since they bonded after their Winter Wonderland roof adventure.

Courtney is spending a lot of time getting dressed when you consider she hates the Tom. What do you think, Jane?

Look, Beth—*you* dressed nicely when *you* went out with the Tom.

I didn't know I was going to go out with him. We didn't go out, anyway. We made out in like . . . the coat closet.

And on the street. And outside the house. And on the sidewalk.

He was a good kisser. What can I say?

More than that!!!

Tom said things. Nice things. About my hair. My sweater. Junk like that.

Your sweater? Oh, gag, I think I'm going to be sick.

You don't get it, Jane. Nobody gets it until it happens to them.

Exactly why Courtney is wearing her favorite shirt and that flowered mini that looks so good on her. Oops, time to shove this back where we found it so she doesn't kill us this time.

Chapter Number 57
In Which the Tom Lives Up to His Name; Or Not

Yes, I'm home early, and I can't believe Jane and Beth stole this to write in *again*. I'll get them both their own blank books for Christmas. Hold on, let me write that on my list. Okay, so I'm back.

What was I thinking? Was I just dressing up to look good because Dave might be there? He wasn't there. I pretty much knew he wouldn't be—like he was too cool now to go to a (long-distance) high-school party. That sort of made me mad, but I sort of expected it. Anyway.

Did I just want Tom to notice me, like those guys said? I guess so. He'd been acting like I was an asexual ugly freshman. (Okay, like I *still was* one. Because it's true, the apple doesn't fall far from the divorce tree and when I was 14 I had braces and a bad attitude and custody hearings to attend.) And you can't come on to every straight female (like he even asks whether they're straight or not) in Colorado and *not* come on to *me*. So okay, I was flirting a little. But did that give him the right?

We were standing in the kitchen, near the fridge. We were laughing about the sleep-a-thon, how we should have volunteered to sleep in the bookmobile, no, wait, drive it. Or we could have sat in one of those tanks with the bull's-eye and gotten dunked.

He hopped on the counter and said he'd like to see me in the dunk tank, like in this challenging tone, as if I deserved it because I've been so impossible to deal with lately. I sort of leaned against him. Then I got the idea that wasn't it. It was more about me in a wet T-shirt. And I sort of liked that he thought that. Maybe I'm just desperate and need someone to notice me, maybe it was time to end this self-imposed no-dating rule. I mean, I technically don't eat meat, and the other day I had another of Oscar's hot dogs—okay, that was a really bad analogy. But you can't be pure wheatgrass, meat free and clear, all the time.

But wait, that slip doesn't even count, because hot dogs aren't even technically *meat*.

Okay, so back to the story. So then Tom said the party was lame and we might as well go do layout together, it would be more fun. He meant yearbook layout; I knew that, but he didn't *say* it like that, and besides, he was sort of playing with my hair when he said it. I felt like everything was leading to one foregone conclusion. So when he said he was going to the coat closet I said I would go with him—of course. Because I was thinking about it, and at least with Tom, it wouldn't *mean* anything, it would never be a dating relationship for more than a few days anyway, so I wouldn't break my rule.

When I walked over to the closet, Beth was dancing in the living room, waving her arms frantically. I think she had too much coffee at work today. It was really weird. She was just hanging with Jane, not trying to hook up with a guy or anything. Totally unlike her.

The closet was packed, unlike the party. We sort of bumped into each other when we went for our coats. Something could have happened right there. But it didn't. We put on our coats and then he walked me to my car and I kept waiting for him to do something. And it was really cold. So eventually I felt really stupid and I just got into the Bull and drove home. Alone. Him not following me. He probably went back into the party and picked up someone else.

What the?

Would it be so awful to make a move on me? Since when is playing with someone's hair *okay* if you don't plan on kissing them later? Maybe he wasn't playing with it, maybe he was taking a tortilla chip crumb out of it. Still!

What am I talking about? It's Tom. *The* Tom. Like I *care*.

Dave called this morning. He started off by saying, "Yes, is Mr. Novotny in, please?" That was pretty funny. He said he was sorry about not meeting me at the party the night before. I was glad he hadn't been there—he would have seen me get blown off by Tom, which is something that's like never happened before. Ever. It would have been really humiliating. Then again, if Dave had been there, I might not have wanted anything to happen with Tom. Not sure.

Then Dave said he really wanted to talk to me, but it was hard with all those people around. And he knew I was leaving town for Thanksgiving in a few days, so could I come up there?

But when I got there, he had nothing to say. Maybe it was because Chad was giving this other guy a haircut and a platinum bleach in the room. We didn't exactly have much privacy.

"Then, Dave," I said, trying to be mature, "why did you call me?"

"I miss you?" he said with a sort of shrug.

There was this unbelievably awkward silence. I kept playing with this tassel thing on his bedspread. He's had this blue-and-white-checked bedspread since he was 8. He's the only boy I know who has one at all in his dorm room—not that I know a lot of guys with dorm rooms, but. You get the picture. I think his was actually a table-cloth once upon a time.

"So do you want to get something to eat?" one of us finally said. We ended up walking over to the Hill. We were leisurely strolling along when I saw an empty storefront and a giant sign: DENVER'S VERY OWN TRUTH OR DAIRY—COMING SOON TO BOULDER! WATCH THIS SPACE!

How could Gerry do that to me? I mean, how could he do it without telling me—and Beth? I hate when people do things without telling me! What is he thinking, anyway? Okay, we're a popular store, but I think what makes us special is there's just one of us.

Dave was psyched, though. Can't wait for his favorite smoothie to be back in town.

We walked around, and it seemed like it used to be between us, but it wasn't. We were all limp-like, droopy, lifeless. Especially when we went to say good-bye and gave each other this half hug. Our relationship (if we still have one? If we have one again?) needs a high-energy power powder infusion. The more bee pollen, the better. Any kind of pollen.

Maybe we should just let it die.

So Dave called tonight while I was in the middle of my new Turbo Yoga (it's the pumped-up version of relaxation) tape and told me he's been seeing someone. He was trying to tell me all day, but he didn't know how. That's why he didn't go to the party—he had to go back to Boulder to see her. "But it's no big deal," he said. "It isn't anything serious."

I sat there clutching the phone wondering why I'd ever given him my control plus code. This felt more like out-of-control. Sweat was running down my wrist. I started writing things with it on my forearm, like YOU SUCK. But I ran out of sweat.

I hate being told important (ugly, horrible) news on the phone! I hate it whenever and wherever I get it. Especially when it's from Dave.

I asked if it was that resident adviser person. He said no, it's someone else, a sophomore. Then he actually started to *tell* me about her, like I wanted to know, like I'd asked. I hung up as soon as I could.

I flashed back to the night in August out by the BBQ when he told me he wanted to be free and clear. Is dating someone else being free and clear?

I had him so close to a burning hot fire that night. Why didn't I *do* something?

I HATE HIM!

When I got to work, completely dragging my heels, fifteen minutes late, I asked Gerry why he hadn't told us about the new store. He said he wanted to surprise us—also, the lease almost fell through. But he said more exciting details would be coming soon. I asked if he meant more stores. He said we were going to start offering more choices "within the Truth or Dairy tradition of good fruit and good food."

How about the Truth or Dairy tradition of crazy owners?

Jane picked me and Beth up from work. We went to this new coffee place where we could be guaranteed privacy—it's in one of those new developments where they don't even have street names yet. We barely found our way in. But Jane has this nose for coffee, she could probably find her way to Starbucks if it was located in a landfill. Survival instinct.

"We shouldn't even be here," Jane said. "We should be somewhere we can meet guys. Because that's what you need, Courtney—a new guy."

"No, I don't think so," I said. I started building an anthill of raw sugar on the table.

"Listen to us. Dave's seeing someone else. So should you," Beth said.

"I can't," I said. "I told you guys, I don't want a relationship this year. I'm not looking for a boyfriend."

"Come on. Don't be silly." Jane tossed a stirrer at me. "You said that in the heat of the moment—"

"Ahem, you have it in writing," I said. "I wouldn't have written it down if I didn't mean it. That's why I'm vice

405

president with the Tom, that's why—"

"Courtney, come on. It was funny when you said it," Beth said. "Remember? We laughed about it. I told you about the advantage of flings, remember?"

"It wasn't funny to me," I said. "I was completely serious. Look, you guys. I appreciate what you're saying. But could we just complain about Dave and not talk about me? Because I'm not changing my mind. I never change my mind once it's made up. Can I have a sip of your latte?"

Beth and Jane looked at each other.

"What?" I said.

"Oh, um, nothing. Here." Beth pushed her cup toward me.

"So do you want to eat lunch together?" Grant asked me today.

Unbelievable! I glared at Grant. He *knew*. He had to know. And he never mentioned a word to me about Dave seeing someone new! And I was supposed to be nice to him? And he expected me to wait until he got his lunch, then eat a mustard sandwich, and suffer through his sympathetic looks and I-knew-before-you sighs?

"I can't believe you," I said. "I thought you were like . . . my friend. Sort of."

"I am. Sort of," Grant said.

What? Was he my friend, or wasn't he? "With the emphasis on the sort of," I said.

"What's that supposed to mean?" he asked.

"I don't know. Like I told you a hundred times, Grant, I don't understand guys. Especially you!" I said.

"What are you talking about? What did I do?" Grant asked.

I glared at him. I was seething. All that overly dramatic stuff because I felt so incredibly humiliated and he had a part in all this. Then I said something I probably shouldn't have.

"So now I know why your nickname is Lake Superior."

He stared at me like he'd never heard that before.

"It's because you're so like . . . gray and vast and *cold*. You sink ships. You don't care about anyone!" Then I stormed off down the hall. Then I realized I forgot my courier bag, which was in the student council office. I hate not being able to exit when I want to.

I ran up the stairs. Tom was sitting at his desk, being

presidential. He was writing checks to pay for the New Year's party we're planning—we need to make deposits on all this stuff.

"Courtney, I thought you left," he said.

"I wish," I said.

"Where are you going again?" he asked.

"Nebraska," I said. "I told you ten times—"

"Where in Neb—" he started to say.

"Yeah, well, *bye*!" I ran out of there before he could talk to me about the fun vacation he had planned.

Thank God it's Thanksgiving (is that redundant or what) vacation. I really really really really need to get out of here and away from all these jerks!

This will probably be illegible. I am writing with ice-cold hands—and gloves on. So is Bryan, in a notebook. He won't show me what, though. I asked and he got all snippy about it.

"You're not keeping a *journal*, are you?" I asked.

"Shut up," he said. "Anyway, if you can, why can't I?"

I don't know. He just can't.

We're sitting in the Taurus. We're stuck. The Bull is not going anywhere. And there is a certain contingent in the car right now who think this is all my fault: Bryan, Mom, and Oscar.

Never mind that there's a severe blizzard happening. That the road is closed now. The problem is that we skidded off the road because I was going too fast for the conditions and also I was thinking too much about Dave and last Thanksgiving and Dave and this Thanksgiving and what I was doing with my life, and how he was seeing someone new but that didn't upset me as much as my fight with Grant, but why did I have to keep thinking about Grant, plus I kept eating jelly bean after jelly bean, I was on quite the sugar rush.

Next thing I knew there was this 18-wheeler in front of me and I swerved to miss it and I went off the road in this long skid and thwacked into a snowbank. There's a billboard for a Motel 6 in the distance, but no Motel 6. We're way too far from anywhere to walk, as if we could. Lots of other cars are stranded, too—when the blowing snow lets up, it's going to be *hours* before anyone comes for us.

Mom is surprisingly calm considering that we're going to miss the pie schedule.

"Courtney? More cheddar?" she just asked me, holding out a giant bag. Mom's excessive planning comes in handy because of the stockpile in the cooler.

"Mom. No," I said. "I don't want any cubed cheese. Can I have a carrot?"

Bryan's crunching on wheat wafers. "If we had a cell phone, this wouldn't be happening."

I can't believe he had the guts to just say that!

Mom's arm is twitching where it's resting on the back of the seat. "We'll be *fine*. All those other people with cell phones can call *for* us. All right?"

Bryan isn't having any of it. "No one's going to call. They can't even see us, Mom. The snow is covering our car!"

"Well then, get out and brush it off," Mom just said. "Make sure you uncover the tailpipe."

We're running the heater once every half hour. When you get stranded in a blizzard you have to remember to clear the tailpipe or you'll die. Either way it feels like we could die, though, if you want to know the truth.

Bryan's trying to open the door, but it's nearly frozen shut. The wind is blowing so strongly that ice is forming on the inside of the windows. Bryan wrote HELP ME in the frosted glass with his finger. The cranberries in the trunk are definitely frozen, and I don't want to even think about "all the breads for the meal" that I spent hours baking last night.

"I'll take Oscar," Bryan just said. "He probably needs to go." We gave him a glass of snow about an hour ago. I'm watching the two of them. Bryan is kicking the tailpipe so hard it might fall off. Mom's arm is still twitching. Oscar raised his leg and it seems frozen in that position.

Uh-oh. There he goes!

No one's going to believe this. I don't believe this. I'm writing this in the bathroom, for one thing. That's pretty strange. But I didn't want to turn the light on and wake Grandma, and I can't sleep, and every other room is taken.

So here's what ended up happening this afternoon after I jumped out of the car to save Oscar from running away (and let's face it, he wasn't scared this time—he was just sick of being in the car, like we were—and decided to strike out for freedom).

First of all, the snow was too deep. Oscar's legs got stuck. Bryan and I picked him up and put him back in the car. Then we started clearing off the car. Bryan took the sides and top; I was clearing off the back. It seemed silly to clear snow off the bumper stickers, but hey—if you're going to be stranded, why not give people a political message to read while they creep by, going 20 MPH, totally ignoring your plight?

I was brushing off the TRUTH OR DAIRY—FRESH FROM THE FARM AND GARDEN! sticker when all of a sudden this new, souped-up black pickup with gigantic snow tires pulled up behind our car. Someone was coming to help us! I was so excited.

Then who gets out of the truck? TOM DELANEY.

"What are you doing here?" I think I asked. A really dumb question. I know.

"Driving to North Platte to see my dad for Thanksgiving. Wow. This is wild, huh? You guys stuck?"

"Why did you stop?" I asked. "I mean—"

"I saw you," Tom said. "Plus I recognized your car. You have that Truth or Dairy sticker. And that tofu sticker.

You have to be the only one in Nebraska right now with that sticker. Where are you going?"

"To visit our grandparents," I said. "And the Von Dragen cousins. Remember?"

"Oh, you're going to the V.D. homestead." Tom smiled.

"Ha-ha," I said as I glared at him.

"Chill, Courtney. I'll help you move the car."

We tried, but the Bull wouldn't budge. Plus we only had a couple of ounces of gas left. So then Tom ends up offering to take us all to the Von Dragens. We can go back and get the car after the storm, he says.

So then the only problem is how we're all going to fit. If we're going to fit. We all had to sit up front, even Oscar. Good thing Mom is so tiny. But they made me sit next to Tom. I was crammed against the gearshift. A wet and thawing Oscar was lying across Bryan's and Mom's laps. All our luggage was in the back, under one of those black plastic truck boxes.

I thought of how Beth said the hailstorm was a sign that I *shouldn't* get to Boulder and reconnect with Dave. So then was this a sign that I was supposed to hook up with Tom? I'd have to call Beth.

We got to my grandparents' four hours after we were supposed to be there. Because of the snowstorm, everyone was worried sick about us, and it was a big party when we finally arrived. We kept thanking Tom—me, Mom, Grandpa. Grandma made him drink three hot chocolates. He tried to leave, but everyone insisted he stay for dinner—it was all hot (and overcooked, I was thinking) and what was one more place setting for the boy who'd saved our lives, etc. etc. etc.

"Thanks for everything, but I should really get going,"

Tom said at about nine o'clock. "My dad's expecting me, so—"

"Don't be ridiculous. In this weather? You're staying the night," Grandpa declared.

"But it's only fifty miles—"

"Do you know how many people's last words have been 'It's only fifty miles'?" Grandpa asked. "Listen, son, I've seen more accidents on this stretch of road than world wars."

I thought to myself, two? More than two? Because I think Tom can take his chances. The thought of him staying here is really bizarre. But I didn't want him to get into an accident, and the snow really hasn't let up yet. So he's sleeping downstairs on the sleeper sofa.

I was trying to fall asleep, but then I realized what I thought was a stomachache from Grandpa's pre-Thanksgiving meal—Cornish game hens, "a little warm-up for the big bird!" he said (no wonder he and Grandma sleep in separate beds)—wasn't going away, and was in fact another kind of ache altogether.

So now I'm sitting in the bathroom, looking at a box of tampons that for some reason has all of the warnings in French.

Question: Why does Grandma still have these and how old are they? Wouldn't she have gone through "the change" about 20 or 40 years ago?

Question: Do tampons expire?

The box is warning me of *Syndrome de Choc Toxique*.

Why does *death* sound good in French? Like an exclusive all-night dance club.

Question: Why would anyone ever want to go to

www.tampax.com? And what links would it have? I sort of don't want to know.

Dear www.tampax.com: Are you there, God? It's me, court364@netcom.com.

There are a bunch of prescription bottles in here, stacked like cans at the supermarket. All my grandparents'.

Don't let me get old.

And don't let me write in my journal in the bathroom again. Extremely depressing.

THANKSGIVING MORNING (pre-poultry)

Oh God. I thought I'd noticed this weird vibe with Grandma and Grandpa. Like maybe they were a lot more interested in each other than Mom said. So I was in the bathroom for a little while, so I was contemplating the Tampax box. Did they think I wasn't coming back?

I walked back into the bedroom and they were like . . . making out. On the bed. Completely oblivious! Completely about to have sex! Grandma's needs *completely* being met.

So I ran downstairs, totally freaked out. And I ran right into the sleeper sofa and toppled onto the Tom, knocking my shins really hard against the metal frame, and falling onto him.

He opened his eyes and said in this Austin Powers voice, "Hello, hello, what do we have here?"

I only took a second to see whether he had as much chest hair as Austin Powers. His chest was bare. And tan, like he went to a salon and had a fake bake.

I leapt off him immediately after that and sat on the recliner. It was so embarrassing, how could I tell him? But I told him. My grandfather would probably be his idol now, but what the heck. I said how it was weird because they hadn't slept together in a long time, and they actually had been sort of cold to each other the last time I saw them.

He said it was probably the Viagra Effect.

"Is that a science fiction movie?" I asked. Because Grandma and Grandpa being sexy . . . that was sort of science fictionesque.

Look, I *know* it's natural, and I'll probably want to do it when I'm seventy-five, too. But I won't want anyone to know about it!

So Tom went upstairs to the bathroom and came back with this bottle of blue pills. "Just what I thought. Viagra." He shook one into his palm and stared at it. Then he lifted it to his mouth. "Bob Dole would be so proud of my courage right now. These things cost like ten bucks a pop, did you know that?"

I begged him not to take one. He just kept laughing and holding the bottle over his head so I couldn't reach it. We wrestled for a few seconds, laughing hysterically, then the bottle popped out of his hands—Viagra pills went flying everywhere, and we fell on the bed again. This time there was a sort of intense moment where he had me pinned.

But he was more interested in saving the Viagra. He let me go right away so he could scoop them all back into the bottle. Then he tucked a couple into his duffel to take home. "Just in case I start aging really rapidly."

You know those scared-straight movies about kids doing drugs? Like heroin and coke and pot? How about *Teenage Boys on Viagra*!!! This one boy in particular.

We started watching TV and I fell asleep on the fold-out couch beside him. We both had sweats on, it was a completely chaste event, and nothing happened. This is the second time this month I've slept next to him, and it's becoming a really weird habit. Not that unlike having Oscar sleep next to me in bed. A little less furry, a little better breath.

THANKSGIVING AFTERNOON (post-poultry)

Let us *not* give thanks. It wasn't even a free-range hen, like Grandpa promised he'd get me. He went out to the turkey farm and got a fresh kill. "Check out that rotisserie action!" he kept saying, as the turkey turned on the metal spit.

"I'd rather not," I said. I kept staring out the window wondering when the snow would stop.

Remember that movie about people being trapped inside during a blizzard? And they all went crazy and started killing each other? *The Shining*. Set in Colorado. No surprise. Okay, so we're in Nebraska and there are no mountains, but still. We haven't been able to leave the house since getting here, and if we eat any more poultry, we're going to start laying eggs.

Tom is about to lose it. Grandpa started telling him how to "truss a bird." (You'd think Grandpa had a turkey farm his whole life instead of an accounting firm.) I guess we're having . . . what? Roast pigeon tomorrow?

Grandma and Grandpa usually sit at either end of the table, but today they had to sit next to each other so they could play footsie. We're all leaving really soon, I wanted to say. Could you just maybe . . . wait until then? For your love fest?

It is so sad when your grandparents are more romantic than you are.

THANKSGIVING NIGHT

We're all sitting around in the living room trying to breathe. The house is hot and stuffy and we're all so full we could burst. Leftovers IV: The Saga Continues. I just called Gerry and told him I probably won't be back to work on Sunday. He said that he'd work for me. Poor Beth.

Bryan is trying to teach Grandpa how to use his new computer, how to get on to the Internet. Probably so they can go to hotchicks.com together.

"The storm is just not letting up," Tom said. "But I have to get out of here."

"Tell me about it," I muttered.

"Hey, Courtney. You want to come with me?" Tom asked. "I know we can make it to North Platte. But if we want to blow that off, we could just head back to Denver."

I wanted to. *So* badly. But Mom needed me to help her drive home (if she was still going to let me drive.) Finally, there was a break in the onslaught of snow and you could see okay. Tom called the roads hot line and they said the interstate was open again, so the Tom made a break for it before Grandpa made him snowshoe home. This was good news for us, too—the car might get towed to us in the next few days or so.

I walked Tom out to his pickup and thanked him for rescuing us from the snowbank. He gave me his dad's number in North Platte and said to call if there was anything I needed, like a ride back. "Or a meal that isn't turkey," he said, and we both laughed.

Could it be that Tom and I are actually sort of becoming friends?

I wondered if I should hug him good-bye. Or maybe

kiss him. I must have been desperate. I sort of leaned against him and squeezed. I felt really stupid.

Right after he left, Grandpa realized Tom didn't give back this antique sterling silver lighter he was showing him. He threw a fit about it. I promised him I'd get it back when I saw Tom at school in a couple days.

I can't wait to be back at school. I can't wait to see Jane and Beth and tell them about the trip and how I slept next to Tom.

There is one person I really am dreading seeing, though. Not because I don't like him, but because I sort of messed up the last time we talked. Maybe he didn't necessarily deserve to be compared to a rocky Great Lake that sinks ships. In fact Grant had been nothing but nice to me before I left, except for that Dave incident. I'd hardly thought about Dave on this trip. Was it Grant's fault he wanted Dave to tell me about what's-her-name in person? Of course, he didn't do it in person, he did it on the phone. Loser.

I started feeling so bad, I decided to call Grant. Of course I couldn't say I was sorry, not really. I started talking about Oscar.

"Oscar tried to run away, but he got stuck in a snowdrift," I said. "He ended up with really, really cold feet and wet fur, but we saved him. Then all he's been doing lately is eating turkey and gravy. Do you think that's okay?"

"He can eat whatever he wants, really. It's just that he has to have his pills."

"Right. Well, seeing as how it was a holiday, I put his pill in a dinner roll instead of a hot dog. He didn't really notice. So, um, what are you doing?"

"Hey, Court—oh, you're on the phone. Who are you

talking to?" Tom suddenly appeared in the room.

Haven't you left yet? I wanted to say. "Nobody," I said. "Did you forget something?"

"Yeah." Tom picked up something off the top of the fridge and slipped it into his jacket pocket and then waved. "See you!"

"Who was that?" Grant sounded very offended all of a sudden.

"Oh, just a cousin. One of the infamous Von Dragens," I said.

"It sounded like Tom Delaney," he said.

"Oh. Well, no, it wasn't," I said. Why did I say that? He'll only find out what happened the next time he sees Tom. And then he'll know I lied to him. But how could I tell him I'd slept with Tom the night before—well, in the same room anyway.

Because nobody would believe you'd spend the night with Tom Delaney and *not* sleep with him. No matter how well Grant knew me or Tom. Tom had a certain reputation, and there was a reason for that. And if anyone found out Viagra was involved in the evening, my story would become completely unbelievable. And if anyone found out that I sort of wanted something to happen, that would be even more unbelievable—

Well, Grant was never going to hear that from me. It was too embarrassing. So I sort of changed the subject and started to explain the car skid, and how we had to get towed, but there was a blizzard, etc. (I didn't mention it was kind of my bad driving that did it.)

"So what have you been up to?" I asked.

"Actually . . . I don't know if I should tell you this." Ooh! Intrigue! I thought. "But I've been hanging out with

Dave," he said.

Go ahead. *Ruin* my holiday via long-distance. He has some nerve. Can't he be on my side and just ban all contact?

"Well, I have to go," I said. "The gravy is burning."

Grant said how he didn't think I ate gravy. "Of course I don't *eat gravy*," I said. "But I can still cook it."

Actually, neither is true.

Bryan has been on the phone ever since the rest of the Von Dragen clan left. All five of them.

Our family doesn't reproduce well, let's face it. How will the Von Dragen name survive?

By forcing young women like me to have it as a middle name, I guess.

Anyway, Bryan keeps laughing, and he has this bizarre smile on his face. Is he in love or something? He's acting like I've never seen before. I asked him what was up, and he said, "Never mind, you won't get it."

"I'll get it," I said, desperate for some real conversation. "I will! Just try me."

He shook his head. "Nobody will ever get it, so—"

LATER . . .

Sorry, I was interrupted in the middle of that fascinating update. My mother came upstairs and insisted we go down and join in the giant gin rummy round robin.

Some of this stuff doesn't even sound so bad until I write it down.

After Bryan lost, he got on the phone right away again. I asked who he was calling. He said it was none of my business. Is that rude or what? He used to tell me everything. Sure, he was six at the time, and a horrible liar, but come on.

He must have a girlfriend at home. He doesn't want me to know who she is because he's embarrassed.

This is going to be fun.

Since when does Bryan have a calling card?

Whoa. Just woke up from a dream where I was making out with Grant in storeroom at T or D. It was very intense. Tom was over by the counter, grinding Viagra pills into an additive and putting the powder into smoothies!

"They have drinks for chicks," he was saying. (We do have this one called Ferocious Female that's supposed to help curb PMS.) "Why not drinks for us? It's virility, baby. I call this a Manly Mango Mojo." (Austin Powers influence again.)

Have to stop sleeping on this foldout couch where Tom slept.

Right away.

Made it home tonight. The less said about the trip, the better. Let's just say that Oscar should not be allowed into a car after eating birds at Grandpa's for days on end. Not in the winter, not when you can't open the windows.

As soon as I got home, I called Beth to tell her the whole story.

She didn't seem that surprised. Like this was a normal chain of events??? Grandparents getting it on? Being stranded on I-80? Nearly sleeping with the Tom?

Well, okay, it wasn't "nearly." Close to nearly, though.

"Are you okay?" I finally asked when she didn't even laugh about Bryan keeping a journal and pining away for someone at home.

"Um . . . yeah," she said. Then she said she was sorry she was kind of out of it, she had to work extra hard at T or D because she was working with Gerry, etc. He kept going over all the procedures with her, hovering over the blenders, etc.

"Don't ever get stranded again, okay?" she begged.

It was great to go back to school today. I felt like I was never going to have my life back.

We had a student council meeting to talk about the New Year's blowout. We've done some fund-raising, plus we're selling individual tickets at $3 a pop, and now it's time to reap the benefits.

Asked Tom about Grandpa's lighter. He said he doesn't have it. I called Grandpa to tell him that. There was a message on their answering machine that they've gone to Hawaii for 2 weeks. *"Aloha!"* my grandfather said in this happy voice. I guess he hasn't noticed the missing Viagra yet. Must have enough to tide him over, through the luau with Grandma.

Hey, if I were them? I'd *move* to Hawaii.

Dad called to tell us that his stepdaughter Angelina had her baby last night. It's a girl! Cool. Her name is something like Bellarina. (Doesn't she realize everyone's going to call her Ballerina? And that she'll have to go through life explaining that she's not a dancer? Unless, of course, she becomes one, due to the power of suggestion.)

Dad got all emotional because it reminded him of when we were born and blah blah blah. Then he and Mom started talking about it and they had this really fun conversation and then Mom was crying. Bizarre.

I need to write this down so it makes sense. I was going to call Beth, so I picked up the phone in the kitchen. I heard Bryan's voice and realized he was already on the phone. This must be his dream date, I thought, because Bryan was talking in a low voice. I was about to hang up when I heard the other voice.

I kept staring at the phone as I listened to her. Not getting it, like Bryan always says. But wanting to get it this time.

I stood there unable to move. Completely shocked. Stunned. Deer in headlights etc.

Beth and Bryan were talking to each other about how much they had missed each other, how they couldn't wait for Christmas vacation, blah blah blah BLAH!

"Hey—is someone on the line?" Bryan asked. "Hey, hang up!"

"Gladly!" I said. I dropped the phone and ran into my room and closed the door. My best friend . . . and my little *brother*? Since when?

They're dating . . . they're in love . . . she's the one he kept calling and writing in Ogallala, that's how she knew about the trip before I told her . . . that's why she hasn't been interested in anyone lately, it's because she likes Bryan . . .

I felt like Oscar, standing there with my tongue hanging out, about to go into a grand mal seizure.

She barely just got over having a fling-a-weekend.

He barely just got over Power Rangers.

What the? Talk about *choc toxique*. I can hardly *breathe*.

I knew Bryan had a crush on her, but that's been for decades. Now what? They've been seeing each other—and not telling me. How could they not tell me? Why?

I went back to my computer and sent an instant message to her: "CRADLE ROBBER!" I wrote in all caps, even though that's bad netiquette, I couldn't stop to think about that.

Then I logged off. I didn't want to know what she'd say. I didn't want to hear about it.

Study Hall. Blah.

Beth came over to my locker before school, but I didn't know what to say. Why does her being with Bryan bug me so much? I think it's because they didn't tell me. Why should I be the last to know? Did they think they couldn't trust me or something?

"What's your problem?" Beth said. "Jane's okay with this."

"You're not going out with Jane's brother," I said. "It's different. And I'm not okay with it."

"Obviously," Beth said.

"Anyway, you don't *have* relationships. You have one-nighters," I said. "Are you going to dump Bryan?" Because one depressed person in the family is enough.

"No, of course not," Beth said. "God, Courtney, haven't you noticed? I haven't had any flings this year. It's a resolution I made, to give that up like I gave up smoking."

"Right . . ." I said. "And *that* worked. I saw you smoking last week!"

"I was only doing that because I was freaking out about Bryan!" Beth said. "I wished I didn't like him so much—it was scary. And then the idea of telling *you* about us was even scarier. So I had a couple of cigarettes—but that's it, and I was just trying to escape."

"So when you slip up and make out with some other guy, and totally ruin Bryan's life—"

"That won't happen!" Beth said. Her teeth were clenched like the way the dentist makes you do to check your bite. "I've changed," Beth said. "Just like you."

"I've changed?" I said.

"Yeah. Into a real bitch," Beth said.

Whoa. No one's ever said that to me, to my face. I could see Alison doing it, as a joke. I called her when I got home to tell her what was going on. She wasn't home so I sent an e-mail. She didn't write back yet.

No one ever writes back.

Dinner tonight was hell. Mom was in a rotten mood. Some stuff got delivered tonight from a company that called to sell her the Century's Greatest Figurines. She said she didn't want them—so they sent them with a bill. She told them to get lost—they said "thank you for your order." I made her open the package so we could have a good laugh at the things, to cheer her up. But they had been packed really badly and were totally shattered. Seemed like a metaphor or something. Smashed little people.

After that I was in a worse mood than Mom, which is saying a lot.

Bryan was sitting there whistling, looking like he'd just won the lottery. He even *cooked*. Last thing I knew, his favorite meal was cinnamon-sugar toast. Now he's making pesto pasta surprise, or whatever he called it. Oscar was running around the kitchen in circles he was so excited about it.

Bryan also made this crunchy Italian bread with spices. The entire meal had a very distinct flavor to it: BETH.

"This is wonderful." Mom looked like she'd died and gone to heaven. A heaven with no phones and no telemarketers. "And all vegetarian, Courtney—no dairy, even. Aren't you impressed?"

"Are you guys in a cooking class together?" I asked, my eyes narrowed at Bryan. "Is *that* how you met?"

Bryan frowned at me. "We met when you brought her over here to play Barbie about ten years ago."

"All right, you two—no arguing. This is a delicious meal, and I don't want it spoiled."

Then Mom's smile warbled into this look of torture because the phone rang. She grabbed the receiver and was about to yell when she said, "Oh, *hi*, Beth, well we're eating, but since I love you so much, you can talk to Bryan."

I glared at Bryan as he took the phone from Mom. I never got to talk to Dave during family meals.

I glared at Mom. What about her family-politics-school rule? Did Beth fit in there? I felt like I was underneath the family and the school rock. Smashed like an ugly figurine.

Why am I posting this e-mail in here? In case Alison ever tries to say she's never done anything mean.

Courtney:*
*[Note: not even a "dear"!]
I don't know why you're so upset. Okay, it's kind of weird, Beth and Bryan dating, and Grandma and Grandpa sleeping together. And maybe it's annoying when Dad goes on and on about Sophia. But you can't go around hating people because they're happy. Just because they found their soul mates, and you haven't found yours yet, doesn't mean you can rain on their parades. It's not fair, Courtney! We were all happy for you and Dave. What's his new girlfriend like? Have you met her?

Would you hate *me* if I told you I might be in love, too? And that's the real reason I didn't meet you for Thanksgiving? And that I've never been happier?

I'll tell you more about it at Christmas. Hang in there until then. I know you're a better person than the one who wrote me that hateful e-mail. I'm deleting it.

Love,
Alison

I think she wants to delete *me*.

We're all in trouble now. Some telemarketer told Mom he got her name from the phone company. "That's how it's done," he said. "Wake up, Mrs. Smythe." He mispronounced her name. Smith. How hard is it?

So now telemarketers are off the hit list.

MegaPhone is on it.

"They have no conscience!" she kept saying, as we sat in front of the TV, watching and eating dinner. Bryan went out with Beth; Mom and I were left to our own devices, which means pizza. About every half hour a new MegaPhone ad came on.

"We keep in touch" is their new slogan. (Their old one, "For the love of talk," got them in trouble with a bunch of religious groups, something about how they were saying they were equal to God, or the phone was equal to God.)

"They keep in touch all right," Mom kept muttering. "With our *wallets*. Stupid figurines. Stupid phone company!"

When I got to school (late and frozen, because Mom is making me ride my bike in subzero temps) (I wouldn't ask Beth for a ride because she was already giving Bryan a ride.) (What kind of relationship can they have if only one of them is old enough to drive?), Tom was waiting out front for me. He dragged me over to a corner by the entrance. This is it, I thought. He's going to make his move. Kind of bizarre at 7:45, but at least I'd know he was attracted to me. And if I could look good with ice chips on my cheeks, and some stuff coming out of my nose, well then hey.

"I have something really serious to tell you," Tom said. "I don't even know if I *should* tell you, but it affects both of us, so you need to know." He reached into his pocket. Here it comes. The standard Tom Delaney jewelry gift, I thought. I wouldn't accept it, of course. But the point was that he was finally making the offer. What's he going to tell me? I wondered. About his deep feelings for me? Yeah, right, like he has feelings. But he is cute.

He pulled out this sheet of paper. "What's that?" I asked.

"It's about the student council," he said. "We're being investigated."

"What? Is it Jennifer? Is she suing you for sexual harassment?" I'd seen this coming. As a future lawyer, I see lawsuit opportunities everywhere.

"Who?"

"*Jennifer.* You went out with her for a few months, and then she transferred to private school?"

"What?"

"Never mind," I said. She could sue him for being thoughtless and cruel, but that was about it. "What does that letter say?"

"We're being investigated. There are like, some, discrepancies. They did some sort of study of us, and they checked our books. They think we stole all this money—they think we did all these volunteer things for show to cover up the fact we were . . . embezzling or something."

"Embezzling? That's crazy," I said. "We haven't been doing anything like that." Only Tom and I had access to the checkbook. Then I looked at him. "Have we?"

"No, of course not. It's probably a clerical error or whatever. But the thing is I applied for early decision. I'm going to find out in days whether I got in or not, and I—I mean, we—have to keep this thing quiet. Keep it out of the papers, you know?" He was almost panting with nervousness.

"Like our school paper has ever broken a story. On anything?" I reminded him. "Don't sweat it."

He was so lost and desperate. I didn't know what to do. I sort of wanted to kiss him, but I also felt like telling him to grow up. This was nothing he'd go to jail over.

So the Duck informed us later that we're going to be reviewed by the Student Honor Committee (not to be confused with the National Honor Society—this group checks out *lack* of honor). And guess who's the head of the SHC? I don't know why I never noticed, maybe because I never had a problem with my HONOR before. Anyway, the committee has a member from each class, and then an "arbitrator" to lead them (they need 5 total so they can have votes). So Mr. Honor of the Year turns out to be Grant. And we have to tell him everything (except maybe the fact that I think I'm getting a crush on him) (hope he doesn't subpoena this journal).

He came to investigate and check our office. We opened the supply cabinet to show him everything we have. It was totally empty.

Mrs. Martinez is horrified.

I'm horrified.

Now we're all under this "umbrella of suspicion." Only everyone suspects me the most, because I'm the new girl. I think I'm going to be impeached.

Remember what Jennifer told me? "You have to watch everything he does." I thought she meant the backrub thing. She was probably talking about Tom's money management, or lack thereof—and that's why she left.

"Courtney! Talk to me," Beth said. She was holding a knife to cut strawberries, so I didn't stand much of a chance. She demanded to know what was going on with the student council, and why I was still so upset about her and Bryan seeing each other.

I started out going on and on about the student council. She interrupted me—she didn't really want to hear about that at all. "Why are you unhappy for me and Bryan?" she asked.

"Because it's wrong," I said. "Because you guys have known each other for too long. Because—Beth, do I really have to *explain* this?"

"Um, yeah, you do," she said. "I'm always happy when you hook up with someone. So why can't you be happy for me?"

"You're like a sister to me. And Bryan's like a brother to me—"

"He *is* your brother," Beth said.

"I know! I know that! But see, with the transitive property, you're like a sister to him—"

"No I'm not! Don't say that. Courtney, we've hardly spent any time with him for years. We've ignored him and made fun of him—"

"And what was wrong with that?" I asked her. "Can't we just go on doing that?"

"You don't get it," she said. "Nobody gets it."

Oh my God, I thought. She's starting to talk like him!

"He's changed," she went on. "He's older now—"

"So are we!" I said. "So that still makes us two years older than him!"

439

"You like Grant," Beth said. "He's younger than *you*."

"What? I do not. And he's only . . ." I tried to remember when his birthday was. At most, he was two *months* younger than me. Then for some reason I got this picture of his body in my head instead of his birthday. "Just forget it!" I told Beth.

We worked in frozen silence for the rest of the afternoon. Wheatgrass Woman came in at 3:40, stared at our name tags, and said, "To tell you the truth . . . this wheatgrass sort of . . . sucks today. Are you concentrating . . . Courtney? Beth?"

"I'll make you another one," I grumbled.

"I sense hostility here," she said. "It could be the result of one of you having unsafe sex."

That's exactly it, I thought. Beth having sex with Bryan—probably not, but even if they kissed? That was definitely unsafe.

Grant is sitting by the window. WWW is hovering over him, like he's invaded her space. He's on break. She's still waiting for that bus. Please don't ask him about safe sex, I thought. And please don't ask *me* about it while *he's* here.

I went over when he first got here and sat with him for a while. He was mad because a shipment of Science Diet came in and he was the only one there to unload the truck. He was sweaty in a clean kind of way. We talked about the student council thing. "I can't really comment," he said. "Me being the arbitrator and all."

"Right. Of course," I said. "But the Duck—she's going to listen to reason, right? She won't expel us or anything." He wouldn't answer.

Oh crap. Imagine me working here forever. Growing old(er) with WWW. Fruit and sundaes being my life. On the Banana Wheel of Fortune.

Oh my God. It *all* happened today. Still can't believe it. I got to work; Beth and I still weren't talking; then Gerry told me this would be my last day "at this location." The Boulder store is ready to open, and he wants me to be the "point person" there, work 3 afternoons a week plus Saturdays, etc. etc. etc. What? I told him I didn't want to, that I couldn't. How could someone who pretends to be into peace and harmony even suggest splitting me and Beth up? Maybe we're not talking now, but still, we have a history, we'll work it out eventually. And Boulder??? Where Dave lives??? No.

"Gerry, how can you make me work there? I can't! Absolutely not," I said.

We went back and forth. I told him I didn't have time, he told me he'd sent me to that seminar so I could do this, he explained it to me back then, he's been talking to me about it for weeks, blah blah blah. "That was before I knew about Dave and what's-her-face!" I said.

Beth was out front helping customers. We were having one of those Front Range wind blasts so no one was really rushing in. Then this kids' birthday party showed up. Gerry had completely forgotten they were coming. Ten kids. They were supposed to have a frozen yogurt cake, but it hadn't been made.

Gerry panicked. He told me and Beth to make the kids whatever they wanted—no charge. The kids were cool, but the 2 moms with them were insane. They had me make, remake, triple-make their sundaes.

I lost it when one of them complained about the pecans on her Banana Splitsville not being pecans but peanuts instead—I was so flustered I'd used the wrong bin. This woman got hysterical, and accused me of trying to give her an allergic reaction, didn't I know she could die if she ate peanuts, blah blah blah.

I told the woman *she* was nuts. Then I quit. I threw my Holstein apron on the floor and marched out, nearly knocking down Wheatgrass Woman. She looked more upset than I felt.

No way am I working in Boulder and waiting on Dave and what's-her-name. *Never!*

Home, home on the Front Range . . .
Where the deer and the antelope play
Where seldom is heard
An encouraging word
From any of my friends or ex-boyfriends or prospective
boyfriends
Or even siblings
And the skies are cloudy all day

So here I am sitting behind the counter at the new Truth or Dairy II. In Boulder. All alone.

I gave in, okay? I had to think about everything I'd be giving up. The free smoothies (like I've had one in 6 months). The endless requests for less or more ice.

Half the stuff here is still in boxes. There's a very annoying new paint smell that won't go away.

This is the opening before the Grand Opening on Saturday. This is like . . . a preview. A run-through so we can see what we've forgotten. Um . . . my guess right now would have to be: customers.

"I knew you'd come back!" Gerry cried, this giggly sound coming out of him. I'd never heard anything like it. "Oh, Courtney, I'm so proud of you. You slew the demons!"

What demons is he talking about? Dave? The fact I had to drive the Bull to Boulder and am commuting 30 miles for a $7 an hour job? The fact I hate change of any kind? Or was he talking about jealousy, hatred, dislike of other girls who date Dave . . . *Those* demons?

I'm supposed to be working with somebody named

Trent. Hasn't shown yet. Don't think he will. I'm supposed to be the one who trains him. I wish he would show up so I could leave him out here by himself when Dave and Pretty Woman come in. She's probably like . . . 20 or something. Experienced. And yet still less jaded than me.

Gerry just called to see how it's going. "How come I don't hear anything in the background?" He expected blenders whirring, ice-cream scooping, nuts being chopped, I guess.

"I think you're going to need to advertise a little more," I said.

Oh hell, the door just opened and like an entire sorority is coming in. Bye for now.

LATER THAT SAME DAY

Back home, in bed. I don't know what came over me today. It was like having a high fever, the kind that gives you really weird thoughts and fears.

I got so nervous about Dave coming in, it was like I had to do something to protect myself. A shield. And I made it out of butterscotch and hot fudge. And chocolate chocolate chip ice cream.

I raced into the back room and started devouring this Turtle Shell Sundae. I *hate* butterscotch. And I hate eating around the smell of new paint.

Grant called while I was there—he'd stopped by to see me at the old store and Beth told him I was working in Boulder and gave him the number. Not that she'd use it.

"It sucks that you have to work up there," he said. "No more Canyon Boulevard." He said he'd miss seeing me around.

He was being so nice, I was afraid I was going to start crying. Or it could have been the new paint giving me an allergic reaction. Anyway, I told him I had to go because the hot butterscotch was boiling over.

"Okay, but before I go, I have to tell you that you got such a glowing recommendation from Gerry and Beth and some customers in the store. So that's going in my report—that everyone thinks you're very trustworthy."

I'm so thrilled with his dumb *report*. Can't he ask how *I* am?

Things can get worse! Who knew?

Was working in Boulder again today. Gerry doesn't seem to notice I am the only one doing a horrendous commute. Beth doesn't seem to care.

So there I was. Trent not showing again. First some guy came in and asked all about the history of the store. He asked if we were kosher vegan, whether we used the same blenders for dairy and nondairy. I had to admit that we crossed the line back and forth, though I personally tried to—

Anyway, that is so not the point.

The big drama (after the woman came in and asked if we had any hot dairy drinks) (and when I said no, she asked if we had any hot smoothies) came next. Grant came in. With Dave.

My scoop slipped into the pineapple sorbet. I don't think I ever found it, I was so flustered. That has to be a health code violation.

SO ANYWAY, there they were. I guess I was glad that Dave was with Grant instead of his new girlfriend. But why was Grant in Boulder and why was he coming here and why wasn't he at work and why did he drag Dave in to see me? Was Grant the one who wanted to see me or was Dave? Was Grant only trying to be a Good Samaritan, get us to talk? Total mystery. Goes along with theory of boys needing to travel in packs, though.

But it wasn't fair because Beth wasn't there to back me up, to be *my* pack. All of a sudden I realized how much I missed her. But there wasn't time for anything like that. I had to freak out.

I took a deep breath and put a very phony smile on my face. I asked if I could help them. Politely. Really!

"Hi, Courtney," Dave said. "Wow, your hair's getting really long."

I didn't know if that was a compliment, but since I didn't know what else to say, I said, "Thanks."

"Must be all the healthy eating you do," Dave said.

Is he trying to win me back? I wondered. By talking about my healthy hair? Or is he being sarcastic because he knows I'm not always healthy? Is he obsessed with my hair?

"Must be," I said. I turned to Grant and smiled. Even though I sort of wanted to hurl a blender at his head. What was he thinking, coming in here with Dave on a smoothie field trip? Did he have no heart?

"So how's it going?" he asked. He immediately looked down at the ice-cream tubs. Like he didn't know what chocolate chip was.

Then they ordered really easy stuff, I think they were nervous. Dave passed on the Coconut Fantasy Dream. That was like a slap in the face. He opted for the Seasonal Cranberry Splash (turkey not included).

"Couldn't get enough at Thanksgiving?" I said as I poured it into a cup. He didn't bring his refillable cup. Another slap in the face. Probably threw it out. Probably has a new refillable cup from new girlfriend.

"You know me. I love cranberry," Dave said.

No. I thought I knew you. I was wrong, thought the jaded bitter dramatic side of me.

The playful side of me said, "You do *not*."

Grant got a Banana Splitsville. Then he sat there and only ate about two bites. Don't know what's wrong with him. He kept looking over at me and smiling and then looking away like he knew he'd done the wrong thing, bringing Dave here.

Dave looked incredibly uncomfortable the whole time, too. Good. I guess it's the first time I've seen him since he started seeing what's-her-name. Well, he definitely doesn't look *happier*. Paler, maybe, and like he's got a head start on those freshman 15 everyone talks about.

I helped him along by putting extra body-building power in his smoothie. After I took their money, I felt really stupid standing there in my apron, so I went into the back for some supplies I didn't really need.

After a minute or two Dave actually came back there, following me. He said I was being very rude. Like a customer who happens to be an ex-boyfriend coming into the storeroom isn't rude? Excuse me!

"Could you just talk to us for a second?" he said. "I mean, I guess it's fine if you want to be mean to me—"

"Oh, thanks." I was so mad, I was squeezing the handful of wheatgrass so tightly that juice was almost dripping onto my shoe.

"But could you just be a little nicer to Grant?"

"Could you just *leave*?" I said.

"Courtney, come on. Why can't we be friends?" he said.

Naturally he has to use a line from a Smash Mouth song. He has no original lines!

"Oh, I'm sure we can be friends," I said. "Just not . . . maybe not for six months or so. Yeah, that sounds right. Of course your time line might be a little different—"

There was a "Moo" out front, which meant the door had opened (dumb new feature Gerry added to the new

449

store—good thing door doesn't open as much as store back home). "Excuse me. I have customers," I said.

Dave tossed his cup into the trash. He'd hardly drunk any of his cranberry. I knew he didn't like it. Just like I knew he shouldn't have ever come in!!!

"You need to lighten up a little," he said. "Are you going for smoothie server of the year or something?"

I went out to the front and Grant was sitting there, chewing on his spoon, the Banana Splitsville totally melted in the dish. There weren't any customers. I guess someone came in, saw Grant not eating, and left.

So I walked over to Grant. "Didn't you like it? Want me to make you something else?" I offered.

"Um . . . no," he said. Then he looked up with this really pathetic look. I can't even describe it. In the meantime Dave stormed past us and went out onto the street to wait.

"Are you feeling okay?" I asked Grant.

"Sure. I just sort of wanted to . . . see where you worked. So, um, well. Here it is, right?" He seemed to come to his senses then. He got up and walked to the door. "See you later!" He waved and then went outside. Two guys were skateboarding down the sidewalk and nearly ran him down.

Grant came up *here* to see me? Sort of like when Dave drove down to the other T or D to see me? So he likes me. Grant, I mean. But when Dave drove down to Denver for a smoothie, it was to yell at me for being on student council.

I'm totally confused.

What would happen if Gerry opened a new store in Pueblo? Who would drive down then?

I hate working at this new store. Later in the afternoon, I had my back turned because Gerry bought these used blenders from a smoothie place that was going out of business, and half of them don't work, so I was using the one that did work, and someone came in and stole the stupid tip jar.

I didn't have to work today so I went to see Grant. I figured one work visit deserved another. Also I actually missed the Canyon Boulevard crowd. I never thought I'd miss that stupid strip mall, but I did. It was weird parking at that lot and not going to work myself.

Anyway, I found Grant at Pet Me. I asked him what he had in mind, bringing Dave to the store.

But I wasn't even thinking about Dave. I was worried about Grant and how he was acting and how he hadn't eaten anything. But I couldn't say that. It was like the only thing we really knew how to talk about was Dave. And we couldn't stop.

He said it wasn't his idea. He also said not to worry, that he met Dave's new girlfriend and she wasn't anything like me. (And why wouldn't that make me worry?)

"Anyway, they're on-again, off-again," he said.

"I'd rather they were off-again. Period," I said.

"Courtney, come on. It's not that bad. Anyway, I think in a way Dave did the right thing," Grant said. "Because you guys might not be happy together anymore. You've both changed a lot since the summer."

Uh-oh, I thought. He's going to call me a bitch, just like Beth! But all he did was sort of put his arm around me. Or I thought that's what he was doing. But at the same time he was also sort of adjusting this leash display rack, putting the right lengths on the right hooks.

"So, did you um . . . have a good time yesterday?" I asked.

"Oh, yeah. Definitely," Grant said. "And don't worry, I bet that store will take off soon."

"I don't want it to succeed," I said. "I want to come back and work over there." I pointed toward the original T or D.

"Yeah. That would be cool," he said. "Well, I have to go unload another truck. But I'll see you later."

"Right. Okay." I went outside and stood in the doorway for a second. Something was definitely happening between me and Grant. But we were both totally not willing to admit it.

I took a deep breath. It smelled like a mixture of stinky cages and fresh snow.

I'm writing this on the bus. It's stopping every half block and taking forever.

Mom paged me this afternoon and told me to meet her downtown. She implied it was important. I assumed it was holiday shopping, maybe she wanted to lift me out of my funk by taking me to dinner at a hot new restaurant, then we'd cruise to Larimer Square, hit some cool clothing store. But no. That isn't her style, anyway, so I don't know what I was thinking.

I met her outside the city and county building, which was all lit up for Christmas. Very festive.

Except that Mom was staging a major protest there. And she marched with a group of people from there down to MegaPhone headquarters.

"Mom. You can't yell at MegaPhone *using* a megaphone!"

"That's the beauty of it!" she said. "Fight fire with fire!"

Then she and her group started chanting: "Hell, no, we won't call! We won't use the phone at all!"

Mom was carrying a sign saying, *Hang Up On MegaPhone*! The woman next to her had one that said, *Automated Directory Assistance = Death*.

I could hear a bunch of disgruntled ex-employees ranting behind me about getting fired and replaced by computers. Then there were some current employees wearing name tags (Duh! Do you want to get fired when this is on the news?) who were complaining about how there was a cash bar at the Christmas party that year and how expensive it was.

"Mom, this is going to be on local TV," I said.

"With any luck!" she said. "Exposure is just what this cause needs right now."

"And if you stay out here all day, you're going to *die* of exposure," I argued. "You don't even have a warm coat on!"

She didn't care. About humiliation, about frostbite, about anything. Except getting the MegaPhone practices changed. I wandered around the stone steps, thinking how I could convince her to leave. I once had a friend who yelled at the phone company, and they screwed up his service, his listing, everything in retaliation. We had enough problems when MegaPhone was giving us "quality service."

That's when I saw Witchy Wheatgrass Woman, with the purple-silver magic purse. She was standing behind Mom, chanting, and holding a sign that said *Privacy Is Our Most Important Natural Resource*. Whatever that meant. She saw me and ran over to tell me how proud I should be of my mother, how she set a good example for all of us. Yes, but did you ask her if she practices safe sex? I wanted to ask her. You sure check up on me and Beth all the time about it.

Suddenly there were TV cameras swarming around Mom. "Ms. Smith! What do you have to say to the executives?"

She gave a very impressive speech. She was completely composed, like she'd been building toward this moment for years, like she had the whole thing prewritten and rehearsed. And maybe she did.

I was really proud of her. I kind of got tears in my eyes. There was a lot of dust and soot blowing around, too, so it could have been that.

Then across the way I saw the Tom show up with a bunch of his friends. I couldn't deal with them—they'd probably only make fun of Mom. The Tom isn't exactly someone you could turn to for support. So I turned to run—and I crashed right into Mr. Novotny. He was in full Broncos regalia—Broncos winter jacket, stocking cap, etc. I was surprised he had come so far into town on a game weekend. Wasn't there a playoff game happening somewhere?

"Not so fast," Mr. Novotny said when I tried to brush past him with a polite wave.

What was he going to do, *CSP on me? Wait a second, I thought. He loves those cell phone features. What's he doing here? So I asked him.

"Those features are fine—but that's through another company. How about the week when all your family's calls came to my house? That is not any way to run a business," Mr. Novotny said. "You know who they need at the helm?"

"John Elway?" I guessed, figuring this had to relate to the Broncos somehow, or his entire day would be wasted. Besides, the man is like a god around here.

"Mike Shanahan," he said. "The man can coach a Super Bowl–winning team—he can run a phone company. They ought to get his input."

"Right . . ." I said slowly. Out of the corner of my eye I saw Mom heading into the building, trying to get past Security. I ran over to her and asked what she was doing.

"I got the idea from you," she said. "I'm going to sleep on the roof until they change company policy and improve customer service."

"What policy? What service? Anyway, we weren't

protesting anything!" I said.

"Same difference," she said. "You made a statement."

"But Mom, that was a school roof. This is a sky-scraper! You'll be sleeping on the helicopter launchpad. You'll get crushed by executives and Flight for Life! You'll get struck by lightning!"

"It's December," she said. "How much lightning can there be?"

"This is Colorado," I said. "The weather changes really quickly, Mom."

The woman does not listen to reason.

I have to get Bryan to help me. And I have to go to Beth's house to get him.

"So. Are you going to quit being weird?" That was the first thing Beth said when she opened the door yesterday.

"No," I said. "Probably not." Then I laughed. And she said something like that was probably too much to ask for. Was I there to apologize, she asked. Actually no, I said. I'm looking for Bryan—is he here?

"I can't believe you're not going to apologize!"

"Sorry," I said. "But I'm not."

"Hm." She stood in the doorway, not budging, her Beth stance on. She should play for the Broncos. They could use her. She looked like this impenetrable offensive line.

"It wasn't so much you guys going out . . . as how you didn't tell me," I said. "I hate when people don't tell me stuff. Like Gerry, and the new store in Boulder!"

"Yeah, but that's Gerry. We're talking about us. How could you be so mean to me?" Beth asked. "I can't believe you'd write me off for going out with Bryan."

I didn't know what to say. "I'm sorry. But it's weird."

Beth shrugged. "Yeah, I kinda thought it was weird, too. I guess that's why I couldn't tell you. So come in, and I'll get Bryan. What's going on?"

I told her about Mom and her crusade for 5-cent Saturdays. Bryan was lying on the sofa in the basement, reading. Beth grabbed her coat and told Bryan to get his and we were out of there.

By the time we got back downtown, Mom was nowhere to be found. I thought maybe they were holding her in the MegaPhone headquarters. Subjecting her to really loud dial tones.

Turned out she gave up and came home. "They agreed to a meeting," she said. "With me and any other consumers who have complaints. I hope they have a big enough building."

"They could use Mile High Stadium," I said. It seats about 80,000.

We laughed.

Then Mom picked up the phone to call Dad and finalize the Christmas plan. And there was no dial tone.

Beth called me at the T or D II, since our phone at home is still not working. Mom is considering legal action, but then, when isn't she? I think we're switching to some tiny telephone company that has zero features and isn't even legal yet. Whatever. She has her meeting at MegaPhone on December 30. I think they gave her that date because everyone's out of town on vacation and nobody else will show for the meeting.

"Listen, Courtney—I have a plan. We're getting you out of that Boulder store," Beth said.

I asked her how. She made it sound like a top-secret plan, as if we were going to strike in the middle of the night. Mercenaries. Smoothie mercenaries. Watch your back and also your nonfat raspberry sherbet.

"We've worked at the place for two years," she said. "We've shown Gerry nothing but loyalty. We've invented drinks. We could have gone and worked for any other smoothie place in town. But did we? No. And we can tell him we were even like recruited by these other places," Beth said. "They *begged* us to work for them, but we said no, even though they pay 75 cents more per hour."

"Hey, wait a second," I said. "So then . . . why aren't we working there instead?"

Hm. We both thought about it for a second.

"Maybe we should," Beth said. "But we stay at T or D because we like working together, and we like guaranteeing freedom of frozen choices, and um . . . we sort of like Gerry. Because we like his nonstandard approach to life."

"And we like banana splits," I added.

"But if he wants us to stick around, he has to let us

work together, at the Canyon Boulevard location, and this is like nonnegotiable."

Girl power!

Then Beth asked me something else. "Can you work for me Tuesday night so Bryan and I can go to a movie? We want to celebrate the last day of school before vacation."

It was like swallowing wheatgrass juice on an empty stomach with no water back. But I can handle that. And I could handle this, I told myself. Just . . . not all that well.

"Sure," I said.

Beth and I gave Gerry the ultimatum. He said he'd *think* about it! What? How insulting is that.

So I quit again. It's not so hard, the second time around.

Beth quit, too. Gerry pretty much looked shocked.

We figure we'll have a much better vacation. Also, now I don't have to cover for her tomorrow night. "Want to go to the movies with me and Bryan?" she asked.

"Um . . . no, that's okay. I have plans," I said. I kept it vague. She didn't believe me anyway, so there was no point wasting valuable time coming up with a story.

One more day of school before Christmas break. We're meeting tomorrow to talk about the New Year's party. I don't know what's going on with the investigation—I guess it's "ongoing."

Random Nosebleed is playing at the party. My idea. They came up with their name after two of the guys got nosebleeds on stage, out of nowhere.

Well, okay, probably it was because the air is drier than toast out here in the winter. Ick. I got one at work once. Blood fell into the smoothie I was making.

Gag. Just thinking about watching the drops fall into the blender could make me puke now. I'll have to finish this later. I feel really ill.

Grant and I had lunch today. He asked how I was doing (fine, considering I had no job), whether I was going to the big Lebeau Christmas party tomorrow night (yes), and what I had planned for tonight.

I felt this utter panic. He wasn't asking me to lunch anymore. He was asking me to do stuff outside of school. He was asking for a date. Tonight! And I couldn't go. I liked him too much.

"Nothing," I said. "I mean—because I have to work for Beth."

Then he asked if I wanted to go skiing over Christmas vacation.

"I can't," I said. "We're not supposed to fraternize, right? You're still investigating us."

"We'll be on vacation," Grant said. "I won't be thinking about your case. It should be wrapped up by then anyway."

"Oh. Really?"

"Sure. So do you want to go?"

"Well, um, I don't ski much," I said. "It's bad for the environment."

"Snow is bad for the environment?"

"Driving up to the mountains is. There's so much traffic and then you have to go over those passes, and—"

"I'll drive. We could take the Ski Train," Grant suggested.

He wouldn't stop.

"I actually haven't skied in a really long time," I said. "I'm really bad, so . . . I'm sure I'd just hold you back." I smiled uneasily. I knew from ski trips with Dave and his friends that Grant was the best snowboarder of all of them. "And anyway, I'll probably have to work, so . . ."

Right then there was this overhead page. "Courtney Smith, please report to the principal's office. Immediately."

"Uh-oh," I said. "I must be in big trouble—the Duck wants to see me."

"Yeah. You must be," Grant said. He was practically glowering at me. What did I do? Just because I didn't want to go skiing—

But I did want to go skiing. But I can't! I can't like Grant. It won't work out.

The Duck asked if I'd seen Tom that day. I hadn't. Then she said that our final meeting, our New Year's party—everything—is off. There will be no Random Nosebleed or even a planned nosebleed.

Six checks we used to pay for the party bounced. The student council fund is completely empty. We have no money left!

Jane and Beth and I met at 10:00 to go Christmas shopping and to buy outfits for upcoming parties like the big one at the Lebeau Mansion tonight. We spent about three hours cruising around the mall—didn't find anything.

"The mall is so bad compared to Discount Duds," Jane said as she trotted around in somebody else's used crinkled black boots. Her outfit was vintage from head to toe. And she was wearing this plastic watch she got for free from the Complete gas station.

She kind of dresses like she's in a band now, and maybe she should be. It's weird, though, hearing Jane say she hates the mall. Talk about a turnaround. Her parents are horrified.

Then we went to a department store cafe where Jane could charge lunch to her parents' plastic, just to let them know she hasn't changed *that* much. I finally told them what had happened with Grant. They nearly fell off their chairs.

"So Grant asked you out. Wow. I don't think Grant's asked out anyone in like . . . a year," Jane said. She adjusted her bubble-gum color plastic glasses. *She* can wear them. She can wear anything. "Not since Beth broke his heart."

"I didn't break his heart," Beth said. "I wounded him slightly. I didn't know he was going to be so sensitive about it."

I knew Beth's angle on the whole thing. I wanted to know Jane's. "How do you know he hasn't gone out with anyone else?" I asked.

"It's obvious." She shrugged. "I thought he was still pining for Beth, but obviously he's been saving himself for you. And then you go and say *no*. Why?"

"Because. I told you, I'm not seeing anyone this year."

"Why? Because of Dave?" Jane asked. "Who you haven't talked to in a really long time and who has a girlfriend and who you're basically completely over now?"

"You're letting Dave ruin your senior year!" Beth said.

"*Our* senior year," Jane said. "This affects all of us. At first I thought your no-dating pledge was sort of cute. Now I think it's ridiculous. Remember me when I was so shortsighted that I wouldn't even shop anywhere but at the mall? I gave that up. You can give up not dating."

"And I gave up running from love," Beth said. "Having meaningless relationships instead of a real connection with someone. Plus smoking. And now I'm giving up gum. So if we can do all that, I think you can consider going *skiing* with *Grant*."

"You guys!" I said. I was drowning in a shower of criticism. "We're not talking about giving up matching handbags and—and—Marlboro Ultra Lights. And as far as this running-from-love bit, we don't *all* have to date—"

"Just to date? No, of course not," Beth said. "But when you find someone—"

"Who says I've found someone?"

"You just did! It's Grant, and you know it." Beth's eyebrow was twitching. Either she's been watching too much TV and has eyestrain or she was getting extremely annoyed with me. "But you're so caught up in sticking to some plan, like you've ever stuck to any of your plans!"

"What? What are you saying?"

All the lady shoppers were staring at us.

"Quit making pledges you can't keep," Beth said. "About campaigns, about food, about boys—about everything!" Then she stood up, tossed her linen napkin onto the table, and went to the bathroom. Too bad she was wearing black pants, because she had a ton of lint on her pants now and looked sort of silly, and everyone was still staring at us.

I pulled my chair closer to the table and sipped my lemon water. "I keep pledges," I told Jane. "I'm *good* at pledges. Like the Pledge of Allegiance. In second grade I was chosen to say it on Parents' Day."

"We're not talking about the *flag*," Jane said. "We're talking about your life."

"My life is fine," I said.

The way I see it, I'm the only one with any integrity. I'm the only one who's kept up her standards. Why does everyone *have* to date? I mean, what is so wrong with being by yourself once in a while, or all the time even?

Except for the fact that it's sort of boring, and I would so like to see Grant on a snowboard.

12/23

REALLYREALLY LATE OR EARLY ON THE 24TH

This is Courney's jrnl. My writing. I'm drunk. Me, Alson, the oldes mos responsbl one.

Is it my fault the punch at the Lebeaus' was spiked? Mr. Lebeau said it was Santa's elfs. Elves. Whatever. I know who didit.

Mr. Lebeau wants to fix me up with his son Mark. Like I'd like Mark. I'm in love with Jessie. And nobody here knows anything about it.

Mom is outside arguing with a man on a telfon pole. Don't knowhy. Courtney do you?

yes, definitely, whatever you say Alison
I love Dave
tom doesn't have a thing for me, but I kissed him anyway
I hate Mrs. Malloy's cookies
I hate Martha Stewart
where is lake superior?

In Canada, stupid.
Happy Holidays,
love,
alison

Complete nightmare. I can hardly write, my hand is so shaky. "You're hungover!" Alison cried, jumping on my bed. "Isn't it cool?"

"No," I said, before running to the bathroom to hurl.

Then the doorbell rang. At the same time, I heard this teensy tiny baby crying. Could it be any louder?

Alison and I crawled downstairs. It's *Dad*. And Sophia. And Sophia's kid, Angelina. And Angelina's new baby. They just drove up from Phoenix.

I guess I knew Dad is now a granddad (which means this baby's *great*-grandparents are having Viagra-induced sex and that's totally disturbing) (or wait, that's the other side of the family—am I still drunk?), but it still seems very bizarre. He was so excited to see us. He gave me a huge hug. And I'm really glad he's here, don't get me wrong. But when he hugged me I knew right away I was going to hurl again. But he wouldn't let go, and Alison was in on it, too, of course *she* doesn't have a throbbing headache and the seasick feeling I got when I went rafting on my 14th birthday and got my period in the middle of the Arkansas and had to turn the full-day rafting trip into a half day. I wanted to put myself into a dry bag.

Anyway, Mom was out shopping for food, so Sophia came running after me when I sprinted to the bathroom. I told her to go away—that Alison could take care of me. But Alison was busy talking to Angelina and playing with the baby. Whatever her name is. So I spent some quality time with the dry heaves. Now I'm lying on my bed. Mom will be home soon, and then all hell will break loose.

I have to hand it to her, actually. The woman has

nerves of steel, inviting Dad and his new family to her house. I can't even handle seeing Dave at a party.

Speaking of which, I still have to write down what happened at the Lebeau Mansion.

Alison is so different! She confessed to me that *she* was the one who spiked the punch. Very impressive. As long as we were all walking to the party, I guess it's okay. She kept talking about some guy named Jesse. She was so lit she even spelled his name wrong in here.

What a night. I still can't get over it. I don't know what to do.

Everyone was there. I mean, the place was so crowded, full of everyone I know from school and their parents. Alison and I went together, sort of late. She immediately headed for the punch bowl. That skinny Mark Lebeau made a beeline for *me*. So I looked around and saw Beth and Jane. They were talking to Grant!

I kind of panicked. I hadn't *seen* Grant since turning him down a few days ago. And Jane and Beth were probably telling him to ask me out again, encouraging him to like wear me down. The fact he was even talking to Beth again was weird. I wanted to go home. But the crowd pushed me forward, a surge for the fruitcake and eggnog table.

I ended up right in front of them. They were in the middle of telling him how I've decided to be a nun this year. But the way they said it made it sound incredibly stupid instead of brilliant.

"Look, here comes Sister Courtney," they teased me.

"Shut up," I said, not meeting Grant's eyes.

"You look incredible—for a nun," Jane said. "Love that green velveteen. Totally matches your eyes."

"Um, thanks," I said. Don't draw attention to me! I thought. We want Grant to think I'm unattractive, so he can move on, forget about me, quit asking me out.

Because it's going to mess everything up for me if he keeps asking, because I don't know how many no's I have in reserve.

I glanced at him. He looked really cute, he had a tie on and everything. He was looking around the room, not at me. Perfect, I thought. Then he said, "So, Courtney. Do you want to get some punch?"

"Ah, well, ah," I stammered. Beth grabbed my arm and shoved me toward Grant. It was like we were in junior high again. "Sure."

So we went over to the punch bowl. Alison was there, which was great. We hung out with her, laughing, and she kept filling our glasses and we kept drinking punch—only because it was so crowded and hot in there, not because I knew it was spiked, honestly. When we thought about moving, we couldn't, because of the crowd. So there I was, trapped with Grant.

Mom came over to get punch and we laughed with her. Grant's parents came over, and I met them (have no idea what their names are now). Off in the distance I could see Bryan and Beth, cuddling on a sofa by the fire. "They're so cute!" I said to Alison. Getting a little tipsy, so I loved everyone.

"I'm so glad Bryan found someone," Alison said.

Then I looked over at Grant. Was he still pining for Beth? Did seeing her with my little brother give him a jealous fit?

"Your brother's a really good runner," he said.

"Oh, yeah," I said. "He's *so* good."

Then I had to find the bathroom, so Alison went with me. We were wandering around the party, and I was feeling a bit dizzy. The Tom waved to me from across the dining room and I was just about to stop and say hello when I saw Dave come around the corner. PANIC!

I hadn't seen him since that awkward day in Boulder when he yelled at me. I hadn't talked to him since then, either. But I knew one thing. I was *not* about to let him see me being Sister Courtney.

I'll show him, I thought. He's not the only one who can move on and grow!

I grabbed a hunk of mistletoe and shoved the Tom under it. Then I started kissing him.

Oh no, I realized. I'm kissing a boy. I'm kissing THE TOM. This is wrong! No boys no boys no boys! This alarm went off in my drunken head.

I shoved Tom away and he knocked the Sangria bowl onto the floor, taking three plates of Mrs. Malloy's special Christmas spritzes with it. They landed cookie-side up, but then the sangria drowned them. She got so mad! But then she went out to her Volvo and brought in 3 more trays. She's like this traveling Martha Stewart. I'd like to see them in a bakeoff.

So then Tom is looking at me all weird. Well, sure, I made a pass, and that was pretty much a shock to both of us. Grant is there, too, and he looks completely upset.

"How could you *do* that?" he asks.

And me, drunken girl, says, "I'm sorry, but they're only cookies, she can make more."

Then Grant looked furious.

And Dave is looking at me like I've just taken off my shirt and am dancing topless on the buffet table. Like he's appalled and intrigued, all at the same time.

And then this woman comes around the corner, reaching for Dave's arm like he tried to ditch her but she isn't going to let him. She's about six feet tall, like him, with blond hair and this holiday ensemble that's a little too coordinated.

Seeing them together made me want to kiss Grant again—I mean Tom—but he was kind of covered in sangria. So instead I ran outside, and started sprinting down the street for home.

"Courtney!" Tom came out after me. "Courtney, wait!"

I turned around to wave at him, and my legs went out from under me. I fell right on my butt, in the middle of the street. That's where I was sitting when Dave ran outside, too.

They both started to help me up, like chivalry wasn't dead, like they were competing to see who could help me up faster, with which arm. I looked back at the house, wondering if Grant was going to come after me.

Instead Alison came running out a second later. "I'll drag her home," she said, taking my hands from both of them. "She's *my* sister." Her voice was this slurry mess, it came out more like "shemssis."

Dave gave me this sort of forlorn look as he let go of me. Then Tom did the same thing. Like maybe I'm a lost cause. Grant was nowhere in sight.

Alison and I skidded the entire five blocks home.

LATER THAT SAME DAY

I'm upstairs after spending half an hour sitting with Angelina in the living room. Totally awkward. Not because we're stepsisters now, but because we don't have anything in common. Not even close.

She was sitting there, nursing her baby.

I was sitting there, nursing my Mountain Dew.

Still can't believe I made out with the Tom in front of a crowd. Grant was so mad at me! He probably won't talk to me again.

There's more!

Christmas Eve. Sitting in front of the fire, waiting for dinner. Hangover fading. Mom and Sophia are cooking dinner together, so civilized you can't believe it.

Here's the setup for tonight (does it get more complicated than this?):

Dad, Sophia, Angelina, Babyrina

Mom, Alison

Grandma and Grandpa Callahan (just back from their second honeymoon in Hawaii, looking very tan and skin-cancerous) (and SATISFIED)

Bryan, Beth (just back from their honeymoon at the Park Meadows Mall)

Sorry, that was catty.

I think I've left someone out. Oh, right. *Me.*

And Oscar, who with any luck will lie under the table and not across Babyrina.

Dave called earlier to say Merry Christmas. I wished him one, too.

Tom has called three times today. I don't know if I can talk to him yet. My hangover went away, but then the memories came back. Me grabbing him. And me kissing him.

Screw the rules. They don't apply at Christmas parties. Right?

We heard a clatter of footsteps during our dinner—not on the rooftop, on the sidewalk. Grandpa started to recite the Christmas story about creatures not stirring and mice and reindeer, but then the doorbell rang. I heard my mother say, "Well, hello there, Tom!"

Tom? I thought. Oh no, what is he doing here? I did not want to see him. What if he expected me to kiss him again?

"I just need to talk to Courtney," he said when Mom brought him into the dining room.

"Well, that's fine, but why don't you join us for supper?" Mom got an extra plate and some silverware and Bryan pulled up a chair. Beth shot me this look, like: *You realize what you've gotten yourself into. Don't you?*

"Who *are* you?" my father asked.

"This is Tom," I said. "Tom Delaney. The president of the student council."

Someone kicked me under the table, then Tom whispered, "Not anymore."

"He's the boy who rescued us on the way to Ogallala," my mother explained. She handed him a giant plate of food. "When Courtney drove us off the road."

"Mom! I didn't try to," I said. When is she going to stop bringing that up???

"Does he have to eat every holiday meal with us?" Bryan mumbled to me.

Meanwhile, Tom was making himself at home. I guess whatever he needed to talk to me about could wait. Which was fine.

"Can you pass the bread?" Tom asked Grandma. "And

476

the relish plate, if you don't mind. And the salt and pepper, Beth?"

"Where's my silver lighter? I want my lighter," my grandfather demanded, staring at him.

"I don't have it," Tom said, calmly clearing off the relish plate onto his plate with a knife. "I did have it, but then I sold it." He dug into his chicken cordon bleu.

"What?" I thought my grandfather was going to have a stroke. I was pretty appalled, myself.

Grandma kept patting his knee and urging him to have another bite of the excellent mashed potatoes. "There's chicken broth in there, Stanley, try it," she urged.

My grandfather ate nothing. Tom cleaned his plate.

I had some green beans and spent a lot of time looking around at everyone, hoping they didn't hate me because Tom was here. After a while it was too much to take, so when Mom made a break for the kitchen and the pies, I asked Tom to come into the den with me.

"So what's the big emergency?" I said.

He paced around for a minute and then he dropped onto the sofa, facedown, and mumbled something into the pillows.

"What did you say?" I asked.

A muffled voice came out from the chenille. "I took all the student council money."

"What?" I cried, yanking the pillow out from under him. He sat up and looked at me like he was about to cry.

"I spent it all, Court. On myself. And it's wrong, I know it's wrong, I kept trying to stop, but I couldn't. I have a problem, I need help!" Then he went on and on about how he was never going to get into college now, and his life was over. "Courtney! You've got to help me, I'm going down in flames!" blah blah blah.

The door opened and Angelina came in with a crying Bellarina and started to feed her. We ignored her.

"Tom, you were only in charge for a few months," I said. "How did you manage to blow all that money—"

"I act fast, okay? In all things. It's a character trait. I bought stuff. Gifts. That sleeping bag—"

"You bought a dumb extralarge sleeping bag with everyone else's money?" I cried.

"Hey, you slept in it, too," Tom said. "And if you don't help me get out of this, I can tell everyone you were an accomplice—"

"I'll help you, I'll help you. So, okay, let me get this straight," I said. "In addition to being a sex addict, you're a kleptomaniac, a thief—"

"Hey! *You* liked me. *You* kissed me," he said.

"Under duress!" I said.

"Oh, right. Sure," he said. "It was all about Dave, wasn't it?"

I ignored him and told him I was sure he could make an arrangement to pay the money back. I'd negotiate on his behalf. He'd be my first client. (Figures. Most clients are reprehensible and guilty.) He'd probably have to resign as president. I could take over for him, and maybe we'd keep this out of the papers—

Then I realized that as I was talking, all he was doing was staring at Angelina, who was sitting on the couch, breast-feeding Babyrina. His mouth was wide-open—he was nearly drooling as much as Babyrina.

I just couldn't believe him! I was getting completely outraged on her behalf. Then I realized they had made eye contact, and she was like . . . enjoying this. As much as he was.

I had to get out of there right away. I went back to the dinner table and smiled uneasily at everyone. "Sorry about that."

"You're not . . . dating that young man, are you?" Grandma asked.

"Oh, no," I said. "Not at all." I chewed a bite of chicken cordon bleu and thought for a second. Not about the fact that what I was eating went against everything I believed in. Not about the fact I'd been really dumb to even spend five seconds wishing I were with Tom and wanting him to notice me. Not even about the fact that I had seen skis under the Christmas tree and they were probably for me and why had I told Grant I couldn't go and was it too late to say yes.

But what I kept thinking was: If Tom hooks up with Angelina . . . if he marries Angelina, and she's my stepsister, then what would he be to me? (Besides an ex-student-council-president.) My second stepbrother-in-law once kissed and twice removed?

Merry Christmas, Part II. Fa la la la! Got exactly what I wanted from Santa: a surprise. (Not the skis, which are way cool and which Dad and Sophia got for me.) (And did I mention Bryan, Alison, and I pooled together and got Mom a cell phone that comes with no features at all except an unlisted number?)

This friend of Alison's came tonight. She drove all the way from California, through the night, straight through.

Though maybe that isn't the best way to say it. Straight through. Because I realized as soon as she came in the door and hugged Alison that *this* was the Jessie Alison was in love with. A *girl*! Not a Jesse at all.

How dumb of me not to get it before this! Can this family not clue me in once in a while? Must people hit me over the head to tell me who they're dating?

They're in this band together: Alison plays cello, Jessie sings—they played a tape for me of them. Jessie sort of sounds like Sarah McLachlan. (Wonder if they'll play at our party—for free.) She has long blond hair and is very short and petite and has six piercings in one ear.

Alison is into girls. That's why she never had a boyfriend. She doesn't like boys.

Talk about a boy-free zone. My own sister, out of the closet, and I didn't even know she was in it. Am I dense or what?

"Don't feel bad," she said. "I didn't tell anyone in the family yet—nobody knows."

"But Mom—Dad—"

"I'll tell them," she said. "Just not on this trip. I figure

I can wait until the timing's better, and we have more time to talk."

"More time? You mean, you *want* more time to talk to them about it?" I said. "Because I can't stand talking with Mom and Dad about who I like and all that."

"Courtney, I was talking about five minutes, that's all," Alison said.

We both cracked up laughing. Then all of a sudden we hugged again and we were both almost bawling. I realized how much I love her and what a jerk I've been lately.

"And don't hate guys because of Dave or because of me or Dad or anything. Just do what you want to!" she told me.

It was like this Power Bar speech.

Suddenly I knew exactly what to do.

I think.

I went to find Grant to tell him about Tom confessing the day before, how the generous holiday brought out the truth in him. I wanted to ask him what we could do about still holding the New Year's party. And also to say I got skis for Christmas and did his offer still stand of going skiing together.

Day after Christmas: biggest shopping day of the year. Even Pet Me was packed. People using gift certificates for collars and hairball remedies. So I thought I'd wait for a lull. I thought I'd stand in the parking lot for a couple of hours, actually. The whole idea of seeing Grant petrified me.

I walked over to Truth or Dairy and peeked in. Gerry was behind the counter, and he had a line. I felt kind of bad for him, he was definitely flustered.

Back at Pet Me I found Grant stocking shelves. "Hey," I said. "How are you?"

He glanced at me. Briefly.

"I came by for a couple of things," I said.

He pointed across the store. "Oscar's food is over there."

I laughed. "No, not that. I mean, I had some things I wanted to tell you. And ask you." My voice was starting to sound weird and thin and shaky. "First off, Tom confessed to taking all the money. And I called Mrs. Martinez and left a message about how he'll resign and how the Duck—with your guys' input, of course—can decide on his punishment. Maybe he can pay it all back eventually." I looked around the crowded store. "Hey, are you guys hiring? Maybe he could work here."

Grant just kept shelving cans of cat food. Chicken mushroom flavor. He wouldn't even look at me.

"So I don't know if I told you, but Beth and I quit at Truth or Dairy," I said. "So I won't get to see you as much anymore, which is too bad."

He didn't blink. "I know you quit. I found out when I decided to drop by and visit you Tuesday night. You said you couldn't go out with me because you had to work? And you weren't there. And Gerry told me you *quit* on Monday."

Turns out Grant is really mad at me for lying to him not once but many times.

He said I lied to him about not knowing how to ski well. (He saw me ski once, when we all went together.)

He said I lied to him about Thanksgiving in Nebraska and how Tom was there.

He said I was a total hypocrite; I wouldn't go out with him, I said I wouldn't go out with anyone. But here I was, making the moves on Tom, who is only the worst living example of the species, a liar, a cheater, a philanderer.

A what?

"But see . . . I'm not interested in Tom, and that's why I kissed him. And I did it because I panicked when I saw Dave, so I had to kiss someone, so there was Tom, and—" Saying it out loud was so embarrassing. It made no sense. "So anyway, I don't care what they think."

"Really? It doesn't seem that way to me," Grant said, still sticking price tags on top of cans.

The thing is, the kiss meant nothing to me. Or Tom. Or even Dave, who could see it was false. But I guess it meant something to Grant. I've never seen him look mean before. It was awful!

"Grant, come on. I was sort of tipsy that night, remember?"

"Of course I remember. I was *with* you, remember? And I thought we were sort of hanging out together," Grant said. "I thought we were having fun. But as usual I guess I was wrong, and you didn't mean anything you did or said that night. Just, you know, like a *guy* would do."

Whoa. Talk about harsh!

I couldn't think of what to say. This was it. I had to tell him that I was wrong and that I did like him and that I was getting too wrapped up in a dumb self-imposed regulation which didn't take into account the fact I'd get to know someone like Grant this year, just like my nondairy rule didn't take into account the fact that Ben and Jerry would come up with new irresistible flavors every year.

"Excuse me, young man, but is anybody else working here?" a man in a plaid coat asked. "Because I need some help picking out the right cat litter. Now, I've got the clumping kind at home, but it gets tracked all over the house and it's like living at the beach, so I thought—oh, I'm sorry. Are you still helping her?"

Grant turned to me. "Am I?"

I couldn't even answer him. I couldn't speak. All I knew was that I'd ruined everything. "No," I mumbled.

Then I tried to run out of Pet Me, but the place was so crowded I couldn't get through to the exit. I tried to hurdle a scratching post and nearly fell into a fish tank. People were laughing at me. I was crying.

Spent all last night mulling over all the things I've done wrong lately.

Woke up with a brilliant idea today. We can have a school fund-raiser at the Canyon Boulevard strip mall, while everyone's out spending Christmas bucks and prone to blowing money on nothing. We could coordinate the effort, me and Beth and Grant and whoever else can help—Jane can stand on the sidewalk looking like she does and cars will pull in. It's too cold for a car wash; people's locks will freeze. But we can offer free smoothies with every pet grooming/dog wash/etc. Not full-size smoothies; maybe half-size. We can offer photos of groomed pets with ribbons, etc.

Two problems with this plan:

(1) Beth and I no longer work at Truth or Dairy.

(2) Our Pet Me connection, Grant, no longer speaks to me.

I have to try anyway, or my entire fall will be a waste.

Yes! I went back to Truth or Dairy, found Gerry. He was miserable and about to call me and Beth to ask us to come back. I said we could, but I made the school fund-raiser part of the negotiation, convinced him what good publicity we'd get, and told him it was time for him to give back to all the students who worked so hard for him. He caved. Then we set my work schedule for next week.

"Courtney, I hope you come back here feeling refreshed," he said. "Ready to throw yourself back into the job with the same enthusiasm you're showing for this school event."

"Oh, I will," I said. "And about me not working in Boulder and all that . . . no hard feelings, right?"

"Right," Gerry agreed. "Just . . . hard ice cream. And a real soft spot right here—" He meant to pat his heart, but he hit his stomach— "for you and Beth. You have done a lot for T or D, and the regulars have been asking for you. Promise me you'll stay until you graduate!"

So I did.

Then I ran over to find Grant again. He wasn't working, but I talked to the manager about my idea. He said he'd offer the grooming services for half price and the other half could go to Bugling Elk. He said to work out the details with Grant and then call him. I told him the event has to be, like, tomorrow. Or the 30th at the latest. Grant might not return my call by then. He said he'd call Grant now and let him know I'd be calling to follow up later. "Your mother's been buying dog food here for years. It's the least I can do," he said.

I called Beth, Jane, then rest of student council. That was easy. Talked with Mrs. Martinez, and she said the principal was willing to make a deal where Tom did hours and hours of community service, *plus* he had to write a letter to the school newspaper admitting his guilt and apologizing, *plus* he had to pay back all the money, and then *maybe* she wouldn't let the colleges he applied to know about it. It would go on his record, though. It sounded like Tom was going to be awfully busy for the rest of the year.

Grant finally called me at the end of the day. I told him about the fund-raiser idea and he said he thought it was cool, that he'd think about helping. "But you're like the cornerstone of this whole thing," I said. "I can't do it without you!"

"Oh. Really?" He sounded more interested after that.

"You and I have to do it together—I mean, we'll have help, but you need to be there," I said.

"Why?" he said.

"Because you're *honorable*. And nobody's going to hand over any money to me—I've been tainted," I said.

He laughed, and we got into the particulars. Like how it's supposed to be really cold tomorrow, "polar bear weather" they said on the news.

Then I went out on a major iceberg. I asked if he wanted to go to the zoo with me and actually *see* the polar bears. "Since it's polar bear weather, they'll be out playing and swimming. We can see all the other animals, too. We can walk around and talk about the fund-raiser." While I waited for his answer I pulled a tassel off the end of the couch. Oops.

"No, I'd better not," he finally said. "It might be a date or something, and you'd hate that. Let's just do the fund-raiser. I'll see you tomorrow."

He's still mad. Still not forgiving me.

Damn.

Event is tomorrow. One pet who won't be groomed is Oscar. He's gone again. He was outside playing in the new snow and Mr. Novotny came roaring out of the garage with his snowblower and Oscar got so freaked out he ran away.

He went down the snowy street like he was in *Call of the Wild* and he was heading for the mountains and wasn't coming back. Only he should, like White Fang. Only White Fang would eat Oscar in about two seconds.

Oscar won't make it in the wild. He won't even make it at someone else's house, because he needs his medication. And I found his collar on the street. So nobody will see the tag that says that. They'll know when Oscar has a grand mal seizure that something is up.

I was posting signs for MISSING—SICK DOG when Grant drove up beside me. "Can I help?" he said.

"Are you following me again?" I asked. Trying to make a joke. Failing.

"Your coat's kind of bright. Couldn't help seeing you," he said. Like I was a dog myself—my "coat?"

Then I looked down and realized I had this bright pink jacket of Mom's on. I'd run out the door in such a hurry, I'd grabbed it. Me. In bright pink. In broad daylight. No wonder Grant saw me.

"We'll find him. We will," Grant said. "Did you check the pasta factory yet?"

I nodded. "The brewery, the supermarket warehouses—everything bright and flashy I could think of. Even the X-rated theaters on Colfax."

"I didn't know Oscar was into that," Grant said.

"It's the flashing lights, not the porn!" I said. Then I realized Grant was only joking.

He was in a good mood again. He didn't hate me. (Wherever you are? Thanks, Oscar.) He's completely in on the Smoothie Out Your Pet plan for tomorrow. Have to work on the slogan, though.

Have to find Oscar.

Other possible slogans:

"Truth or Science Diet"

"Clean Up Your Pet and Your Diet"

"Fluffy and Smoothie—Together Again!"

Temperature dropped about twenty degrees today. Not a good sign for (a) Oscar's survival, (b) our class fundraiser. If Random Nosebleed doesn't get their full money, they won't play. Very hard-nosed about it considering they are prone to unpredictable nasal bleeding.

We still need to buy everything else for the party—with cash, because no one will take our checks now.

Everyone really pitched in: Jane getting people to bring in their dogs and cats, two guys giving complimentary flea dips to all pets, Beth and me making smoothies, Grant and this guy Larry grooming them—the dogs, I mean, not the smoothies. It was fun. We didn't even get any dog hair in anyone's drink or sundae.

But at the end of the day, when I looked at the proceeds, I could tell we wouldn't be able to pull it off. Our New Year's party was dead in the water. Or frozen in the blender, more accurately.

"We don't have nearly enough money here. You know what I need to get this party off the ground?" I said. "A grant."

Beth started laughing. "You know what you just said?"

"What?"

"You need *a Grant. Him!*" Beth pointed at Grant, who was busy trimming a Portuguese water dog with black hair.

"Quiet," I said. But it was true.

I'd been worried about Mom all day, how her meeting went with MegaPhone. When I got home, she wasn't there. She came in about an hour later, completely happy. She hadn't been there at all. She'd been shopping—buying cell phones for all of us. The meeting was called off because the level of consumer complaints was so high, the state has created a special commission to investigate.

MegaPhone offered to give every consumer a $10 credit for the inconveniences. Governor said no, that wouldn't even begin to cover it. He turned it over to the consumer attorney general, or someone like that.

Ha! See how *you* like being under the umbrella of suspicion.

Mom and I spent most of the night calling each other on our new cell phone numbers from different rooms of the house. Cracking up.

I only got Mr. Novotny's house once when I tried to call Mom. I didn't tell her about it.

An absolutely incredible thing just happened! Grandma and Grandpa Callahan greeted me at breakfast with a huge surprise.

"We don't want your party to be canceled." They handed me a check for a lot of money, made out to the student council.

"Especially not because of that Tom person," Grandma said. "He ought to be arrested, that's what they should do with him."

"I want my lighter," Grandpa said. "But if I can't have that, I want you kids to have fun tonight."

My eyes widened as I stared at the check. "But—but—this is too much money," I said. "Don't you need this?" For your Viagra prescription? I thought.

They said they wanted to be involved in my life and do something for the community. And they could see how hard I was working, and how I could make a difference, how everyone needed to have a good time now and then. I had to promise them a hundred times that none of the money would go toward alcohol or drugs.

Having sexually satisfied grandparents is not a bad thing at all!

Happy New Year!

Sad, isn't it? The beginning for some is the end for many. Like this sketchbook. Only 5 pages left and I have to cram in everything that happened and then put you in a time capsule so someone can find you in 50 years. Like they'd want to.

Better make it 100 years—that way I won't be around when it's opened. Spare me the pain and humiliation. Decompose or something, will you?

Well, the party went great. Mrs. Martinez made an announcement about everything that had happened with student council, and she said how I'd managed to turn lemons into lemonade and the next thing I knew she had appointed me interim president, meaning I'll probably get to keep the job and run student council for the rest of the year. Everyone cheered. It was unbelievable.

I knew Tom was at the party somewhere, hiding in a coat room or a locker or something. He'd come out when Mrs. Martinez wasn't around to yell at him. I just didn't want to see him.

Random Nosebleed was awesome. Everyone danced. Jane, Beth, and I danced together, like usual. Bryan sprained his ankle running the other day, so he was out of commission. Which was cool, not that I want him to be hurt, but it was fun to just be the three of us.

"You really made this happen," Jane said.

"The lead singer keeps checking you out," I told her.

"He's cute," she said. "I want his leather jacket."

"Okay . . ." I said. It was this scuffed-up thing that looked like it had been run over by a truck and then singed with cigarette burns.

When the clock struck midnight the band threw all these noseplugs and little packets of Kleenex into the crowd—that's their trademark. Jane, Beth, and I hugged each other, and then the crowd broke up.

When I was leaving, Grant stopped me. I'd been avoiding him all night. I couldn't ask him out again, it nearly killed me the first time.

So now he asked me if I wanted to go to the zoo with him. I said we couldn't; it was closed. But I had another idea. I told him we should wait until tomorrow though, (or at least later today) (technically) because New Year's Eve is a really bad time to drive anywhere.

Then he asked if I wanted to go skiing New Year's Day, so I said yes. "Just like that? Yes?" He was pretty much stunned. So was I. I never say "yes" without thinking something through.

Running out of space here and will have to keep this brief. Or insert extra pages.

I picked up Grant yesterday morning, but then told him he had to drive. Not having much luck lately in that department, why risk it?

"We're taking this car. Into the mountains?" He gave the Bull a disparaging look.

"I know, I know, it's hideous and skids easily. But it does have a ski rack," I pointed out.

We went to Breckenridge and skied and boarded. So much fun, I couldn't believe it, like I hadn't really been outside in months. Of course, I hadn't. Really. Unless you count commuting and driving, being stuck in hailstorms and snowdrifts. We only skied for a few hours, but it felt great.

New Year's Resolution: Cut back on hours at work. Add hours outdoors. Break it to Gerry gently, though.

After skiing we were driving back on I-70 and I made Grant stop to see the buffalo.

Resolution Two: Organize school event involving saving more buffalo in the wild. Perhaps free the buffalo at the Denver Zoo. Which reminded me.

"I still want to see the polar bears," I said. "It isn't that far out of the way, right?" Actually it was quite a few miles away from our neighborhood, but I didn't want the day to end.

We were there at 4:00 when the sky got dark and they turned the holiday lights on; it's this thing they do every year, and you walk through and see all these cool light displays in the shapes of animals. Tonight was the final night—they held it over longer than usual because the weather has been so unusually crappy lately and people had stayed home. And they turned the lights on early so you could see lights plus animals. Perfect.

First we went to the Northern Shores area, where all the Arctic animals are. We still had our skiing clothes on so we looked sort of Arctic ourselves. We checked out the polar bears right off. Two little ones were walking around the display, and the mother was swimming.

Every time I said something about them, from what I'd learned on TV, Grant would say something, too. Like we'd watched all the same shows. And we both knew they were only a pound or two when they were born and that they make a loud noise like bees buzzing when they nurse and how their fur is hollow like straw and that the adults don't eat for several months every year while they're waiting for Hudson Bay to freeze up so they can walk on it.

I was so excited to be there with someone who actually *got it*. Who cared. The cubs started playing, and I grabbed Grant's arm.

Then he put his hand over my hand. I was getting really nervous, I was afraid the polar bears would sense it and freak out.

"Come on, let's go see something else," I said, dragging Grant away.

"Okay . . ." he said.

We were going down this path admiring more of the lights when we saw the biggest light of all, this giant giraffe, towering into the sky. And who was sitting at the bottom of it, gazing up at it, looking forlorn?

OSCAR!!!!!!!!!

Grant talked to him nicely, in this quiet voice, very

calm—like that guy who whispers to horses. He got close enough to pet Oscar on the head, then he grabbed his neck—gently, of course. We got him! Once Oscar knew it was us he jumped up on me and licked my face.

I was so happy I threw my arms around him and kissed him.

Not Oscar this time—Grant. He looks a lot more huggable these days.

He kissed me back. He kept kissing me. And it felt incredible. And I didn't even have my pager on.

We walked to the car sort of hugging, our arms around each other, with Oscar trotting between us. I kept wondering how Oscar ended up way over here, and Grant asked if we ever lived near here, and I said no. And how come he hadn't been picked up by the zoo? What if he got into a fight with an exotic animal?

"It's Oscar," Grant said. "I'm sure he ran away whenever anyone tried to catch him—animal or human."

"They could have used a tranquilizer dart!" I said.

"He's a dog, Courtney. And let's face it, people care a lot more about exotic animals than they do about plain old dogs like Oscar." He started going on and on about how when he becomes a vet, he's going to spend all his time and money on educating people on how to treat their pets, he has horror stories from working at Pet Me blah blah blah.

It was all fascinating, and I agreed with him a hundred percent and admired him even more than before. But I wanted to get back to making out.

So, okay. I only have one page left. And I know I said I wouldn't go out with any guys this year, that I pledged this back in September. And it might seem like I broke my pledge. A little bit.

But if you think about it, technically I did make it through "the year" without dating. You know—because I didn't say I meant the academic year. I meant until the end of the *calendar* year, and this is a new year, right?

Oh wait. I just found my old floral diary where I made that so-called pledge. I did say something about not dating anyone "senior year."

Who cares?

I'll just rename the next several months precollege-freshman year.

That is, if I get into a college.

If I don't end up being the poster girl for Truth or Dairy.

Which reminds me. I'm late for work. Gerry's going to give me another motivational speech about promptness being related to smoothieness, and I don't think I can stand listening to that again. I'd better go.

Resolution Three: Never be late to work again.

I hope WWW comes in today. When she reminds me to have safe sex, I will just say yes with a smile. Maybe give her an extra wheatgrass punch on her card.

Resolution Four: Go to First National Blanks on the way home from work and pick out a new journal. Am ending this one just when things are getting (more) interesting.

Don't miss any of these must-reads by *Catherine Clark!*

Better Latte Than Never

This is not how Peggy Fleming Farrell planned to spend her summer—being the barista in a gas station coffee shop. But she's sure that she can turn the summer around if she could only get a certain waiter to look her way.

Rocky Road Trip

Courtney survived senior year in Banana Splitsville. But at college with her boyfriend 1,000 miles away, only one thing is certain: Long-distance romance is a bumpy road.

Picture Perfect

On the beaches of the Outer Banks, North Carolina, Emily meets a way-too-photogenic guy, and her picture-perfect summer starts developing quickly. Will this one be Prints Charming?

Icing on the Lake

Kirsten's New Year's resolution is to find a hockey-playing, winter-loving hottie to invite to her weekend cabin. No problem...right?

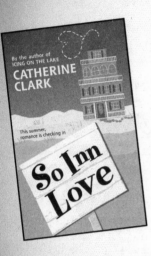

So Inn Love

Liza has finally landed her dream job at the Tides Inn on the Rhode Island shore. Now she just needs to figure out a way to get in with the in crowd.

Wish You Were Here

Ariel is stuck on an "America's Heartland" bus tour with her family for four weeks! But then she meets intriguing, also-miserable Andre. Who has a plan to escape.

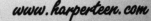